THE LEGEND OF
MILDRED WELLS

THE LEGEND OF MILDRED WELLS

BY MICHAEL CLARK

Edited by: MJ Pankey
Formatted by: Stephanie Ellis
Cover illustration by: Francois Vaillancourt
Cover design by: James Helps of GoOnWrite.com

First Edition: September 2024
Previously published as The Patience of a Dead Man series:
      The Patience of a Dead Man
      Dead Woman Scorned
      Anger is an Acid

ISBN (paperback): 978-1-963355-10-9
ISBN (ebook): 978-1-963355-09-3
Library of Congress Control Number: 2024942439

BRIGIDS GATE PRESS
Overland Park, Kansas
www.brigidsgatepress.com
Printed in the United States of America

This book is dedicated to my family, immediate and extended (Josi, Mom, Ed, Addison, and Olivia are the center of my universe).

Special thanks to MJ Pankey for foot-stomping her way into my permanent memory. That's an inside joke, but what a talent. And it is a pleasure working with you.

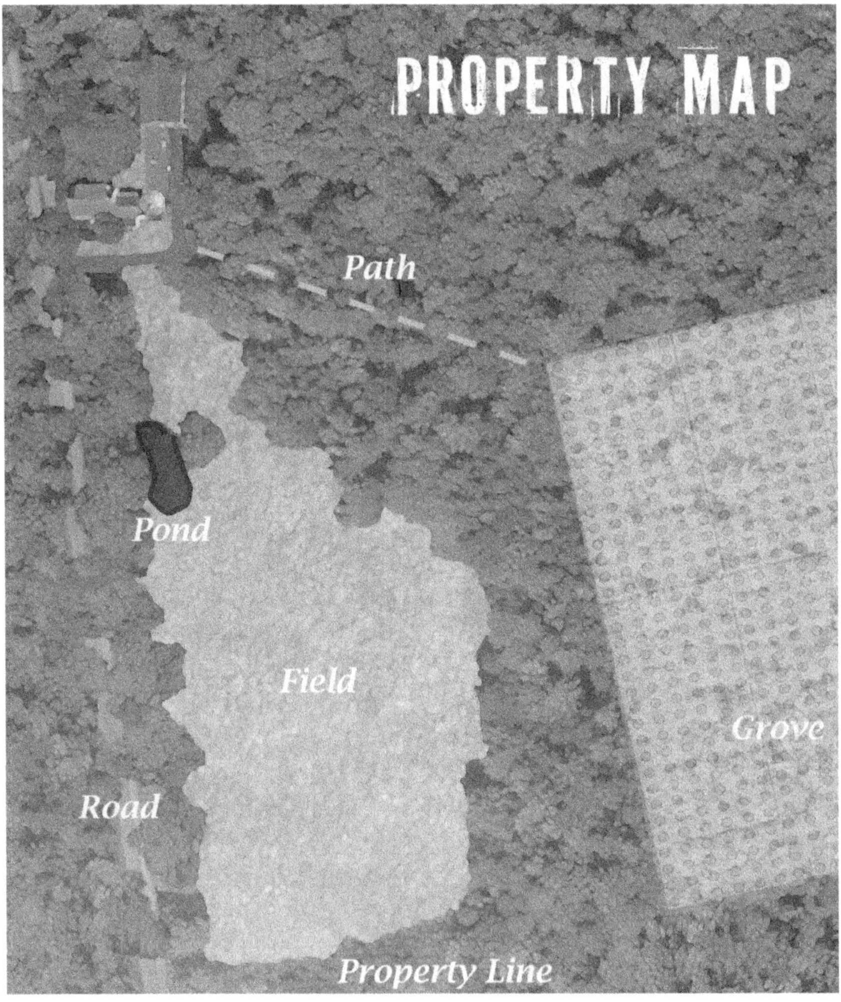
PROPERTY MAP
Path
Pond
Field
Grove
Road
Property Line

HOUSE PLAN: FIRST FLOOR

1. Barn
2. Carriage House
3. Breakfast Area
4. Kitchen
5. Dining Room
6. Porch
7. Living Room
8. Den/Office
9. Bathroom
10. Room by the Road
11. Horse Stall
12. Barn Storage
13. Front Door under bedrooms
14. Front Porch Door

HOUSE PLAN: SECOND FLOOR

1. Hay Loft
2. Turret
3. Master Bedroom
4. "Sunny" Bedroom
5. Back Bedroom
6. Back Bedroom
7. Bathroom

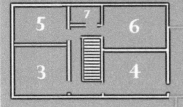

CONTENT WARNINGS

Child death
Rape
Murder
Blood
Corpses
Human bones
Death
Drinking (recreational)
Drug use (mentioned)
Insects
Kidnapping
Cult
Suicide
Violence
Weapons

CONTENTS

Foreword   1

Intro: Lord of the Flies   3

Part One: The Persistence of a Dead Man   9

Part Two: Mary   175

Part Three: Dead Woman Scorned   277

Part Four: Anger is an Acid   307

Part Five: The Patience of a Dead Man   437

Epilogue   547

Acknowledgements   549

About the Author   551

More From Brigids Gate Press   553

FOREWORD

By Michael Clark

I'll be brief. After you read this, you'll understand why.

When I decided to write my first book in 2017, I thought reverse engineering a Stephen King novel would be the best place to start. I chose *Pet Sematary* for its medium length. It sounded like a good plan, but bear with me.

The next thing I did was choose a setting. In 1971, when I was five, my family moved into a farmhouse in central New Hampshire with a grove hidden in the woods. Being in those long, empty hallways when no one was around raised many a goosebump. My setting was chosen.

I made a detailed outline of scary scenes and wrote as much as possible about each bullet point. When the outline was complete, I began to type, stretching those bullet points like taffy. When Mom and Dad liked it, I showed it to friends, and they liked it too. And since I didn't know anything about submitting a manuscript, I self-published it. Once published, I sent it to as many BookTubers and Bookstagrammers as I could, looking to pile up reviews.

Head swelling, I continued begging for attention and was eventually invited to a Night Worms Book Party, but it was here that I was held to a higher standard. While the group's reaction was split, the message I heard was that my book needed at least one more round of edits. Disappointed but undaunted, I revised and republished the book—by myself—not only once but several times. To this day, I have no idea how many versions of Book One there are. There were even two different covers.

Meanwhile, still naïve enough to hope my book could be made into a movie, I continued writing and turned it into a trilogy (Book Two was called *Dead Woman Scorned*, and Book Three was *Anger is an Acid*.). But somewhere along the way, I heard a podcaster mention that the second and third books of trilogies don't sell as well as the first, and I found out the hard way that he was right.

To solve that problem, I combined all three books into one volume and called it *The Patience of a Dead Man COMPLETE*. It was a three-pound, 800-page doorstop—roughly 220,000 words—the kind of book no one wants to read in the age of TikTok.

Deep down, I knew my story had still not been told the way it should. Thankfully, I met Heather and Steve of Brigids Gate Press and pitched the idea of a professionally edited *Patience of a Dead Man* omnibus, and they liked it. They paired me with MJ Pankey (who edited my other novel, *Hell on High*), and we were off to the races.

The days of stretching my prose so that the finished product was as thick as a Stephen King novel were no longer the goal. Very early in the process of working with MJ, I knew *The Patience of a Dead Man* had become an inferior product, so I unpublished it. We even gave it a fresh title and had a new cover created (by François Vaillancourt).

Readers, the book you hold is Mildred Wells as lean and mean as she's ever been. If you read Book One and stopped, here's a great second chance to see what happens in a better-written book free of cliffhangers and recaps. There are even new characters and an extra murder! Need I say more?

Thanks so much for reading, and pay no mind to that fly on your window, it's probably nothing.

INTRO: LORD OF THE FLIES

Horror fiction, in my humble opinion, hits like no other genre, whilst, in a way, it encompasses all genres. Romance, science fiction, mystery, thriller, fantasy, and more: all of these genres can be found within the horror sphere, but finding horror (*true, unrelenting horror*) in another genre is often a tall task.

Finding something truly terrifying in a book possibly entitled *Seven Years of Walking Over Lemons Barefoot* is a tall task and one which I can guarantee doesn't exist, and if it did, I'll go out on a limb and say it wouldn't be executed well.

What I believe makes horror the ultimate genre is that every reader, regardless of race, sexual orientation, gender, and economic status, can relate to being scared at some point in their life. Not every reader can relate to falling in love, getting married, or traveling across an orc-infested landscape in search of some sparkly jewelry that will bring an end to a thousand years of tyranny or a car that can shrink down to the size of an atom and travel around a person's vascular system.

If I were to ask a reader of any genre what truly scares them, they'd be able to give me one or a handful of answers; we all get scared, and that's okay. Even you are scared of something. Don't be shy. What scares you?

A writer of horror has to strike fear and dread into the reader, which sets the genre apart in exploring the darkest parts of human existence (that which makes monsters of men and women) and keeps us, you and me, coming back for more. Your fear could be my fear; your fear might also conjure something within me that I've never known I've feared, and with this, the writer is giving us new fears, new atrocities, and new scares.

Everyone fears something, but not everyone (sadly) loves something.

Horror authors have been defining this genre for decades, reshaping it and remodeling it to changing trends, always keeping ahead of the game while incorporating other emerging tropes and pulling conventions from other genres where necessary.

3

Horror has changed over time, we've had the early oral traditions of storytelling, folklore, and myths (*Grimms' Fairy Tales*, 1812), the Victorian Gothic (*Frankenstein*, 1818), scientific advancements, and the human experience (*Dracula*, 1897, *The Strange Case of Doctor Jekyll and Mr. Hyde*, 1886), Creature Features of the '70s and '80s (*The Rats, 1974; Night of the Crabs*, 1976; *Cujo*, 1981; *Slugs*, 1983).

Horror, unlike other genres, is always treading new ground, it doesn't ever appear to grow stagnant or comfortable (other genres tend to stick to a tried and tested approach with little deviation to the *'rules'*). Horror, however, is constantly evolving, metastasising, and becoming something *other*. Maybe it has to, maybe it's forced on the genre and the author in the way we've become desensitised to the horrors we've seen in the world, needing to up the ante and draw on that wellspring of real horrors that get beamed into our living rooms or printed in the papers each week; and from that mess, we're pulling out new fears and new nightmares.

If we look at recent history and the COVID-19 pandemic, we can see its effect bleeding into the genre only a few years after that great tragedy and loss of life, and why shouldn't it? Humans are the dominant species, after all, and we were not so long ago looking at a mass extinction event; this fear, this true horror, which has grown over time with issues of global warming and such, has started a spate of books that look at our own demise from an ecological perspective.

Books such as Paul Tremblay's *Survivor Song* (2020), although written before the pandemic, detail a pandemic that hit hard given the pandemic we'd lived through. I read it a few years after COVID-19, and it affected me in ways I didn't expect. I had an almost traumatic response to it, and his latest offering, *In Bloom* (2023), takes us back to an ecological landscape too. Tim Lebbon's *Eden* (2020) again shows what our strain on the planet has caused, and his latest *Among the Living* (2024) follows a similar path. Naomi Booth's *Sealed* (2017) showed us something equally as terrifying and ecologically devastating with a body horror element that still haunts us today.

It takes a great horror writer to truly scare us. Trust me; thousands try their hand at it, and many succeed in some capacity, but only a limited handful really get beneath your skin and make their fear *your* fear.

Stephen King, Peter Benchley, William Peter Blatty, Robert Bloch, Josh Malerman, and Bret Easton Ellis are a few household names, but they are also, for me, my fearmongers. They tap the vein time and time again, bringing to the table lasting, penetrating terror.

I will never look at a clown the same way again because of Stephen King and *IT* (*1986*). Pennywise lives rent-free in my mind, and that was

King's gift to me; I used to love clowns, not anymore. Peter Benchley and *Jaws* (*1974*) and Stephen Spielberg's adaptation (*my favourite film of all time*) gave me a fear of the water and of sharks. Now I can't set foot in any body of water without an irrational fear and the theme music from *Jaws* entering my head (*even in swimming pools – you heard it here first*). William Peter Blatty and *The Exorcist* (*1971*) gave me the fear of losing my agency, of becoming a pawn to an outside, invasive entity. Robert Block and *Psycho* (*1959*) and Hitchcock's masterful adaptation gave me a fear of showers and shower curtains and what lurks behind them. Josh Malerman's *Incidents Around the House* (*2024*) has caused me to fear going to the toilet (*trust me, you'll know when you read it; good luck taking a dump after that*) and the silent whisper of my daughters saying '*Night, Night, Daddy …*'. Bret Easton Ellis and *America Psycho* (1991) gave me the fear of losing my mind and Phil Collins (*laugh it up, why don't you?*).

I wasn't scared of these things before, yet I'm terrified of them now, and I've a good idea some of you also hold similar fears.

The thing about my particular examples is that they've successfully reached further than the books that contain them, their horrors have bled into popular culture: 'We're going to need a bigger boat …'; 'What an excellent day for an exorcism …'; 'We all go a little crazy sometimes…'; 'We all float…'. We've somehow tried to trivialise these horrors into T-shirt slogans in a vain attempt at normalising the horror that's terrified us, with the sole aim of making them *less* scary … I've got news for you, it doesn't make it any less scary.

This all brings me on to talk about what I'm here to bend your ear about: Michael Clark and his masterful *The Patience of a Dead Man* series (I wanted to call it a trilogy, but I'm hoping he'll write more in this macabre sandbox in the future; hopefully, *this introduction, and my calling it a series, might force his hand*).

Mike (*we're friends, so I'll refer to him as that from here on out*) has become the Lord of the Flies. If you've read the series, you will know what I'm talking about; if you haven't, well, you soon will. Flies have their part in horror history; there are a hundred examples, but most notably, *The Amityville Horror* (1977) used them to great effect in both the book and the film, yet in Mike's books, they became something *other*, a harbinger of something utterly terrifying and unrelenting.

You see when the weather starts to heat up and we open our windows to let in a cool breeze, you can bet your arse that within moments of cracking the window open, our house will have a number of flies flitting around inside it (*so peculiar is the occurrence I've often gone in search for a dead animal in the garden or under the floorboards*); flies, yep that's right, small ones, big fat ones too, the bluebottle kind.

I never minded them before now. However, even the sight of one or the insane buzz as it zips past my head causes me to break out in a cold sweat; not for fear of what it will do to me, but because what is a measly fly going to do to me? It's what they represent.

My fear comes from what Mike surgically implanted in my soul all those years ago at their appearance because, with it, I'm nervously looking over my shoulder, peering around a door which is partly closed as I'm sat writing at my computer, alone in the house; or when I'm listening intently to the house settling around me, checking beneath a drawn curtain, expectant to find someone lurking, feet, a dress, the bone-white skin of my unwelcome guest, Mildred Wells.

Mike has crafted something truly terrifying with these books. They haunted me when I first read them and still do to this day. Mildred is that terrifying entity. She's a thing of nightmares; trust me, you do not want her coming to pay you a visit. But it's more than that. It's her story and Tim's story that continue to haunt me, and all those pesky flies.

I've read a lot of haunted house stories over a great many years, and *The Patience of a Dead Man* (now *The Legend of Mildred Wells*) continues to be the best in the show. Honestly, I've never been more terrified, more on edge, or more panic-stricken than I was when I read these books. There are a number of scenes throughout the series that caused me to jump while reading them. Yeah, can you believe it? Jump scares in a book—who would have thought that possible? But it is.

Mike is not only a great guy—one I'm delighted to call a friend—but he's also a phenomenal writer, and I believe he doesn't get the credit he is due. My hope is that this new edition of his collected trilogy will bring a wider audience, one that is thirsty to be haunted, one that wants to discover true fear. I know for a fact that when you start seeing those flies in your house, you will be looking over your shoulder, praying that Mildred hasn't decided to visit.

The Legend of Mildred Wells is a masterful tome of horror fiction, intrinsically terrifying, utterly beguiling, and full of tension, horror, and fear. In my opinion, this is the best horror series I've ever read, and here it is, in your hand, in one volume. It also might be the most terrifying tale of a haunting put to paper.

Many have called this series a haunted house story, and I, too, have fallen into that bracket; having marinated on the series for a while, to call it a haunted house story somehow belittles the scope of Mike's work and limits it to four walls.

The Legend of Mildred Wells is more than just a haunted house tale; it's a real, personal haunting of heart, mind, and soul, and reminds us that you don't have to be a home to be haunted.

Ross Jeffery
Bristol, February 2024

PART ONE:
THE PERSISTENCE OF A DEAD
MAN

CHAPTER 1

Sanborn, New Hampshire
November 29, 1965

The sun was low in the sky on another perfect New Hampshire day as Henry Smith washed and brushed his favorite horse, Fiona, inside the old red barn. After ensuring plenty of hay to munch on, Henry dumped the bucket of soapy water into the lawn. The workday was over. Farming was not as mentally stressful as his previous banking job, but it was much more physical. Since changing careers, he hadn't suffered one night of insomnia, and his heart was on the mend.

Things were different here, in a good way. Every minute on the farm was about working together. The animals had timely needs, like food, water, and sleep, and they did the timekeeping with the sun. It was remarkable how accurate their body clocks were. If, by chance, one overslept, the geese showed up outside at 7:00 am, honking for breakfast.

In a little more than a week, he would take Fiona to Concord to be auctioned off. His little horse breeding hobby had taken off, and he was beginning to build a reputation around town and throughout New England for his show horses. He and his wife Annette were making enough to pay for their happy country lives without tapping into the nest egg his banking career had provided.

Henry shook the excess soap from his hands and wiped them on his jeans. It was getting close to dinnertime, so he headed for the house, but just before turning the knob, something out in the field caught his eye. Letting the doorknob go, Henry walked around the front of the house. Perhaps it was nothing, but just the same, he stood there for a few seconds, scanning the tree line where he thought he'd seen her.

Sometimes, they saw a woman cutting the corner of the field into the woods. Dusk was an odd time of day for a walk, especially for someone who did not live nearby. The nearest neighbors were more than a mile away.

Henry and Annette had even speculated that the woman might be a friend or relative of somebody, but they were only grasping at straws. All of the neighbors had meadows full of wild grapes and blueberries, so why come here? It would be one hell of a walk home in any direction.

Annette asked him yesterday to start looking for a suitable Christmas tree. *Why not kill two birds with one stone?*

Henry returned to the barn, grabbed his hatchet, and set off down the front lawn past the pond and the garden on the way to the meadow, where the horses spent most of their day. A hundred yards past the pond, he turned into the forest.

He'd known about the hidden spruce grove since the day they bought the place, and it had enamored him ever since. *It's a damned shame it went to seed. If this grove had been cared for, I'd have my pick of trees every year. I could even make a few bucks selling to the townspeople.* Unfortunately for Henry, the trees had long since become towering spruce, each at least forty feet tall, standing in symmetrical rows, but some wild evergreens made great Christmas trees. They were easy to spot too, so out of place, like shooting fish in a barrel.

Henry made his way through the first few yards of natural forest, and as always, the entropy gave way to perfect hallways, which never failed to raise goosebumps. Because of their busy farm life, he rarely had time to make it out here, but when he did, he was always alone, which added to the solitude.

Henry cut diagonally through the forty-plus rows, ever deeper into the woods. *Where'd she go?* The woman was making better time than he was, probably because he was tree shopping. Maybe he would have to postpone meeting the mystery woman for another day, as sundown was approaching.

Before Henry knew it, the grove ended, and the deep woods began. *Too distracted. I probably passed some keepers already.* In the final rows of the grove, the forest had reclaimed large patches, making it an even mixture of man and nature. Scrub brush, briars, poison ivy, and vines grew along the grove's edge. The forest floor wasn't just a bed of spruce needles anymore. Leaves from a hundred autumns had blown through, leaving piles of natural mulch.

As Henry was about to turn for home, something caught his eye. Nestled under the brush were two pronounced mounds. At first, Henry thought it might be leaves covering a stone wall, but he was nowhere near the property line. He checked the sky. The last minutes of the day were ticking down, and it was doubtful he would find a tree.

Squinting in the dying light, Henry plotted a path through the thorns and made his way forward, folding the spiky plants over with his boots and wishing he brought his gloves. As he closed in on the mounds, a section of gray stone peered out between the twisting vines, much whiter than anything in the area.

Gravestones, he recognized. *Thirty-one years. I never knew I had neighbors.* Henry looked down at his hatchet, wishing he could trade it for pruning shears. He forged on, hacking the bases of the sharp plants so the way out wouldn't be as rough as the trip in.

The prickly patch was thicker than he'd estimated, and time was a factor. The sun would be gone in minutes, and the Christmas tree would have to wait for tomorrow, even if he happened to find the perfect one on the way out. Dinner might be on the table right now, and he hadn't told Annette where he was going.

As soon as he broke through the last of the thorns, Henry put down the hatchet, dropped to his knees, and began clearing vines, taking care not to disturb the stones in case they were poorly anchored. Both were leaning from years of frosts. To the left was a larger one, and to the right, a smaller one. Perhaps a child's grave? *How the hell did I miss this?*

Twilight began to fade. The sun had set, and only its glow from beneath the horizon kept the sky alight. There was so much moss on the headstones he couldn't read them. Concentrating on the bigger one, Henry scraped, taking care not to dig too hard. A minute later, he'd cleared the top two lines. The first, in smaller letters, read: "Here lies." The second line, where the person's name should appear, was taller than the first, but he still couldn't read the inscription.

Suddenly, a twig snapped, and Henry spun, attempting to see in the dark. *It must be her,* he thought. The perfect aisle was all shadows. Henry took off his glasses and squinted. Someone was there.

Twenty feet away stood the woman from the field. All he could see was her silhouette, the long dress, and pale hands holding what might be a bouquet. Her hair was pinned up, as unkempt as the surrounding woods, with strands and bunches pushing out in all directions.

Her face was lost in shadow, but he knew it was her. His heart pounded. Why hadn't he introduced himself years ago? *Why's she in the woods after dark?* Henry looked for his hatchet.

"Hello," he said. "I'm Henry Smith. We're neighbors, aren't we?" The woman said nothing and was impossible to read without seeing her face. Finally, Henry stood, his knees cracking, his back slowly straightening.

"What's your name?" *She must be a Simmons*, Henry thought. The family down the road had a reputation for being slightly off. Henry took a step forward. "Did you have a nice Thanksgiving?"

No response.

"Are you a Simmons?"

Still no response.

With ten yards between them, Henry opened his mouth to speak again but froze. There was an odor. A farm has many unpleasant aromas, but this was the smell of something dead, like the time a mouse died inside their bedroom wall. Something was ripe, and that something was her.

The woman trembled as Henry hesitated, pulling her shoulders back as the flowers fell to the ground. Her right arm twitched, and the shape of Henry's hatchet appeared. Henry turned in panic, even though he knew he wouldn't find it. All at once, he realized that talking wouldn't work. This person wasn't his neighbor. She wasn't even alive.

The woman dropped the hatchet and lurched, closing the distance between them in less than a second. Henry heard a *pop* but felt nothing. Gray static filled his vision as his nervous system shut down. Gray faded to black and didn't even have time to regret leaving Annette behind, unaware.

CHAPTER 2

Essex County Probate Court, Salem, Massachusetts
January 10, 1971

Tim Russell took a breath, picked up the pen, and signed at the X. Was it finally over?

"That's it, buddy, you have officially beaten the Devil," said his lawyer, Frank Turnbull, celebrating the windfall of a day in court. Calling Tim's ex-wife *the Devil* was a phrase he'd coined to play with the emotions that came with divorce. It stoked the fire and made his clients more amenable to fighting people they used to love. The angrier they were, the more they paid. Tim, however, wasn't biting anymore.

"Woo-hoo, I won," said Tim in a monotone, feeling in no way victorious. One of his friends had told him that only the lawyers win, and he was right. But Frank kept on:

"We're almost done. After today, take a few days off and get your courage back. Wait for your tail to come out from between your legs, and when you're feeling right, get back out there and get yourself a bimbo! Just don't get married again, for God's sake."

Tim had learned on day one that Frank was a male chauvinist pig. Getting a "bimbo" was the farthest thing from Tim's mind right now. He only wanted to spend time with his two daughters.

He wouldn't have dreamed of calling a shyster the likes of Frank if there were a chance the divorce could end amicably, but it didn't take long to figure out that Sheila was fighting dirty. One day, while trying to withdraw money from their bank, he was told by the teller that the account had been closed. Right away, he realized he'd better look for legal help.

Tim thumbed through the Yellow Pages to find a lawyer with a decent-looking ad and picked up the phone. The attorney gave an opening spiel explaining the process, but there was an awkward pause when he asked for Tim's name.

"Did you say your name was Timothy … Russell?"

"Right," Tim replied.

The attorney cleared his throat. "I won't be able to help you, and I can't comment further. I hope you understand." Sheila had already retained him.

Suddenly, everything made sense. Sheila had been distant, playing confused, even suggesting they "take a break." Tim worked long hours, so he thought they were just in a rut, but now he knew the truth. He was being lied to. She had a plan, and he was way behind.

She'd suggested they go through a mediator while she was lawyer shopping. The betrayal was of soap opera quality. It was as if the Sheila he knew was gone, and a stranger had taken her place. She probably already had a boyfriend too, he thought. A short time later, it was confirmed. However, the guy didn't stick around for long, and Tim celebrated with a six-pack when he found out. At least that guy wouldn't be around his daughters.

Tim needed to fight fire with fire, so he called Frank. It wasn't about going on the offensive. It was about girding his loins. Frank Turnbull, the crass bastard he was, could keep Sheila honest.

Tim and Sheila Russell owned a successful general contracting business. They started doing handyman projects, then moved to kitchens and bathrooms and slowly built a stellar reputation. Eventually, they built houses, and Russell Construction grew to six full-time employees.

Sheila was the bookkeeper for two years before becoming a full-time mother. Tim was okay with that until he discovered that part of her *Mommy time* was spent with her new boyfriend. Naturally, after Tim found out, dividing everything down the middle was a tough pill to swallow.

Tim tried to convince her that dissolving the company wasn't in their best interest, but she wouldn't listen. She was pissed that he caught her and made her look bad. Now, she lived to tear him down. "Primary Physical Custody," it said on the courthouse papers, meaning the kids would live with her, but he would have the right to visitation. He didn't like it, but that was the law.

As the lawyers worked to split them apart, the business all but folded. Much of the equipment had to be sold off, and everyone but Tim's number-two-man, Johnny Upson, was let go. Sheila got a hefty child support payment and half of everything by law. She also got to live in their Amesbury house for up to five years, after which it was agreed that she would sell it and Tim would get his half. Tim was left with no choice but to rent an apartment.

Today, the divorce was scheduled to be final. All that remained was a brief ceremony before the judge where all parties agreed to divorce. The lawyers were given a basic set of Permanent Stipulations with only minor details left to settle from separate conference rooms. Both lawyers scribbled on their working copies of the '*Stips*,' meeting in the hallway between the two rooms, ever negotiating, dividing mundane things like furniture. All they needed was two signatures, and everyone could go home, but Sheila wasn't done.

"Okay, buddy, now Satan wants half your dining room set," said Frank.

"Are you kidding me?" said Tim. "We already agreed! What the hell am I going to do with three chairs?"

"The Devil's not done dealing, I guess. Want me to make it difficult and ask for half the bedroom set?" Frank could smell another billable hour.

"She's going to bust my balls until the eleventh hour? Screw it. Give her the dining room set, but if she doesn't sign after that, I'm not signing today, and I'll leave. Tell her that. We can do this some other time, and she can pay her lawyer for another day. Do your job, Frank. Stop the madness."

Frank dispensed with the "devil" talk and scribbled the notes necessary to deliver Tim's request. Sheila realized some worthless furniture was about to cost her a pretty penny and signed the papers.

Less than a week later, Tim began to try to look at the bright side. He could do things now that he never could with Sheila. Cook with mushrooms. Work on his golf game. Leave the bed unmade! With the death of the marriage, all the little pet peeves went away, like how she used to put his stuff away in places he would never look or how bath towels couldn't be hung on the back of the bathroom door. *Silver linings.*

Strangely, divorce was like standing on a cliff, and it was exciting. There was no plan, only today and whatever he decided to do. *Life begins at divorce,* he had heard, but until now, the meaning had never registered. Not knowing where his life was headed was scary and thrilling at the same time.

CHAPTER 3

Haverhill, Massachusetts
March 7, 1971

Since Russell Construction was down to only Tim and Johnny, there would be no more house-building. They were back to kitchens, bathrooms, and handyman projects; small potatoes compared to what they were used to and unappealing to Tim. The thought of repeating the last twelve years was boring. In twelve more years, he'd be fifty for crying out loud.

Johnny was a monster when it came to output. If you wanted to redo a kitchen, you were better off letting him do the whole thing because you'd only get in his way. If Johnny weren't given enough work, he would grow impatient, followed by antsy, and finally, he would get angry, the opposite of a clock-watcher. Johnny's ambition left Tim as the sales guy, which was monotonous but vital to the business's survival.

Once Tim had his fill of mushrooms and had gone a month without making his bed, he realized he needed more. Boredom, he'd once thought, was for children and lazy people. Adult life was supposed to be filled with work and family tasks, but with no family to fill up the average day, he was staring at the wall. The monotony continued for two more weeks, and inspiration struck.

One of the most painful losses in the divorce was the sale of the cottage on Lake Kanasatka. Despite being in the Russell family for generations, Sheila had no qualms about liquidating it. Tim had learned to fish there, caught his first frog, and spent nearly every summer there since age six. Just like that, it was gone, and with it, a piece of his soul.

This new idea was so strong he couldn't sleep, and he leaped out of bed to make notes. He'd return to New Hampshire, where real estate prices were low compared to the Boston area, buy a place on a lake, and fix it up. The best part was he didn't have to ask Sheila's permission.

After three days of brainstorming, Tim decided he could be the salesman for Russell Construction from anywhere as long as he had a telephone, and when he had to meet with people, it was only an hour-and-a-half drive to Massachusetts. He could set all the handy work up for Johnny and let the boy tire himself out.

Tim called Johnny, pitched the idea, and made a few more business calls to fill up the schedule. When he was finished, Tim dialed zero and asked the operator to connect him with the best real estate agency in the Lakes Region. Tim's next several child-free weekends were spent meeting with Holly Burns of Depot Realty.

Before pulling the trigger on a purchase, however, Tim needed to speak with his accountant. Tim hated going to see Stanley Brown, CPA, who looked to be one hundred years old. Four times a year, he gathered his receipts and drove to Gloucester to sit across Stanley's desk as he crunched the numbers. It was agony every single time. Waiting an hour in silence to determine how much he owed the government was never fun.

Stanley hunched behind his desk, poring over the numbers while tapping his adding machine. He had a cup full of pencils and highlighters and wore bifocals on the tip of his nose. Stacks of files and folders on all edges of his desk reduced his workspace to no more than two square feet. For all Tim knew, Stanley was working a crossword back there. Tim's eyes wandered the room as Stanley worked, reading client names on the spines of binders and notes taped to seemingly everything.

Tim always focused on Stanley's body language as the moment of truth approached. Every time the old man was about to finish, he would clear his throat, rip the paper off the adding machine, and staple it to the paperwork. This year would not be pleasant. Legal fees and a divorce settlement on top of declining sales meant he would stop for a bottle of Jack Daniel's on the way home, no doubt about it.

"Uh … Tim, is this everything? Any savings accounts, cash flows I don't know about, perhaps?"

"That's it. Stanley, give me the bottom line. I know it was a bad year, and I know Sheila gets half of everything. How much?"

"You aren't going to like this. You might have to consider bankruptcy if things continue on this trajectory. Your revolving debt concerns me, and your income is down almost sixty percent."

Tim shifted in his chair, heart racing. *Bankruptcy?* "I know. I'm lining up work again, though. We're only two employees, so things will be different, but I have new goals. I'll get this turned around."

"And pay off this debt? It looks grim from this side of the desk, Tim. You're not my first client who's gone through a divorce. Sometimes, it's the best option; bankruptcy, I mean. It might even lower your child support payments."

Child support. A brand new bill to pay, and it was a big one. Fifteen percent of his gross salary, and Sheila controlled where the money went. It wouldn't be as hard to swallow if he'd been the cheater, but that was the law.

"I can't go back to working for someone else. I have an idea for a new venture, though."

Stanley looked at Tim over his bifocals. "A new venture? I don't mean to rain on your parade, but this is your bottom line after Sheila's half and taxes." Stanley turned the paper around and handed it to Tim.

The number was worse than he thought. Tim's stomach flipped. On paper, three years ago, Tim and Sheila had been millionaires. Now, most of the equipment was gone, the Kanasatka cottage was too, and they wouldn't sell the house for up to five years.

"Eighty-five thousand? That's it?" Tim had estimated he would need about twenty thousand for a house refurbishment, which didn't include the asking price. His heart sank.

"After taxes, yes. What's this new venture you're talking about?"

"I've been looking at properties in New Hampshire. I want to buy something and fix it, but eighty-five grand is cutting it close."

"You don't have to buy the house outright. Get a mortgage."

"Do you think they'd give me a mortgage now? After all the destruction Sheila caused? Plus, I don't want to pay 7.5 percent. You're telling me I can't afford it."

"Fixing this house in New Hampshire means you won't have any money coming in for how long?"

Tim rubbed his temples. "It depends. I don't have a property in mind yet. I wanted to buy something lakefront, but ..."

"Pfff! You don't have lakefront money, Tim."

Tim gritted his teeth. Tax time was bad enough. He didn't come here to be laughed at. "I know that *now*, Stanley. But I'm still in business in Massachusetts. I'll keep Johnny busy while I tackle the New Hampshire project myself. A year and a half, and then I'll sell it."

"A year and a half! And in the meantime, your income is dependent on one employee? Don't forget the child support. If your employee gets sick or quits while you're halfway into your project, you'll be in trouble. How about your truck?"

"I'm in trouble already. My truck is seven years old. I know where you're going with this."

"And gasoline back and forth to Massachusetts?"

"I know. Maybe I'll find the perfect house and money won't be so tight."

"Don't buy a log cabin and expect a windfall."

"Don't worry about me, Stanley."

Tim abandoned his dream of finding a shorefront property on the ride home. He'd have to lower his expectations after the bad news in Stanley's office. Nostalgia was a luxury he couldn't afford. Every dollar was on the line.

He needed a property that could double or triple his money, which eliminated anything on the water and, in fact, entire towns. Gilford, Center Harbor, Laconia, and Wolfeboro were too pricey, so he looked at places off the beaten path. Two weeks later, Holly Burns called him with good news. She'd found a house with a pond.

CHAPTER 4

Sanborn, New Hampshire
April 3, 1971

Technically, Sanborn was part of New Hampshire's Lakes Region, but it didn't have much lakefront. Downtown Sanborn was tiny, consisting of a town hall, a post office, and nothing else. However, it had some charm.

The house Holly found was an old horse farm about an hour and fifteen minutes from the kids. He could cover that distance easily when visitation weekends came up, plus he could spend those visitation Fridays back in Massachusetts touching base with Johnny and meeting with clients before picking up the girls.

Tim drove up rural Route 14 for two miles past the center of Sanborn and took a left onto a dirt road. Lancaster Hill Road cut through a forest that eventually led to the town of Meredith. Occasionally, the trees surrounding the road would open up to reveal a meadow, but otherwise, it was like driving through a tunnel of foliage. Tim noticed early on that he hadn't passed many houses, and grass was growing in the middle of two tire ruts.

Tim's truck bounced along at twenty miles per hour when he noticed a woman in a farm dress walking through a meadow about a mile in. *Howdy neighbor*, he muttered. The woman turned her head, but the gap in the trees passed, and Tim drove on. His mind was on the house, and he was ready for his tour.

Even though he was looking for it, he nearly missed the beginning of a driveway sloping up between two maples. It was April, and the leaves were filling out the trees. At this rate, the house would be all but invisible by June. Tim steered his truck between the two trees, pressing the gas to make it up the incline. Suddenly, there it was.

To his left was the farmhouse, and to his right was a pond in the middle of a field. Tim had to look in his rearview mirror to see how well the barrier trees closed off this sprawling open space. The listing said the building was three thousand square feet and came with twenty-three acres, half field, and half forest.

The front lawn was as overgrown as the meadow and sloped down from the house about fifty feet to a stone wall that enclosed the small frog pond. Two weeping willows were on each side of the water, their branches hanging to the ground.

Beyond the pond was the meadow, which went for about two hundred yards until it hit the forest. Tim wondered for a moment if this was where the woman was walking. If it was, she was gone now. The phrase *Get off my lawn* came to mind, and Tim smiled at his joke. He liked the place already.

Tim observed the house as the engine idled, and it stared back. The paint was peeling, and the exterior was weathered. All the windows were empty, with no curtains or shades. *Don't worry, we'll put some life back into those eyes,* he promised. There were two front doors, one close to the road under the bedrooms and one inside a closed-in porch halfway down the house.

According to Holly Burns, the house had been empty for three years and was previously owned by a widow who had passed away. *Three years,* Tim thought. *That's a long time. The place needs a ton of work, but it has potential.*

The house had a 360-degree octagonal turret at the far end. As Tim pulled around the far side of the building, a big red barn came into view. He hadn't seen it from the end of the driveway because of the turret. Connecting the barn to the house was a one-story carriage house with another entrance.

Parked just in front of the barn waiting for Tim was Holly, his eyes and ears in New Hampshire. She'd shown Tim dozens of properties, and they'd gotten to know each other in a professional yet slightly flirtatious way. She was an attractive, sandy-haired thirty-something, and Tim, shaking the cobwebs, couldn't help but notice. Nevertheless, he had not attempted anything, still gun-shy. *Consequences,* he reminded himself.

"Good morning, Tim. How was the drive up?"

"No traffic! You gotta love New Hampshire." Tim had spent countless hours of his younger years stuck in traffic on Routes 93 and 128, the Central Artery, all over Massachusetts.

"Yes, it's quieter up here. Now we have to find you something so you can stay."

"I'm counting on it. What's the story with this place?"

"Let's walk."

Holly unlocked the side door and pushed it open. A musty waft escaped the building, and Tim stepped in, sniffing for mold. They entered a utility room that, while only about ten feet deep, extended almost thirty feet to his right. It could be a racquetball court if the ceiling were higher. Holly told him the room's original purpose was to park horse carriages and was currently unheated. Once inside, they turned left and opened an out-of-place sliding glass door into the main house.

"That's an odd choice," said Tim. "I might change that to something that matches the house better."

"I agree. As you can see, this room is the breakfast area connected to the kitchen." Tim ran his hand along the counter separating the two rooms. In the kitchen was an old stove against a wall, and on either side were separate passageways to the next room. Hidden behind the wall were two staircases: one to the cellar and the other to the turret. While standing in the breakfast area, Tim noticed he could look all the way down the length of the house to the room by the road.

"I can't wait to see the turret," he said.

"Oh, it's nice up there. It's a good place to drink a coffee—or a beer."

Tim led the way, and they climbed into a small room with eight windows in all directions and an old desk. To the front were the pond, the field, and the forest; to the rear were the barn and a small backyard.

Tim felt disconnected from the rest of the house up here, but it was nice, like an escape. Together, Tim and Holly descended the stairs and took a left into a darkish dining room, and Tim noticed that one of the windows in the back was boarded up.

"What's with the floors?" asked Tim. The wide pine planks were water-stained in places. "Leaky roof?"

"I'm not sure, but the place needs some TLC. Come see the porch." Holly turned the knob and stepped out. Tim noted that the walls were not insulated. The porch might be useful for two seasons, maximum.

Back inside, after the dining room was a living room with a fireplace and a built-in bookshelf. Tim looked closer and saw a World Atlas from 1925 amongst other ancient reads. Behind the living room was a den-like room. Nothing fancy, just a pair of windows looking out into the backyard. Tim peered out. The backyard was nothing special: tall pines and too much shade over a postage-stamp lawn covered by decades of spruce needles. The beauty of this property was clearly in the front.

Tim walked back to the living room, catching a glimpse of the pond through the window in the distance. *Ah, my water view.* To his right was a doorway to another stairwell. To his left was the front door under the bedrooms, and straight across the hallway was the room by the road. Tim was sure he'd close it off in winter to save on the heating bill. This house was too big for him and his daughters. Under the stairs was another bathroom.

Tim looked up the staircase to the bedrooms, wondering if the widow had died up there, and his imagination got the best of him. For a moment, he pictured the body crawling with beetles after months of waiting for someone to find her, which probably wasn't even close to the truth. Tim pushed the thought from his mind and followed Holly up the stairs.

Like the dining room, the upstairs hallway was dark for ten in the morning. Only one window at the front of the house provided light. Tim reached the top of the stairs and stepped into the back bedroom that overlooked Lancaster Hill Road.

"The floor up here needs work too. It looks like they used a wet mop on pine. Not good. The ceiling is in good shape, so it can't be the roof," said Tim.

"This place is a handyman's special," said Holly. "All it needs is a handyman. By the way, that's Mount Kearsarge." In the distance, Tim could see a hill slightly taller than the other hills. "That's twenty miles away," she added. Holly stood close enough to Tim that he caught a whiff of her shampoo. *What is that? Flowers? Or fruit?* Whatever it was, it made Mt. Kearsarge more pleasant to look at.

He blinked semi-hypnotized as they left the bedroom to walk the balcony to the main bedroom. A freestanding full-length mirror was the only piece of furniture in this part of the house. One of the maples at the end of the driveway was right outside the window. Then, something caught his eye. Flying over the field was a red kite.

"Holly, I didn't see many houses. How many neighbors are there?"

"Good question. You have the third house on the road. You might have missed the first two at the beginning because they're set back. But go a half-mile in the opposite direction and you'll see two more farms, and then Lancaster Hill Road turns into Abbott Road between here and Meredith. So, what's that, four houses?"

"So, looking past the pond, it's nothing for a mile, and behind us, nothing for a half-mile?"

"I think that's right," said Holly, tilting her head. "I can double-check. I live about twenty minutes away. This property is my only listing in Sanborn."

Tim looked for the kite, but it was gone.

"Tim?"

25

"Huh?" There was an awkward pause as Tim realized he'd tuned out.

"Sorry. I was just wondering, did that widow die here?"

Holly grinned. Tim was interested in the house. Now came the tough questions. "I knew you'd ask. I'm not sure. Why? Do you believe in ghosts?" Holly continued to smile, daring him to say yes.

"Haha, no," Tim answered. "I'm not sure why I asked that. I don't care, but I suppose it's on my mind. It's weird being in a room you know someone passed away in."

"It is. A few years back, I drove down to Fall River and visited the Lizzie Borden house, you know, the girl that chopped up her parents back in 1892. Of course, it's just a bed and breakfast today, but seeing the crime scene is spooky."

"I keep wondering how many days it took to find her. Morbid, I know."

"Morbid for sure! That's why I paid to sleep in the Lizzie Borden house. I've always had trouble putting that feeling into words, but 'morbid fascination' is it. I'm going to remember that."

Across the hall from the main bedroom was the fourth bedroom, perhaps the sunniest room in the house, as no trees blocked the windows. It had a straight-on view of the pond and a side window facing the turret. From here, Tim could see the top of the barn.

"Don't forget this property comes with twenty-three acres. Come outside. If you like morbid fascinations, I have something up your alley, no pun intended."

"What pun?"

"It's better if I show you."

Holly led Tim back through the house, stopping at the cellar, a tiny dugout of a room under the kitchen with a dirt floor, undoubtedly 1860 original. Its low ceiling housed an old furnace and a well-worn snow shovel. It was musty down there but nothing terrible.

Tim looked at the furnace and clenched his jaw, concerned. "Wow, that thing is old." After searching the beast, he found the date of manufacture. "1911. Damn. Does it work?" Tim added the furnace to his mental list of expenses and swallowed hard.

"It must. I didn't see anything about it in the listing."

"I'm going to need to be sure before I make an offer." Holly and Tim left the cellar and went outside.

"You've got a nice big barn here," said Holly. Tim looked up at the large sliding doors rusted halfway open and wagered it would take several cans of *3-in-1* oil and a lot of determination to close them. The hayloft was above the barn doors, with a rusty pulley-post for lifting bales into storage.

The back of the barn was shadowy, featuring a workbench and an old rowboat. Above all were a cavernous ceiling and a cupola. Tim didn't have to wonder if any bats were up there. It was broad daylight, and they were already circling.

"Do they come with the property?" said Tim.

"Uh, yes, they do. You might want them around, though. Some say the New Hampshire state bird is the Black Fly, and bats eat them."

Tim laughed.

Tim and Holly walked the driveway, crossed the front lawn, and went to the pond. Four Canada Geese were there, preening feathers. A gap in the stone wall served as a gateway to the water. Once through, the geese took off, and as Tim got closer to the water, the ground squished beneath his feet.

The cattails seemed taller at eye level. It wasn't fit for swimming but was more of a haven for frogs, snakes, and water bugs. The stagnant water was ripe with algae, frog eggs, and goose dung. Tim imagined falling asleep to the song of horny bullfrogs when warmer weather arrived. Holly continued past the pond and into the field, and Tim followed.

"This field is multi-purpose," she said. "It could be a garden or a grazing area. Are you ready for the fascinating part?"

Tim looked around. An old pumpkin patch was certainly not his idea of excitement. Fifty yards later, Holly stepped into the woods, and Tim followed.

After ten yards of ducking through branches, she spoke up. "Wait here a second." Holly studied him, smiling as if he was supposed to notice something. When he didn't get it, she laughed. "Nothing?"

Holly backpedaled, exaggerating her steps, waiting for a reaction. Tim began to feel foolish, and Holly started to count. "One! What's the matter? Can't see the forest for the trees? Two!"

Tim stopped, frustrated, but then his eyes focused on everything behind Holly. At first, it wasn't there, and then it was, like looking at colored dots on paper and seeing a hidden picture. The wild woods had given way to an overgrown grove, or timber plantation, entirely invisible from the field. If he turned left or right, he was in the middle of an aisle, an undisturbed carpet of brown needles between every row.

Holly was excited to see his face. She was correct. It was weird here, but he wasn't sure why. *Oasis? Sanctuary?* No, that's not it. Wait, *secret.* Perhaps that was part of the description he was looking for, or maybe it was *abandoned?* Sunlight trickled through the canopy, leaving the atmosphere forever dusk.

"It's cool, right? Creepy, maybe? I didn't want to try to describe it."

"Yeah, moody," said Tim.

"I think about this place every so often. I dreamed of buying it, but I could never afford it."

Tim stood silent for a few seconds, taking it all in—the atmosphere, the perfect rows, and Holly's company. He was being seduced, and he wasn't sure if it was her shampoo, the property, or both. They didn't go much deeper into the woods and left before he could see how far back it went. Meanwhile, he began to worry that his bid would not be accepted.

"I suppose we need to look at the numbers then?" said Tim, to which Holly recited the basic terms. The bank was asking $75,000, but that would only leave him with $10,000 to refurbish. Tim planned on double that amount initially, and now it looked like he needed a new furnace. It was time to negotiate.

CHAPTER 5

Sanborn, New Hampshire
December, 1965

Annette Smith convinced her husband Henry to give up city life after his first heart attack. Henry had done well in the banking industry, but it was more than his body could take, and she felt he should get out while he still could. The Smiths had always loved horses, so in 1933, they searched for an available farm in northern Massachusetts and worked their way north, eventually finding their dream farm in Sanborn, New Hampshire.

Once they'd moved, Annette, a former nurse, volunteered at St. Mary's Nursing Home to stay current with her profession and maintain her social skills. Henry and horses all day would leave her wanting for conversation. They were blessed with their first child, Julia, in 1934, and two years later, Henry Jr. came into their lives.

Time passed quickly, and Julia married in 1953 and Henry Jr. in 1957. Thankfully, the horse business took off, growing so much that they had to hire two employees. They ate homegrown produce almost every day, and what they couldn't finish, Annette canned for the winter months. They could even cut their own Christmas trees from the property, and it was a perfect life until the day after Thanksgiving, 1965, when Annette found Henry on the lawn.

Annette didn't know it, but Henry wasn't killed next to the barn, but out in the grove, nearly a quarter mile away. She did her best to revive him but to no avail. Finally, the ambulance arrived twenty-five minutes later, but Henry was gone. As much as she wanted to, Annette couldn't blame the paramedics. He'd been at risk for years, and despite his change of lifestyle, the old vices had done their damage. The autopsy results confirmed as much.

Marjorie, Annette's sister, took two weeks away from her family to comfort and help Annette adjust to a widow's life, but when her time came to leave, it was the single loneliest moment of Annette's life. Suddenly, the farmhouse that was too big for two became a mansion for one, and after only two days of solitude, Annette felt as if she might be the last person on Earth. However, her loneliness was put on hold when she saw the little boy.

CHAPTER 6

Sanborn, New Hampshire
April 17, 1971

Tim powered up the driveway and parked in front of the barn. Thankfully, negotiating had resulted in a five thousand dollar discount, and he could spend the rest of his afternoon purchasing building materials before heading back to Massachusetts to meet a client. *Day One of the Lancaster Hill Road refurbishment begins tomorrow.*

Something, however, caught Tim's eye at the far end of the field: the same woman he'd seen on the day of Holly's grand tour, standing still, knee-deep in the grass, looking away. *Hello again,* he thought. *Help yourself to whatever you're doing. I'll be too busy to pick blueberries, so knock yourself out.*

Tim pulled a small envelope containing two freshly cut house keys from his pocket and slid one into his palm as he walked to the front door beneath the bedrooms. Thankfully, it worked on the first try, and he stepped in. The house was his now, and with it, all twenty-three acres.

He'd been pondering his plan of attack on the drive-up and decided it was wiser to save the exterior work for the summertime. For unpredictable April, he would begin inside, re-insulating the outer walls. The living room had two windows that needed replacing and ancient plaster walls, so Tim decided to start there and began moving anything not nailed down to the next room over.

As he worked to clear the bookshelves, he read the titles. On the top shelf was a World Atlas, a set of encyclopedias, some novels, a book called *Inspirational Quotes*, and a book on the history of Boston from 1630 to "modern day," which, for this book, meant 1930. He found a nondescript black hardcover on the middle shelf that looked like someone's handwritten journal. Tim cracked it and read the first page.

Thursday, February 17, 1966

Today, I sat and waited for the boy to come to the field to make his snowman. I waited until noon, but he never showed up. I even stayed an extra hour and rechecked the calendar to ensure I had the correct date. So, I wonder if my theory is off.

Losing interest, Tim clapped the book shut and moved it to the dining room. Thirty minutes later, he called it a day and walked the length of the house to the side door, realizing he hadn't been in the kitchen since Holly's walk-through. He sniffed the air. There was a musty odor. His heart sank. Water problems weren't cheap to fix.

Sniffing like a dog, Tim backtracked to the kitchen, where he heard a splashing sound from somewhere beneath his feet. *One, two, three, four, five, six* times. The sound kept repeating. Tim looked down. *It's coming from the cellar.*

Tiptoeing over the floor, Tim eyed the cellar doorknob, listening carefully for whatever it was. It sounded like someone wading in a kiddie pool or bathtub. As if on command, the splashing started again. Remembering every dollar he'd bet on the house, Tim grabbed the knob and turned. The stairway began in the shadowy corner of the kitchen and ended somewhere in the pitch black of the basement. The light switch was a foot inside. Tim reached in and flicked it on.

Tim watched as the last ripples bounced off the bottom stair and went still. The dirt floor was under an inch of water and smelled like a marsh. Crouching, Tim craned his neck under the kitchen floor and looked around. A single bulb provided the light. The old furnace occupied a third of the room, leaving the rest in shadows. Nothing moved.

Uneasy, Tim fetched a hammer and, after a moment's hesitation, took his first step downstairs. The temperature dropped with every step. Tim splashed around the ankle-deep water, searching for the source of the flooding and tapping pipes to scare potential rodents, but found nothing.

I can fix it, he told himself, wondering why whatever it was sounded so much like human footsteps. Bewildered, Tim climbed the stairs, flicked off the light, and closed the door, willing his heartbeat to slow. The water was a problem, but not the end of the world. *Every house has issues,* he told himself. Peeved, Tim walked to the sliding glass door, ready to lock up. He would spend one more night in his Haverhill apartment, gather the necessities, and move to Sanborn tomorrow. The stuff in storage, however, would take several trips.

As Tim reached for the handle, he heard another noise, this time from deeper in the house. This sounded like footsteps, this time coming down the bedroom stairs. *Six, seven, eight, nine, ten, eleven.* The hairs stood on Tim's arms as he wondered what the hell was happening.

He gazed down the length of the house, through the kitchen, dining room, living room, and hallway, to the last room by the road. The living room wall obscured the stairs, but he knew from years of contracting that staircases had roughly a dozen steps. Whoever had paused their descent on step eleven had to be around the corner.

"Who is it?" he bellowed, hammer held high. As he waited, he questioned himself. Perhaps being alone in the country was too different. It was quiet out here. Maybe he wasn't ready for little noises to sound like big noises, especially in a house with a mysterious past. *No*, he corrected himself. *All seventeen footsteps happened.*

Gritting his teeth, Tim strode through the dining room and then the living room, hugging the front wall, hammer raised. Finally, he peered around the threshold into the hallway and up the stairwell. *Empty*, as was the balcony above.

Tim called out: "I can hear you up there. Come out, or I'm coming up." The hallway was cold like the cellar, and the balcony over his head was the last place he wanted to go. An hour-and-a-half drive with a beer between his legs sounded like heaven. After listening for a full minute, Tim started up. Although he didn't believe in ghosts, he was scared like he did.

In a controlled panic, Tim barged through each bedroom, hammer raised, and cleared the second floor in less than twenty seconds. He stood between the two front rooms, watching the hallway and the staircase. Sweat dripped from his forehead, and his heart pounded. *Enough.* He'd never leave if he checked out every little creak.

Tim hated unfinished business, and this would bother him. He heard a sound or two on the way out but no footsteps, so he ignored them all and locked up. Once on the highway and after half the beer was gone, Tim wondered: If he had heard more footsteps, would he have chased them?

CHAPTER 7

April 18, 1971

Tim returned to Lancaster Hill Road the following day and went straight to work, determined to ignore any strange noises that might interrupt his day. The first thing he checked was the cellar to see if the water had risen, but to his ecstasy, the marshy funk had drained away. The floor was barely damp, freeing him up for the actual work. *I dodged a bullet there.*

He got a lot done, stopping only to eat a sandwich, and before he knew it, it was evening. As always, there remained a half-hour of cleanup. Tim's stomach growled, and he headed to town to grab a burger before crashing on the mattress upstairs. Maybe he'd call Holly tomorrow and tell her how things were going. *It couldn't hurt.*

As he emptied his last dustpan of plaster, the phone rang, startling him. The line had only been activated this morning, and it was the loudest thing he'd heard all day. Only Johnny and Sheila knew the number. Tim answered, but there was nobody on the other end. *Telemarketers,* he reasoned and placed the receiver back in the cradle. No sooner did he touch the broom than he heard the footsteps again.

Thud-thud-thud-thud-thud-thud-thud-thud.

Grabbing the painter's light, Tim peered around the corner, past the staircase to the hallway above. He tried the light switch at the bottom of the stairs, but nothing happened. *Oh, no,* he thought. *Not enough lights!* The wide beam made elongated shadows up the staircase. The railing had a long double that moved with it, but nothing else moved. Tim's heart raced. At a loss for what to do, he rested his shoulder against the threshold and waited.

THUD-THUD-THUD-THUD-THUD.

Tim spun. This time, the footsteps came from the kitchen. *Are there two?* He lifted the light high, hoping it could carry into the breakfast area, but the beam died in the middle of the dining room. There were so many places to hide: the kitchen, the cellar, the turret, etcetera. He waited, uncomfortable being the only light source in the house. *I'm like a damned beacon,* he thought. *Note to self: Bring the baseball bat and tons of light bulbs.*

Were there gypsies out here? The house had been empty for three years. Someone, at some point, had broken the back window in the dining room. *There can't be anyone in the house,* he thought. *You've been here all day.*

Anxious, Tim decided to move and snapped the painter's light off, leaving him blind. *The wrong move,* he thought, as his eyes took forever to adjust. Even though a near-full moon came through the front windows, his vision was near zero. The entrance to the dining room had become a dark mouth. Tim moved to the back of the house, praying whomever it was had lost sight of him. Tim snapped the light back on half a minute later, blinding himself again, but he didn't dare blink. Suddenly, he heard the footsteps again:

Thud-thud-thud-thud-thud-thud-thud.

Holding the painter's light over his head, Tim stepped toward the dining room. The short-range beam reached halfway through the kitchen, and there, in the far corner of the breakfast area, shined two eyes, swaying back and forth.

The boy entered the light and stopped, thin and pale, roughly eight years old, wearing overalls, a white shirt, and leather shoes. His skin was bone-white, and his hair stringy. The eyes were lifeless, yet Tim sensed caution. There was a chill in the air as the boy approached, and a smell reached his nostrils: musty, like the cellar.

"Where are your parents?" With Tim's words, the boy turned and ran back to the breakfast nook beyond the limits of the painter's light. Tim listened for the sliding glass door, but it never came. In a panic, Tim bolted out the front door and into the night. *Dammit;* the truck was in front of the barn! With little choice, he rounded the corner at top speed, yanked the truck's door handle, started the engine, and threw it in reverse.

Tim spun the truck in the driveway's bend and floored it, barreling for the road, watching the house for signs of the boy.

You're running, Tim. It's Day One, and you're quitting! What about providing for your daughters? Don't ever tell anyone how you lost everything.

Ashamed, he slammed on the brakes. Nervously, Tim checked the rearview mirror and bit his lip. This house was his future. Every dollar was here in Sanborn. If he left now, he would be penniless, and worst of all, Sheila could tell everyone she'd known for a long time what a loser Tim Russell was.

Tim put the truck in park and opened the door. Standing on the lower lawn, he stared into the living room, watching the orange glow of the painter's light and trying to get the nerve up to go back in. *That kid was dead.*

Tim hopped back in the truck and drove down Lancaster Hill Road until the painter's light disappeared, then pulled over and cut the engine.

This panic attack was uncharted territory, and no one could help. Getting out of the truck, Tim walked the ditch back toward the house, the gravel crunching like coffee grinds beneath his feet. He hadn't grabbed his jacket, and as the adrenaline ebbed, the cold crept in.

Two minutes later, he crossed the property line where the forest became his pasture. Feeling his way across the ditch and over the stone wall, he walked midway into the field and stopped. The moon cast a hazy glow as he watched the house for signs of movement, the aura of the painter's light turning the living room into a fishbowl. *Seventy thousand dollars, and it's haunted? You've got to be shitting me. What now? Check in to a hotel?* He could go to a bar for liquid courage, but then what? Go back? *Sure, Tim, things will be much better after midnight.*

Indecision was rare for Tim, and the chilly evening made things worse. Suddenly, a light went on in the turret, dim and flickering, different from the steady beam of the painter's light. *What's that, a candle?* Again, he felt a chill, this time more than just the April weather. *Damn it, there's an open flame up there. Wait any longer, and your investment goes up in smoke.* Oh, the garbage Sheila would plant in the girls' heads if he failed! The last thought did it. Tim returned to the truck, ready to stare death in the face.

Tim turned on his headlamps and drove back, announcing his arrival. Forty feet ahead, candlelight danced on the ceiling of the turret, and his heart pounded. *I'm betting my life. Let's be friends.* Tim exited the truck and opened the front door under the bedrooms. The painter's light spilled into the hallway. He could see up the first six stairs, but after that, nothing but darkness. Tim fetched the lamp and two extension cords and began rigging them for an extended search.

Five minutes later, he climbed the turret stairs, praying nobody would unplug the cord. The candlelight shimmered on the ceiling. There had been no candles in the house that he was aware of, certainly not in the turret, one more thing that defied explanation. As Tim's eyes cleared the top of the stairs, his head swiveled to cover all angles, and thankfully, no one waited for him.

The candle's flame and the painter's light reflected off the eight windows, making the yard below invisible. He knew full well the opposite was true for anyone looking in. The candle was sitting atop a book he recognized from earlier. It was the journal from downstairs.

CHAPTER 8

December 16, 1965

Annette sat in the turret with a cup of tea. Things were difficult without Henry, and she missed him terribly. There was a lot to do on a horse farm, especially alone. Several horses were considered works-in-progress; Henry's expertise, not hers. Very soon, she would have to sell them off at a discount.

Annette's sister Marjorie had left three days before, and the two weeks she afforded Annette had been accommodating, albeit brief. So many unpleasant yet necessary tasks were completed for the care of Henry's body: the funeral arrangements, the life insurance, and so forth. The painful transition from life with Henry to life without had begun.

Annette considered selling the farm and moving closer to one of the kids, but it didn't feel right. Annette loved living here, and moving away would not help anything. Henry Junior stayed for a week, but he had young children and had to return to Cambridge. Julia came for the funeral but lived in Illinois, so her visit was even shorter.

Annette knew she could always spend more time volunteering at the Sanborn Nursing Home if she got too lonely. She enjoyed helping the elderly, and why not? Maybe they would help her, too. The patients were as lonely as she was and had similar stories. Misery loves company, and there was much to commiserate.

It was nearly 3:30 pm, and sunset was only forty minutes away. Nothing was left in Annette's day but a lonely dinner and sleep. She hadn't eaten much of late. No matter how hard she worked, the appetite wasn't there, at least not yet. It was then that she caught something in the corner of her eye.

The little boy ran past the pond, directly between the two willows. Perhaps she'd seen this boy off and on for years, but was it always the same one? The Simmons family had a compound down the road, and she'd always assumed it was one of them. But she'd lived here twenty-nine years. It had to be a grandchild. *Time flies.*

The boy trudged through the snow, pulling a toboggan sled bigger than he was. The wind blew, and the hair on his forehead with it. To her surprise, he was not wearing a coat. Moving quickly, she grabbed her sweater and descended the stairs, leaving the house in a run and trudging across the snowy lawn toward the pond, but she'd already lost him. He'd disappeared. The wind picked up, and the willows danced.

Annette looked left toward the forest, hoping to reacquire him. In the time it took her to descend the turret stairs and leave the building, somehow, he'd covered four times the ground she had, which was all but impossible. She stopped and turned, scanning the tree line and the pasture, and went back to the pond, but there was still no sign.

Annette struggled to catch her breath and arrived at the spot where she'd seen the boy, but there were no footsteps and no sign that anyone had crossed the field. Just then, she sensed movement by the trees and turned quickly but saw only a rabbit lurching across the meadow, breaking through the icy crust with every step.

The speculation began. This sighting gave birth to a theory that sparked much-needed purpose. Annette had always believed in spirits, and her mind shifted to something meaningful for the first time since Henry's death. A widow with a hole in her life had found a mystery to solve.

Annette got into her truck and drove to Newman's Stationery. On the wall just past the cash register by the pastel paper was a shelf full of blank journals, from which she chose the most ordinary-looking book and grabbed two of them just in case they went out of print.

CHAPTER 9

April 18, 1971

Tim's nerves were fried, but he was proud of himself. He'd returned to the house even though gathering the courage took an hour. But the night wasn't over. In fact, it wasn't even midnight. Which would he rather have: financial death and Sheila's poison tongue or death itself? After thinking about it, Tim chose death itself.

Bringing the journal with him, Tim descended the turret stairs and made his way through the living room to the bedroom stairwell, extension cords trailing. The process of moving the cord was harrowing, twice leaving him in darkness. Fumbling for outlets was excruciating, all the while thinking of the woman who probably died in his bedroom.

Sweat broke out over his drywall-caked skin. He needed a shower, but there was no way he would risk standing naked behind the curtain tonight. Tim climbed the stairs, eyes on the two dark bedrooms on either side of the hall. As he brushed his teeth, he realized that the top of the stairs would be an ideal spot to get ambushed, as it was vulnerable from almost every direction.

Once the bathroom rituals were complete, he crawled into bed with the journal. The only sound was his beating heart. It would be near-impossible to hear something in the kitchen from here. Tim did his best to relax and opened the journal.

Friday, December 17, 1965
My Journal
By Annette Smith

While having tea in the turret, I saw the little boy on our property again, walking through the snow, dragging a sled past the pond. I'm always so busy I never have time to go outside and flag him down to ask him who he is and where he lives. It seems like he's been around for a while. How many years? I couldn't begin to guess. I wish Henry were still around. I would ask him.

Since we are so isolated from our neighbors, it's shocking to see a boy his age alone. I know country folks are more naïve than city folks, or maybe they know more than we do. It's hard to say.

Anyway, I left the turret to catch up with the boy and pick his brain, but he was gone! Oddly, he didn't leave any footprints in the snow, so I am either losing my mind or may have seen a ghost. In my heart, I hope he IS a ghost. If he is, he must need help, and I would love to help. Yes, I am so heartbreakingly lonely that I would befriend a ghost.

Tim's first thought was not about the boy but of "Henry" being dead, too. What happened to Henry? *And who is this kid?* Maybe he should call Holly tomorrow and ask all the questions he should have asked before buying the place.

Tim didn't read much further. The house had been quiet for nearly three hours, and his heart rate was back to normal. If something wanted him dead, it could have killed him by now. Tim fell asleep with the painter's light on and the journal on his chest. *Take me if you want me,* he thought. *Take me out while I'm at rock bottom. You'll be doing me a favor.*

CHAPTER 10

April 19, 1971

Tim woke at 5:24 am the following day, but it took him a moment. Where was he? *My house, my haunted house.* His first thought was of the ghost boy, and that shook the cobwebs. Butterflies fluttered in his belly as he stood, his heart racing again.

After listening to the house, Tim's second thought was to get to work. His original plan was to work on a wall, but things had changed. He would have to drive to Amesbury and haul as much as possible for the coming evening. Suddenly, he heard pounding in the distance. Still clothed in yesterday's filth, Tim looked out the window. He searched for something to wield, grabbing the only thing he had brought upstairs: his hammer. *It probably won't work on ghosts, but whatever makes you feel better ...*

Tim crossed the hallway to the sunny bedroom, which looked across the roof to the turret. The barn was behind and to the left, nearly seventy-five feet away, and the banging was coming from that direction. He descended the stairs, head on a swivel on his way out.

Tim scanned the kitchen and breakfast area and exited through the side door. The pounding was louder out here, and Tim confirmed the hammering was coming from the barn's roof. Since the barn was attached to the carriage house, walking around was not an option. The right side was pressed against the forest, so getting a view from a distance was also impossible.

Tim walked to the front of the barn and looked up. With no clear vantage point, he followed the front wall and turned the corner. Wild vines and thorns made passage nearly impossible. There was simply no good place to look at that side of the roof.

Suddenly, a metallic rattle came from overhead, and one by one, six nails plopped next to him in the weeds. Tim picked them up and examined them closely. They were square, tapered to a point on two sides, and made of iron, yet they were oily and brand new in appearance. This type of nail hadn't been available for a century. Tim returned to the driveway. When he was thirty feet from the barn, he called out:

"Who's up there?" The pounding stopped. "Who are you? Let's talk!" Nothing happened. Determined, Tim went into the house, climbed into the turret, opened a window, and lowered himself onto the roof as the hammering continued. He had to be careful where he stepped as the shingles were old, some tearing under his feet. Finally, Tim transitioned from the carriage house onto the much steeper barn, and as he reached the peak, the pounding stopped.

The roof was empty, and it was no surprise there were no ladders anywhere. This part of the roof was in the same disrepair as the rest. *I need to read that journal.* Tim hadn't read a book in thirty years and was up to his eyeballs in things to do. There were not enough hours in the day, but he would have to find the time.

CHAPTER 11

Laconia, New Hampshire
April 19, 1971

Holly had just arrived at her office when the phone rang.

"Hi, Holly, this is Tim Russell. Do you have a minute?" Holly was just about to sit down and organize her day. It had been over a week since Tim bought the house, and since then, she'd come to think of their flirty vibes as the heat of the moment. Holly had dropped some hints but never asked him on a date. The man was barely divorced and probably damaged goods anyway.

This phone call was interesting, however. By coincidence, Holly had planned to check back with Tim today to see how things were going and ask for referrals. It was something the boss required all of the agents to do.

"Hi, Tim. Kicking up the dust? Ready to re-sell?"

"Haha, sure, Holly, I'm just about finished. One more coat of paint in the living room, and we can put it back on the market."

"Well, I hope you aren't calling for help. I hate painting."

"You sound like some of my former employees. No, I was calling with some questions, but it can wait if it's not a good time."

"I have time. Coincidentally, you were on my list of callbacks. I'm mailing you a tin of cookies from Depot Realty later today. They aren't fresh, though, I must warn you. I've heard they must be dunked in milk to get them down your throat."

"Thanks for the warning." An awkward pause followed before Tim spoke again. "Holly, we discussed it briefly, but how much do you know of the house's history?"

Buzzkill thought Holly. It didn't sound like the phone call she hoped it would be. *Buyer's Remorse, here we go.* "You mean the Smith woman?"

"Yeah, I guess so. I found a journal and read some of it. Annette's husband, Henry, also died, and I wasn't sure if you knew that. Not that it

43

bothers me, but, you know. First, there's Annette, and now the husband. I just wanted to get your thoughts."

"To be honest, Tim, I avoid looking into this type of thing. I don't know if your house has a history, but that house is over a hundred and ten years old. Several people might have died in it, and perhaps a birth or two! What's in this journal you're talking about?"

"I've only read a page or two. This is a strange phone call, isn't it?"

"What are you trying to say, Tim?"

"Well, Annette Smith wrote the journal, and she says she saw the ghost of a little boy on the property. I never believed in that stuff, but laugh all you want. She was right." Tim exhaled as the words left his mouth, both cathartic and embarrassing. He hadn't planned on spilling the beans, but he ran out of words. He waited for the giggle on the other end.

"You did?" said Holly, a note of surprise in her voice.

She didn't laugh at me. "There's no doubt. I even have physical proof, more than just the journal."

Tim didn't realize, but he'd lit a fire under Holly's chair. As a little girl, she and her grandfather shared a fondness for ghost stories and scary movies. It started with a Saturday afternoon movie on TV called "The House on Haunted Hill."

Grandfather and granddaughter watched the movie together, and when he was sure Holly hadn't suffered any nightmares, he let her watch more, starting a tradition. From that day on, the two spent their days looking for scary things to share the next time they got together.

"I just got a chill. Hold on a second." Holly put her hand over the mouthpiece so she could hear her boss calling to her from the other room. Listening to him was the last thing she wanted right now. "I'm sorry, what, Marty?"

"There's a meeting in the conference room. Can you call them back?" said Marty.

"It's my latest buyer, but, sure. Five minutes."

"We'll be waiting."

Holly flashed a fake smile and took her hand off the mouthpiece. "Tim, I hate to cut this short, but my boss is calling a meeting. I want to hear your story. How about I buy you a burger tonight? Do you know the Bunkhouse Bar?"

"I don't, but I'll find it," said Tim.

"It's close to you, on Route 3. 7:00 pm?

"7:00 pm!"

CHAPTER 12

April 19, 1971

Holly was not wearing work clothes when they met at the restaurant. She'd finished her workday early to go home and dress properly. Tim, too, had driven a little faster down to Amesbury to ensure he returned on time after acquiring plenty of light bulbs, batteries, and flashlights. When he arrived at the house, he showered with the curtain half-open and a baseball bat leaning against the tub. He told Holly everything at dinner, from the boy to the roofing nails and the journal.

"So, where is it?" Holly asked.

Tim's face paled. "I can't believe it. I forgot the damned thing. I put the nails in my pocket and forgot everything else."

"Well, I guess dinner's over then," said Holly, straight-faced.

"Are you serious? I can drop it off."

"I'm joking; of course not! The nails are proof enough. You can stay."

"Dry humor always gets me," said Tim.

"Yeah, well, you still have to earn your burger. Tell me what you saw." Holly watched Tim's smile fade as he sat up straight and serious.

"The first time I saw the journal was the day I got the house keys, and it was in the living room," Tim told his story in the order everything happened, explaining the footsteps he heard, the sighting of the boy, his sudden exit, and the candle in the turret.

"The next time I saw the journal, it was under the burning candle, and I took it to bed. Annette writes that she saw the kid running in the snow, and he didn't leave any footprints."

Holly stared back, astonished. "And you just had to forget it back at the house."

"Don't remind me," said Tim.

Holly examined the roofing nails again, feeling their oily texture. They talked for an hour and a half, but it felt like fifteen minutes. Tim insisted on picking up the check, and when he returned to the table, Holly made her second proposal of the day. "Tim, I want to help you figure this out. Do you mind if I stop by to grab the journal? That is, if you're not planning on reading it tonight. We have a Xerox at the office, and I can make a copy of it. Divide and conquer, compare notes."

"You want to go there now? Are you sure? That would be helpful, but last night wasn't fun. Fair warning."

"Hit and run. I'm nervous just thinking about it!"

"All right, then. I'll show you the journal, the turret, and the candlestick. If you're lucky, there might be three of us." Holly froze, and for a second, Tim wasn't sure if he'd scared her away. "Look, you don't have to come. I'll drop it off at your office tomorrow. No pressure."

"No, let's go. I might be naïve, but I'm betting we don't see one."

With that, they left in two cars, but Tim wanted to approach slowly, keeping engine noise to a minimum. They parked Holly's car at the end of Lancaster Hill Road, then rode the last mile together. When she climbed in, electricity was in the air. Holly seemed excited, but neither said a word until they arrived at the property line.

"I'm going to shut off my headlights, and depending on what we see in the next fifty yards, I'll know how to proceed. I spent a lot of time today rigging the place with lights, so at least there's that. Two lights are on timers and were set to turn on at 8:00 pm."

Tim put the truck in gear and crept forward, driving by moonlight. Every so often, they saw a flicker of light through the foliage. *Good,* the timers were working. Then, sixty yards from the house and dead even with the pond, a gap in the trees opened up. Tim stopped. They could see almost the entire front of the house.

Tim had placed the timers in the living room and main bedroom, and thankfully, both rooms were illuminated. However, the bad news was twofold: The turret was flickering again, and even more alarming, a shadow was moving in the main bedroom.

Holly gasped. "Who is that in the bedroom?"

"Black dress. I think that's the woman I've seen in my field." *Thank God I went out for dinner,* he thought.

"Do you know her?"

"You know more about my neighbors than I do, Holly. I didn't light the candle in the turret either."

"If this is a joke, Tim ..."

"It's not, I promise. I'm wondering if the whole town isn't pranking me."

They locked eyes, and Holly saw he was serious. Meanwhile, the woman in Tim's bedroom paced back and forth.

"Tim, this is creepy. Let's go!"

"Wait, I don't think she knows we're here. I don't know if that's a ghost or a thief, but maybe she'll leave so I can put the candle out. I've got a baseball bat in the back."

Holly looked at Tim, then back at the house. The woman in the black dress appeared to be talking to herself. "She looks angry."

Tim's mind raced. Even if it was a thief, there wasn't much to steal in there. He would have to trust the candlestick to do its job. Decision made, Tim put the truck in gear, but the engine died. He tried again, but all they heard was a series of clicks. Tim looked at Holly in disbelief but said nothing. One more time, he exhaled, rested his forehead on the steering wheel, and turned the key. Nothing. *Of all the damned clichés.*

"Get the baseball bat," said Holly.

"All right. We'll run back to your car."

"What, like a mile? Are you sure? What if we … Oh, I don't know."

Tim checked their surroundings, then grabbed the flashlight, holding it like a club. "Are you ready?"

"Okay, but be quiet!"

Tim grabbed the handle and pulled, but it wouldn't budge. He checked the lock, which should push and pull freely, but the handle was frozen. "It's stuck!"

Holly tried hers with the same result. In a panic, Tim tried his window, but it, too, was jammed.

"Is she doing this?" said Tim as he removed his jacket and wrapped it around the flashlight. "Shield your eyes." Tim swung, and what should have been an explosion of glass was only a loud *crack*: the flashlight bounced off the window as if it were made of cement.

"Son of a bitch!" Pain shot up Tim's arm as he shook his hand, rubbing it, feeling bones and tendons for damage. A trickle of blood dripped between two knuckles. The window was cracked, but the glass didn't move.

"Are you okay?" she asked.

"It won't break." Tim didn't care about the woman in the window for a moment as he wondered if his hand was broken. She seemed oblivious to them anyway, walking back and forth, talking to herself or someone they couldn't see. Tim studied the driver's side window. The shattered glass was opaque with spider-web cracks, yet nothing had fallen onto the road. He poked the center gently, and six chunks dislodged. He placed his hand flat and pushed, and half the window crumbled.

Encouraged, Tim finished clearing the window and prepared to climb out, but as soon as he attempted to get up, something pressed him back into his seat. A palpable weight held him down, pushing around his shoulders and chest. He struggled, testing the unseen force, but it was like trying to lift his body weight.

Holly saw everything happening to Tim and tried an escape of her own but was forced back the same way, the air pushed from her lungs. Separately, they struggled in silence. The more they fought, the heavier it felt. Finally, Holly surrendered, and the grip loosened, then returned when she tried to open her door.

"Stop fighting," she instructed. Tim listened and felt the pressure yield. The two of them panted, sucking air. "Are you okay?" whispered Holly, and Tim nodded, shifting his weight and still feeling the invisible grip.

"How are you?" he asked.

"I'm scared."

"Is she coming?" Tim looked up at the main bedroom, and the woman passed the window again.

"What is she doing?"

"I don't know, but I'm fine with her staying there." Suddenly, the woman left the window and disappeared into the house.

"Is she coming?" asked Holly.

Tim felt helpless. If she was coming, they were fish in a barrel. "I don't think so," he lied. All they could do was wait. Tim paid attention to the darkness around the truck, praying she would not emerge. Then, suddenly, all the lights in the house went out except for the candle in the turret. The road went dark, and Tim checked his watch: 9:37 pm.

"What time are the lights supposed to go out?" she asked.

"5:00 am." As soon as Tim spoke, the weight holding him down disappeared completely. Holly sat forward and drew in a slow breath. Their hands searched their bodies instinctively.

"Let's try again," said Tim, turning the key to the sound of … still nothing. Their best bet was to run to Holly's car. "What do you think?" he asked.

"I don't know. I want to leave, but walking this road won't make me feel any better." Suddenly, the turret went dark. The only light on Lancaster Hill Road was the quarter moon.

"Oh shit, Tim, let's run!" As soon as the words left Holly's mouth, a match flared, followed by the familiar steady flicker.

"I think there's something we're supposed to see."

"In there? Are you sure? Where's the woman?"

"They left something for me last night. Maybe they did tonight, too, but I'm fine with going to your car." They tried their doors, and this time, it worked. Once outside, Tim hand-signaled: *Ready? One ... two ... three.* They began to walk, but the pressure returned as soon as they passed the tailgate. Holly stopped, and the pressure faded. Tim took two more baby steps to be sure, and it was clear there was only one option. Holly wasn't happy.

"If I had known it would get physical, I wouldn't have let you come. Nothing like this happened last night," said Tim.

"Six hours ago, I thought you were going to tell me about things you thought you saw, like footsteps and doors creaking. Things that happen in the first half-hour of a horror movie. Instead, I feel like a ghost is touching me."

Tim reached for her hand, and she let him take it. "Ready?"

"Not really. Where is that woman? Keep watching."

"Maybe if we see her, she'll tell us what she wants."

"I don't want to see her," said Holly.

Tim and Holly walked hand in hand between the two maples at the beginning of the driveway. Tim watched the dark windows for a staring face as they made their way up the slope. Which door should they enter? He moved for the first front door, and Holly yanked his hand back.

"Too close to where we saw her!" she mouthed. It was a bonus Holly knew the house as well as he did. Tim had a feeling the woman upstairs was gone, but Holly believed otherwise. Tim unlocked the side door, turned on his flashlight, and stepped in. Quietly, they opened the glass slider to the breakfast area, checking every shadow. They stood where Tim had seen the boy's eyes the previous night and attempted to see down the length of the house. As the beam painted the walls, Tim couldn't help but wonder if things like this happened every night.

Knowing a candle was burning in the room above them, they passed the cellar door to the turret stairs and climbed up. Holly stayed close, holding his hand tightly. The déjà vu was intense as Tim ascended into the turret for the second consecutive night. Again, on the table was the candle, and beside it, the journal, this time open to a page.

Holly took the flashlight from Tim's hand.

Tuesday, January 18, 1966

Today, I saw the woman out in the pasture again from the turret. Not that I think she is a living person now, of course. She can't pick our wild blueberries or grapes as we first suspected as the seasons have passed. In this January freeze, she wears no overcoat, walking primarily from the far tree line to the pasture and into the woods.

Perhaps I was bored, but I decided to tempt fate and ask her some questions, maybe see if I could help her find comfort or talk the way I do with the ladies at the nursing home. So I threw on my overcoat and went outside quickly to catch her before she disappeared.

I called out, but she seemed focused on her destination. Either that or she didn't hear me. Finally, I passed the pond, still calling after her to stop. She was almost to the woods, but a hundred yards of field was still between us. I was going to shout one last time, but I was suddenly pushed to the ground from behind. Before I knew it, an invisible weight pressed my face into the snow. It was hard to breathe, and I couldn't scream. I had no idea what was going on above the surface.

When I quit struggling, the weight released me, and I picked myself up. The woman was gone, and my face was numb with cold. I went home crying, but after thinking, I had to wonder. Was it her that pinned me to the ground or someone else? I wasn't harmed, other than the initial shove.

As I have little to do but think for hours, I have come to believe that the woman in the field is unhappy. The boy is distracting but not as disruptive. Perhaps she wants nothing to do with me. I suppose if this is true, we may be able to coexist. But maybe it's the opposite, and someone else is telling me to keep my distance from the woman in the field.

"I told you I didn't like her," said Holly. "And I'm not the only one. Tim, she was in here not ten minutes ago. You can't stay here tonight, and that's not a come-on. Let's grab the journal and take it back to my place. You can sleep in the guest room."

The topic was not open to discussion, not that he protested. Holly picked up the journal and blew out the candle, and Tim led the way downstairs, praying they'd be able to drive. Thankfully, the truck started perfectly. Tim had to smile as soon as Holly was in her car, leading him back to Laconia. *That was one hell of a first date.*

CHAPTER 13

April 19, 1971

It was getting late, but Tim was exhilarated. It was a tremendous relief not to brave another night alone. His eyes were bloodshot-tired. He knew, however, that he had to be a gentleman at Holly's house.

The house was Cape Cod style, and he would later learn that she, too, was a divorcee. Holly married a man who ended up spending too much time at the pubs, and when the relationship failed three years ago, Holly won the house as part of the settlement. She referred to it as a "starter marriage," as it had lasted less than two years and there were no children. As they parked, Holly opened the door and invited him in.

"How are you feeling?" she asked.

"I feel like my brain is in a blender. I'm on the hook for $70k and can't abandon it. I hope this journal can point us in the right direction, but I'm skeptical because Annette's situation didn't seem to end well. She might even be one of the ghosts, for all I know. How about you?"

"I think I'm in shock, but I don't think that was Annette we saw. That woman's dress was not from this century."

"That's true," said Tim. "Holly, don't feel bad about selling me the house. I can tell you feel guilty."

"I do. I'm so sorry, Tim."

"No one could have known."

"Who do you think left the book open?"

"I have no idea."

"Annette also mentioned someone else. And they might have kept her away from the woman in the dress."

"Who was she? Annette, I mean. Do you know any details?"

"No, but I will do some digging." Holly opened the journal, skipped past the sighting of the boy in the snow, and read aloud.

Saturday, December 18, 1965

As I wait for the next sighting, I will explain myself in case this journal goes unfinished. I am Annette Smith, and I have lived in the house on Lancaster Hill Road since 1933. My husband Henry and I have lived here for 29 years without a supernatural occurrence, or so I thought. Unfortunately, Henry died a little over a month ago outside our barn from his second heart attack, and I miss him terribly.

I never thought we were being haunted, but now I'm sure I was wrong. If you're reading this, you have most likely read the first page with the sighting of the little boy. It may not sound like much, but I'm sure he's a ghost beyond the shadow of a doubt. Maybe you're asking if the wind filled his footprints with snow as I left the house to search for him. All I can say is no.

The wind was not strong that day, and I have had other sightings over the years, more years than I realized! I feel so ignorant. I should have noticed he never grew up, but honestly, for all I knew, it could have been two or three different little boys over the years. I'm busy, and it's not like we saw him all the time.

For years, we had seen the woman in the long dress (old-fashioned, to be sure, but then again, we live in New Hampshire). She would walk across the pasture from time to time. We thought she wanted to pick fruit or had a favorite walk, and we didn't care.

One day, Henry asked out loud why he had never seen the person flying the kite, and it got us thinking. We even ventured out to try and find the kite flyer, but it always disappeared on our way.

I hope to find out more, and I will report it here. If you haven't seen anything yet and don't believe me, save reading this for the day you do.

"What the hell! She said she'd been there since 1933. I've been there less than a week and seen everything she's written!"

"Relax, Tim, we're only four pages in. I want to know how she put up with it. How could she sleep with them running around? She must have been either very strong or eccentric."

Tim chuckled as he yawned. He was running on fumes. Holly continued skimming. "What's tomorrow?" Tim asked. "It feels like a Saturday because I went on a date."

"Oh, was that a date?"

"Well, you invited me back to your house, didn't you?"

"I do this as a courtesy for clients I sell haunted houses to. Tomorrow is Tuesday. What's your plan?"

The smile disappeared from Tim's face. "I'm refurbishing an old house I depend on for my financial future."

"What if she shows up? Annette wrote that you should steer clear."

"Yeah, I know, and Annette got pinned down in that field like we did in the truck."

"Shouldn't you wait and see if we can figure this out?"

"The short answer is no freaking way. Money is an issue." Tim sat up, elbows on his knees, clearly stressed. "If I see her, I'll keep clear, but I need this place to sell for double what I paid. I made noise with saws and hammers, and she didn't bother me. I've only ever seen her in the field, never in the house. Well, until tonight."

"Yeah, that's what I'm talking about. You don't know where she'll be!"

"I don't mean to play the macho man, but I'm more afraid of losing my shirt than I am of death." Suddenly, the blood drained from his face. "Oh, no."

"What's wrong?"

"I have my kids for visitation this weekend. My ex is going away."

"Well … you don't have to figure that out yet. Friday is four days away."

"Look, Holly, it's not the stuff you like to talk about after a first date, but I had an ugly divorce. The kids were used as weapons by their mother. She put ideas in their heads about Daddy having better things to do than spend time with them. She's fought me at every turn, even though she was the one who blew it all up.

"I realize this is he said/she said crap, but at the end of the day, molehills turn into mountains very quickly in Sheila's world because she wants them to. Sorry to dump my problems, but my better judgment fell asleep a few hours ago."

"My ex had a similar situation going on. As far as this weekend goes, you can always get a motel, take the kids to Funspot, and you'll be a hero. Tell them you had to fumigate the house or something. Let them tell their mother how much fun they had when she picks their brains about your new house."

"That might take care of this weekend, but I can't afford to do that every two weeks for a year and a half. There's no kitchen in a motel, for starters. I know it's not sexy to talk money, but I took a gamble buying that place. Sixty-five nights a year in a hotel is not in the budget.

"And Sheila will be relentless. She'll hound them with questions and use whatever they tell her to crawl up my ass, trying to find out why my house is so unsafe. If she takes me to court once, I'm in trouble. Do you want to know what my divorce cost? Ten thousand bucks. That's half of what it will take to refurb the house. It's cheaper to walk on eggshells."

"How about you take it one weekend at a time? Maybe the journal will help."

"Sure, like a *Hardy Boys* mystery. Maybe there's a treasure map in there, too." Tim caught himself. "I'm sorry. Talking about Sheila is never fun."

"I guess," said Holly. "I've never seen Mr. Negative before."

"Yeah, well, pleased to meet you." Tim held out his hand as if to shake.

"Ew! I don't want to meet Mr. Negative!" Holly giggled.

"It's been two jam-packed nights, but I had fun tonight," said Tim.

"That's what you call fun?" Holly kissed Tim on the cheek, then went to the linen closet and got him a towel. Tim followed as she led him to the guest room. "Here you go. There's an extra toothbrush in the bottom drawer of the bathroom vanity."

"Thanks for being there. At least now I know I'm not going crazy."

Holly smiled. "I had a nice time, too."

CHAPTER 14

April 20, 1971

Tim woke slowly, remembering where he was. Despite the ghostly encounters, there were very positive memories. He rose, stripped the linens to show he made no assumptions about staying over again and laid the quilt back over the bed. When finished, he went downstairs, sat on the couch, and waited for Holly to come downstairs. The journal was sitting on the coffee table, and his spirits sank.

Holly hit the bottom stairs smiling and lightened the mood. "Good morning! I'm sorry, but I don't have much food in the house. I usually grab my coffee on the way to work, so I can't even offer you that."

"Don't worry about it," Tim replied. "I can grab something later. I'm grateful for the good night's sleep. I needed it."

"Tim, be careful today."

"I will."

"Stay near the telephone. I'll take the journal to work and copy what I can when the boss isn't looking. We'd better get reading. Anything Annette learned could help. Do you want to lock up here when you're ready to go? I have to run."

"No, I'll walk out with you. Hey, are you doing anything tonight? Do you want to get some dinner again?"

She smiled. "I was hoping you'd say that. I asked last time, after all."

"Yes, because your boss rushed you to get off the phone. You didn't give me a chance!"

"Oh, so you were calling to ask me out? I thought you were angry with me."

"You like to give me a hard time, don't you?"

"Maybe. Think about what you want to eat. I know the area. Just make sure you make it to dinner. Be safe."

Tim touched her arm and stepped closer. When Holly didn't flinch, he kissed her, this time on the lips.

He followed her to a fork in the road, where they each went their separate ways. Tim enjoyed the drive. It only took one night with Holly to remember how things were supposed to be. *Cooperative* was an everyday, simple word that only the divorced truly understood. He and Sheila had lost that spirit of cooperation, and he saw that now. The doldrums were over, it seemed. He was feeling better about life, and Holly was a big reason why.

Tim kept his eyes peeled as he coasted down Lancaster Hill Road. As he passed the pile of shattered glass, he realized he'd been holding his breath.

Tim pulled up the driveway slower than ever. He scanned the windows for watchful eyes, but reflections impaired their transparency. Tim looked up at the turret, turned left at the bend, then turned around and pointed the truck toward the road. Grabbing the flashlight, he entered the side entrance and paused to listen.

Tim sniffed the air. *Is it marshy again?* He hadn't checked the basement in a while. Grabbing a hammer from the toolbox in the dining room, Tim flicked on the light and headed down the rickety staircase. Thankfully, the floor was dry. The low ceiling left the naked bulb at eye level. *I need to be careful not to take that out with my head.* Tim clicked on the flashlight and peered behind the furnace. Spiders ran the place. He would have to clear decades of webbing to see anything. One of the vertical beams blocked his view, so he went to the other side. The passage here was tight, so he turned sideways and shimmied in, clearing cobwebs with the shovel.

A stack of lumber scraps was in the corner, so Tim pulled them out and tossed them into the center of the room. Next, he found a toy drum, a rocking horse, and a large toboggan sled. *Must have belonged to the boy,* he thought.

One of the runners on the horse was broken. Perhaps the child's father intended to repair it somewhere down the line. Tim cleared the rest of the spider webs and went back in. Now, he could see the other side of the support beam, against which leaned an old rifle. Tim grabbed it and backed out, careful not to scuff it on the wall. Once under the bulb, he took a closer look.

The rifle was surprisingly long and was fixed with a bayonet. The metal on the side was stamped *1861 U.S. Springfield*, along with an engraving of a small eagle, the steel rusted by a hundred years of damp basement. The stock was warped and swollen, and the butt plate had rotted away due to what he assumed was periodic flooding. The word "Millie" was carved into the wood. He ran his finger over it. *Wife or girlfriend, most likely.* He was no historian, but he was embarrassingly ignorant. *Wasn't the Civil War in the 1800s?* His school days were so far behind that he'd forgotten almost everything unrelated to construction.

He hadn't pounded a nail, and it was almost 10:00 am. At noon, the phone rang. Nobody was there the last time he'd answered the phone, and not long after, the boy had appeared.

"Hello?"

"Are you still alive? What's happening?" asked Holly.

"Still alive. I'm glad you called, but I got a late start."

"Anybody there? Any sightings?"

"Nobody. I was nervous coming down the road, so I swept the house before I started work. I found a couple of antiques in the cellar behind the furnace that nobody's seen in a century. I'll show you later. How's work?"

"The morning was slow, but the good news is my boss is out of the office, and I copied a chunk of the journal."

"Thank you! Were you able to read while copying?"

"Not much. I was dodging coworkers because I didn't want to answer any questions. I did gather that Annette did some research on previous owners. She may have saved us some time."

"Did you learn anything about her death?"

"I did ask one person, but there's not much to report. One of my coworkers was friends with one of Annette's kids. Her death shocked everybody. She was young and in good shape. They think she just fell asleep and didn't wake up. I didn't ask how long it took before they found her."

"Hmm. Did you pick a restaurant?"

"I know a place if you like Chinese food, and I'll pay this time. As for sleeping arrangements, you were a perfect gentleman last night, so I think I can trust you. You are cordially invited to sleep in my guest room again."

"Well, that's mighty nice of you," Tim replied. "Holly, I complained about money last night, but I promise I can afford dinner. Thanks for the offer, though. I have another favor to ask. Do you mind if I shower at your place before we go out?"

"I give you an inch, and you take a mile. Are there any other requests, or will that be all?"

"That'll do for now, but thank you for your hospitality."

"Sounds good, Mr. Russell. Call me when you're done, and I'll quit when you do."

As Tim hung up the phone, something flashed by the window. Instinctively, he ducked down, heart racing, looking out just in time to see the boy cross the driveway and disappear into the woods. There was no time to think. The boy hadn't hurt him the other night. He'd follow at a safe distance and see where he went.

Tim ran out the front door. He would have a story to tell at dinner and perhaps another piece of the puzzle. Behind Tim's truck was an overgrown trailhead where the boy had vanished, heading toward the grove. Tim stepped in and looked around. The forest was near-silent, there was no breeze, and the birds were suspiciously quiet. Two hundred yards in, the grove opened up, and Tim stopped cold. He knew it was coming but was still stunned by the grove. In the silence, Tim listened.

It was hard to tell how many rows there were. Padding through spruce needles, Tim was grateful for the lack of noise they made. One row passed, then two. Finally, in the third row, sixty yards away, was the boy. From this distance, his features were indiscernible. Tim could see two darkened spots where his eyes should be. He looked like a skeleton.

They stared at each other for an uncomfortable minute. Spooked, Tim raised a hand. *Hello.* The boy didn't move, and it took all of Tim's willpower to stay put. *He approached me the other night. Why not now?*

Suddenly, the boy turned and began to walk, cutting through aisles, and Tim followed parallel. As he crossed through the first row, Tim lost him for a second, then found him again in the next hall. The boy waited for Tim before moving again and repeated the process, row after row, deeper and deeper into the woods.

Tim stared down an empty hallway along the edge of the wild forest. He poked his head back into the previous row but saw nothing, then down the last one again, but the boy was gone. There was something there, however.

A mound of leaves was at the far end, and Tim felt a chill. It was time to go. Perhaps he had seen enough for one day. The wise thing would be to read more of the journal before any confrontation. *She's going to flip when I tell her,* he thought. Suddenly realizing how far away he was from his truck, Tim ran back through the rows until he found the path to the driveway.

The woman in the black dress watched from the hayloft as Tim emerged from the woods, checking behind himself as if he had seen a ghost.

CHAPTER 15

April 20, 1971

Tim met Holly at her house, where they showered separately. Before dinner, they made small talk, as Holly requested that they save the juicy bits for the actual date. They took her car to the restaurant because Tim's window was broken.

"If you liked last night, you're going to love the second date," said Tim, and without missing a step, Holly faked as if she was walking away.

"I can't wait! Last night, I was trapped in your truck. What will tonight bring?"

Heads turned.

"Hey, not so loud, you're going to ruin my reputation," said Tim.

Holly blushed.

"Just kidding. Nobody heard that."

"Me and my big mouth! Okay, now we can talk. Tell me about your day."

Tim knew the question was coming, and there was no perfect way to break the news. "I saw the boy again."

Holly's eyes widened. "What? Did you get the hell out of there?"

"Well, it was broad daylight."

Holly stared as Tim reported the whole story. "Tim, don't be a hero! We've got to read the book first!"

"Tonight, after dinner, we'll dive into that journal."

"Are you a stubborn man, Tim Russell?"

"Sometimes." Tim reached over and squeezed her hand. "I saw something else, too, but I'm not sure what it was."

Holly's smile disappeared. "What?"

"Uh, maybe nothing, but I think the kid led me to something in the last row of the grove. It looked like a pile of leaves, but I didn't check it out. That's when I got out of there."

"Well, it will be interesting to see if Annette knew anything about it." After sharing the discovery of the rifle and the toys and despite having brought the journal, Tim and Holly enjoyed each other's company, even talking about normal things unrelated to ghosts.

CHAPTER 16

Saturday, January 20, 1966

Last night, I heard the little boy running around. At first, I was upstairs and heard him moving around downstairs. I thought an animal had gotten into the house, so I went down and grabbed the fireplace poker. When I reached the kitchen, I heard the same footsteps upstairs.

For a second, I thought I might be losing my marbles, so I cautiously made my way back up. The footsteps started again as I crossed the living room but stopped as soon as I touched the first stair. After returning to bed, I heard him again downstairs.

I didn't get much sleep. I miss Henry so much. I wonder why we've had so many sightings since his death. Now, they seem to be around the house at any time of day. As a result, I am suspicious. It seems more than coincidental that he died and they started showing up.

To this day, I have not seen either of the ghosts up close. Perhaps I won't ever see her in the house, and that's fine. However, all this activity has helped me decide to do some digging into who they were.

Monday, January 21, 1966

I could barely wait for the Town Hall to open to start my research. The rest of the weekend was quiet, ghost-wise, but I had trouble sleeping, wondering if they would show. What I found in the town records gives me goosebumps.

Joseph and Rebecca Hobson, the previous owners, moved here in 1894 and stayed for thirty-nine years. Before the Hobsons, it was Robert and Katherine Miller, and they lived here a total of thirty-one years from 1863-1894. Before that, I have no idea because here is the part that chills me.

The records were there but illegible, all smudged and blackened by something soot-like. It was as if someone had scrubbed the page with a charcoal pencil. I showed the damaged records to the clerk, but she had no answers. I believe some deceased soul doesn't want anyone to remember who they were. My next step is the library.

Tuesday, January 22, 1966

I know the house was built in 1860, and the smudged records ended in 1863, so I went to the library and began scouring the microfilm of the _Sanborn Crier_ for those years. I made it through 1860 and 1861 today, just skimming, but I didn't see anything that caught my eye. This project is more time-consuming than I thought, and some of the work around the house went undone. I'm discouraged.

Wednesday, January 23, 1966

To my horror, I woke this morning with my journal on my chest, opened to January 19 (the day I decided to start my investigations). I did not bring the journal to bed. I think the page it was open to was a message. January 19's entry expressed my desire to explore the occurrences in the house.

Now, I fear I may have inspired someone else. Why so many ghosts? Well, because you, Annette, are taking an interest! I don't feel I have a choice anymore. What have I gotten myself into?

Wednesday, January 23, 1966 (night)

Today's trip to the library was more productive than yesterday's. I may have scored my first clue. In the obituaries section of May 12, 1861, I read that a soldier from Lancaster Hill Road was killed in preparatory exercises here in New Hampshire and shipped back to Sanborn for burial at Tower Hill Cemetery. His name was Thomas Pike.

Tonight, I will experiment. I will write five names in this journal, each across two pages. Then, I will close the book and leave it in the turret. I'll also leave a pen. I feel so silly trying this.

Holly sat on her couch with Tim and turned the pages. Page one said "John" only. The next said, "Sherman." Following were: "George," "Brown," "William," "Lincoln," "Thomas," "Pike," "Daniel," and "Boone."

"Hey, Annette thinks the ghost of Daniel Boone is haunting us," Tim joked, and Holly elbowed him in the ribs.

Thursday, January 24, 1966

I woke early with a purpose. Thankfully, my journal was not on my person or in the bedroom. I rose and headed straight for the turret, fireplace poker in hand, mindful of my surroundings. I loathe the presence of ghosts. They can be anywhere at any time! I opened the door to the turret stairs and ascended. The journal was open to "Thomas Pike."

I looked behind me as it seemed someone might witness my discovery. My eyes searched the pond and the field but saw nothing. I turned to the left, looking over the *roof and the barn, but still nothing. I relaxed somewhat, picked up the journal, and sat down. As I examined the pages, there were no marks of any kind. The pen I left for Thomas lay where I had placed it, untouched.*

After getting some things done around the house and buying groceries, I stopped at the police station and asked where Tower Hill Cemetery was. For your information (you, the reader of this journal), it is on the north side of town, on Old Range Road off of Tower Hill Road. It is a small cemetery surrounded by trees, easily missed if you aren't looking. It's about a half-acre. The stones are all ancient and illegible.

There are only about two hundred or so stones in the yard, and I looked at all of them. I learned in the library that a Civil War soldier's headstone frequently has the outline of a badge around a simple epitaph. I found the grave of Thomas Pike in the back row, under the limb of a pine tree.

My best guess is that I have at least two ghosts on the property (the boy and the mother) and perhaps one more still unseen by the name of Thomas Pike.

Holly sat back. "That's a pretty good start. What compelled her to stay? I mean, to do so alone is very brave."

"I agree. It would have been so easy to cut and run, but Annette's not in danger, right? Other than maybe 'stay away from the woman?' She's just scared. But we—*I*—still need to be careful." They read for another fifteen minutes, but it was getting late.

Holly yawned, leaned into him, and looked up at his face. "We both have to work tomorrow."

Tim smiled. "You're right. Point me to the towels again, and I'll set up shop."

"They're in the hall closet," Holly hesitated, dropping her eyes. "Tim, ghosts aside, I'm enjoying our time together."

"Me too. Thanks for giving me a safe place to sleep."

Holly smiled but said nothing, and Tim pulled her close, looking for lips. They kissed until their eyes glazed, and Holly frowned as she stepped away, implying it was time to say goodnight.

"Goodnight," Tim turned and began to unfold the bedsheets.

"Goodnight," she said and closed her bedroom door.

After brushing his teeth, he turned off the light. Then, as his eyes adjusted, he relaxed and stared at the ceiling, collecting his thoughts. *Things could be a lot worse. Tomorrow, I'll start in the room by the road.*

Suddenly, Holly appeared over him and tapped him on the chest. "Come with me."

He didn't need to be asked twice.

CHAPTER 17

April 21, 1971

Tim opened the side door and stepped into the carriage house room. It had been roughly eighteen hours since he had locked up and left. *What's happened since?* Today's goal was to rip out the walls in the room nearest the road, directly beneath the main bedroom, and he started with the noisier tools. Tim was nervous about running the Sawzall, a high-powered blade that would cut through anything. As it screamed its way through the antique walls, Tim was all but deaf to the rest of the house. He kept the cutting sessions short, stealing glances at his surroundings, which was nerve-wracking. Work would have gone twice as fast without all the pausing.

Halfway through the day, Tim caught a whiff, as if something had burrowed into the house and died inside the wall. He stopped the saw and sifted through chunks of plaster, looking for remnants, but found nothing. Several houseflies confirmed Tim's suspicions and bounced against the windows, looking for food. Tim crushed them with a newspaper and opened the windows. Thankfully, the smell dissipated.

When five o'clock came, Holly called to check on him, wanting to know the plan. She didn't have to ask twice because Tim was ready to drop the tools and celebrate the good things in life. She was relieved to hear he had worked all day without interruption. They chose a restaurant in Gilford called O'Steak, and there was no wondering about the sleeping arrangements.

What Tim didn't know was that the woman in the dress had eavesdropped on him all day long. She began in the kitchen, observing from afar, gauging the timing of his machines and the silence between cuts. She used the noise to advance on him because he was more alert when things were quiet.

She got very close, even watching from the doorway at one point, anticipating the moment he would pick up her scent and retreating before he could pin it down. She didn't mind his presence here as long as he didn't get too curious. The house was more interesting with people in it.

When the phone rang in the living room, she descended quietly and observed the conversation while his back was turned. He didn't smell her this time. He also didn't hear the flies, many of which disappeared when the cold front moved in.

Like the previous owner, this new man didn't know who she was. None of them knew her business, and that's how she liked it. There was work to be done to correct past mistakes, and she felt she could be forgiven one day. Her guilt and the solitude were crushing.

CHAPTER 18

April 22, 1971

Tim and Holly enjoyed another near-perfect evening followed by more sex. They had so much fun they didn't get to Annette's journal. Things were going exceptionally well, to the point that nothing else mattered. But that was all right because there weren't enough hours in the day, and one of the ghosts was trying to help them.

The phone was ringing when Tim unlocked the side door on Thursday morning. He burst through the door, looking right and left for danger, jogging with caution. When he arrived in the living room, he grabbed the noisy phone.

"Hello?"

"Tim?" The female voice on the other end made it sound as if she was surprised he answered.

"Yes?" He didn't recognize the voice after just one word.

"Where have you been? I've been calling and calling. I almost had to cancel your visitation this week. I've got a situation, and I need you to be there for your daughters, or I'll have to make other arrangements."

Oh no, please, God, no. It was Sheila, and as always, she was ready, willing, and able to disrupt his life in the name of her schedule, using the girls as pawns if necessary. She had no right to change his visitation but acted as if she did, almost daring him to take her to court.

"You have no right to cancel my visitation. I was getting breakfast," he lied where he was because telling her he was getting laid would redouble her efforts to make him miserable. If she knew he had someone, the girls would be pushed on him every weekend to pressure the new relationship. If she thought he was lonely, those opportunities would dry up. *Daddy's too busy to be with you.*

"I've called you four times! Is there going to be a problem with communication going forward? I'd hate to think you were unavailable to your children. You should have bought a place closer. The girls can't understand why you're so far away."

"Stop telling the girls your personal opinions."

Sheila changed the subject, deflecting. She wasn't used to Tim's new habit of questioning her. "I need you to take them tonight. I have a seminar at the bank, and if you can't come, I'll have to call a sitter, and she won't work for less than twelve hours' pay. You'll have to pay the difference if you want them before 8:00 pm."

Tim's blood pressure spiked. He'd been slow to learn that Sheila was a control freak. Mandating that he pay for her sitter was a first, a slippery slope that set a costly precedent. He would be, in effect, enabling last-minute schedule changes. "Sorry. All I hear is your last-minute crisis and how I'm supposed to drop everything to bail you out."

"I told you I need you tonight at 5:00 pm! You're self-employed, Tim. You're the boss. You get to make your hours." Of course, she had not told him any such thing. Sheila was the queen of gaslighting, even though gaslighting hadn't been invented yet.

Tim rubbed his temples. He hadn't yet had the chance to scout the area motels to keep the girls away from the ghosts. He didn't even have a phone book! Tim saw red. "That's the first time you've mentioned time at all!"

"Judy is sitting here. She heard it too, and—"

Tim had heard this all before. Judy Larson might not even be with Sheila right now. Oh, if he could only turn back time and not marry her. Unable to withstand the surprise attack, Tim caved. "I can be there at five."

Olivia and Vivian (a.k.a. "Liv and Viv") were coming to Daddy's house. He'd been sucked into Sheila's vortex and had forgotten everything else. To make matters worse, he'd sabotaged his evening with Holly, who had slipped his mind in the hypnosis. Never a good thing with women, he knew.

Now, he would have to ask for forgiveness after only their second night of intimacy. It wouldn't fly. She wouldn't believe him, thinking he'd gotten what he wanted and was on the fast track to becoming an inattentive asshole. Tim dialed Holly's number. After exchanging pleasantries, he got to the point.

"Holly, I messed up. I got a phone call from my ex-wife right after arriving at the house. She needed me to take the kids spur-of-the-moment. She needed an answer."

"Tonight?"

"Yeah," he exhaled. "I said 'yes' too soon. Sheila caught me off guard, and—" Tim was repeating himself.

"Uh-oh," said Holly, letting her words hang.

"Maybe the four of us can eat dinner together if you're up for it. I promise this won't be a problem in the future."

Holly cringed. "So, what's the plan? Where will they sleep?"

"I don't know. She just called two minutes ago."

"Are you sure you want to introduce me to your daughters so early? What if we don't make it work? Then, they'll meet the next girlfriend, too. You don't want to be Daddy-can't-get-it-right, do you?"

"Daddy can't get it right. That would be not good. Sheila would have a field day. "No, Holly, I messed up. You're my first and only girlfriend, post-Sheila. I'll be ready for her next time."

"I'll give you a Mulligan, but I don't think we should mix with the kids yet, right? Where would I sleep? Where are they going to sleep? You'll get a hotel, right?"

Holly was right. It was too soon for her to meet his daughters and to have Sheila in their business. But if they slept in a hotel, Sheila would want to know what made Tim's new house "so unsafe." *I can't have the girls breathing paint fumes, Tim. Does your place have asbestos in it? How old is that furnace? Carbon monoxide is a killer.* He should not feed the Sheila Monster. These ghosts were semi-understandable, and the girls were heavy sleepers. *That's it, rationalize, Tim. You have to.*

CHAPTER 19

April 22, 1971

Sheila's phone call shortened the amount of work Tim could complete that day. All of his Friday plans suddenly became Thursday plans. He gave up and drove to Massachusetts to visit his lone employee, Johnny, who was installing a kitchen in Topsfield. While there, he made some Russell Construction phone calls, lining things up to keep Johnny busy for the next two weeks.

"You're here early. I was expecting you tomorrow," said Johnny.

"Sheila called with one of her emergencies, and I'm picking the kids up tonight."

Johnny shook his head. He'd witnessed his boss battle through the divorce and stuck with him through the darkest days. "Oh, no school tomorrow?" said Johnny, squinting one eye quizzically. Tim stared blankly. Immediately, Johnny knew Sheila had pulled the wool over Tim's eyes. "Man, you need to take a class and prepare yourself! She got you!"

Tim hung his head and changed the subject. "I'm going to need those beds you were talking about. They're in storage, right? Salisbury?"

"Right, Newbury Road. Here's the key: number 217. Use them for as long as you need. I don't think we'll need them back. How are things besides Sheila, Boss?"

"So far, so good."

"Is it in worse shape than you thought? Do you want me to come up on the weekend and help you?"

"No, no, no, I can do it. I lost a day because of Sheila, but I'll catch up." Tim didn't mention his date nights with Holly, which contributed to the slowdown. *But they were so worth it.* He also didn't say anything about the ghosts. The absurdity of the situation hung in his mind. The original plan had been to work late into the evenings, alone, with no interruptions. Eighteen-hour days, work like a bastard on the cheap, and sell the house in a year. He never anticipated he'd be dating so soon and had budgeted zero time for it. He also hadn't budgeted any time for ghosts.

"You looked stressed, man. Grab one of those Cow Hampshire women by the hair like a caveman. I heard they like that. I also heard they still churn their butter, too." Even though Sanborn life was not that different from Methuen life (where Johnny lived), he loved to razz Tim for moving to the country. Tim ignored Johnny's comment, and Johnny picked up on it.

"Wait, are you already scoring? Who is she? Is it the girl at the hardware store or something? A farmer? A maple syrup maker? A farm animal? Who the hell could you meet so fast? The real estate lady? She was pretty hot. What was her name?"

"Holly."

"Holly! Wow! It's her, right? I knew it! Did you make her breakfast? Chicks like that."

"Shut up, Johnny. No, I didn't make her breakfast. We slept at her house." Tim wasn't used to taking advice from Johnny. It had been the other way around for almost a decade.

Johnny's eyes bugged out, and he clapped for Tim, an official standing ovation. Tim ignored the digs.

"Yeah, she's cool, but I messed up with Sheila today, taking the kids early. I had to break some plans."

"Oh no, no, no, no." Johnny dropped his hands and hung his head. "When are you going to take your balls back, man? She still owns you. Enough is enough! Kids or not, they'll always love you as long as you do the right thing. Slow the conversation down and *think*."

Tim listened to his third lecture of the day: First Sheila, then Holly, and now Johnny. They were all correct, too, minus Sheila. "I'm pissed at myself and don't want to discuss it. But, hey, I have to go. Are you all set with your schedule for the next two weeks?"

"Yeah. I'll finish in Topsfield and start at the Mills house on Tuesday. After that, you let me know."

Tim nodded as he looked down at the doorknob but didn't turn it. Taking a breath, he turned back around. "Johnny, do you believe in ghosts?"

"Say what?"

"You heard me. Have you ever seen a ghost?"

"No, man. Is this a joke or something?"

Tim sighed, wondering where to go from here. He'd cornered himself. "Johnny, I've got ghosts." He readied himself for the razzing, but Johnny didn't laugh.

"What do you mean?"

"I'm not joking. I've got a little kid running around and some other stuff. No shit."

Johnny's eyes bored into Tim's, suspicious. "Okay, I lied. I thought you were setting me up. I have seen a ghost, and it messed me up. My grandmother stuck around for a while after she died. I'll tell you about it sometime. It wasn't fun. She wasn't the grandma I knew. What do you need? Help or something?"

"Would you know what to do?"

"Not unless you know why your house is haunted. We had to figure out why my grandma was still around. We knew her through her sickness and all the crap she went through with my grandfather. We had to put two and two together to get her to go away. Ghosts don't speak up and ask for help. I can't say I'm an expert, but another set of eyes couldn't hurt. I'll tell Maria you need me overnight."

"I'm good for now, Johnny. But I will take you up on that soon. There's also a woman ghost and maybe one more. The previous owner left a journal behind, who also saw them. She left some notes."

Johnny's face lit up. "Did Holly see them, too?"

"Yeah, she saw the woman."

"Wow. So you've got a whole family up there? It's been less than a week, and you've seen all that?"

"Yeah, it's nerve-wracking, especially the night I stayed there. And it's a huge pain in the ass, robbing my time, and the girls are coming this weekend. So, that's it? With your grandmother, I mean? All I have to do is figure out why the ghosts are sticking around?"

"As I said, I'm no expert. I'm just telling you what happened with my grandma. I wasn't the one figuring it all out. I was just a kid. Do you want me to tell you the whole story?"

Tim looked at his watch. "Yeah, but I can't do it right now. I'll call you later, though. Thanks, Johnny, I appreciate it."

"No problem, Boss."

Tim left to run his errands, picking up the beds from Johnny's storage in Salisbury, stopping at the hardware store for some things, and when that was done, he picked up the kids. He was always happy to see them. Tim turned onto their street in anticipation of the handoff. Pulling into the driveway was always a crapshoot because he would have to talk with Sheila, which could lead to anything.

"Olivia shouldn't be allowed to watch TV because she lied and said her homework was finished," or "Vivian has a project she needs to do by

Monday." Pain-in-the-ass monkey wrenches designed to hamstring his already limited time with them. Tim got out of the car and knocked on the door. Vivian answered. *Thank God.*

"Daddy!"

"Hey, Viv! Ready to go? Where's your sister?"

"She's in the bathroom."

Oh, no, thought Tim. Olivia was famous for her bathroom time. "All right, well, how about your suitcase? Where's that?"

"Right here." Vivian pulled a small yellow suitcase with Tweety Bird to the door.

Tim grabbed it and turned for the car. The more time he stood in the doorway, the more likely he'd have to talk to Sheila. "Go get your sister!"

"Okay." Vivian disappeared into the house, and Tim lingered by his truck. When four minutes had passed, he began to get antsy, but then the screen door opened.

"Hey, Liv! Ready to go?"

"Yeah. I was in the bathroom." Suddenly, Sheila was in the doorway.

"Hi, Tim." She always used her motherly voice around the girls.

"Hi."

"Be careful around the house, girls. Watch out for nails. You don't want to step on one."

Tim managed to keep a straight face. "Are we ready to go? Say bye to Mom."

"Bye, Mom!"

As he was backing out of the driveway, relief washed over him. "Are you guys ready to see the new house?"

"Yeah!" they replied in unison. The three of them had a great time catching up on the way back to New Hampshire, but they first talked about the Plexiglas patch job on Tim's window. He told them he'd locked his keys in the truck. When they were a half-hour outside of Sanborn, thoughts turned to dinner.

"What do you guys want to eat?"

"Pizza!"

Tim took pleasure in spoiling them when they were together. They got pizza, dessert, and whatever else they wanted. When the meal was over, he headed for Lancaster Hill Road. Home Sweet Home, he hoped. *Please be good hosts, Pike family, if that's who you are.*

The girls were wide-eyed, excited to see Daddy's new digs. "Wow! It's bigger than Mom's house! There's a pond! Hey, where's our bedroom?"

"You're going to love it. It is unfinished, though, and messy. I just moved in, and I'm working on it."

"Yay!" said Olivia.

"Yay!" mimicked Vivian.

Tim gave them the fifty-cent tour, but they cared most about their bedroom. He wanted them close, so he put them across the hall, in the "sunny bedroom," as he had come to refer to it. Strangely enough, he felt safer with the girls in the house, as if their love had power over the supernatural.

They went back to the truck to unload it. "I need you guys to hold the doors open," was the excuse, and that's about all they did as Tim lugged the mattresses upstairs almost single-handedly. Next, they showered while he assembled the beds and were tucked in at around nine o'clock. After that, Tim took his time showering and brushing, shortening the night as much as possible. Finally, after ten o'clock, he went downstairs to the living room (with the hammer) and called Holly.

Tim looked at the darkness outside as the phone rang and realized he had not thought things through. All the lights in the downstairs were off, including the living room. He had never reset the timers after the ghosts shut them down three nights ago. The room was dark, and the lamp was out of reach. He stood near the staircase, resting his shoulder on the doorjamb, looking through as many dark doorways as possible. Holly picked up.

"Hello there. How's the family?"

"Hi, Holly. The kids are in bed. I put them across the hall. They were excited to see their room, and now it's Nervous Timmy time."

"I bet. Listen, I'm going to put the phone next to my bed. If you need anything, call. I'm twenty minutes away. Get out of there if things are happening. I'll leave the door open."

Tim took a few steps toward the kitchen. "Thanks, I appreciate that. I think we'll be all right, or at least I hope so. What are you doing tomorrow? Do you want to meet for lunch? I could say you were the real estate lady."

"I have a showing at 11:00 am, so you go ahead. We can talk in the afternoon and see what's happening."

Tim heard Holly's hesitation as he turned toward the dark den behind the living room, exploring the space without pulling the cord out of the wall. "Okay, sounds good. We'll catch up. And I'll bring the phone upstairs to the bedroom." He couldn't wait to unplug and head up. He should have moved it earlier. Holly said goodnight, and Tim hung up. As the receiver hit the cradle, he listened to the house. In a way, even though the girls were here, Tim felt alone. He was the only person with his guard up. Since the sun went down, he'd begun to regret his decision to bring them here.

Tim reached into his pocket and pulled out a folded piece of paper with the names of the only two motels within fifteen miles. He looked at his watch: 10:27. The first number rang sixteen times before he gave up. On the second call, the operator informed him that the Leisure Motel telephone number was out of service.

"Operator, can you give me the names of some other hotels in the Sanborn area?"

"I see three listings, but one is the Leisure Motel, and we know that's not going to work."

"What are the other two?"

"The Belmont Inn. Do you want that number?"

"I just called them. It just keeps ringing."

"They probably have limited check-in hours. The other number is, oh, I'm sorry. The Burke Hill Resort is closed for the month of April. Do you want me to try Concord?"

"No, that's all right, thank you, operator." Tim crouched to unplug the phone and backed out of the room. Tim checked on the girls, returned to his bedroom, and dragged the mattress to the doorway. He was twelve feet from their bed. He left all his clothes on as he had the other night, then shut off the light and attempted to sleep. Thankfully, the house was quiet. Despite his nerves, he was exhausted.

CHAPTER 20

April 23, 1971

The sun woke Tim, and he remembered that the kids were there. His watch said 6:30 am, and for the moment, he was excited the night was over. When he pulled the blanket off, however, he noticed blood on his arm. A long scratch ran down his forearm, jumped the crook, and continued down his bicep. Worse, he was still bleeding. The front of his t-shirt had dots of blood in four different places, with two small pulls in the cloth.

Immediately, Tim crossed the hall to the girls' room to check on more precious cargo. Thank God, their heads were peeking out from under the covers, and they were still asleep. He relaxed as he lifted the blankets and checked their bodies. No blood.

Tim returned to the main bedroom to check himself in the full-length mirror. It looked like he'd lost a fight with a house cat. In addition to the scratches on his body, he had a nasty cut across his nose and cheek.

Confused, Tim began to clean himself before the girls awakened, but as he closed his eyes to splash his face with water, his memory flashed, and he saw a pair of headstones between two perfect rows of trees. *Was I there?* Suddenly, his heart beat harder, and he wondered what was happening. Tim cleaned his wounds, put on some band-aids, changed his clothes, and headed to the kitchen. Thankfully, the downstairs was clear. After sneaking back up to retrieve the telephone, he plugged it in and called Holly.

"You survived!" she proclaimed.

"We did, but something happened. I think I sleepwalked."

"You what?"

Tim had only been awake five minutes and was still piecing things together. *Was it even true?* "I think so. I think I went into the woods!"

"What? Do you remember anything?"

"I think I saw two gravestones. I'm scratched up. My arm is bleeding."

"Gravestones? Was it a dream? I haven't seen gravestones in your woods."

"I don't know! Maybe I should check while it's daylight."

"No! Don't you dare, at least while the girls are there. And not alone, either! Have you ever sleepwalked before?"

"Never."

"I don't know what to say."

"I have a scratch on my face. The girls will see it. I'm going to have to make an excuse."

Holly wanted to get in her car and make breakfast for everybody, but real estate agents didn't just pop in for waffles with single dads. "Well, no one saw a ghost. Make breakfast, and try to enjoy the day."

Tim mixed the batter, cracked the eggs, and lit the burner. He whistled, even if it was a blatant attempt to push dark thoughts away. The kitchen smelled like banana pancakes in minutes. He'd even bought real maple syrup from Abbott's Farm.

The girls asked about the scratch on his nose, and Tim told them he bumped into a post while checking the furnace. After breakfast, the girls went upstairs to get dressed while Tim did the dishes. Ten minutes later, he went upstairs to check on them, and the girls were gone.

In a panic, Tim checked all the rooms and closets. Were they hiding on him? He called out using his serious voice, but there was no answer. On his way down the stairs, he noticed the front door ajar. After scanning the pond area, Tim jogged around the house to the barn, listening. His stomach turned as he looked at the path in the corner of the driveway.

"Liv! Viv!" There was no sound but the chirping of robins, and he decided to check the barn first. The doorway engulfed him, and the musty atmosphere dampened outside noises. Tim passed the empty horse stalls and stepped into the shadows. Bats circled high overhead.

"Olivia? Vivian!" Tim stepped into one of the dark corners and looked under the workbench along the wall. Most of the tools that had once adorned it were gone. Tim looked in the first drawer to find spider webs and a couple of nails. The second drawer held a mason jar half-filled with orphan screws.

"Liv! Viv! Enough! Game over!" Suddenly, he heard a giggle from the loft and breathed a sigh of relief. "I hear you up there! Be careful, I don't want you to fall." The girls were under an old, filthy horse blanket, and Olivia struggled to keep Vivian quiet. Crisis averted, Tim opened the third and final drawer of the tool bench.

Tim pulled a well-worn hatchet from the drawer and examined it.

"Come find us!" giggled Vivian.

"Shut up!" scolded Olivia.

Tim put the hatchet back, climbed the ladder into the loft, then crept toward the blanket with the two wiggling lumps underneath and attacked. "Come on, let's go have some fun!"

The three left the house and began the day at Funspot, an arcade with pinball machines, go-carts, batting cages, and the like. Nine dollars of game tokens later, Tim took them on a drive around Lake Winnipesaukee. Visiting the lake was anticlimactic for the girls, and Olivia deemed it "boring" because it was too cold for swimming. Before calling it a day, he treated the girls to some penny candy at the Old Country Store.

When they arrived back at the house, Tim wanted them close until he'd checked everything out, so he told them he saw a mouse and needed help looking for it. It would have been wise to bring the TV from Massachusetts to keep the girls in one place, but he hadn't. They finished the night playing a slow game of Monopoly, eating chicken nuggets, and getting ready for bed. Finally, he kissed them goodnight and returned to the main bedroom.

Tim installed a screw eye hook directly into the baseboard next to his mattress with a string attached, then tied a double square knot around his wrist. Remaining dressed, Tim checked his front pocket to ensure the jackknife was there. He didn't want to sleepwalk again.

CHAPTER 21

April 24, 1971

Tim raised his hand the following day, relieved to see the string still tied to his wrist. Before celebrating, however, he examined his clothing for signs of travel, and everything checked out. *Thank God.* After cutting himself free, he went to check on Olivia and Vivian. They were safe and sleeping.

It was only 5:15 am and too early to call Holly, but he was done sleeping, so he put on the coffee and began preparing breakfast. Tim left the kitchen to listen from the bottom of the stairs every two minutes. Every third trip, he would climb the stairs and look in on them, just to be sure.

After three cups of coffee and twenty trips, he heard them talking and fired up the burner to prepare today's breakfast, *blueberry* pancakes. Like all kids, no matter how little they weighed, they sounded like Frankenstein overhead. All Tim could hear was *thud-thud-thud-thud-thud-thud,* and it brought back an unpleasant memory. Tim stepped away from the stove to peer through the house.

Vivian rounded the corner, followed closely by Olivia. Their hair was mussed, and Olivia was yawning. Something seemed off as they cruised through the living room and into the kitchen. At first, he couldn't place it, but then he realized. The girls had gone to bed in the nightgowns Sheila had provided. Olivia had Barbie, and Vivian wore Bugs Bunny. Now, they had on full-length formal nightgowns. Tim realized he was looking at clothing from another era.

"Daddy, what are these? I don't like it! It's too much clothing! I feel all hot!" said Vivian.

"Yeah, these are weird, Dad. Did you put this on me?" added Olivia.

Tim's blood boiled. Someone had changed their clothes—and they thought it was him. "What? Don't you like them? It's what they wear in New Hampshire!"

"Then why didn't you just give them to us before bed?"

"Well, I thought I would surprise you."

"Boring," said Vivian, pulling a stool up to the counter. Tim grabbed her face, pretending to ask for a kiss while checking her skin for marks. He faux-tickled her to see if she winced. Nothing, thank God. He did the same thing to Olivia, and she shooed him away. Tim's good mood was gone.

"Do we have to wear them every night?" said Olivia.

"No, you don't have to. You can change before the pancakes are ready. Go, go, go! You have two minutes!"

"Pancakes again?" complained Vivian.

"Blueberry this time!"

After breakfast, Tim checked the gowns while the kids went outside to explore. Olivia's was on the floor, and Vivian's was on the bed. The fabric was uneven and frayed in spots, clearly not modern. The Barbie and Bugs Bunny t-shirt nightgowns were nowhere to be found. Tim looked out the front windows at the girls in the driveway playing hopscotch on an imaginary court. He tossed the gowns on the bed and went downstairs to call Holly.

"The girls woke up in nightgowns that I've never seen before, and I think they're from the 1800s."

"What do you mean?"

"Somebody changed their clothes in the middle of the night, but they didn't appear to be touched or marked. Too close for comfort."

"Do the girls remember anything?"

"No, they think I changed their clothes while they were sleeping and that I'm weird. Sheila's going to ask questions. I can't find the nightgowns they brought."

"Who cares what Sheila thinks? That's the least of your problems. You've got somebody changing your children's clothes in the middle of the night!"

"I used to see my daughters every day, and now I see them every two weeks. If she can tear me down, she will. When I fail, she tells herself she did the right thing. The ghosts are creepy, but at least they're peaceful."

"She did a number on you, but you're allowed to be human, Tim. I mean, bring them here if you want. We could make up a story. We had to test the house for radon gas or something."

"I appreciate that, Holly, but that's not what you want, and I'm not convinced we're in danger. I'm more worried about them seeing something and telling Sheila. I'll sleep with the girls tonight. If I sleepwalk, I'll wake them up, and vice versa."

"Well, the invitation stands," said Holly. "If you need to come over, come over. If it gets hairy over there, get out."

"Thanks. One more night, and I can return the kids tomorrow. After that, we'll catch up on the journal and figure this mess out."

"I'll leave on the outside light and put a key under the mat just in case. I'll also set up the guest room and pull out the couch."

"Holly, I appreciate everything."

CHAPTER 22

April 24, 1971

"Dad, what are you doing?" asked Vivian.

"I'm setting up a giant's bed!" Tim pushed the girls' beds together, dragged his mattress across the hall, and piled it on the other two. Now, they had a towering queen-sized bed. Tim compared it to the one in The Princess and the Pea, and the girls ate it up.

"Where are you going to sleep, Daddy?"

"With you!"

"Why?" said Olivia.

"Why? Because this bed is awesome! You don't want me to sleep on the floor, do you? You have all of the mattresses!"

Tim kept them up until 9:30, after showering, brushing their teeth, and a lengthy pillow fight. Eventually, it came time to turn out the lights.

Tim insisted on sleeping in the middle. He knew their wiggling would allow him little or no sleep, but he couldn't bear being too far from either daughter. The whole story about the girls waking him if he sleepwalked was for Holly's benefit. They were such heavy sleepers they would never see him leave.

CHAPTER 23

April 25, 1971

Tim was still awake at one in the morning. Something was bound to happen, as it had every night thus far. Aside from the crick in his neck, the first three hours were uneventful. He wanted to stretch and roll over, but the girls were pressed tight against him. Tim had closed the door before coming to bed, which, in retrospect, was a bad idea. Now, guessing what was happening in the rest of the house was much more difficult.

He thought he heard footsteps downstairs at a quarter past one, walking back and forth, then moving away until they disappeared. Ten minutes later, they were back. It wasn't the boy. They were too even, too calm. Tim's held his breath as they paused, perhaps at the bottom of the stairs. *Is she listening?*

Tim heard the stairs creak. At step number eleven, the house went still, and Tim pulled the girls closer, lifting his head to hear better. Things were quiet for so long that he hoped whoever it was had left, but then the railing down the hall groaned.

The footsteps began again, slower this time, and the balcony creaked as it did when he walked it. The hair stood on his arms. Seconds passed, and the muscles in his neck began to burn. Tim adjusted his arms, imagining her outside the door, listening with the patience of a cat.

Tim relaxed his neck against the pillow. The stress was too much. He had to reposition without waking the girls. Just then, a light flared to his left, illuminating the room. It came from the turret again, just across the roof. Tim retracted his arms from under his daughters and separated quietly. As soon as he escaped the sandwich, he peeked out the window. Sure enough, the candle was lit—but it went out as soon as he saw it.

Tim stood motionless at the foot of the bed, listening, waiting. He peered out the two front windows, but nothing moved outside. So much time passed that Tim considered opening the bedroom door. Perhaps he should search the upstairs.

But Tim couldn't leave the girls. The thought of the door shutting behind him crossed his mind. He would rather die than have it locked behind him with the girls on the other side.

Vivian snored, and Olivia breathed deeply. His adrenaline faded to fatigue, and Tim returned to the bed, careful not to make a sound. Frazzled, Tim prayed for the stress to subside. He'd been on edge since day one, and it was eating him up. Half an hour later, he began to drift.

CHAPTER 24

April 25, 1971

Tim dreamed he was a raven circling over the house. As he flew, the orbit widened until he was over the grove. The raven banked and dove, landing on a mound of leaves and using his beak to undo a tangle of vines. The epitaph was revealed.

Here lies
Elmer Pike
Abandoned by his father,
A casualty of his mother's broken heart.

Suddenly, a terrible odor caught his nostrils, and the raven took off before he could uncover the second stone. There was no more soaring. The bird flew directly back to the house, pumping its wings as if his life depended on it.

Just as it seemed Tim would collide with the outside wall, he was back in bed with the girls. The odor was stronger here, and as the dream faded, he heard a series of clicks. At first, he couldn't place it, but then he remembered where he was. Someone was turning the doorknob. The latch cleared the strike plate, followed by the protest of hinges. Tim opened his eyes and saw the door swing open.

There, in the hall, was the woman in the dress. Moonlight from the hall window outlined her silhouette, and her hand still clutched the doorknob. Tim tensed and pulled the girls closer, trying not to wake them. The odor was not pond water or marsh. This smell was rot, like the dead mouse in the wall. *Dear God.* Tim coughed, and the girls stirred, crimping their noses as they managed to sleep through it. What was that sound? Flies. *Don't wake up, girls. Not now.*

The woman released the knob and let her arm drop. Tim strained to see her face but could only make out a cheekbone. The woman moved again, rolling her neck as if to ease stiffness. She finished the head roll, looking down, rocking it left and right, working an ancient cramp. She put her face in her hands.

Tim braced. He might have to break the silence and try to talk his way out of this. Then, suddenly, he heard the footsteps of the boy.

Thud-thud-thud-thud-thud-thud-thud.

The woman perked and turned to the hallway, leaning over the balcony, listening. Then she left the doorway out of sight, but Tim heard a cacophony of bounding footfalls down the stairs as she chased the tiny footsteps out the front door.

Tim left the bed, afraid to breathe, and peered down the hallway. A breeze came up the stairs from the front door. Quickly, he ran down and locked it. Exhaling, he wiped his forehead and checked his watch. It was a quarter past four.

CHAPTER 25

April 25, 1971

Sensing the danger was over, Tim passed out. He'd changed his t-shirt and laid a towel between the girls over the sweat-soaked sheets. Hours later, Tim sensed the sunlight through his eyelids and a ringing in his ears. The sound was important, he knew, but his body would not respond.

"Hello?" said Vivian from downstairs. Tim sat up straight. The shades were up. "Yes, but he's asleep. Who are you?"

"Viv! Who is it?" Tim shouted while working his way to the edge of the bed. *At least it isn't Sheila.*

"It's the real estate lady. Her name is Holly!"

"Okay, hold on, I'm coming!" When he rounded the corner, Vivian was there, phone to ear, dressed for the day. "Where's your sister?"

"I can't tell you. It's a secret!"

"Vivian, I—" Tim heard pots and pans clanging in the kitchen. "Olivia?"

"Don't come in here. It's a surprise!"

Tim sighed, relieved they weren't outside exploring the property.

"Okay! Don't start a fire in there!" Tim rubbed the top of Vivian's head and hugged her as she passed him the phone, his mood suddenly excellent. "Hi, Holly. How are things?"

"How am I? How are you? It's Eleven-thirty! Something must have happened. Tell me what happened!"

Tim pictured the woman in the dress, her hand on the doorknob and the moonlight behind her. "Is it eleven-thirty?"

Tim told Vivian to help her sister, then whispered the details. So much had happened.

"Oh, my God. They go home tonight, right? You can't let them stay again until we figure this out!"

The back of Tim's neck began to stiffen. "Yes, thank God."

"I read a lot last night and learned some things, but I didn't see the name Elmer Pike anywhere. Annette calls him 'the little boy.'"

"That's interesting. Do we already know more than she did?"

"We have to read on and figure it out."

"I haven't had the chance to read all weekend. I'm going nuts," said Tim.

"We'll get you rested. Why don't you take it easy today? Let them play outside and watch from the turret."

"Yeah, I need a break. And sleep."

"I didn't say it was going to be all about sleep. You must pay the toll if you want to use the bed."

"How much?"

"You'll have to wait and see. I'll talk to you when you're back from Amesbury. Stay safe!"

Tim stayed on the couch for another minute and rubbed his eyes, smelling the pancakes. They would be black on the outside and gooey on the inside, and Tim would have to pretend to enjoy them. But then he remembered the light in the turret and made a beeline for the staircase.

Olivia protested when he entered the kitchen. "Dad! It's a surprise!"

"I know! I can smell the surprise!"

She was at the stove, which was chest-high on her, and it looked like a fire waiting to happen. Tim wondered for a second if he was a "cool Dad" for letting an eight year old cook or an idiot who was a danger to his children. Tim paused on his way to the turret and reduced the burner's heat by two-thirds.

"Dad, stop! I'm making them!"

"Honey, cook them slower, or they'll burn. I didn't see it. I still don't know what you're making." Tim grabbed the spatula and flipped the suffering pancake.

"Yes, you did! Stop! Let me do it!"

"What time did you wake up?"

"I don't know. You don't have a clock. A long time ago. We watched the neighbor try to catch frogs," said Olivia.

Tim opened the window to clear some smoke. "Honey, there aren't any frogs yet. What neighbor?"

"The little boy neighbor. We went down to the pond, but he wouldn't say anything. He ran into the woods, and a goose hissed at us."

Tim felt goosebumps begin to rise again. "I don't even know my neighbors yet. Don't play with him or anybody else until I say it's okay. How close did you get?"

"How close? It was like from me to the table. But the goose scared us."

"From now on, you stay where I can see you. No more hiding in the barn, going down to the pond, and no woods. Not until I know this place better." Tim headed to the turret as Olivia pouted and watched the pancake cook.

It was sunny in the turret; however, Tim was nervous. On the desk was the journal. *Doesn't Holly have it?* Tim picked it up and realized it was not the same book. The word *Anniversaries* was written in red ink on the inside cover in Annette's handwriting. The first page had the header "January 1" and then listed all of the happenings Annette had witnessed on January 1 for four years.

Saturday, January 1, 1966
  No sightings.

Sunday, January 1, 1967
  Possible footsteps upstairs, but I am not sure.

Monday, January 1, 1968
  No sightings.

Tim felt a twinge of hope. Someone was helping. He recalled the epitaph:
  Here lies
  Elmer Pike
  Abandoned by his father,
  A casualty of his mother's broken heart.
The father didn't write that. The third line made it clear. "A casualty of his mother's broken heart." What did that mean? It sounded selfish, like something Sheila would say. Annette's work pointed to Thomas Pike as the driving force. Perhaps Tim needed to put more faith in the man.

Tim was in no mood to invent an activity that Sunday, so with no further hesitation, they all piled into the truck and drove to the Radio Shack in Laconia, where they bought a small black-and-white TV. They spent the day in the spare room at the bottom of the stairs, and Tim decided to get some work done, saving his noisy tools for the commercials.

After a quick macaroni and cheese lunch, it was almost time to drive them home. Thankfully, they didn't have any eyewitness accounts to share with Sheila. The weekend could have been so much worse. When five o'clock finally came, he struggled to keep his eyes open on the highway. Once the kids were dropped off, he found a payphone and called Holly.

"You did it. How are you feeling?" Holly asked.

"I'm tired and relieved. I need to stop for coffee. How are you?"

"I'm good. You won't cry for me, but I could also sleep. I was up late reading."

"Wow, you're the best. Did you finish?"

"Not quite, but I did get through three-quarters of it."

"Oh, that's great. Thank you, Holly. I could kiss you."

"You have to ask first," she flirted.

"Okay, I'm asking. Can I kiss you?"

"Maybe. How long until you get up here? And you're coming to my place, not your place for anything, right? I have everything you need right here."

"For sure. My house is not as relaxing as yours."

"All right, but bring some energy. I said I was tired, not exhausted."

Tim grinned. "It's nothing coffee can't fix."

"Get your coffee, and then get your buns back here. And a word of advice: if you want to stay awake, don't stop to pee. It'll help during those last twenty miles."

Tim laughed. He would need every trick in the book to stay awake. Then suddenly, his eyes opened wide. He'd forgotten to tell her something.

"I didn't tell you about the journal, did I?"

"No, I told you about the journal. Wow, you are tired."

"That's not what I mean. Someone dropped off another journal in the turret just before my encounter with the ghost woman. Thomas Pike, I'm guessing? It's different from the other one. In this one, Annette breaks everything down by date. Like, January 1: 1966, 1967, 1968, all on one page."

"Another journal? I'm not done with the first one, and you haven't read more than three pages. We can't keep up!"

"Yeah. Somebody likes us."

CHAPTER 26

April 25, 1971

Tim knocked on Holly's door at 8:18 pm, and she greeted him in her bathrobe.

"You don't have to knock, Tim. We're past that point, aren't we?"

"I didn't want to assume." Tim placed the new journal next to the first and noticed the dining room table was set for two, complete with candles and a bottle of wine. He exhaled for what felt like the first time all week. "What's all this? Wine and everything? I'll pour!"

"I've been waiting for you to say that, but truth be told, I already had a glass."

"I don't blame you. Let's celebrate."

Holly and Tim caught up as they ate. Her food was good, and the wine made it better. She got a little tipsy and knew Tim was too. Unfortunately, Holly saw his eyelids begin to droop. He was still chatty but exhausted after all he'd been through. She looked at the journals sitting on the table, and guilt set in. Reading them would have to wait.

Tim offered to help clean up, but Holly told him to shower. Listening from the kitchen, she heard the water shut off upstairs and gave him five more minutes. The bathroom door opened as she turned out the kitchen lights, then went upstairs to intercept before he got too comfortable.

CHAPTER 27

April 26, 1971

The alarm went off at 6:45 am, his first good sleep in four days. But even with the rise-and-shine attitude, he found something to complain about. "I need another weekend."

"That ended yesterday," she replied. "Life is cruel. What are you doing today?"

"Ripping my house apart."

"How about tonight?"

"Tonight is all about you. Want me to cook? I'm not bad in the kitchen."

"Good answer. I have a grill in the garage if you want to use it, but it's charcoal, not propane."

"I'll think of something."

Tim jumped in his truck, knowing they hadn't even cracked the second journal. The nerves returned the second he passed between the two trees at the beginning of the driveway. Tim pulled around to the barn, cut the engine, and heard a pounding hammer. Tired of the games, he called out.

"Thomas Pike? Show yourself!" The pounding stopped, and Tim waited, imagining a corpse with sunken eyes and wispy hair, but nobody showed. *Don't you need me? Don't ghosts want something? Skip the puzzles and tell me.*

"Are you sending me journals? Is there a better way for us to communicate?" Nothing happened. Maybe he scared Thomas away again. "Thomas, I saw the gravestones in the grove. I'm going to check them out. I hope you'll tell me if this is a bad idea."

Tim headed up the trail, hoping for some interaction. The sunny April morning dropped a few degrees under the tree canopy, and three minutes later, the grove opened up. The chill in Tim's belly returned. Holly would hate this. He looked down the trail for a sign, but there was nothing. Tim turned to the grove and walked the same path he had a few days before. The boy wasn't here, at least not yet, so Tim walked briskly, head on a swivel, counting rows, as scared as a deer. Beyond the grove was nothing but uneven ground, fallen foliage, and thousands of wild trees. Finally, Tim reached the last hallway. "Here we go," he muttered.

The closer he got, the more he thought about the footpath back to the barn. The woods were silent, and a tangle of vines had the gravestones in a choke hold. Only a fraction of one of the stones was visible, like a bone poking from an open wound. Suddenly, Tim lost his confidence, and depression coursed through his body as if it had been injected. *It's not going to work.* The thorns made the approach dangerous. He'd have to return with the proper tools.

Then, he smelled decay, the mound of leaves flashed, and the forest went dark. It was nighttime, and the vines covering the stones were pulled back. He looked down and realized he was wearing the clothes from the night he sleepwalked.

Suddenly, he was pushed from behind, and with his second step, he met the thorn that ripped his arm. When he turned to look, no one was there. Tim tried to wake himself up, but it didn't work. His sleepwalking body forged ahead, penetrating the circle of thorns, catching them painfully as he relived his steps. The briars bit through his t-shirt and drew blood, leaving the stains he'd found the morning after.

Dripping blood, Tim reached the headstones and knelt. He already knew Elmer Pike's epitaph, so he focused on the second stone, which sat at an eighty-degree angle, pushed and pulled like a loose tooth over a hundred frosty winters. Tim grabbed the flattest stone he could find and scraped the moss away. The light was poor, and the mildew on the marble made it all the more difficult. *Who are you?* Tim shifted his weight, anxious to finish, and finally, there it was:

Here lies

MILDRED WELLS

As soon as he finished reading the name, the forest flashed again, and Tim was blinded by sunlight. As quickly as it came, the night faded, and he found himself just outside the field of thorns. He looked around. He was back in his clothes from this this morning, , and the two headstones were still buried in compost. As fast as he could, Tim ran back to the house.

News this juicy couldn't wait, so Tim called Holly at work.

"Tim, do I need to chain you to the floor? You keep going out there, and it makes me nervous! You're going to get yourself killed, and no one's going to know where to look!"

"It was an attempt to get Thomas Pike to talk to me. I thought he would warn me if it wasn't a good idea. He wants something from us after all, doesn't he?"

"We aren't sure about that!"

"I saw her headstone. Her name is Mildred Wells."

"Not Mildred Pike?"

"I guess not."

"That's not in Annette's journal, at least not yet. I wonder if I could look her up in the library."

"Let's finish the journals first, as you said. What about dinner?"

"We'll order takeout. I don't want to put this off. I'm starting to care whether you live or die."

Tim grinned. "Well, I guess you fell under my spell. So, by 'takeout,' do you mean a bucket of fried chicken?"

"Ew, no fried chicken. Never take me to a place where the food is served in a bucket."

"I was kidding. I've never met a woman that likes fried chicken. Whatever you choose. What time?"

"I had an appointment fall through, so I'll call it a day around four. I'll be in Franklin before that, so I'll stop by. But Tim, seriously, stop with the adventures to the grove."

Tim looked at his watch. It was 11:17 am. *Already?* How long had he been in the grove? It was beginning to look like today would be another washout. "No more grove. I haven't even started on the house. Come get me when you're done."

"Good! Get busy." They hung up, and Tim worked like a maniac for three hours to make up for lost time. Finally, it was time to clean up. Tim coiled the cords and swept up the dust. As he did, he glanced out the front window.

Mildred Wells was in the pasture. *I know your name,* he thought. She moved right-to-left, coming out of the woods, cutting the corner of the meadow, and back into the woods. A thought struck him: What if he'd left evidence at the grave? Would she know? The original sleepwalking incident was days ago. Did that matter?

Tim dropped the dustpan and bolted through the front door to the road. He dared not run for his truck—it was too close to the path, and she might be coming. Instead, Tim sprinted the two hundred plus yards to the property line at the far side of the meadow and waited behind the stone wall.

Now that he was here, he wished he wasn't. Why hadn't he parked by the road? *Thomas Pike and his hammering, that's why.* Mildred Wells emerged from the woods halfway between Tim and the house. Her back was to him, but she must think he was still inside. Tim sank behind the stone wall. *What now?*

Mildred began to walk toward the house, and Tim held his breath. *If she goes inside, I'll lose my mind.* Then, something strange happened. Mildred planted her left foot and fell, then picked herself up and continued. Tim couldn't believe his eyes. *What the hell was that?* When she reached the driveway, Mildred went around the side of the house, and he lost her somewhere near the barn.

Several minutes passed, so much time that Tim began to watch the woods behind his back. No sooner had the thought entered his mind than Tim heard a car engine behind him, coming down Lancaster Hill Road. Holly's VW buzzed past on the way to the house, oblivious to his hiding place behind the stone wall. He glanced at his watch: 3:22 pm. *No! She's early.*

There was nothing to do but try to get to her before she went inside. Holly pulled up the driveway and drove along the front of the house, turning the corner to park behind Tim's truck.

Tim pumped his legs, sucking wind, bounding over the tufts of tall grass, hoping to remain upright, not yet halfway to the pond. "Holly, don't go in!" he screamed, but Holly didn't hear. "Holly!"

Unaware of Tim's shouting, Holly entered through the side door, close to the last place he saw Mildred. Tim powered on, past the pond, falling twice, twisting his ankle on the uneven ground. Tim picked himself up and burst through the front door, nearly bowling her over. Holly had made it to the living room. She screamed.

"Oh my God, Tim! You scared me!"

"Shhh, I saw her. Follow me."

Holly saw the look on his face and panicked. Tim grabbed her hand and led her outside, around the house, to the vehicles. "Drive to the diner. I'll follow you." Holly obeyed, checking her rearview to ensure he was behind her.

Fourteen minutes later, seated at the diner, Tim was still catching his breath.

"What the hell happened? You weren't in the grove again, were you?"

"No. I saw Mildred in the field heading toward the grove and got a little paranoid, wondering if I might have left some evidence. Now I'm sure I did."

"Where were you coming from?"

"As soon as I saw her walking toward the grove, I ran down the road. I thought she'd see my blood or something, and I think she did. She might have been in the house when I met you at the front door."

Holly went pale. "She might have?"

Tim lowered his voice. "I'm not sure. I thought you might run into her in the kitchen."

Holly slumped in her seat. "So you might be on her shit list. What now?"

"Ah, yes, it is time to abandon the house. It always comes back to this."

"Of course it does! You have your health and your daughters, and I'm not sure how you feel about us, but I'm having fun."

"I am, too, but I need that house, or I'm no longer the happy guy you see before you, and I refuse to live a less-than-excellent life. I'd rather be dead."

"Dead? That's the most selfish thing you've ever said to me."

Tim sat silent and stirred his coffee. "Mildred Wells didn't hurt us. Maybe it's just me being paranoid."

Holly let Tim's words hang. "You're nuts. Your trips to the grove are driving me crazy. Don't forget: Henry and Annette didn't live happily ever after."

"We don't know that anything sinister happened to them." Tim sipped his coffee, still trying to calm down. *Maybe coffee wasn't the best choice.* "Oh, and I almost forgot. I don't think Mildred Wells is a ghost."

CHAPTER 28

April 26, 1971

Holly changed the dinner plans so they could get down to business. They got takeout with zero alcohol. The two journals sat side by side on the coffee table, and Holly began.

"I read most of the first journal and gathered that we're dealing with the same three ghosts Annette did. Mildred Wells, Elmer Pike, and Thomas Pike. Annette never learned Elmer's or Mildred's names, so we are breaking new ground. We see Mildred and Elmer but never Thomas. Additionally, Annette saw some things we haven't yet. She talks about 'anniversaries,' where the same scenes play out annually like clockwork.

"That's the title of the second journal: *Anniversaries*," Tim added.

"Pass me that, please." Tim had filled her in briefly over the phone, but she had yet to crack the book. "This is stuff I've already read, but more organized."

"Hooray for small miracles!"

"Be serious, Tim. You don't want ol' Millie to sabotage your nest egg."

"I just realized something when you called her Millie. That rifle I found by the furnace has 'Millie' carved into the stock."

"See? We should have read this days ago. Thomas was killed during training exercises here in New Hampshire while getting ready to go to the Civil War, and that must be his rifle. We should double-check that."

Despite the help Annette's anniversary journal afforded, they still didn't have an answer for Mildred's fall in the field. Holly's first theory was that Mildred might be a living woman attempting to scare Tim into abandoning the property, like in an episode of *Scooby-Doo*. Tim shook his head, reminding Holly of the terrible stench and swarm of flies that followed Mildred around. There was no explanation for her tumble, at least not yet.

"Okay, where was I, anniversaries?" Holly continued checking her notes. "Right. According to the journal, there is some crazy stuff that happens here every year. For instance, there is a funeral march, and Mildred is the only one who shows up. It took Annette a few years and a lot of detective work to figure it out. She says you can even hear a horse if you listen closely. And there's a boat on the pond and many other things that we should be ready for. So maybe if we know when the ghosts will be here, we can work around them."

"Who was the funeral for, did Annette say?"

"I was guessing it was for Thomas."

"Makes sense."

"The last page underlines my point. She goes on and on, making it sound important." Holly flipped to the back of the book and showed Tim. The last two pages were in red ink.

VERY IMPORTANT: To whomever this journal finds, be warned that many events repeat themselves annually, so you might want to note where the events occur to avoid encounters.

If you have read this, you know about the woman and the other two entities I am dealing with. I see them almost weekly now. I will write more as I go to keep you informed.

"'Almost weekly basis'? Good Lord, I see them every day!" Tim complained.

"Do you think they're working together? I don't. Thomas wants us to solve it, maybe Elmer, but not Mildred. I think she's the one that destroyed the town hall records," said Holly.

"Thomas's gravestone isn't with them in the grove, and she put Wells, not Pike, on her headstone. That can't be good," said Tim.

"Maybe Thomas doesn't want to deal with her. I wouldn't blame him." Holly continued thumbing through the Anniversaries journal until she reached January 23, 1966, when Annette woke up to find her journal on her chest. Holly then found the same date in the anniversary journal. The page was much neater, and under "January 23" were three short paragraphs to separate the years.

January 23
1966
I woke with my journal on my chest after I had left it in the turret the night before. I believe Thomas Pike placed it on my person to encourage my interest.

1967
No sightings today. There is no reason to repeat this day as an "anniversary" because it was an interaction between Thomas and me and not something the ghosts would remember to celebrate as a milestone in their lives. Not part of the history I am trying to uncover.

_1968_
   Same.

Holly flipped ahead to April 20, which was a few days ago. "Tim, what did you see ghost-wise on Tuesday the 20th?"

Tim sat on the couch, bleary-eyed. April 20 wasn't even a week ago, yet it seemed like a decade had passed. "All the days are running together. That was my third day, so that was the day I followed Elmer into the grove."

"Oh, right." Holly shot Tim a disapproving glance and turned the page to April 20.

April 20,
_1966_
   No sightings.

_1967_
   I volunteered at the nursing home. No sightings that evening.

_1968_
   Same.

"No answers there." Holly read through the rest of the week, but there were no anniversaries. Annette hadn't seen any ghosts this entire week in any of the years. Holly flipped forward until she saw a date with something other than "no sightings" and stopped on April 25.

April 25
_1966_
   Today, I woke to a thunderous banging noise out by the barn. I stopped in the turret to see if I could get a look from that vantage point, but no luck. From there, I descended and went out the side door in front of the barn. I could not get a look at the other side of the barn roof due to the proximity to the forest, and I dared not call out to whoever might be up there. I guess the barn was built in April, which was important to somebody.

_1967_
   There were no sightings, although I volunteered most of the day at the nursing home. Feeling lonely.

1968
   Nursing home all day.

Holly's pulse quickened at the recognition of an anniversary they'd experienced. Perhaps Thomas had fond memories of that day. Or was it Mildred? Maybe building the house was important to one of them. Holly looked up. Tim was asleep in his chair. *Meeting adjourned,* she thought.

Tim was being pulled in every direction between kids, work, dating, ghosts, and diaries. Even if she woke him, he wouldn't absorb it. However, Holly would fill him in tomorrow morning. She flipped to April 27, tomorrow's date, to set him up.

April 27
1966
   The mother was in a small rowboat on the pond. She remained almost motionless except for the drifting of the boat. It went on until I grew tired of watching. I let down my guard and started some menial tasks on my to-do list, checking back every few minutes. I'm unsure how long it took, but I checked on her roughly half an hour in, and she was gone. For the next hour, I wondered if she would show herself again, but that was it for the day.

1967
   Nursing home.

1968
   No sightings.

It was odd to say that Tim might "only" be seeing Mildred in a boat on the pond tomorrow, but a boat ride sounded like a day off after the previous few days. Holly closed the book, put the wine glasses in the dishwasher, and shut off the kitchen lights. She was relieved that the next day seemed safe enough to let him work at the house alone, but still, something bothered her, and after racking her brain, she had to let it go.

Holly woke seven hours later with the same lingering feeling. Once again, she put it out of her mind. "Keep an eye on the pond. Annette saw Mildred in a rowboat on one of her years here."

"Only one? What happened in the other years?"

"One year she was at the nursing home, and the other year says 'no sightings.' I don't understand it, either. Take a look." Holly turned the book around so he could read. Tim had yet to make a dent in his coffee.

"Did she mean to write 'nursing home, no sightings' on the last one? Or does it mean she was home, and there were no sightings? Anyway, I never go near the pond, even on my grove trips."

"Yeah, well, don't go to the grove, either! Not today, and not any day until we fully understand!"

"Holly, I'm so behind I'm thinking of calling Johnny up here to put my mind at ease. I'll see if he can spare a day between the paying projects. Speaking of that, I need to play salesman soon to keep him busy. Man, I'm so busy."

"What are you doing tonight?" asked Holly.

"Hanging with you again, right?"

"I think we should do the same thing we did last night. I'll get takeout, and we'll finish our conversation. Tim, I'm forgetting something, and I was hoping you could help me figure it out. I thought, at first, it might be that Annette spent a lot of time at the nursing home, and she missed a lot of sightings, but that wasn't it."

"Something about the house, you mean?"

"I'm not sure. You fell asleep, and I don't blame you, but we must catch up. Take pictures of the pond. Here's the agency's Nikon. Be careful, and don't break it. It won't zoom in much, but don't you dare try to get closer."

Tim took a closer look at the Nikon, and Holly was right. The lens would offer little or no zoom, and the pond was too far away for a good picture. They'd be able to see a boat with a person in it, but not much else. "Alright, I'll try. I have a question: if I call Johnny up for tomorrow night, would you be okay with that? I'm not even sure he'll want to come. I told him about our ghosts and was surprised to find out he's had some experience."

"That's fine, but you'll warn him first, right? You've got to give him every chance to back out. Does he have a family? Wife, kids?"

"Yeah, he's got a wife and kids. I'll make sure he knows everything. That's why I said I wasn't sure if he would come."

They finished breakfast, cleaned up, and left for work. Tim followed her until the fork: right meant Sanborn, and left meant Laconia. As she turned, he waved through his Plexiglas patch job, another thing he had to get done.

Holly waved back, but as soon as Tim's truck disappeared, her smile did too. That thing still bothered her, and she couldn't figure it out.

CHAPTER 29

April 27, 1971

Tim cruised down Lancaster Hill Road, slowing to twenty miles per hour. He craned his neck, looking for a boat, but the cattails were too high. Seeing no reason for concern, he pressed on. After pulling into his usual parking spot, Tim reminded himself to face the truck toward the road. He got out, scouted, and stopped in the turret for potential correspondence.

When all was clear, Tim went to the barn to retrieve the hatchet he had found the morning the girls hid on him. He removed it and locked it in the toolbox in the bed of his truck, then went inside. The sunny bedroom had the best straight-on view of the pond. Two maples grew along the stone wall before the pond but were far enough apart to provide the optimum angle.

The first step was the noisy part of the wall refurbishment, and he had it torn out in less than an hour. Tim took frequent breaks to walk the hallway and test the air. The thought of being watched was discomforting. Every nail the crowbar pried released a cringe-inducing whine, and he prayed it wouldn't call her attention.

The day was gray, and distant clouds threatened to bring the April showers everyone in New England complained about. *April showers bring May flowers, but what do Mayflowers bring?* "Pilgrims," he whispered out loud. *Mayflowers bring pilgrims. Good one, Tim. Good joke. Everybody in New England knows that. Probably the whole country.* Tim was nervous.

An hour passed, and the tension mounted. Under normal circumstances, Tim would bring a radio to pass the time. If he were lucky, he might catch a Red Sox game.

But Tim didn't want to be deaf to the sounds in the house, and it always made plenty. Even the false alarms were stressful. Every minute or so, Tim shot glances at the pond. Holly's Nikon was within reach, awaiting the photo op. Noon came and went.

At 12:30 pm, Tim went to the living room to call Johnny. He'd almost forgotten. It was Tuesday, and Johnny would work on the Mills' kitchen in Topsfield. Mrs. Mills picked up on the second ring, and after Tim made small talk, she passed the phone.

"How are things down there, Johnny? Ahead of schedule, as usual?"

"Yeah, hey, I was going to call you. I'm done here after today, or at least as done as I can be until Mrs. Mills' exhaust vent arrives. When's that?" This exhaust vent was a thorn in Tim's side. The manufacturer had sent it to the wrong address, and the result was a work stoppage, pissing off Mrs. Mills and delaying her payment.

"It's coming Friday. I told them I'd order from China directly next time if they couldn't get the shipping straight. I always speak to some guy named Larry, and Larry doesn't know his ass from his elbow." Tim paced the living room, stealing glances at the pond.

"I know that guy. He's terrible. I always ask to speak to someone else," Johnny replied. "So, where do you want me?"

"That's why I'm calling. If you could come up and help me, I might do some catching up." The telephone cord was driving him crazy. He'd twisted it so much the handset began to fight him.

"Is Holly slowing you down, Boss?" Tim could hear Johnny's grin through the telephone line.

"Uh, funny, I can hear your smile through the phone, my friend, and you're right, that's part of it. That's a pretty good chunk of the problem, but that's the good problem. I need to tell you the whole story."

Johnny knew the ghost conversation was coming. There was a noticeable lack of gutter humor, which was okay because Mrs. Mills was in the next room, and he couldn't respond in kind. Mrs. Mills was a stay-at-home housewife who employed a cleaning lady and read romance novels. Contractors were a nuisance, and the quicker they left, the better. Johnny continued: "So, is this about the other thing you talked about the last time I saw you?"

"Yeah, it's about the ghosts. I see them every day. We even have a couple of journals somebody left that tell us when things will happen."

"Did someone give them to you? Or, let me guess, they're not around anymore."

"Right, she's dead. She died in her sleep at the age of sixty. And I know what you're thinking, and that fact never sat well with me, either. Johnny, we've been physically touched by these ghosts, or at least one of them. I couldn't even move, man. I'm serious. I was pressed back into my truck seat like a pancake. So was Holly, so it's not just me saying so." Tim looked left and right, down to the kitchen and back to the room by the road. All clear.

"Well, what are you still doing there, then? Just leave, man! It's not worth it!"

Here we go again, thought Tim as he looked toward the pond. "Yeah, right. You want me to move in with you?"

"No, just sell it."

"Would you? I don't think so. You go to church, don't you? Selling a haunted house isn't the moral thing to do." Tim checked: still no boats on the pond.

Johnny lowered his voice so that Mrs. Mills wouldn't hear. "I guess not, but what about this ghost pushing you around?"

"Hold on, Johnny. I need a second." Tim's telephone cord had become so twisted he couldn't stand it anymore, so he pulled the handset from his ear and let it spin until it was right again.

"I don't think he was trying to hurt me. Maybe he was trying to help. I'm not sure." Tim walked into the den and checked out the backyard.

"He? Like you know this guy, Tim? How's that?" Johnny asked.

"I'll tell you more when you get here if you still want to come. It's weird up here, and it's for real."

"Tim, I'm going to give Mrs. Mills back her kitchen until Friday when the exhaust fan comes. I'll be up tomorrow morning first thing. Give me the address again, and I'll buy a New Hampshire map." By Johnny's tone, Tim could tell Mrs. Mills was within earshot.

"As I said, you don't have to do this. I would understand."

"I'll be up there by eight o'clock, and we'll go from there. I have to go. I don't think Mrs. Mills knew the exhaust fan was coming on Friday. Thanks for letting me break the news, old friend. Oh, and Boss, if you happen to talk to my wife for whatever reason, do not mention the pollen count up there if you know what I mean. She's concerned about my allergies. Understand?"

"Right. Don't mention the ghosts. I got it." Before they hung up, Tim heard Mrs. Mills say, "*Friday?*" Tim was thankful to have Johnny. Not only could he outwork anyone he'd ever met, but he was good with customers. Tim hung the phone up and looked at the pond. The water's surface was dull gray but also free of boats, so he was happy. *Fine by me, but what's wrong with your journal, Annette?*

Just then, something caught the corner of his eye. Tim turned and looked into the breakfast area. Whatever he sensed was gone, but the hairs on his arms confirmed what his eyes had missed. Quietly, he backed away to avoid being visible from the kitchen and huddled against the den door. He thought he heard someone cooking, specifically a knife tapping a cutting board. *Click, click, click.*

It had to be Mildred. Tim's heart pumped harder than on any of his trips to the grove. *What the hell is this? Where's the damn boat?* All bets were off. He needed to escape if he should be so lucky. He would exit through the front door by the road. Suddenly, her voice disrupted his train of thought. She was crying, an odd, low sob with pauses between breaths.

To call it sadness was an understatement. This was grief. Between wails, the house went silent but for a boiling pot. Tim began to sweat, bracing for the next round of lament. The realization she possessed a knife terrified him, as did the fact he was weaponless.

Another groan broke the silence, and Tim raised his hands to his ears. He wanted nothing more than to leave, anything to avoid the next shriek. Holding his breath, he prepared to run. Suddenly, there was a loud crash in the kitchen, followed by another. Dishes were smashing on the floor and against the walls. A wail filled the air as sorrow turned to anger.

Suddenly, some members of her swarm crossed into the living room, and he knew she couldn't be far behind. Tim was in the wrong spot, backed against the den's wall, and cut off from his truck. Even if he escaped through the window into the backyard, he would have to circle the house.

Another dish smashed, but this time it sounded different. It might have been a window. Tim's eyes darted to the front door, calculating distance, about to cross her line of sight. Then, the front door swung open.

Outside on the front step was Elmer, as glassy-eyed as Tim remembered. The clouds hung in the sky as if they delivered him. The boy looked at Tim, raised a finger to his mouth, and then held up his other hand, suggesting Tim stay put. Tim waited, shocked. Mildred's rant continued, increasingly frantic. Raspy sobs and shrieks pushed fetid air from her dried-up vocal cords.

Tim watched Elmer, nervous that his life depended on the dead boy in the doorway. Suddenly, the telephone rang. The piercing tone filled the house, and the noise from the kitchen stopped. Time stood still, and Elmer lowered his hands. A fly buzzed Tim's ear. Tension was thick as he monitored the two doorways, frozen in fear.

CHAPTER 30

April 27, 1971

Holly pulled into her usual spot at Depot Realty, named after the real-life train station where the business was housed, and slid the gear into park. The outside of her workplace looked rustic, but Holly hated the cramped quarters. She removed the key from the ignition and realized she couldn't remember one detail of the morning commute. The thing bothering her wouldn't go away.

Holly dropped her bag on her desk and sat down. Evenings with Tim were fun, but they cut into her prep time, which was a good problem to have but a problem nonetheless. Holly kept a rolling to-do list, and yesterday's was still taped to the light on her desk. Taking it down, she grabbed a new piece of paper and recopied the unfinished items. Then she pulled out her call list. Today, there were eight phone calls to be made, two showings, and, thankfully, a signing.

She glanced at her bulletin board, which had a twelve-month Depot Realty calendar pinned to it. She didn't use this calendar, but her boss, Marty Dubois, gave one to every employee. The calendar was the only holiday "bonus" Marty ever offered. It earned him several nicknames, "Frugal Frenchman" being one of the kindest.

April was almost over, and she still hadn't flipped from March, so Holly sat up, pulled the pushpins, and corrected it. Sitting back, she stared at the unmarked pages. There were only three holidays in April: April Fool's Day, Passover, and Easter. Holly was surprised that Easter had already come and gone. Why hadn't her mother reminded her? *Easter,* she thought. *It's hard to keep track of. It's always on a different day.*

All of a sudden, Holly knew what was bothering her. It wasn't something she'd forgotten but rather something she'd gotten wrong. She had to get her hands on some old calendars. On her way to the library, Holly wondered how she would look up old calendars and decided to use microfilm and search through old newspapers.

Holly opened a blank notepad and drew herself four empty April calendars, then gave each one a year: 1966, 1967, and 1968 for the Annette years, and 1971 for Tim. After filling in the dates, Holly opened Annette's anniversary journal and transferred all the ghostly occurrences onto the dates they occurred. She began with the fourth week in April for Tim's immediate safety.

April 25
1966
   Today, I woke to a thunderous banging noise out by the barn. Holly remembered reading this passage and moved on to the next.

1967
   There were no sightings, although I volunteered most of the day at the nursing home. Feeling lonely.

1968
   Nursing home all day.
On the 1966 calendar, in the Monday, April 25 box, Holly wrote "roofer." On the 1967 calendar, in the Tuesday, April 25 box, she wrote a small question mark because Annette wasn't home that day. On the 1968 calendar, in the Thursday, April 25 box, she drew another question mark for the same reason. After that, Holly moved to April 26, and something wasn't right.

April 26
1966
   I volunteered all day at the nursing home.

1967
   The mother was again seen in a small rowboat on the pond. No moving, no nothing, just drifting, and she disappeared after I couldn't watch anymore. She was out there for over an hour! No further sightings after that.

Here was the problem: According to what Holly had read last night, *April 27* was the day Mildred went boating.

April 27
1966
   The mother was in a small rowboat on the pond. She remained almost motionless except for the drifting of the boat. It went on until I grew tired of watching. I let down my

guard and started some menial tasks on my to-do list, checking back every few minutes. I'm unsure how long it took, but I checked on her roughly half an hour in, and she was gone. For the next hour, I wondered if she would show herself again, but that was it for the day.

1967
  Nursing home.

1968
  No sightings.

Had Annette made a mistake, or did it happen on different days in different years? Holly's eyes raced across the pages as she flipped back to April 26, a knot tightening in her stomach:

April 26
1968
  It was a very upsetting day! The mother was berserk with emotion. It was so loud I couldn't get her screaming out of my head. Thank God she didn't see me. I was upstairs making the bed. Then, a howl came from the living room and nearly scared me to death.
  I listened to her footsteps as she ran around sobbing. She left through the front porch, bursting through both doors, and I'm surprised they're still on their hinges. She stood in the driveway, facing away from the road. Her hands were out straight as if attempting to keep someone back.
  She looks dead, for lack of a better word, and I'm sure that seems obvious to the reader, being that she is a ghost, but I mean to say that she looks like a corpse. Her motions are stiff and jerky, and her face is blank despite her vocal emotion. She is a terrible sight, covered in flies, hundreds of them.
  Her body jerked as if someone had pushed her or she had choreographed it. I think it was a reenactment of the morning Thomas left, and if I'm right, that will place the year in 1861. The ordeal ended when she collapsed near the road in sobs. Eventually, she stood up and slow-walked around the building toward the barn. I hid, hoping she was gone for good.
  What are the five stages of grief? Anger, sorrow, depression— I can't remember them all (I knew the list very well right after Henry died). I understand the last one is "acceptance." I am sure this woman has not gotten there. Her emotions are powerful, the epitome of unrest. I hope if you find this journal, you can avoid this day.

Holly's heart raced as she filled in the calendars. *April 26 is always different.* Tim heard the *Roofer* on April 26, 1971. Annette saw a *Boat* in

1967, and *Thomas Leaves* happened in 1968. But it wasn't just April 26 that was different from year to year. Every date was different.

"Anniversary journal" was a misnomer. The date didn't matter. This ghost problem worked more like Thanksgiving, the fourth Thursday in November. Getting increasingly anxious, Holly filled out Tim's experiences in the 1971 calendar.

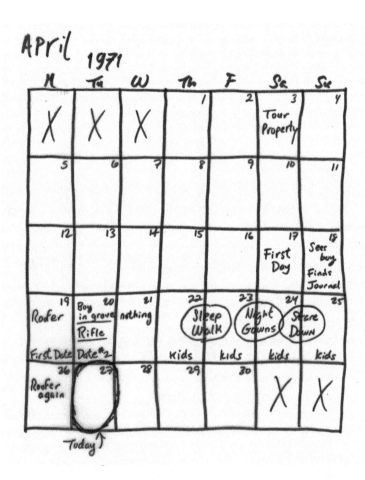

After she finished Tim's calendar, Holly referred to Annette's notes and filled out 1966, 1967, and 1968. After completing everything, Holly stacked the pages together and held them to the light.

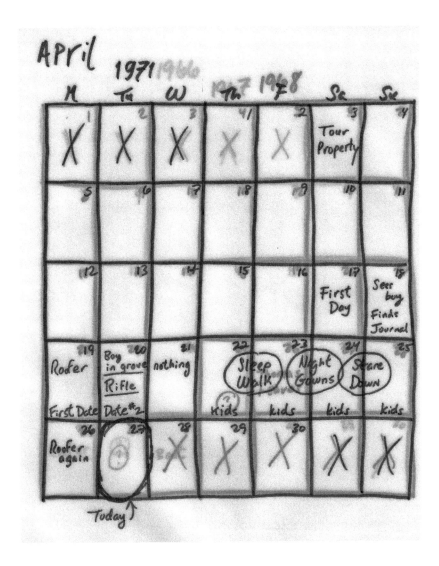

The fourth week of 1968 did not align with the fourth week of the other three years, probably because the first row of April 1968 was seven full days, and on the rest of the calendars, at most four. Holly slid the 1968 calendar down a week, and when two *Roofer* dates matched up, she knew she had it right.

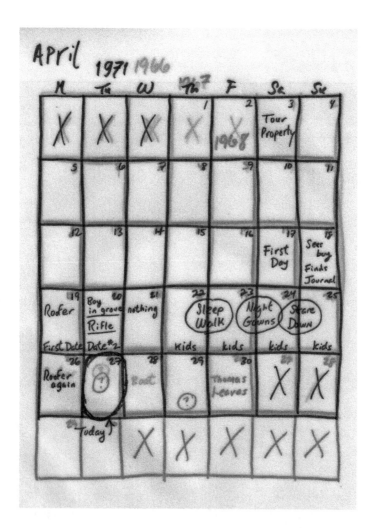

Two question marks shone through the pages on April 27. Those were two days, in different years, that Annette had not been home. Why two question marks and not three? Because April 27, 1971, was April 23, 1968. Holly hadn't looked at Annette's April twenty-third entries because she thought they were in Tim's 1971 past.

Suddenly, April 23, 1968, was the most important date in the world, and she couldn't flip through the journal fast enough. Holly frowned as she saw the April 23 page included an extra-long fold-out. *Annette needed extra space to write it all down.*

<u>April 23</u>
<u>1968</u>

Awful, awful day! I was changing the bedsheets upstairs when a cacophony of crying and screaming came from the kitchen, followed by crashing dishes, pots, and pans. I know this house is haunted, so I stayed upstairs. The "sorrows," I will call them, went on for several minutes, and the gloom in the woman's voice was the most depressing thing I have ever heard. At one point, I heard her moving toward the staircase, which terrified me, but I was relieved to hear the porch door open. She left in a rage, a hatchet in her grasp, on her way to the pond. I hid behind the curtain, watching.

Then, I saw two Canada geese grazing. She was quiet, like a hunter, no longer wailing. I realized her intent, turned away, and then felt a hand on my shoulder. He turned me around and made me watch.

I could not see Thomas, but I'm sure it was him. I have never seen him in any shape or form or from any distance, and this was only the second time I have been close enough to have been touched. I pray it never happens again.

The woman slaughtered the beautiful creatures by cutting their heads off on the stone wall. She picked them up by their feet as they died, wings flapping, and stood there, arms out, a headless goose hanging from each hand, spraying blood everywhere. It was all over the geese, the grass, her hands, face, and dress, and it didn't bother her. It was the messiest, most unnecessary act I have ever witnessed, even though I am a farmer and no stranger to putting meat on the table. The look on her face was vengeance. I will have to refer to my notes, but this is my third April alone here, and I have never seen this happen. Today must have been when he broke the news that he was leaving for the War.

Holly closed the book and ran to the payphone. The house phone rang once and then disconnected. Holly dropped another dime and dialed again, getting a busy signal. Panicked, she bolted out of the library and ran to her car.

CHAPTER 31

April 27, 1971

Tim silenced the telephone and froze, listening. Everything in the kitchen stopped. No more wailing or smashing. Mildred had no doubt heard. So that it wouldn't ring again, Tim unplugged it. Two flies buzzed into the living room, and Tim looked to Elmer on the front steps. Suddenly, a door slammed.

Unsure of where to be, Tim stayed put as Elmer turned to face his approaching mother. The boy turned and ran as Mildred appeared outside the living room window. Suddenly alone, Tim sneaked into the kitchen, and it looked like a bomb went off. The floor was covered in broken dishware, and the windows were smashed. A lone pot boiled on the stove.

Blood and feathers were everywhere, splattered over every surface: walls, countertops, floors, even the ceiling. Tim gagged, unsure if it was her stench or the contents of the pot. He kicked the broken glass aside and stepped through to turn off the burner.

The cutting board was piled high with goose meat, spilling onto the floor. Tim took a closer look and saw it move, then jumped back. He was tired, perhaps even hallucinating, but no. Maggots crawled through the pile. Some had escaped her blade, others were still writhing, chopped in two. The simmering pot spattered the stovetop. Tim looked in. Within the crimson broth bobbed the heads of the two geese.

Tim had seen enough. He'd given it a gallant try, but being at the house on Lancaster Hill Road was no longer worth it. It was time to abandon the plan, money be damned, but first, he had to survive. Tim peered through the broken windows to the pond. No one was there, but he couldn't be sure. Tim left through the side door, and for the hundredth time, he'd forgotten where he'd parked.

As if on cue, he heard Holly's Volkswagen. Tim rounded the corner to see the driver's door open and the engine running, but Holly was gone.

The porch door slammed. Tim knew Holly shouldn't see the kitchen, so he rushed back in the side entrance to intercept. He found her in the doorway to the dining room, horror-struck.

Breathing through the sleeve of her jacket, Holly spoke. "Tim, there won't be a boat on the pond today. She'll be closer than that, but you already know. We have to go, please, right now."

"Okay." Tim tiptoed through the blood, being careful not to slip. "She left the stove on. They'll probably burn the house down one of these days anyway."

"Tim, she's outside!" Mildred was on the upper lawn, covered in blood. It had begun to rain, and she stared at the house. Her shoulders rolled as if to ease stiffness, and it was then that Holly noticed the hatchet.

Tim saw it, too, dripping goose blood into the grass. Holly grabbed Tim's hand and led him through the broken shards toward the front door by the road. Tim whispered: "That hatchet was locked in the bed of my truck."

Holly's eyes widened, but she didn't speak. As they passed the living room windows, Tim looked out. Mildred hadn't moved, still standing by their cars, the rain sticking her dress to her body. Her head turned, and their eyes locked.

"Oh, shit," said Tim.

Holly huddled by the window, hiding, studying Tim's face for a reaction. *It can't end this way,* she thought.

"I think she's coming," he said.

Holly looked out. Mildred stared back, glazed eyes unblinking.

"Get back, Holly!" said Tim. Suddenly, Mildred marched, gray-white knuckles gripping the weapon, and headed for the porch door.

"She's going to the porch," said Holly, moving toward the door by the road. Tim followed but stopped when he heard a rumble over their heads. He grabbed Holly's arm, pulling her back, a finger raised to his lips.

THUD THUD-THUD-THUD-THUD-THUD.

Elmer came bounding down the stairs as loud as could be. Tim watched the front door as it opened itself, and the boy ran out into the rain. Immediately, Mildred turned and dropped to her knees, arms outstretched. Elmer looked her way but walked past the dead geese on his way to the pond. Halfway there, he looked back, and Mildred followed as if trying not to scare a deer.

Tim and Holly kept still, relieved to be forgotten. Once Mildred had passed the pond, they ran through the downpour to their cars and sped down Lancaster Hill Road as fast as the potholes allowed. Just before they reached the property line, Elmer broke into a run and turned into the woods.

The last thing Tim saw was Mildred as she turned her attention from Elmer to his taillights. Having her attention was terrible. As the house blurred in his rain-blurred mirror, he wondered if he would ever go back.

There it goes, he thought: *My money, pride, and future.* The worst part was nobody would believe him. Not only would he embody Sheila's description of her loser ex, but she could now add the word lunatic.

CHAPTER 32

April 27, 1971

Tim pulled into Holly's driveway and parked behind her Volkswagen. His Plexiglas window had leaked, but that was the last thing on his mind. He got out of his truck and went right to the built-in toolbox. The lock was still in place, yet Mildred had gotten in. As the rain soaked his clothes, he ran to the front door, where Holly held it open. As soon as they were inside, they hugged.

"How are you doing?" said Tim.

"Shaken. That was terrible."

"I'm done with the house. I'll take the loss but give full disclosure to potential buyers and sell to the first one that doesn't believe me."

"Hold on. I can't believe I'm saying this, especially after today, but you might want to look at what I learned in the library. Annette's anniversary journal has a flaw."

Tim listened impatiently, his mind made up. "Holly, you just said, 'That was terrible.' Did you see all the blood? She has a hatchet!"

"I know, I sound like you, and you sound like me, but we can avoid her. Let me finish. You've seen Mildred three times, right? Not counting the times she was walking through the field? There was our first date, where we think Thomas held us in the car, and then there was the night she looked in on you and the girls, and then what I call today's cooking show."

"Holly, visitation is around the corner. What if today's cooking show had been the day my daughters made pancakes? It's like a bad movie. I don't want to be the dumbass that doesn't leave."

"All I'm saying is, we should reassess. Johnny is coming, correct? You said he had a ghost situation with his grandmother, so he won't think we're nuts. He'll have a fresh perspective."

"Oh shit, I need to call him. I don't want him showing up at the house. Otherwise, I'll have to go back and intercept him." Tim called the Mills residence, and of course, Mrs. Mills answered. The good news was that Johnny was still there.

"Johnny, don't go to my house. I won't be there. Let me give you Holly's address. Got a pencil?" Tim kept it short and sweet, saving the details for later.

When Tim hung up, Holly pulled out her calendars and shared what she learned in the library. She also showed Tim Annette's take on what happened on this day in 1968.

"Wow, that's what happened, alright," said Tim.

"Yeah, I've only had time to figure out a few days. Tim, we haven't done our due diligence. You could get so much more done if you knew she wouldn't show up on a given day, and vice-versa."

Holly had a point. If Mildred hung around on any given day, he shouldn't even go to work. He'd be better off driving to Massachusetts and lining up work for Johnny. "All right, I can't believe this is you talking, but what else does Annette have to say?"

Holly picked up where she left off and read aloud:

"I was forced to remain at the window, Thomas's hand on my shoulder, until the woman returned covered in blood. He let me go after that, but I had questions. I ran into my bedroom and grabbed a blank journal that I had yet to write in. Turning to a random page in the middle of the book, I wrote "YES," flipping about fifty pages forward, I wrote "NO." I closed the book and returned it to the guest room across the hall.

Knowing that the woman might still be downstairs, I held the book in my hands up to the air and whispered: "Thomas, is she angry that you are leaving for the war? The answer is written in this book." Then I set the journal on the guest bed and peered out the window to see if she was still outside. The two geese were piled on the grass, but I couldn't find her.

I took twenty minutes to sneak downstairs, but the anniversary was over, thank God. I picked up the geese by the feet and brought them to the compost. As I dropped the bodies on the pile, something caught my eye. Up in the turret was a lit candle. I entered the house, knowing what I would find. My journal of two words was open to the word "YES."

I think Thomas hides because he doesn't want her to know he's here. She haunts this place, but he wants something. As for the boy, I know very little, but I can tell he doesn't want his Mommy.

Who is the ghost woman? I assume she smudged the town records. She must have a history. I will ask around at the nursing home. There wasn't much of anything in the microfilm unless I missed something.

Another important thing happened today: Thomas has turned the pages of my books twice now. I will fill up my yes/no journal with words that might be useful, and perhaps communication will improve.

Until then, I reiterate: My anniversary journal has a flaw. Anniversaries do not go by calendar date. Just because it happened on the 23rd of this year doesn't mean it will occur on the 23rd of next year. For the "Goose Murders," watch out on the fourth Tuesday in April!

"What the hell! Why didn't she put that on the first page?" Tim griped.

"She ran out of time, Tim. That journal is far from complete. Thomas Pike has been waiting for someone like us."

"But he only gave us the journal forty-eight hours ago!"

"After waiting a hundred years, I bet Thomas Pike doesn't care about our schedule."

CHAPTER 33

April 27, 1971

Johnny was on his way, and Tim prepped for dinner. He'd decided on Chicken Marsala, his go-to dish because everything else in his repertoire was mediocre. Holly bought a pad of tracing paper to make seeing through her calendar pages easier. When Johnny arrived at six o'clock, he saw Tim with his apron on and laughed out loud.

"Half day, Chief? How many nails did you hit today? Can't be many." Johnny started with the taunts as if they hadn't spent a day apart. Each man would brag how they'd outworked the other, and God forbid one took a day off. Johnny had once cut himself on a table saw, and Tim razzed him for the missed time.

"Johnny's already ragging on me, and he hasn't started drinking. Holly, this is Johnny, and Johnny, this is Holly. Honey, turn your bullshit filter to high. Anything out of his mouth is questionable."

"Pleased to meet you, Holly," Johnny said as he shook her hand. "Smells good. You let him cook?"

"That's right, a real man cooks, Johnny," said Tim. "This is the seventies. Women's Lib. Equal rights." Tim knew Johnny would be a gentleman in front of Holly but would exact his revenge later. Tim had never cooked for Sheila, and Johnny knew it. "What are you drinking, buddy? We have beer, and we have red wine."

Johnny surprised Tim when he opted for the wine and sat on the couch opposite Holly. Tim pulled a chair over, and they began to talk. "So, how are things?" said Johnny. "I mean, I know you're running behind, but in general?"

"Johnny, Holly knows everything. It's terrible up here, and today was the worst. I might have to sell the house. I'm not going to ask you to help me tomorrow. Today, we saw a woman with a hatchet." Johnny's eyes narrowed as he looked at Holly, who stared back dead serious.

"I'm not kidding. Dead geese, too. Blood was everywhere, and I don't mean just a few drops. It was disgusting. The smell …"

"Whoa, whoa, whoa," said Johnny, "Where's the ghost? No, forget that. Just start from the beginning. Like, Day One."

"Johnny's right, Tim. Start over," said Holly. "This story builds. Does he even know about the journals?"

"I know there are ghosts and journals, but that's about it," said Johnny.

Holly started by explaining their first date, and Tim filled in the parts when Holly wasn't there, like when the girls visited. Over the next hour, they recounted the previous ten days, from the property tour to the cooking show.

When they were finished, Johnny stood, walked to the table, and grabbed the bottle of wine. After he'd refilled everyone's glasses, he turned to Tim. "What's today? April 27? And you moved in when?"

"My first day was the 17th," Tim replied.

"All that in ten or eleven days. Wow, that's heavy-duty. My first reaction is that the man ghost, the unseen one, is the driver, and you're working for him. He's using the journals to communicate. He's the one that talked to Allison."

"Annette," Holly corrected.

"Right," Johnny continued "Annette laid the groundwork. I'm guessing that the happenings went from zero to sixty because Thomas thinks he can use Annette's journals to get what he wants. Thomas sees Annette investigating and protects her when Mildred is around because, after today's happenings, you know she's insane."

Tim took another sip of wine, beginning to feel the effects, and put some breadsticks and olive oil on the coffee table.

Holly spoke up: "Do you think he's helping us too? Like the night in the truck? At first, I thought it was Mildred."

"I'm not sure, but it could have been," said Johnny, fingers already covered in oil.

"That little kid has saved me twice," noted Tim. "He showed up today and got her attention, and he started running around downstairs the night she looked in on the girls and me. Do you think the father and the kid are working together?"

"They might be looking out for themselves, so be careful. Annette and her husband are dead. What was his name? Henry?"

"Yeah, but Henry died of a heart attack. Annette's death is the one I wonder about."

"Maybe it's time for me to tell you about my grandmother."

"Yeah, right after I get you a napkin. Do you see what I have to deal with, Holly? It's like he's five years old," said Tim.

"Oh, come on. Who serves olive oil on a coffee table?" Their laughter broke the tension for a moment, and it felt good. When his hands were clean, Johnny told his story.

"I was eleven years old, and my grandmother was sick with cancer. We would visit her in the hospital almost daily. She was in there for a long time, too, like it must have been a few months. As a kid, I had always assumed that Grandma and Grandpa were that cute old couple that fed pigeons together on park benches. Boy, was I wrong.

One day, I was with my Mom visiting Grandma when my grandfather walked in behind us. Grandma's mood immediately turned sour. We'd been having a normal chat, and when he walked through the doorway, her eyes turned black, huge pupils and shit. I don't know if I was the only one to see it, but it scared me. She looked mean. Grandpa pretended not to notice and started acting weird. He sounded fake.

"He seemed full of shit but also scared. It changed the mood, and I wanted to leave, but Grandma pulled me close so Grandpa couldn't get near her. He didn't seem to mind, either. He hung back and made small talk with my Mom.

"I had no choice but to look at her. I couldn't even turn around. She stared up at Grandpa with those dark eyes like she hated his guts, and when he and my Mom were out of things to say, he turned to my grandma and said, 'How are you feeling today, Isabella?' And then, I'll never forget her face or her words because I had a front-row seat. She said:

'I'm not done with you, motherfucker.'

"Grandma didn't raise her voice or anything, but it was terrifying. I mean, she hated him. I had never heard her swear before. I have not used that curse to this day. It reminds me of her, of the real grandma."

"Oh my God, what did your Mom do?" asked Holly.

"Hold on. My Mom didn't have time to do anything because right after Grandma said that, her head rose off the pillow a good three inches like she was sitting up, and then she hung there and started moaning. She squeezed my hand tight, and it hurt, but I just stared, and she let out this big moaning breath like she was in pain and then fell back to the pillow, dead. My mom had to help me pry my hand out of hers. I had nightmares for months."

Tim and Holly were speechless.

"But that isn't the half of it. Several hours later, after a long car ride home and a barely touched dinner, I asked my Mom if Grandma hated

Grandpa. Mom's eyes were red. She'd been trying to hide that she was crying. The death of her mother was upsetting, but the three of us had heard Grandma's last words."

"What did your grandfather do?" asked Holly.

"Mom tried to get him to come over, but he wouldn't. I found out later he had a girlfriend and wanted to be with her."

"Oh, that's why Grandma was pissed off," said Tim.

"Right. And that's how my Mom answered my question. She told me Grandpa had done a bad thing and started seeing another woman, and Grandma knew all about it. It made me feel weird. It was like I had been tricked. You want to think your grandparents love each other, but then you realize they're messed up like everyone else. I never looked at him the same."

"Not to rush your story, but she becomes a ghost, right?"

"A week later, my Mom told me that Grandpa's girlfriend died and that he would be coming to live with us. I didn't like that because I didn't know how to feel about Grandpa anymore. The guest room became his, and he didn't want to be there either. Two nights later, I woke up, and he was screaming. Mom and Dad were already in Grandpa's room, so I stayed in bed.

'It was her! She killed Dorothy, and now she's going to kill me!' he said.

'No, Dad, stop it! Keep your voice down, Johnny is sleeping, and you're going to scare him. You must have had a bad dream. Mom is dead. You saw her die in the hospital.' Johnny paused. His emotions were creeping up on him, so he took a breath and a sip of wine.

"My Dad got mad at him and told him to shut up, or he'd move him down to the basement, but Grandpa was spooked."

"Why didn't they just put him in a nursing home?" asked Holly.

"Money, mostly."

"This doesn't end well, does it?" Holly's question was more of a statement.

Johnny shook his head, took another drink, and put the glass down. "Three nights after Grandpa's meltdown, I woke to strange noises. It sounded like the fan in Grandpa's room was vibrating or something. I had to pee anyway, so I got up. His bedroom door was ajar, so I pushed it open.

"Grandma was standing over the bed, but at first, I wasn't sure it was her. She was hunched over him, but I couldn't see what she was doing. Stupidly, I stepped closer. Grandma was shoving a rolled-up newspaper down his throat, really jamming it in there, back and forth, putting her weight into it. I had never seen her move that way. It was like she was changing a tire or something.

"Grandpa was gone, or at least I hope he was. His arms were down at his sides, open wide as if to surrender. A noise came from his mouth, and I'm not sure if it was him or the newspaper thrashing his throat. When she saw me, she dropped what she was doing and smirked, pretending to act all dainty again. She even winked at me.

"I peed myself, and she reached back and pulled the newspaper from his mouth. Grandpa made a noise like a deflating raft, and he went still. Grandma dropped the newspaper, put her finger to her lips, opened the closet door, and left like it was an emergency exit. I never went in that room again."

"I never mentioned Grandma's ghost to my parents, but I looked in the room when the ambulance arrived. You'd think his mouth would be all newspaper ink, and the newspaper itself would be crumpled and wet with saliva, but the murder had been covered up. I can't help you with 'ghost physics,' sorry. Some things just can't be explained.

"The cause of death was ruled a heart attack. My grandparents died a week apart. People who didn't know about his affair thought it was romantic, like he couldn't live without her or something, but I knew better. And I never told a soul, just in case Grandma was listening. I hope I didn't just jinx myself." The living room went quiet as they waited to see if Johnny had more.

Finally, Tim spoke. "Got any more boring stories?"

Johnny laughed. "Yeah, right. I pray that Grandma understands I'm trying to help you guys."

"Did you have to figure out how to get rid of her?" Tim looked at Holly, who looked like she had become part of the couch, fingers gripping the soft arm.

Johnny sat down. "No, Boss. A quick double murder, and she rested in peace."

"I think Henry and Annette were murdered," said Holly out of the blue.

"Are you serious?" said Tim. "You told me an hour ago I should wait to sell it!"

"Sell it? You can't sell it," said Johnny. "You told me it's unethical. You're better than that."

"I'll tell them it's haunted, and then they can make their minds up."

"Yeah, right. How much detail will you go into? Are you going to tell them that you saw blood boiling on the stove and a woman with a hatchet? Or are you just going to say it's haunted? I know you, man. Why don't you demo the place? Too expensive?"

"Exactly. What the hell should I do? What would you do?"

"Well, first of all, don't lose your shit. Panic never helps. And second, please, can we eat dinner? I've got a buzz, and my stomach is empty. Third: What makes you think Thomas Pike will let you stop, even if you want to?"

"What do you mean by that?" asked Holly, eyes wide.

"Well, remember how you told me that Thomas hadn't bothered the Smiths for most of the time they lived there? And then Annette started making progress, clues started popping up, and physical contact was made?"

"Yeah," said Tim.

"And how infrequent Annette's sightings were compared to yours? You've been here a little over a week and found two journals with candles to light your way. Do you think he's not invested? When did Thomas die?"

"1861," said Holly.

"1861. So, Thomas Pike has been waiting a hundred and ten years. Is he losing his patience?" Johnny's words were a cold slap. Johnny's grandmother died in the hospital, yet killed his grandfather and the mistress in different places. Even if Tim and Holly left, they could be followed.

Tim stood up, suddenly feeling older, and made his way to the kitchen. He wasn't hungry anymore, almost sick to his stomach. Opening another bottle of wine, Tim lit the burner and cooked as he drank.

"Hey, Boss, don't give up hope. I imagine Thomas has a plan, or he wouldn't be directing you. Maybe your goals are not mutually exclusive. That means there could be an answer. I mean, why would you have to die for his family to be put to rest? He has no gripe with you, right?"

"Okay, let's speculate. What does Thomas Pike want from me?"

"Well, he's invisible, and the other ghosts are not. That's strange. They're from the same family, after all, right?"

"Right."

"And she's always chasing the kid, who doesn't want to be caught. And she's crazy. Chops up toads in your kitchen."

"It was geese, not toads," said Tim, and Holly chuckled.

"So, what happened to the kid? How'd he die?" asked Johnny. Tim put his wooden spoon down and turned to Holly, and they blinked at each other. Great question. How had they not thought of this?

"I'm so tired I don't remember. Holly, what happened to Elmer?"

"We don't know, and now I'm not sure I want to know. Elmer died early, after all. I think I'm going to be upset."

123

"So, something bad happened to the boy, and she did it. That would make a lot of sense," said Johnny.

"If she killed him, that would be a good reason for Dad to be mad at Mom."

"Okay, here's another question: Does Mom know Dad is around? He doesn't show himself, right? They're never seen together, blah, blah, blah."

Tim and Holly looked at each other again, grateful to have someone better rested helping.

"Probably," said Tim, feeling stupid that Johnny was on top of everything. Holly nodded.

"Did you already know this? Or am I just catching up?" Johnny asked.

"I hate to give you any credit, but you're kicking ass, Johnny. We're frazzled. It's been a hell of a ten days." It was nearly nine o'clock, and dinner was finally ready. Holly opened the third bottle of wine, worried they might lose focus, but the mood had lightened, and a celebration was in order.

As they ate, Holly showed them her calendar. When it was complete, she explained it would hold every incident from Annette's journals on one convenient April 1971 calendar, and if needed, she would continue as the months progressed. The calendar provided a forecast of annual events but did not include random sightings. The ghosts could still pop up on any given day, but *anniversaries* should be predictable regarding time and place as long as Annette wrote about it.

April 1971

M	Tu	W	Th	F	Sa	Su
			1	2	3 Tour Property	4
X	X	X				
5	6	7	8	9	10	11
12	13	14	15	16	17 First Day	18 Sees boy Finds Journal
19 Roofer First Date	20 Boy in grove Rifle Date #2	21 nothing	22 Sleep Walk Kids	23 Night Gowns kids	24 Scare Down kids	25 kids
26 Roofer again	27 Mildred "Cooks"	28 Boat	29	30 Thomas Leaves	X	X

Today

"Can I see that?" asked Tim.

"Why, Boss? I thought you were selling the place?" ribbed Johnny.

Tim ignored him and went right to April 28. April 28, 1971, was the fourth Wednesday in April and the same day as April 27, 1966, April 26, 1967, and April 24, 1968.

April 27
1966

The mother was in a small rowboat on the pond. She remained almost motionless except for the drifting of the boat. It went on until I grew tired of watching. I let down my guard and started some menial tasks on my to-do list, checking back every few minutes. I'm unsure how long it took, but I checked on her roughly half an hour in, and she was gone. For the next hour, I wondered if she would show herself again, but that was it for the day.

"That's what I thought would happen today! Instead, I got a blood-sprayed kitchen and a woman with a hatchet. Holly, are you sure?"

"Yeah, I'm certain this time. All three match."

Johnny spoke up: "Okay then, Chief. That means I'm coming with you tomorrow. Let's get up early, finish some things, and get you back on track. Good meeting?"

"Good meeting," Tim echoed.

"Good meeting," said Holly.

CHAPTER 34

April 28, 1971

While Tim and Johnny went to work on the house, Holly called in sick to spend time on her calendar project. After the hatchet, there was no room for ignorance. She was also excited to skip her phone calls. Her first task was to finish reading Annette's original journal. It had only been eight days since she knew of its existence, but it was long overdue.

Tomorrow was once again the most important day of their lives. She looked for any information on April 29th but came up empty. Annette had been busy or elsewhere like many other days. Tim would not be happy, but they could do nothing about it.

Holly read through a part of Annette's journal written in interview form, guessing Annette recorded the conversations and transcribed them later. Thinking ahead, Holly pulled out her notepad and began to summarize.

Annette knew a patient in the nursing home named Martha Simmons, whose family lived at the beginning of Lancaster Hill Road near Route 3. Martha Simmons's mother, Emma, had been a schoolmate of Elmer Pike's. According to Martha, her grandmother Elizabeth was upset when Elmer went missing in 1862, a year after Thomas Pike died in training for the Civil War. Elizabeth knew Mildred and disliked her so much that she started rumors.

The truth was Elizabeth was jealous. Thomas Pike was a handsome young man, and many local ladies, including young Elizabeth, hoped to one day become Mrs. Pike. Mildred, a sixteen year old orphan, arrived out of nowhere and married Thomas two years later. Elizabeth settled for a consolation prize named Frederick Simmons, and they had their daughter Emma not long after Elmer Pike was born.

Elizabeth's obsession with the Pikes continued, and in the depths of depression, she started a scrapbook. According to Martha, Elizabeth would write her feelings, detailing encounters and run-ins with the Pikes. Elizabeth quit on the scrapbook after Thomas' death, as no one was left to covet. Her last entry was a copy of his obituary. After that, the book collected dust. She almost threw it away.

An undetermined amount of time later—Holly couldn't tell— Elizabeth's father, George, a policeman in Sanborn, was called to the Pike house because something happened to Elmer. For reasons unknown, the local press did not cover the story in depth. All Holly could gather was that the boy was found dead on the property.

Elizabeth, of course, suspected Mildred, telling anyone who would listen what a coincidence it was that a widowed woman was suddenly free to find new romance without the baggage of a child. These happenings inspired Elizabeth to dust off the scrapbook and return to her passion.

Elizabeth learned through her father that he had suspicions about Mildred and the Chief of Police, Abner Wallace. Chief Wallace was a single man, having lost his wife to pneumonia several years back. Once or twice, Officer Simmons witnessed Mildred stop by the station at odd hours. Chief Wallace died falling off a ladder at his home in late 1862. George Simmons checked on Mildred's whereabouts on the day of his death but found no reason to pursue his hunch.

Elizabeth wrote everything down, wondering if, before his death, Chief Wallace had pressured Jacob Callan, editor of the *Sanborn Crier*, to keep the details of Elmer's death quiet for his girlfriend.

After the death of the Chief, things at the Pike estate got even quieter, and Lancaster Hill Road became a darker place. What was once a lively homestead with a young family became overgrown and unkempt. The Christmas tree farm, where people would flock after Thanksgiving, had gone to seed. Elizabeth couldn't stifle herself, renewing her obsession so emphatically that even her granddaughter Martha remembered some of the rants.

As passive as he was, Frederick Simmons began complaining that her infatuation was taking away from their happy home. Still, his concerns were pushed aside as she approached a full-blown conspiracy theory. Because there was no public funeral, Elizabeth believed Mildred had him stuffed and moved him back and forth from sofa to bed daily. Later, she changed her theory, now proclaiming that Elmer's bones were buried somewhere on the Pike property. It wasn't long before she lost her audience, and not long after, Elizabeth Simmons went missing.

Emma was the one who called the authorities, having come home from school to an empty house. The town searched for the policeman's daughter, Emma's loving mother, and Frederick's devoted wife. Everyone opened their hearts and doors, putting aside their belief that Elizabeth had a screw loose and had found trouble.

During the search, Mildred Pike was one of the most benevolent townspeople, donating her time and volunteering while inviting others to search her property. Throughout the debacle, George Simmons watched with suspicion. While the property was open, he walked the entire twenty-three acres himself.

What was left of Elizabeth's body was found in early May of 1863 in the woods across the road from the Pike estate. By then, she was hair and bones spread across half an acre as the coyotes had found her. Mildred wasn't even questioned, as it had nothing to do with her property, and she had been so helpful the previous fall.

CHAPTER 35

April 28, 1971

Tim and Johnny arrived at the house just before seven o'clock and parked at the end of the driveway, nose-out for safety. Tim noticed the kitchen windows as soon as he stepped out of the truck.

"Son of a bitch."

Johnny looked around wildly. "What is it?"

"The kitchen windows are still broken. I thought everything would be back to normal. My God, she's even haunting my wallet!" The house had been wide open all night.

Before entering, Tim gave Johnny an introductory tour from the hood of his truck, including the pond—where today's main event was supposed to happen—the field, the woods, and the house itself, window by window. When Tim was done, he took Johnny to the barn.

"Where does that go?" asked Johnny, pointing to the path at the bend in the driveway.

"It takes you to the grove."

"Want to show me?"

"Hell no. We don't know where she is right now."

"Well, haven't you been there two or three times?"

"Yeah, but that was before yesterday. I'm not taking any more chances. It's terrible, Johnny. The smell, the flies, she's scary, man. And dangerous."

"I may be naïve, Boss, but I believe in Thomas Pike. He wants something and will protect you until he gets it."

"I ain't chancing it."

"You're the boss." Johnny left it at that, and Tim took him in the side door, where they paused at the sliding door.

"Are you ready? It's going to be gross in there."

Johnny nodded, and Tim opened the slider. It smelled terrible, and Johnny wrinkled his nose as both men rounded the counter into the kitchen in silence. Everything was as they'd left it, including the smashed dishes and the goose heads in the pot, but what was red yesterday was now brown and swarming with flies.

Tim poked his head into the dining room and looked around, then crept through the living room to the end of the house. When he reached the bottom of the stairs, he held his finger to his lips and waved Johnny through. Together, they searched the four bedrooms. The house was empty. Finally, standing in the sunny guest room, they looked out at the pond.

Johnny broke the silence: "We never finished our talk. We didn't figure out Thomas Pike's end game, the thing that could set you free."

"Welcome to my world, Johnny. The days are never long enough, you get tired, and the next day is exactly the same."

"Fix that attitude, Boss. There are two graves out there, right?"

"Right."

"Mildred and the kid, right? So, where is Thomas? Maybe he wants to be buried with them, or if not, maybe he wants to be buried with the kid."

Tim stared at the pond, mulling it over. "I bet you're right." He turned to face Johnny. "I don't want to inflate your ego, but that could be it! So, do we move the kid or move her? Shit, maybe we move Thomas, too." The thought trailed, and Tim realized he had more questions than ever.

"Hey, I just got here. Give me a minute. By the way, you haven't done shit to this place! How much is the ghost's fault, and how much is Holly's?"

"None of your business, and don't forget it's Sheila's fault, too. That's ten percent of my time right there." The manly banter died as the two men returned downstairs to clean up the mess, throwing the rancid goose meat into the trees around the side of the barn. The kitchen windows would have to wait. New ones had to be ordered, and that would take up to a week. Tim took some measurements and made some phone calls to line things up.

When they were done in the kitchen, Johnny set himself to work in the main bedroom, and Tim worked across the hall. Holly's Nikon was still on the windowsill between the two rooms, sitting where he left it yesterday. As always, the house made noises. Sometimes it came from one of the empty bedrooms, and sometimes it came from downstairs. Johnny frequently poked his face around the doorjamb to check the staircase. As the day wore on, Tim noticed that Johnny was sweating.

"Hey Boss, I'm getting antsy, you know? You see ghosts every day, right? I keep looking out the window. This waiting game is nerve-wracking."

"That's because you're still a virgin. It's different when you're a real man and always see them."

"It's not my first time, my friend. Remem— ah, never mind." Johnny cut his sentence short, but it was too late.

Tim put down his tools and swaggered into the doorway, wearing a shit-eating grin.

"Oh, right. You're not a virgin anymore because your grandma was your first."

Johnny flipped him the bird and dropped his head in defeat. Tim burst into laughter. They worked steadily until noon, then pulled out sandwiches and sat on their toolboxes in the guestroom. Every few minutes, one or the other would peek over the windowsill to look at the pond. Tim stood up, retrieved the Nikon, and kept it close. The day was half over. Johnny took a bite from his sandwich when suddenly Tim whispered.

"Heads up."

Johnny put down his sandwich, and both men knelt before the windows. On the pond was a rowboat, and in it was Mildred Wells. She was in the front seat, away from the oars, and two fishing poles were over the side. She wore a sunbonnet, leaving her face obscured.

Johnny spoke in short, excited whispers. "Oh my God, she doesn't move! Can you see her face? I can't see her face."

Tim snapped five pictures, realizing there would be no prize winners. She was too far away. "No, I can't see her face. She doesn't usually wear the hat. There are two fishing poles. Is she alone?"

"You mean like she's the only actor on the stage today? Yeah, maybe," said Johnny.

"She's not rowing. She's sitting in the front, and the oars aren't beside her," Tim noticed. The two men stopped speculating and watched. Mildred never moved as the boat drifted, never touching the shore. After ten minutes, Johnny repositioned and took a break, leaning against the front wall.

"In one of the journal entries, Annette talks about Thomas Pike leaving to fight in the Civil War. According to Holly's calendar, that anniversary is this Friday. Mildred didn't want him to go and followed him to the road, hysterical."

"Just her? She didn't use a prop for that one? Like the boat?" asked Johnny.

"According to Annette, she does it all by herself, a one-woman show. I guess it was realistic enough that she could figure out what was happening. I wonder if I should skip it."

"Skip if you think it might be dangerous."

Tim looked at the pond again. "There should be two people in that boat, but it's just her. Thomas and Elmer must hate her guts. Otherwise, they'd show up." Tim's back began to stiffen, too, so he stood and set the toolbox on end to use as a stool.

"Right." Johnny let the thought fade and sat up. "Hey, where'd she go?" The boat was gone.

Tim stood and motioned to Johnny. "Watch my back," then left the room, looking in all directions as he went downstairs, going window to window, scanning the property for any sign of her. Two minutes later, they convened in the kitchen. "I think it's over," said Tim, but Johnny couldn't relax.

"Are we in danger? Does she disappear like that all the time?"

"Annette had three years written for this particular date, and she didn't mention anything about her coming to the house, but I'm not going to let down my guard."

"So, how does Thomas talk to you? Remind me," said Johnny.

"Well, one night I sleepwalked, another night I had a dream, and of course, he left two journals."

"That sleepwalking has to be upsetting, man. Holly didn't notice you leaving?"

"No, I was alone with the girls across the hall. The next night, I tied myself to the floor!"

"You left the girls? That's bad."

"That's part of why I was going to quit until you showed up. And you know the girls woke up in old-fashioned nightgowns too ..."

"That can't happen again. When is the next visitation?"

"Nine days."

"Let's hope we figure this shit out soon. Otherwise, you're going to have to introduce the girls to Holly. Have you thought about having a séance? I mean, I don't believe in that crap, but ..."

"I don't either. Sheila did, though. She used to have her palm read every so often. Maybe that's part of the reason I'm against it. Seems like bullshit."

"The Bible says it's crap, too."

"Yeah, I know, like horoscopes."

"Where does Holly stand on the matter?"

"Uh, I don't know. Maybe I should wait until we run out of options. We see enough ghosts without calling them. We're making progress, right?"

"Whatever you think. Hey, Boss, where do you think she went? I can't stop looking out the window. Everything that moves catches my eye. What happened to the boat?"

Tim stared at Johnny, dumbfounded, then smacked his palm against his forehead. "Come with me. I have to check one thing before we leave. Keep your eyes and ears peeled." Johnny looked at Tim as if he had two heads as Tim made his way through the breakfast area and out the side door. "You hold the flashlight, and I'll go in."

"Where? The barn? Cut the shit, Tim, don't do it."

"I won't if she's in there, but I have to check something. Do you hear anything?" They listened for almost a minute before Tim made his move.

Johnny followed beneath the ever-circling bats, trying to light Tim's way. The sunlit entryway gave way to the darker depths, and they were near-blind until their eyes adjusted.

"She's not here. You can relax."

Johnny trained the beam on Tim. Finally, they arrived in the back corner, where they found an old rowboat leaning against the wall.

"Is that her boat?" asked Johnny.

"Yeah, and it's wet."

CHAPTER 36

April 28, 1971

Johnny returned to Massachusetts, but Tim and Holly talked all night. The day's highlight was Johnny's revelation that Thomas might want to be buried with Elmer, but Tim also raved about Holly's calendar. Today had been spot-on, and it seemed they had a reliable tool to figure things out. Tim, of course, also recounted the details of Mildred and the boat. Holly, in turn, brought Tim up to speed on Martha Simmons and her grandmother's scrapbook. Tim had a random thought as they ate dinner: "How did Mildred die?"

"Good question, but unfortunately, we don't have much left to read. We may never know." Tim sat back as the room went quiet. "In other news, I filled in my calendar through May. We have to watch for a few anniversaries, but it's not nearly as intense as April. I'll figure out June, too, when the time comes."

"Honey, I'll take every bit of good news I can. Thanks for skipping work. Here's the million-dollar question: What does the calendar say for tomorrow?"

Holly's enthusiasm fizzled as she read from the page. "Here's tonight's buzzkill. As you know, Annette volunteered quite a bit at the nursing home, so tomorrow is a question mark."

Tim took the news in stride, even though Holly knew he was disappointed.

"I'm sorry. I don't like it, either. Is Johnny coming back?"

"No. Johnny has to finish up at Mrs. Mills' house. She's one of only three clients right now. He may return in a few days, but we'll see."

Holly frowned. "Well, in that case, I have good news. I'm free tomorrow."

Tim put down his chicken wing. "Are you sure? Aren't you going to get in trouble at work?"

"I can spare a day to make sure you're safe."

Tim stood up and hugged her. "You just made my night. So what's the matter, you don't trust Thomas Pike like Johnny does?"

"Not after the hatchet. I can't get that out of my head."

Tim kissed her again, and they remained entwined. He checked his watch: 11:45 pm. It seemed like a week had passed since he and Johnny pulled into the driveway and saw the smashed kitchen windows. "Honey, I need to sleep. Please come to bed."

"Sleep? You only put in twelve hours today. Go shower."

Tim strolled out of the room, smiling.

CHAPTER 37

April 29, 1971

Holly's doorbell rang, and she jumped. She looked at her clock radio: 2:17 am. Tim was sound asleep, so she elbowed him.

"Ow!"

"Someone just rang the doorbell."

Tim snapped to attention, immediately awake. "Does that ever happen?"

"It's two in the morning!"

Tim leaped from the bed and put his pants on. "You don't have a baseball bat, do you?"

"Maybe the garage." Holly grabbed two kitchen knives and handed one to Tim as they approached the front door. Tim flicked on the outside light when they were in position and released the bolt. No one was there.

Tim stepped out, knife at the ready, and something shifted under his foot. He jumped back. It was a book or photo album, just beginning to absorb the rain. After looking around, Tim picked it up and locked the door behind him.

Holly immediately knew what it was, but to be sure, she thumbed through the pages. "Tim, this is Elizabeth Simmons's scrapbook."

"Johnny was right. Ghosts travel. Congratulations, Holly. Thomas likes you, too."

"That's not funny."

"Well, this is proof he knows where we are."

Holly set the scrapbook on the table and opened it. It was much thicker than she'd imagined.

"Remember how I said I would help you tomorrow, Tim?"

"Yeah, let me guess. Now you're staying home to read."

"Close. I'm still going, but I'm not going to help. I'm going to read."

CHAPTER 38

April 29, 1971

It took Tim a half-hour to fall back asleep, but Holly stayed awake longer, upset the privacy of her home had been violated. At 5:18 am, the dream started. They dreamt as spectators, separately but simultaneously, with Mildred walking through a cemetery on her way to a row of headstones by the edge of a forest.

It was a small cemetery with only a hundred graves, and the wrought iron gate said *Tower Hill* in bold letters. Mildred wore a dark dress and brought no flowers and, within a minute, found the grave of the man who'd introduced her to happiness. A man who healed wounds wreaked by her upbringing, then betrayed it all by leaving. Mildred didn't sit, kneel, or pray but stood defiant.

"*Are you there, Thomas? I hope so. I hope you are trapped and all you can do is watch. If, for some reason, you are resting, well, there is no justice, but I believe there is, and I believe you can hear me.*

"*I was happy. You knew that. We were content, but you had to serve. I told you I would not do well. The irony is you don't deserve to be buried here. You have no idea how embarrassing it is to explain your death, but I am every single time I'm asked. I tell them the truth. You died horsing around with a bayonet. There was drinking, and you were the life of the party. It must have been so fun to be away from us. Were you celebrating?*

"*I buried you on Tower Hill because I want you to be alone, as you left me. The things embedded in me are sometimes too much. It's not healthy to be alone for too long. If you don't believe me, ask Elmer. He suffered, too. I'm not sure if you are aware, but yesterday, I ended his pain. He was not the same without you, so I did us both a favor.*

"*I will be cleared of suspicion shortly, but I came here to tell you he won't be with you. He will remain on the property, and when my time comes, I will be buried next to him. You didn't think I put you up here because you're a veteran, did you?*"

Mildred pressed her palms to her eyes, rubbing as if it relieved her pain. *"Elmer will be with me, but you can have his hat. He wore it on the boat. I fished it out of the pond for you."*

Mildred pulled her shoulders back as if the headstone were Thomas himself, then tossed the hat on the grave. After clearing her throat, Mildred spat directly between THOMAS and PIKE and watched as the saliva dripped into his date of birth. When finished, she turned and walked out the front gate.

So angry, thought Holly.

It was quiet for a moment, and then, from out of the woods, came the boy. Elmer, freshly deceased, meandered to his father's grave and dropped to all fours, running his fingers through the grass, thrilled to have found the place his mother would never take him. Elmer crawled forward, picked up his cap, and wiped the saliva from the headstone, and when it was clean, he hugged it.

Holly wondered why Thomas didn't appear. He was dead, and Elmer was dead now, too. Why no reunion? Tim had similar thoughts. Elmer spoke to the headstone too softly to be heard. He stayed for a while, laying on his back and stretching out as if sharing a hammock. Eventually, however, he got up and disappeared into the woods.

CHAPTER 39

April 29, 1971

"What a bitch," said Holly, her first words of the morning.

"What?" said Tim.

"I was dreaming. I saw Mildred in a graveyard, and she—"

"Spit on Thomas Pike's grave, and then Elmer appeared. You saw that, too?"

"Yes!"

"I got the impression Elmer followed her there."

"Yeah, she messed up, though. The kid heard everything."

"Did she kill Elmer? Is that what she said?"

"Yes."

Tim and Holly's first stop was the barn, where, to their relief, they found the old hatchet in its original drawer. The big question, however, was if they could hide it from Mildred this time. How did she get it from Tim's locked truck? It was upsetting, but at least for now, it was in their possession.

Holly put the weapon in her handbag, and Tim set up a workspace in the dining room. Because Tim had a limited view of the front yard, Holly sat in the living room, where she could keep watch. Finally, Tim started work, and Holly opened the scrapbook.

It began as Annette described, written by a young woman with a crush that turned sour when Mildred stole him away. Elizabeth's writing style proved she was obsessive, rambling on for pages on end, frequently without punctuation. Sometimes, the penmanship was so small Holly had to squint to read it, as if the woman's mood had changed.

Near the end of Elizabeth's section (before Emma took over), Holly was surprised to read that she had begun sneaking onto the Pike property after dark. She would "go exploring" after everyone had gone to bed, searching for Elmer's grave, and even went so far as to peer through the windows. Elizabeth wandered the old grove but must have missed the gravestones, merely remarking that her father used to buy their Christmas trees there before Mildred "spoiled that too."

Emma's first entry picked up a month after her mother went missing.

Emma suspected Mildred and hounded Grandpa George, the policeman, to do something about it. When George said he couldn't, it prompted Emma to say a few things she shouldn't have, earning her a hard slap. Grandpa George added insult to injury, reminding Emma that the "whole town knew your mother was crazy" and that trespassing was illegal.

It was clear to Emma that some of her family members expected her mother's death and that the burden of exposing Mildred Wells now fell on her shoulders. When Elizabeth's remains were found across the street from the Pike property, Emma scribbled page after page about how much she hated Mildred and how she knew she had killed again.

Emma had commiserated with her mother the day the news broke about Elmer Pike. Both knew in their hearts that Mildred was guilty. Elizabeth's death was salt in the wound. Desperate for a strategy, Emma weighed her options, deciding she was not ready for trespassing yet. Grandpa George's police connection was no help either. He'd given her nothing since the slap. "The case is closed," was all he would say, so Emma changed her tact.

One weekend in June of 1863, Emma announced she would take a leisure trip to Boston. But what Emma didn't tell them was that her journey was really to Salem, Mildred's alleged hometown. When she arrived, she went to the town hall to dig for information but came up empty. Witches, she deduced, would know how to cover things up.

Holly put the book down and looked out the window. "Hey Tim, Emma Simmons thought Mildred Wells was a witch and even made a trip to Salem to look for clues."

"Oh, that's wonderful," said Tim. "Wouldn't it be nice if our ghost was also a witch?"

"The people who were hanged in Salem were innocent. Emma Simmons was as cuckoo as her mother." Holly continued reading from February 12, 1863.

Emma knew in her bones that Mildred had murdered poor Elizabeth and thought if she learned all there was to know about witches, perhaps one day she could convince the Sanborn police that they had one living right under their noses. Emma looked up all the women executed in Salem to see if any were named Wells but came up empty. Half a day later, she'd learned everyone's backgrounds, but there was still no link to Mildred. A thought occurred to her: What if some witches escaped execution?

Emma rubbed her eyes. Frustration set in as she was no closer to proving Mildred Wells practiced black magic. Defeated, Emma logged her thoughts in the scrapbook, packed her things, and left town empty-handed. Her thoughts turned from Mildred to Elmer, the sweet boy she sat behind in third grade. Handsome, like his father. Here one day and gone the next.

What had Elizabeth written about Elmer's death? Emma's memory was unclear, as she was young when it happened, so she flipped back and re-read. Mildred had been the only one on the property at the time of death, but how about the funeral?

"Private services held on the Wells property," read the newspaper clipping. *Perhaps Mother was looking for the grave, and Mildred caught her.* Emma was still not ready to go searching, but she did have other ideas, beginning with a visit to the Barker Funeral Home. Simon Barker, the director of his namesake business, had been hired by Mildred Wells to arrange Elmer's services.

Emma sat across a large desk from Mr. Barker, a plastic look of peace on his face.

"How nice of you to stop by, Ms. Simmons. How can I help you?" Simon Barker had his finger on the aging pulse of Sanborn and was responsible for over seventy percent of the town's burials. Emma sensed an attitude behind the fake smile and a hint of condescension.

"I won't take much of your time. The reason for my visit is not about my family, but it is close to my heart. I recently traveled to Boston, and for whatever reason, as soon as I left Sanborn, I began to reminisce about my childhood, specifically, my former classmate Elmer Pike. We were best friends, Mr. Barker. I guess I never got over it."

"Oh, yes, what a pity. That one still stings—a tragic loss. I'm sorry to hear you're still feeling the pain."

"Thank you, Mr. Barker. I appreciate it, and I'll get to the point. I want to visit him. His grave, I mean. Also, to pay respects to his father, leave flowers, and tidy the plot if needed, but I don't know where they're buried."

"That's very sweet of you. I can direct you to Thomas Pike's grave. He is located at the Tower Hill Cemetery. Unfortunately, we did not perform the services for that funeral because it was taken care of by the military, but as for Master Elmer, I'm afraid you will need to seek permission. The grave is on private property."

"Private? Oh, I'm sorry. I assumed they were buried together. Is Elmer's grave on the Wells property then?"

"Due to the nature of Elmer's death, Ms. Wells requested the utmost discretion. I'm not at liberty to say where Master Pike is buried, and I would refer you to Ms. Wells. I hope you understand."

"Tim!" Holly called, scanning the scrapbook. "I think we're getting somewhere!" She kept reading. *"I decided to say goodbye to Mr. Barker, who had undoubtedly sold his soul and was too ingrained with the Wells woman's money to help. Instead, I sought out the mason who crafted Elmer's headstone."*

CHAPTER 40

1862

Emma Simmons didn't know what to do. She was not about to go knocking on Mildred Wells' door, and Simon Barker was a dead end. Eventually, her spirits rebounded. Simon Barker's sin was not enough to get her to quit. Instead, she decided to pay a visit to Taylor Memorials in Belmont.

Sam Taylor didn't have to put on a face, as most of his clients never met him. However, those who did usually found him covered in dust while cutting a memorial or manufacturing granite steps. He was a working-class man with rough hands and a blunt way, the opposite of Simon Barker. Emma stood in his doorway and waited as he finished a cut before calling his attention.

"Mr. Taylor? Hello, I'm Emma Simmons. My mother was Elizabeth Simmons. I'm not sure if you remember, but …"

"Yes, I do. I knew your mother from my school days. I was very sorry to have to make her stone. That's the thing about making memorials. It takes so long to carve the words you never forget them."

"I imagine you wouldn't."

"No, ma'am. Most people think we crank these out like writing a postcard, but it's not that way at all." Taylor gestured to his workbench, covered with various hammers and chisels. He was the last of his kind, too old to upgrade to the latest and greatest.

"Thank you, Mr. Taylor, for helping my mother, but I'm here for another reason. Do you mind if I ask some questions about my former classmate, Elmer Pike?"

"Another tragedy. I must say, Ms. Simmons, you're young, but you've already felt some painful passings. Of course, you can ask. What's on your mind?"

"Well, as I understand, you deliver the gravestones and manufacture them, right?"

"Yes, that's right."

"Good. I hoped to visit Elmer, tidy the grave, and pay my respects, but I don't know where he and his father are buried. I was a little girl when they died."

"Sweetheart, they're in two different graveyards, and it's a damned shame if you ask me. She must have hated his guts. Some men hear the call and can't refuse duty or country. Thomas Pike is buried up at Tower Hill."

"And where is Elmer buried?"

"On the homestead, in the last row of the old Christmas tree farm. I'm not sure if you'd remember the place. The forest filled in around it, and you can't see it from the road anymore."

"So, you made both stones for her?"

"I made all three," he boasted.

"Three?"

"Yes. The Wells woman wanted hers done at the same time as her son's. Thomas's was made earlier, of course. She's a real planner, Mildred, a real piece of work, cold fish. I never liked her. She wanted her maiden name on her headstone, which made me feel funny. *Mildred Wells*. I did a lot of thinking as I carved those stones."

"I knew her maiden name was Wells, but I had no idea she had it engraved on her stone! She was from Salem, Massachusetts, you know. You've heard of the Wells family from Salem, right?" Emma searched his face for a hint of recognition.

"Can't say I do."

"Tell me your thoughts as you chiseled *Wells* into her headstone."

"She wanted it in bold letters, more prominent than Elmer's stone. So they're next to each other but don't match. I think it was a slap in the face to the Pike name. It says a lot about how mad she was. I remember them. They were once a happy family. You'd see them in town, and there was no doubt life was good. You could read it right on their faces.

"Then the war started, and he left. That never sits well with women, and that's understandable, but time passed, and some say she got lonely— and angry—and the little boy, your friend Elmer, was her scapegoat. The single-mother life didn't suit her, and the boy looked too much like his father, which might have cost him."

"You think she murdered him?"

"That was the rumor, although it was never proven, of course, or she would have been put away. Oh, they investigated. I believe your grandfather was a part of it, too, but it was kept quiet. You didn't even read about it in the paper. Some say she was sleeping with the editor then, and I don't know how that played out, but the grapevine was buzzing and buzzing good.

"Do you believe she did it?"

"I'm not one to gossip, but yes. You will too when I tell you what Mildred had written on Elmer's headstone."

"Go on, what was it?"

"It said:

Here lies
Elmer Pike
Abandoned by his father,
A casualty of his mother's broken heart."

"A casualty of his mother's broken heart? What is that supposed to mean?"

"Well, I thought about that for a long time, and I'll explain. First, I thought about it the entire time it took me to engrave the words. So, for that particular sentence, you're talking about a quarter of a day. I thought it sounded like a poem at the time, so I took it to mean that the kid was sad because his mother was sad.

"And then, I got wind of the police investigating, which struck me funny. I mean, this lady's name is involved in the only two suspicious deaths in Sanborn in the last forty years, and that would be one hell of a coincidence.

"So I'm done engraving, but I'm still thinking about the words. I began to read it as if the kid suffered because his mom took it out on him, and I felt sick to my stomach after that. Pretty soon, I couldn't read the sentence any other way. I couldn't unsee it. The worst part is I'm one of few people to have seen what was written.

"She dated the police chief, too, right?" Emma asked.

"Oh, more than just him, although he's dead too, right? Anyway, Mildred wasn't investigated for that. She was on a bit of a tear, sexually, some say. The editor of the *Crier* began to take criticism, but he denied involvement. There were other men, too, but none of importance. The town was humming, though. Lots of ugly, dirty talk going on."

"Why didn't you tell them what was written on the headstone?"

"After she slept with the chief of police and the newspaper editor? No, thank you. I need to make a living. Discretion is big in this industry. I minded my own business. I'm not even sure I'm right, but I know I wanted her out of my shop. I still look over at the door sometimes when I'm alone, and it's because I'm thinking of her."

"Wait, go back. What did Mildred's headstone say?"

"It was full of self-pity."

"What did it say?"

"It said:

Here lies

MILDRED WELLS

Born: October 6, 1836

Exploited and Scorned

Resting in Fury

"That's horrible! Is it in the grove, too?"

"Yes, right next to Elmer's. Mildred arranged to be buried with her son, whom she may have murdered, leaving Thomas alone on Tower Hill. Pretty cold if you ask me."

"Mr. Taylor, can I ask you one more thing?"

"Of course."

"Is she crazy?"

Samuel Taylor took a minute to ponder. "Well, I can see how some would think that, but I've looked her in the eyes, and the lights are on. No, I don't think she's crazy. Evil is a better word."

CHAPTER 41

April 29, 1971

Holly closed the scrapbook, digesting the information. The last few pages were blank, and it wasn't hard to guess why. Emma had gotten curious.

Mildred had her headstone made at the same time as her son's. She was angry and planned everything, but it didn't solve her problems.

Tim's power saw whined as Holly waited for the next pause. While she waited, she checked the pond through the living room window. The rowboat was there again.

Holly bounded into the dining room and unplugged the saw, and it took Tim a second to realize she wasn't joking. Together, they hid behind the curtain and watched.

At first, it looked like the day before. Mildred, a couple of fishing rods, and the oars resting on the boat's edge. She wore the same hat, but the dress was different. Today's was black, and Holly wondered if it was intentional. Meanwhile, the boat drifted, allowing the breeze to choose the direction.

Suddenly, the boat rocked, unsteady, and Mildred picked up an oar and jabbed it into the air. A splash disrupted the pond's surface, and Mildred leaped to the bow, leaned over the edge, and plunged both arms into the water, hat still on her head, face inches from the water.

Bubbles thrashed beneath the surface as Mildred wrapped her fingers around Elmer's shoulders, locked her elbows, and held him under. Elmer opened his eyes to the blur of his mother's face between her obstructing arms. He kicked and pulled, trying to break free as her nurturing embrace turned deadly. Realizing his fate, Elmer relaxed, deciding to spend his last living moment staring into her eyes.

Mildred saw the blue of his stare despite the silty churn in the water. *Stubborn, like his father,* she thought, but his defiance would not change anything. She would have her life back soon. Even after the deed was done, as his body lay in the marshy grass, Elmer's eyes were open, almost surely following her every move as she prepped the scene for the authorities. It took forty minutes for them to arrive, and she made it all look perfect.

THE LEGEND OF MILDRED WELLS

CHAPTER 42

April 29, 1971

Tim's heart rose in his throat as the mismatch played out. There were no words. Annette was fortunate to have missed this anniversary. Had Thomas spared her the pain? He had, after all, waited a hundred years. What would a few more be to get things perfect? *Time means nothing to the dead. It's the results that matter.*

"Oh, my God, I wasn't ready." Holly buried her face in Tim's shoulder, and he held her close, eyes on the pond. Mildred stood on the bank and rolled up her sleeves before wading into the mire to drag what must have been, in her little ritual, Elmer's body to shore.

"We should leave, but I don't want to catch her attention when we drive by," said Tim. "What do you think?"

"She's too close. Maybe we should wait."

"What if she comes to the house?"

"I don't like that either."

Suddenly, footsteps bounded down the stairs, and Elmer peered around the doorjamb. Holly shrank against the wall, and Tim froze, wondering what came next. Suddenly, Elmer lifted his arm, signaling to stay put, then left through the front door and headed for the pond.

Elmer had no fear, or at least there was no hesitation in his step. As he stepped through the stone wall, Mildred saw him and stood, dropping the last act of her macabre performance. Body language indicated she wanted him to come closer, but he wouldn't. Instead, Elmer started walking in the meadow on the way to the woods, and Mildred followed.

Tim saw his opportunity and took Holly by the hand. They sped down Lancaster Hill Road as fast as they could.

CHAPTER 43

April 29, 1971

That night, no one could eat. It was no surprise that the boy was murdered, yet witnessing the act was pure heartbreak.

"We still don't know how Mildred died, do we? Annette never figured this out? Nothing in the microfilm?"

"The scrapbook alleged that Mildred was romantic with the editor of the *Sanborn Crier* at one point, which might have kept a lid on her history. I'll look it up tomorrow."

"She racked up quite the body count. There's Elmer, Elizabeth Simmons, and probably Emma Simmons. I'm guessing Emma took the information from the headstone maker and went trespassing like her mother. Add to that the possibilities of Henry Smith, the Chief of Police, and Annette, that makes six."

"One for sure, and we witnessed it." Holly shifted in her chair. "Poor Elmer. I can't get it out of my head."

Tim grabbed her shoulders and began kneading. "You should stay home tomorrow. Call in sick again. Refresh my memory. What does your calendar say?"

"It's the day Thomas left the family. That means Mildred will be wailing across the front lawn at some point. It happened the year before Elmer's death. That's too close, Tim. It's dangerous. You shouldn't go."

"This woman is all up in my business, literally. She's killing my investment." Tim looked at the ceiling. "Thomas, what else do we need? You're the narrator. I admire your patience, but I'm losing mine and my shirt along with it. Annette got you started, and we were passed the baton, so what can we do for you, short of death or financial ruin? Make it a win/win deal, or I'll leave. I mean it."

"If it were only that easy," offered Holly. "Everything is cryptic. Dreams, sleepwalking, journals. There's a disconnect."

"Holly, what if I wake up early, get some work done, and leave before she shows up? Do we know when that is?"

"I don't know, and I don't want you to go. Be smart. Six people died, remember? Don't be number seven."

"All right. I'll drive down to Massachusetts and help Johnny."

"There's nothing on the calendar for May 1 that we know of, but tomorrow is a sure thing."

CHAPTER 44

April 29, 1971

Holly was sleepy but wouldn't shut off the light until she finished Annette's journal. Despite the promises she'd made to herself earlier in the week, the Simmons' scrapbook had interrupted them, as mandated by Thomas Pike. If she could finish, her reward would be a clear conscience. She'd learned all she could about Tim's haunted farmhouse.

Holly picked up just after the nursing home chapters with Martha Simmons. The interview style was over, thank goodness, and the return of Annette's easy-to-read diary was a relief.

Saturday, April 27, 1968

Last night, I had a very intense dream. I saw Mildred, but she was not dead. There was color in her cheeks and life in her eyes, and thankfully, no flies. She sat in the turret, staring at the pond. Mildred was alone as I watched from above as if I were the ghost.

I watched her for several minutes when suddenly she stood, hands balled into fists. Elmer emerged from the pond, his eyes fixed on her as if he'd been watching from the depths. When he was waist-deep, he stood there for ten seconds, staring, then turned back and disappeared in a trail of bubbles.

Mildred began to sob, and I'm not sure why, but she ran out of the house to the pond. I think she intended to follow the boy into the water but reconsidered, realizing the futility. Instead, she walked back to the house in defeat.

Sunday, April 28, 1968

Last night was what I call "Chapter Two!" I'm unsure if it was a dream or if I was witnessing some ghostly replay. I sat up in bed after hearing the front door creak open. I peeked around the doorjamb and saw Mildred at the top of the stairs, watching the front door below, which was outside my line of sight.

She was the same Mildred I had seen the previous day in the turret, still alive, haunted by her dead son, wearing a nightgown, intense focus on her face. I ducked back into the bedroom to avoid being seen and listened as wet footsteps splashed into the house and the living room. Mildred bolted down the stairs and called out: "Elmer!"

I moved to look, but she had moved to other parts of the house. I listened for a minute and, hearing nothing, began to wonder where they went. I couldn't go back to bed without knowing, so I descended, looking down the length of the house to see Mildred in the kitchen facing away, her nightgown illuminated by the moon.

She was whispering, so I perked my ears, but my balance was off, and I took the last step into a giant puddle. The floor was soaked from the front door to the kitchen. Mildred, her back to me, was kneeling, obscuring Elmer.

"Elmer, I was angry,"

"Where's Daddy?"

"He's gone, Elmer. He left us. That's—"

"I want Daddy."

"He's not coming, dear. I told you he left, but we can—"

"I don't want you. I want Daddy!"

His last 'Daddy' boomed through the house, and Mildred seemed to lose patience despite the fact she was scolding her dead son! Back from the dead or not, Mildred didn't want to hear Elmer say "Daddy" again.

She then did some yelling of her own: "He left you! Get out! Go back to the grove!" Her arms were rigid, and she shook as she screamed. It was sheer lunacy, but then again, so is murdering your child.

I wish I could have seen the boy's reaction, but there was silence, and he spoke again: "I'll find him."

Mildred's body seemed to deflate, but then she stood, and I could see he was gone. I went back upstairs before she could turn to me, and a thought occurred as I reached the top: Would she come to my bedroom? No sooner did I think it, I woke up, thankful. Sleep has been difficult ever since. I'm too afraid to close my eyes.

Monday, April 29, 1968

There's no way these are random dreams. It has to be Thomas. I'll call this journal entry "Chapter Three." The boy returned last night, and I saw it from Mildred's perspective. I woke in the middle of the night to water splashing my face, and when I opened my eyes, the boy was there. I backed into the headboard, taking the sheets and blankets with me, and the odor was there, the funk of the pond. I looked at my arm and realized it was not my sleeve but Mildred's.

"Elmer, I told you to leave unless you're here to apologize. What do you want? And don't say—"

"Daddy."

Mildred's hand went to my chest to cover my pounding heart. My legs scissored, kicking me to the far edge of the bed, and I stood in the far corner, heart racing. The boy stared from the opposite side of the bed. "Get out, Elmer. Your father is not here. Go to the grove and wait for me. I'm coming soon."

"I can't find Daddy."

The boy couldn't care less about Mildred's wishes. Visibly upset, she (I) changed into her working dress, left the room, and marched through the house. As we trudged through the dining room, she turned back, checking to see if the boy followed, and he did, although at half speed.

Mildred grabbed a lantern and shovel from the barn and marched up the path. When she arrived at the family plot, she placed the light in front of Elmer's headstone and began to dig, throwing shovelfuls to the side.

I heard a hollow thump as the spade struck the coffin, then took one last look down the row. Elmer was in the lantern's light, a disembodied face in the darkness, freshly soaked as if he'd been in the pond. Mildred paused, stuck her shovel into the earth, and wiped her forehead with the back of her sleeve.

"If you don't change your attitude, I'll put you in the middle of the woods, and you can spend forever alone. I won't even mark your grave. Better yet, I can split you up and bury you all over the county. You can have that, or you can be with me. I told you why I did what I did, and I'm sorry. He's gone, Elmer. What's it going to be?"

That's when I woke up. These dreams are intense. I start to dread bedtime at midday. I think I'm losing my mind.

Tuesday, April 30, 1968

My heart has been re-broken. I can't do this anymore. Today, I saw Henry's death. They were up in the grove, so I'm guessing he was after a Christmas tree. Mildred said nothing as he tried to converse, and she attacked him like a tiger on a lamb. They were so far from where I found him. I have no idea how she got him there. Damn you, Thomas Pike! I don't care how much you're hurting. You aren't the only one who feels pain.

Wednesday, May 1, 1968

And I thought having dreams was bad. Last night, I sleepwalked! I woke up in the grove with a flashlight and shovel, and I saw the disgusting epitaphs, which are even worse in person.

What was I supposed to do, exhume the boy? What will Mildred do if I'm caught? Kill me, as she killed Henry? No. I ran. Our beautiful grove, a place I once found romantic, now only reminds me of Henry's death.

Maybe I'll take this to the police, but how would I explain it? For anyone who reads this, because Thomas is so damned cryptic, or shy, or whatever, I will ask him to clarify. I'll write more full-page word choices in my flipbook journal as I did when I learned his name.

I think I'll put "MOVE" and "BOY" across two pages, and maybe "MOVE" and "WOMAN" across two more, and "MOVE" and "THOMAS" on the next two, then "GUESS" and "AGAIN" across two more, maybe "NO" and "POLICE" and "YES" and "POLICE" and finally (wishful thinking), "DO" and "NOTHING." I'll leave his response here if I get one.

Holly turned the page, but the rest of the book was blank. The first journal's abrupt finish reminded Holly of the scrapbook's cliffhanger ending. *This is where Annette died.* Holly looked at Tim, snoring next to her. Even though she was bursting, she let him sleep. One person rested was better than none.

CHAPTER 45

April 30, 1971 (12:09 am)

Two hours after Holly fell asleep, she became Annette in a dream. Annette sat in the turret after sundown, finishing what would turn out to be her last journal entry. She put the pen down, closed the book, left it on the desk, and headed to her car for the nursing home. She exited through the side door, checking her surroundings, and someone waited for her, staring.

Mildred was near the path, holding the spade Annette left in the grove. Annette was afraid, but her fear turned to anger as she remembered Henry's murder. *It's time,* she thought, and gave Mildred a piece of her mind. *When you've got nothing, you've got nothing to lose.* Annette was tired of the hauntings, the nightmares, the journals, and the woman who treated this property as if she still owned it.

"You're afraid, aren't you, Mildred? You're afraid I'll figure this out and move his bones like you were afraid Henry would call attention to your family plot. You don't want people to read the headstones. You didn't think things through."

Any steam Annette had gathered evaporated as she caught the stench of Mildred's corpse. Mildred, meanwhile, stared, emotionless, flies buzzing. Annette wondered if perhaps she was the one who hadn't thought things through. It had been a mistake to leave the spade at the grave; one should never taunt a hurting mother.

Annette's following words tumbled out, still defiant yet stripped of conviction. "Someone will figure this out. If not me, then someone else. We will figure you out and be rid of you."

Mildred said nothing but brought the shovel up, and Annette felt guilty for not finishing the job. Would Thomas help the subsequent owners, or would they die, too? *God help them,* she thought, *and God help me.*

"It's a matter of time, Mildred. Even Elmer is—"

Mildred swung, and the shovel connected, opening a mortal tear over Annette's collarbone. She followed up with her knife, ensuring the offending mouth was done talking. Afterward, she dressed the body in the main bedroom and left it to the flies.

CHAPTER 46

April 30, 1971 (1:16 am)

Tim and Holly woke simultaneously.

"Oh my God, oh my God, Tim, I just saw…"

"I saw. Annette is dead. Mildred killed her. It was awful." The sheets were soaked with sweat on both sides of the bed because of an eight-minute dream. They hugged, catching their collective breath.

"We can't mess with her, Tim. She's dead! And strong! And she's *magic* too. That knife came out of thin air."

"Pfff. Do we have a choice? The scrapbook was delivered to your house, and we're sharing dreams. Ghosts travel."

Holly started to cry.

"Wait right here," said Tim. He returned a minute later, holding a bottle of Jack Daniel's. "Take this. It's a mood changer."

Holly drank a shot and grimaced.

"Worrying does nothing to strengthen tomorrow. It only ruins today," said Tim.

"Who said that?" asked Holly.

"Not sure. Now, lay back and relax. Don't think. Save that for tomorrow."

CHAPTER 47

April 30, 1971 (5:11 am)

Thomas Pike allowed a four-hour nap before the next dream. Tim and Holly were spectators again, and Mildred was in bed with Chief Abner Wallace of the Sanborn Police.

The new lovers were rounding third base when Elmer's footsteps soaked the hallway floorboards outside the bedroom. The Chief nearly jumped out of his skin as he grabbed his pistol and charged out of the bedroom naked, ready to confront whoever dared interrupt his first sex in more than a year.

As he entered the hallway, it didn't take long to realize it was no burglar. Instead, the Pike boy, the one he and his men had pulled from the pond two months previous, was staring at him from the top of the stairs.

Mildred looked around Chief Wallace and addressed her dead son as if it were no big deal. "Get out, Elmer. Let me live my life!" Chief Wallace looked on in disbelief as Elmer ran, splashing down the stairs, mission accomplished.

"He won't come back. Come to bed," said Mildred.

Chief Wallace got dressed and left. That was the last time Mildred saw him.

CHAPTER 48

April 30, 1971 (5:12 am)

After a brief interlude, the dream continued, and Tim and Holly were spectators in the last row of the grove. Mildred was digging, and the dirt was piled high. A pile of blankets, pillows, and her bedroom mattress sat on the other side of the grave. It had taken her over two hours to lug it all out here, even though she used the wheelbarrow.

Mildred shredded the bedding with a knife and dumped the stuffing into the hole with hay and woodchips. Across the open grave were laid planks, leaving an open space at the bottom to squeeze through when finished. It took another half day to move the dirt back onto the planks, which, in the end, barely held the weight.

When her pyre was finished, Mildred threw the tools into the grave and squeezed through the opening to nest in the bed of flammables. It was dark down there, the near ton of soil already testing the boards. As Tim and Holly watched, Mildred lit a nub of candle, propped it on her chest, and used the knife to open her wrists.

Mildred bled for a while, and as the color drained from her face, the flame lit the feathers, which ignited the hay and woodchips. She was too far gone to feel anything as the pine planks caught, burned, and collapsed according to plan. Mildred Wells was buried.

CHAPTER 49

April 30, 1971 (5:13 am)

Tim woke with a start. The dream was over, and Holly was already sitting up. "She killed herself? What for?" he asked.

"I'm so glad you saw that, too. What is this woman's problem?"

Tim didn't answer.

"Tim, are you okay?"

"I'm okay. I'm just realizing something. It's our turn."

"What are you talking about?"

"Yesterday, I asked out loud what Thomas Pike needs, and today he answered. It's like Johnny said. He wants to be buried with his son. Bodies need to be moved, he can't do it without us."

Holly couldn't dispute the logic. Without saying a word, she got out of bed and left the room. A minute later, she returned with her calendar. "We've been wrapped up in this ghost problem for two weeks, but it seems like a lifetime. Today is the last day we know where she'll be."

CHAPTER 50

April 30, 1971 (7:30 am)

Unable to sleep, Tim and Holly made plans, preparing for what they hoped would be the endgame. They left early, surprising the manager of Aubuchon Hardware as he arrived to open the store. Tim's tools were trapped in the house, and he wasn't about to risk attempting to fetch them. They bought two spades, a rake, a pickaxe, some trowels, a hammer, a crowbar, some burlap bags, a bag of cement, and a tarp.

Light rain started as Tim pulled over into the gulley before the property line. He and Holly got out and made their way into the woods, walking parallel to the meadow for the grove. When they reached the corner of the field, they chose a spot behind the stone wall and waited. Their best guess was that a soldier leaving for war would not leave late in the day. Thirty minutes later, Mildred emerged from the barn, begging an imaginary Thomas to stay home rather than join the Union Army.

Tim and Holly raced to the grove. Mildred would not be at the graves in the immediate future. How much time they had was anyone's guess. Tim estimated they'd need a full hour to dig up the bones and escape. Hopefully, Mildred had other places to be.

The canopy made the grove almost cave-like, blocking the rain somewhat. Tim began digging at Mildred's grave, and Holly started on Elmer's. It wasn't long before he passed through a layer of ashes that turned his boots and shovel black. They knew there would be no coffin, so he looked for bones. Tim checked his watch.

Fifteen minutes had passed. He wondered what was happening back at the house.

Tim pulled chunks of charred planks out of the soil along with several rocks, casting them in all directions, for there would be no reason to fill the grave back in. The plan was to toss Mildred's bones in a bucket of cement and drop it off a bridge anywhere but around here.

Tim looked to Holly, who was nearly a foot down in the soil and due to hit the boy's coffin at any time. He picked up the pace, wondering where Mildred's bones were. Changing strategy, Tim switched to the edge rake and sifted through the dirt, but still no luck. Then he heard a *thunk* of a shovel on wood, signaling that Holly had reached Elmer's coffin. "Honey, let's switch. See if you can find her bones."

Tim dug for five more minutes and managed to hoist the tiny coffin from the grave, but this was a bigger job than he'd expected. After a moment of indecision, Tim changed the plan.

"Wait, Tim, you're not opening it, are you?" said Holly, wide-eyed and dripping sweat.

"It's been a half-hour. For all we know, Mildred is on her way. Getting this thing to my truck will take at least that! Have you found anything?" he asked.

"No. Is she even here?"

All at once, it dawned on him why they would not find any bones. *She isn't a ghost.* After all, he'd witnessed Mildred take a tumble while running through the field. "Holly, wait. There aren't going to be any bones. Let's grab Elmer and get out of here." Tim pulled out the crowbar and began to work on Elmer's coffin. When he got his fingers inside the lid, he pulled up with both hands, and one of the nails squealed loudly. He cursed under his breath.

"Do you think she's a witch?" said Holly.

"I wish I knew," said Tim as the lid popped on Elmer's coffin, and the little boy's bones were there, dressed in a cheap pair of overalls. He was a skeleton with hair, and his bones were in order except for his jawbone, which had fallen agape.

Tim thanked Elmer for all his help. "Don't worry, kid. We'll get you back with your Dad." Starting with the skull, Tim placed it in one of the burlap bags, then grabbed the spinal cord, which fell apart. They soon realized they didn't have time to treat every bone with tender loving care and apologized to Elmer while scooping the rest by the handful.

"Tim, stop," said Holly.

"Why?"

"Stop."

Tim whirled. Mildred was staring at them forty yards down the row.

"What do we do?" Holly whispered. Tim lunged for his spade but tripped and fell into Elmer's open grave. Mildred began to approach and flashed a knife.

Tim stood up and spat the first words that came to mind. "Mildred, stop. You don't want to do this."

Mildred stopped. Thigh-deep in Elmer's grave, Tim tightened his grip on the spade as Mildred dropped her knife.

Holly gasped. "Tim, there's someone behind you."

Tim turned to see the bottom of a boot in his face. Stars exploded as he collapsed in the hole. The man had a rifle with a bayonet attached, and he brought it down on Tim with force.

Holly screamed as Thomas Pike withdrew the rifle and wiped the blade clean, but Mildred was moving again, her ruddy complexion and noxious cloud passing too close for comfort. With little choice, Holly bolted, leaving Tim behind. Tim was hurt or dead, and the best thing she could do was call for help. She ran as fast as she could, cutting through rows, crying, praying Tim was alive.

Thomas met Mildred halfway. Hopefully, stopping the grave robbers proved his good faith, but first things first. Mildred had been angry for a long time, and it would take a miracle to shut that off. Elmer needed his help.

Mildred was over the moon. She hadn't seen Thomas's rifle since the funeral, and back then, the "Millie" monogram riled her. *What good does that do me?* Now, it lay on the ground by her feet, and she couldn't help but see it in a different light. She'd also forgotten how tall he was. He'd just saved the graves, but where had he been all these years? Was he aware of everything that happened?

Thomas whistled, and Elmer appeared at the end of the row. Mildred, overcome, bent to one knee and opened her arms, begging forgiveness. Elmer looked to his father, and Mildred swallowed her pride, irked that the boy required Daddy's blessing. She'd been jealous of their bond for ages but tolerated it once more in the name of family harmony. Thomas extended a hand to Elmer, telling him it was okay, and wrapped the other in Mildred's.

Thomas was the only one who knew of her upbringing. He didn't know every detail, but he knew enough. Her years with Thomas were the best of her life, and he should have known she wouldn't do well if he left.

But it felt good to have the torment dissolve and the psychosis slip away. She could be happy again with proper love and rest. Thomas hugged her. *One hundred and ten years. Where were you?*

Mildred let Thomas's hand go and turned to Elmer, arms open. Once more, the boy looked to his father, and Thomas nodded. Given the green light, Elmer walked into his mother's arms, the family embraced, and Thomas led them to the end of the row, past the graves. As they reached the end, Thomas pointed into the wild woods, suggesting a destination. Hand in hand, they stepped out of the grove and into the forest to a new afterlife.

CHAPTER 51

April 30, 1971

When the crunching of spruce needles stopped, Tim lifted his head. He'd been kicked in the head and had fallen backward into the grave. Along with the headache was a pain in his hand. He'd taken Thomas's bayonet through his palm, and the bleeding, although substantial, seemed to have stopped.

Tim wiped his palm on his jeans and watched as the wound began to bloom again. He'd suffered worse on the job, but Holly probably thought he was dead. Thinking quickly, Tim grabbed the spade and the sack of Elmer's bones and ran to find her. He wasn't sure how long he'd been unconscious. She could be at the house or halfway down Lancaster Hill Road, for all Tim knew, but he had the keys to his truck.

When Tim made it to the house, he called out, and mercifully, Holly exploded out the porch door holding yet another book, thrilled he was alive. She'd been crying. Tim held up his bloody hand. "Thomas didn't kill me, but he could have. I didn't see where they went, but I've got Elmer. What's that?" Tim pointed to the book.

"I'll tell you on the road. Get us out of here." It took them three nervous minutes to get to the truck, and Holly insisted on driving so Tim could bandage his hand.

CHAPTER 52

April 30, 1971

Mildred followed Thomas, feeling better with each step. The woods darkened as if storm clouds had rolled in, but she was comforted that her family was near, like a warm bath before bed. Selfish wants, like apologies, could come later, and, of course, she would have to make amends, too.

Mildred looked to Elmer, who was still closer to his father but constantly glancing at her. *He will come around.* Now that death didn't matter, she could explain things, and he could listen. In time, Elmer would understand. Forgiveness was a sure thing if they felt as good as she did.

But fifty yards into the forest, the hundred year ache returned to the base of her neck. Soft shadows gave way to cracks of light. Panicked, Mildred reached out, searching for Thomas and Elmer, but couldn't find them. Lost, she called out.

The covers had been ripped from the bed. Mildred fell hard and found herself at the bottom of her own grave. The light faded, and her vision returned. Thomas and Elmer were gone.

He lied. Everyone knew but me. Mildred dropped to her knees. She was as alone as the day she escaped the compound. The homeowners were in on it, too. They coordinated with Thomas. She could have killed their entire family, and maybe she still should. How Thomas tricked her, she didn't know, but with nothing but time to think, Mildred crawled from her grave, fuming.

CHAPTER 53

April 30, 1971

It was near midday when Tim and Holly arrived at Tower Hill. The clouds were low in the sky, threatening to open up and make a mess of things as Holly parked the truck a half-mile away to disguise their presence. Tim set to work on Thomas' grave, rolling the grass like a carpet in four pieces. Unfortunately, he'd only grabbed one of the shovels from the grove, so the work went slower than planned. Holly insisted on taking frequent turns digging because of Tim's hand.

"Are you sure this is what Thomas wants?" said Holly.

"Hell, no, but he can speak up any time. I'm all ears," said Tim.

"Because Mildred would take the bones otherwise, right?"

"I wouldn't want her to know where my bones are, would you?"

"No, I wouldn't."

They struck Thomas's coffin twenty minutes later and mixed his bones into the sack with Elmer's. Father and son, together, forever. Tim and Holly covered their tracks, replacing every last bit of dirt over the empty grave. "What now?" asked Holly.

"I need a wood stove. I don't want these bones to be moved again."

"Well, I have a wood stove, but what about a campfire or an acetylene torch? I'm not sure I want to burn human bones in my living room. What if they start haunting my place?"

"I'm just trying to make their bones impossible to be messed with. Do you hear me, Thomas? Speak up if I'm wrong."

"Isn't it going to take a long time to burn them? Does the fire have to be a certain temperature?"

"You're probably right. Forget the wood stove. Let's go to Sears."

CHAPTER 54

April 30, 1971

Tim and Holly walked out of Sears with a hand-crank meat grinder, then went to the supermarket to pick up dinner. Tim assembled the meat grinder at Holly's place and lit her ex-boyfriend's grill, throwing the bones onto the flames to weaken them.

Holly, for the first time, opened the book she found in the turret. She'd fled the horror in the grove, hoping to use the telephone to call an ambulance, but instead, she reached the driveway and found a trail of burning candles leading to the side door.

No, Thomas Pike. We're done listening to you. Instead, Holly headed for the porch, which was the closest entrance to the telephone. When she got to the living room, the phone was on the floor, the receiver was separated from the cradle, and the cord was ripped from the wall.

"You bastard!" she screamed. With little choice, Holly headed for the turret. There was nothing to do but trust him, die, or both. Tim told stories about feeling like he had nothing to lose after his divorce, and finally, Holly understood. *I'm too angry to care.*

Upstairs, she found an encyclopedia volume open to a passage on the term *revenant.*

rev·e·nant

/ˈrevənənt, ˌrevəˈnänt/

Noun

a person who has returned, especially from the dead.

That explains the flies, thought Holly. Suddenly, the candles disappeared, and she heard Tim in the driveway shouting her name.

CHAPTER 55

April 30, 1971

Tim shut the grill down, let the bones cool, pulverized them with a hammer, and put them through the meat grinder twice. When finished, he filled one of Holly's vases with the ashes. "Come on, let's get these gentlemen off your property. Maybe after this, they'll leave us alone." As Tim got into the passenger side, his eye caught the bag of cement in the pickup bed. "Plan A" had been to mix Mildred's bones in a bucket of cement and dump it off a bridge, but there sat the bag, a grim reminder they didn't get it done.

"Where are we going?" said Holly.

"We're taking Thomas and Elmer to a place I used to enjoy."

"Where's that?"

"Lake Kanasatka. You know, Sheila and I used to go there, but they can have it. I'm going to borrow a rowboat, say some words, and hope nobody notices."

"Borrow a rowboat?"

"I've got a set of bolt cutters. I'll break into a shed and leave ten bucks for a new lock."

"Ooh, what a bad boy," Holly teased.

"I'm a grave robber."

Holly laughed.

CHAPTER 56

Moultonborough, New Hampshire
April 30, 1971

They were the only boat on the lake, as most cabins were winterized and would remain empty until the following summer. After one last scan of the shoreline, Tim opened the burlap bag, poured the ashes into the water, and said a short prayer. Tim then filled the bag with rocks and let it sink.

"If Thomas could carry his rifle and move journals around, why couldn't he move the graves?" said Tim.

"I don't know. Too big? What about just speaking his mind? Elmer could talk to Mildred while she was alive," said Holly.

"I have no idea, but Annette had the same problems we did." Tim watched the burlap bag disappear into the depths of the lake as he pondered.

"People are different," said Holly. "Maybe ghosts are, too. Maybe he forgot how, but there's a definite disconnect."

Tim grabbed an oar and stirred the last of the floating ashes. When they disappeared beneath the surface, he headed for shore. *How does that feel, Tom?* he wondered.

CHAPTER 57

October 7, 1972

At long last, Holly was delighted to host Tim's open house on Lancaster Hill Road. The refurbishment was beautiful. Additionally, it was a seller's market, and it seemed that Tim's money worries might soon be over. Holly reflected on how hard it had been to get to this moment. The Mildred ordeal happened over the course of two weeks but felt like much longer. Now, they were accepting bids.

Holly considered hosting open houses her strong suit, but this one was especially nerve-wracking. She recalled the conversation with Tim before their first date about the morality of selling a home that someone died in and wished it were so easy. This time, the dead person was probably still around.

A crowd of nearly twenty people showed up, but Holly had doubts about how many were qualified buyers when she saw a cop with SIMMONS on his name tag, the gossiping family down the road. *A cop like his grandfather and nosy like the women.* For the first time in forever, a Simmons was allowed to wander the Wells property without trespassing, and this one was taking full advantage of it.

She'd already shown the house twice privately, and both couples submitted bids, which Tim was happy to hear. There were two more private showings later in the week, and when that was over, they would select the winner. However, there was a lot of last-minute anxiety, and Holly couldn't wait to get the hell off the property.

There were no grand tours this time, but she let potential buyers feel free to show themselves around. Holly set up a card table on the lawn and served lemonade while she let the crowd meander. It gave her anxiety to see one couple strolling through the field and another circling the pond near the spot where Mildred slaughtered the geese, but when they returned, Holly composed herself.

"My goodness, I love that grove! You were right!" said one potential buyer.

"It's beautiful. Romantic, even?" Holly spoke of it the way she used to see things.

"So peaceful. I can see myself taking walks in there to de-stress."

"Yes, and with the sunset coming through the trees? Wow." Tim's "forest garden" was growing where the graves used to be, hiding the fact that they'd ever been there.

One of the potential buyers approached. "Excuse me, Holly. I have a question."

Holly turned. "Mrs. Wallace. Yes, how can I help you?"

"Who's that lady in the field? She's been staring at the house since we arrived. We said hello, but she ignored us. She smells bad, too. I don't think she's here for your open house. You might want to keep an eye on her."

PART TWO: MARY

CHAPTER 58

Mifflintown, Pennsylvania
1843

On a breezy day in 1836, a dark-eyed girl named Mary, the second healthy daughter of a happy couple, was born in the Pennsylvania countryside. Despite their meager lifestyle, they felt blessed. What they didn't know, however, was they would only get to enjoy their lives together for six and a half years before things took a turn.

The father, Elmer, suffered a fatal heart attack behind the family barn just before sunset on a cold January evening. It was the wrong place to fall. He'd been examining the remnants of a giant hornet's nest that he'd avoided all summer. The hive was up high on the building and hard to reach. It was not a great place to go to war with an army that outnumbered him two thousand to one. He would have taken the hive down in November but had forgotten.

Because he lay dying behind the barn, the family couldn't find him in time, and Alice, the mother, was overwhelmed searching for him while tending to her two young girls and fetching help. When he was found the following morning, Elmer had passed, and his death spelled the end of the happy homestead.

Sarah was nine and old enough to carry loving memories for the rest of her life, but Mary was seven and was too young to remember most of the happiness. Alice, suddenly underprivileged, was forced to sell the farm.

CHAPTER 59

1845

Elmer's death made life difficult for Alice. The burden of her two children and her plain looks rendered her invisible to other men. Money was tight, and resources dwindled. She began to look for work.

Two years later and days from bankruptcy, a knock came at the door. A massive man with a beard towered over Alice, filling the doorframe and introducing himself as Gideon Walker.

"Good afternoon, ma'am. I'm sorry to interrupt your day, but I spoke with our mutual friend, Albert Mongomery, at the general store and heard of your plight. I'm so sorry about Elmer. My condolences."

Alice smiled, enjoying the sympathy. "Thank you. You know Albert?"

"Oh yes. I've been selling Albert my brooms for almost ten years. I live in Pennsylvania. I own a business that makes corn brooms. You might own one if you bought yours from the general store."

"What can I do for you, Mr. Walker?"

"This may come off as personal, but Albert and I are fairly close. He told me you'd fallen on hard times. I came to offer you a job making brooms. Room and board are free for you and your daughters, and the pay is good. Food is also included. I had a family helping me, but they moved west. It's a working farm, a live-in job. Upkeep is part of the deal, but you'll have private quarters. I've been shorthanded for six months, and this scenario could work for both of us."

Alice hesitated. Moving the girls to Pennsylvania would be life-changing, but they were barely surviving as it was. Winter was coming, and she didn't know how she would pay for firewood.

"That's a generous offer, Mr. Walker, but I must sleep on it. The girls were born here. They've never known different."

"I understand. Take the night," said Gideon.

Alice visited the general store the next day and spoke with Albert, whom she'd known for two years. After Albert's gushing review, complete with a demonstration of the quality of his brooms, Gideon Walker didn't have to twist her arm. Not only did the job sound like it would solve her problems, but Mr. Walker was handsome. Might this be the break they'd been waiting for? It almost felt like Mr. Walker was admiring her. She hadn't felt that emotion since Elmer.

Gideon's farm was in the middle of nowhere. The buildings needed work, and there were very few animals. There were no cows whatsoever. They ate meat from goats and squirrels whenever possible. Gideon cooked, which was a surprise. Alice was accustomed to men working in the field, tending to animals, or maintaining structures.

But Alice was happy for the first time in years. Her financial burdens were gone, and the girls would be warm. Making brooms was monotonous, but it was easy and something all three could do. Whenever they finished a batch of fifty, Gideon would leave the farm and take to the road to sell them.

His food was on the lighter side, but it was enough. *Beggars can't be choosers*, she reminded herself. Meat was served twice a week, and most of their calories came from scraps of bread and a pasty potato mixture mixed with bitter herbs. Gideon confessed that money was tight, but things would improve if they worked as a team.

At their first supper, Gideon announced that he had prepared a speech. Expecting a short prayer, Alice was surprised when he started talking about the importance of family, as he had yet to pursue her in any way.

"We are fortunate. All of us gathered here. There is nothing more important than family and community. When I was young, I was an orphan and didn't know what a family was. I had dreams, but I was alone.

"Then, I was adopted, and my new family showed me what it meant to be loved. The whole world suddenly became clear to me. People are meant to be together. As I speak, I feel that love is growing. Let it wash over you. Take it in. Absorb everything as we become family.

"Do you sense it? Soon, we will fill this world with love forever. Forever is not a concept. Forever is real, and we will own it. The world is filled with magic. All we have to do is find it and make it our own. Then, we can grow our family and bend the world to our will.

"The people at this table are just the beginning. I promise there will be more, but it will not be easy. There will be growing pains, but our family will rise above all the rest."

The table was quiet after that, and Alice wondered what came next. "Tell us about the family that adopted you. How old were you?"

"Eat your food," was all Gideon said.

Alice couldn't tell in the candlelight if he was being scornful or if he had gotten emotional. Intimidated, Alice and her girls finished their meals and prepared for bed.

The two girls were slow to warm to Gideon, but Alice knew they would come around, as they hadn't lived with a man in over two years. Sarah was polite but intimidated, and little Mary had yet to speak to him. Gideon, meanwhile, did a poor job of pretending it didn't bother him.

As time passed and Alice got to know him better, she felt pressured to do things his way. One night, she woke up to pee and found him in the hallway. Was he coming to see her, or was he watching them? Mary seemed averse to him. On more than one occasion, Alice witnessed her youngest daughter taking long paths to avoid him. Sarah, however, did everything she could to stay in his good graces.

Alice needed him more than he needed her, so she did her best to herd her children out of his way, fearing they might be asked to leave. The workdays were longer than at any time in her life. The day started at 3 am, and Alice was responsible for getting the girls dressed. Gideon gave them bitter tea and a slice of bread, and when they were finished, he homeschooled them. Alice didn't get to eavesdrop as much as she liked because she was busy washing dishes, doing laundry, and making brooms.

When the children finished Gideon's lessons, they took over for Alice while she shifted her efforts to painting and minor farm restoration projects. On the weekends, they would forage for mushrooms and tend to the garden. Alice was expected to bathe the children at the end of every day. They went to bed after eleven every night, and the days—and her mind—began to blur.

She and the girls were in an enduring daze and never questioned why they never went into town, and at the end of her thirty-seventh day on the farm, Gideon appeared in her doorway. The girls were asleep, exhausted after fulfilling their broom quota. Gideon approached her and began playing with her hair. She was tired and couldn't think straight. Were they finally becoming a couple?

Stars danced in her peripheral vision. Before she knew it, Gideon was on top of her. He made no effort to undress fully. Alice felt numb. The last thing she remembered was Gideon leaving the bedroom, buckling his belt. He and the candle he carried disappeared down the hallway, leaving her in darkness.

He shook her, not three hours later, to prepare for work. She would be alone today. He was headed into town to sell brooms and would return by evening. He told her to work fast to get everything done and that there would be guests when he returned. Exhausted, Alice wondered if she should say something, but, unable to focus, the thought faded. After he left, she woke the girls and didn't think twice about it.

The only food in the house was leftover potatoes and herbs. She wasn't sure exactly what the herbs were and never thought to ask, even though they'd been eating variations of the same thing since they arrived. There were never any fruit or vegetables, at most a squash or a pumpkin, every so often. There were also no fruit-bearing trees in the yard. There had been an apple tree once, but it was chopped off at the trunk. She wondered for a quick second about the farm's history when her mind drifted again. She couldn't seem to concentrate.

CHAPTER 60

1845

Gideon returned that evening with two guests, a mother and son pair, and Alice was too lethargic to be jealous. He carried a slaughtered goat over one shoulder and a small bag of provisions, a meager haul for the first trip to town in over a month.

Alice took the bag and looked inside. It contained more of his herbs, the bitter ones he used to season his food. Just a bag of herbs and a goat, despite the fact there were already a dozen of the creatures on the property. But it took too much energy to care, and food had lost most of its attraction anyway. Thoughts of leaving the farm faded. Where would they go, anyway? Alice turned her back on the new people and brought the herbs to the kitchen. Gideon dropped the goat on the ground and herded the newcomers to the guest house.

He returned a few moments later and gave precise instructions to Alice on how to prepare dinner. Cooking was a new chore, and she accepted the duties unquestioned. Before he left, he opened the bag of herbs and delegated to her how much to add.

Two hours later, when the food was nearly ready, she found him behind the guest house, standing beside the new woman, talking into her face. He was oddly close, filling her field of vision, similar to how he had spoken to Alice when she arrived three, four—*how long ago had they arrived?*

The new mother was humorless, with dark circles under her eyes. The boy was slightly more animated but too thin for his age. He looked about eight years old. Alice, who used to be cordial, was indifferent. Gideon occasionally took his gaze off the woman to intimidate the boy.

Alice announced dinner in a monotone voice and turned back for the kitchen. Dusk was falling, and, in accordance with Gideon's rules, one candle illuminated the dinner table. He controlled the conversation from start to finish, keeping the candle at his face so it would be the only thing anyone could focus on.

"Do you feel fortunate? You should. To everyone gathered here, there is nothing more important than family. Our love is growing. Our family is growing. Embrace it.

"We live modestly, but my goals for everyone at this table are anything but. I'm here to tell you that eternal life exists. Forever is not a concept—forever is real. I have studied magick for nineteen years and barely scratched the surface. First, we will grow our family and then cross over to immortality. The people at this table are the beginning of something special, and there will be more. Our family will one day inherit the Earth, I promise you."

Accustomed to the routine, Alice's girls said nothing the entire meal. The new boy, Marcus, seemed upset that Gideon had snuffed all his attempts at conversation. The big man had stolen his mother's attention. His mother, Martha, appeared desperate, trusting, and hopeful at the same time. Alice, meanwhile, tried to remember through the cobwebs if the words God or Jesus had ever been part of Gideon's sermon.

After dinner, Gideon produced a large cup of tea that he passed around and required everyone to drink. He then instructed Alice to clean up while he helped the new guests settle. He escorted them out of the main building and back to the guest house. They were gone for over half an hour.

Alice's promotion to cook was apparent, but he warned that he would check her work and did so when he was done with Martha. Alice could smell the sex but didn't say anything. She knew better than to pick a fight. Did it matter? It was so hard to concentrate.

Months passed, and aside from sharing Gideon with Martha, Alice was given more and more responsibility, stretching her workday and physicality. Mary, moody on her best day, seemed unchanged, but Sarah was markedly different since her first day on the farm. The laughter and joy in her personality were gone, replaced by anxiety. Her eyes were vacant, but she finished all her chores, so Alice brushed it off. She worried, but for never more than a passing moment.

In the following weeks, Alice was taught to set up the altar in the living room, where everyone gathered every evening. The altar was new to the house. One day, the living room was empty, and the next, there it was. There had been no hammering, construction, or recent trip into town. Alice wondered if it had been in storage and quickly forgot it.

As passive as she was, Alice began to look forward to the gatherings. Anything different made her feel more alive. The sex was numbing, mentally, too. *Eternal life? Living like this? Okay.* Whatever Gideon decided was acceptable. Sometimes, there were rituals. Some days, there were ceremonies or sermons and, on occasion, a baptism. The goblet of odd-tasting tea made the rounds. Sometimes, Sarah, Mary, or Marcus would nod off mid-ceremony, and Alice and Martha would be told to rouse them.

"New Orleans. Salem. Cuba. Brazil. Africa. Haiti. Magick exists, and we will use it to our advantage, no matter how far we must travel." What was Gideon talking about? *Africa? Brazil? Haiti?* Alice had never been outside Pennsylvania.

Weeks later, Gideon returned to town for three full days, leaving the two women in charge. They weren't aware, but he doubled back immediately and set up camp in the woods to watch and be sure they followed his every instruction. Like zombies, their dulled minds completed his to-do lists. They kept everyone awake as long as instructed, and the food was served as ordered. The children were not out in the sun, and he heard the chanting from the living room every evening.

CHAPTER 61

Salem, Massachusetts
1846

One year and eight new compound members later, Gideon left the farm again, this time for a two-week trip to Salem, Massachusetts, several states away. Now that he had a following, it was time to find what he was after. During his journey, Gideon diligently poked around in the local pubs until he came across an old drunk with some information. According to the man, a book existed that could enhance the power of the mind. Gideon's ears perked.

The old man called it the *Book of Shadows* and said it was a how-to guide that offered physical enhancement and immortality to those who followed it. Gideon was skeptical but wanted it to be true. Perhaps this was what he was looking for. The drunk man told Gideon that to "purchase" his copy, he would have to endure several tests by the powers that be, a group of living-dead men who made their home in the woods.

These tests were no joke, and according to the drunk, "many people" had backed away and disappeared when they heard how dire the consequences could be. Disfigurement, torture, abduction, and death were the rumors. Furthermore, the tests were always different, making the road to success impossible to anticipate.

Gideon wanted to know more. He could pass these tests or anything he set his mind to, for that matter. The Book of Shadows called to him. It was real. He knew it in his bones. Suddenly, the drunk gasped. Behind him, the crowd in the busy bar backed away as he slid off his chair and collapsed to the floor, a maroon stain spreading across his coat.

Gideon stood as he scanned the mob for a knife and prepared to fight. At that moment, the crowd parted, and the bartender gathered the dying man by the feet and dragged him away. Gideon backed toward the exit.

"You're a stranger, aren't you?" the man asked.

"I am," Gideon answered, placing the heel of his hand on the butt of his knife. "What's happening here?"

"You just witnessed a fool who doesn't know when to shut his mouth. Forget what you've seen and head back to Pennsylvania."

"How did you know I'm from Pennsylvania?" said Gideon, wild-eyed, more from excitement than fear. *They know who I am*, he thought. The powers exist.

"It's time to leave, Mr. Walker. You shouldn't be here." Nearly a dozen knives glinted in the dim light of the bar. *And they know my name.*

Gideon thought it best to leave and live to fight another day, and there would most definitely be another day.

"I'll leave." With that, he bowed out, and no one followed. *I'm not the first person to come looking.* He smiled, knowing they'd underestimated him. Intrigue became an obsession as he rode out of Salem. As he traveled, he dreamed of the next visit. He was a big man, an intelligent man, and a determined man. Once he got his hands on that book, he would be unstoppable.

After returning to Pennsylvania and checking his flock, Gideon turned back around. This time, he would seek one-on-one encounters where he could defend himself properly and get answers. He would demand to meet the people who held the Book of Shadows.

During his third afternoon in Salem, as Gideon passed several houses in a residential neighborhood, a man popped out of an alleyway and began following him. Gideon listened, waiting for the man to make his move, and eventually, the man called out.

"Gideon Walker."

Gideon turned. Because of his size, most people slowed their approach, but this man did not. Gideon looked him over. The man was thin and bald, with a mouth full of broken teeth, and he resembled a rat. Gideon must outweigh him by a hundred pounds. "Yes, that's me. Who gave you my name, and what do you want?"

The rat man stared, unblinking. Despite the dozen feet between them, Gideon detected an odor. Gideon wondered if it was the rat man or something dead in the bushes.

"We know you've been asking around. We also know about your farm in Pennsylvania and what you did in New Orleans. And we told you to stay away."

Gideon attempted to hide his surprise. No one knew about the sect in New Orleans, and anybody who did was dead. It was an experiment—a first effort. And he thought he had successfully buried it. "I want to learn," said Gideon. "I want to learn it all. I want to read the Book of Shadows."

The rat-man snickered. "There is no Book. Turn around, or you'll end up like your friend at the bar."

"I have a following … If you need resources, I can help."

"We don't need your resources, Mr. Walker. You can keep your mongrels. Leave while you still can." The rat-man had not blinked since the conversation started, and as soon as he finished his sentence, the wind changed directions.

All of a sudden, Gideon realized why the man was not afraid. He was one of the living dead people the old drunk was quacking about before they silenced him. Gideon shivered. He stopped thinking about the book and wondered how this conversation would end. *It could be my death*, he feared.

"Last warning, Mr. Walker. Turn and go."

The rat-man drew a long knife from his belt, and Gideon wondered if he might be slain in broad daylight. But it couldn't end this way. He was destined for more than this. He had seen and done many bad things. He had devoted his life to darkness, and the Book of Shadows was the next step. Why should he fear these people, or anyone for that matter, including the man before him?

The rat-man's element of surprise was over. Who cared if the dead man knew his name or life history? They were nothing more than parlor tricks. Gideon wanted their deeper secrets. Then and there, Gideon decided he'd rather die than live without the Book of Shadows. In his mind's eye, Gideon pictured a fork in the road. He had just chosen the newer path.

The rat-man sprung. His strength was inhuman, but Gideon expected as much. A memory popped into his head, something he had read in New Orleans. A creature like this would get stronger as the fight wore on. Gideon sidestepped the lunging revenant, avoiding the powerful limbs and dangerous blade, and as the rat-man whirled, Gideon sank his blade into the dead man's heart, followed by a powerful kick. The beast hit the ground, and his knife skittered into the gutter.

Gideon kicked the blade away, quickly cutting the heart out as the dying revenant pounded at his bleeding face. It would have been his end if he hadn't known what to do. His life would be over if things had not gone perfectly, down to the quarter-second, and all this in broad daylight. Where were the townspeople? It was a side street, but this was too good to be true. Perhaps another trick from the book. He had to have it.

Gideon sat down, hands covered in blood, arms slashed, nose broken. He decided not to remind himself how foolish he had been and how lucky he was. Realizing he was holding what was once a human heart, he tossed it into the bushes.

Suddenly, another man appeared from between the houses, and Gideon froze. Perhaps this was his last day on Earth. He could not be so lucky twice. If this were the end, he would beg for mercy. He would even ask them to make it quick. The second revenant walked up and stopped ten feet away. "It's time to move your cult to Massachusetts," he said, holding out his hand, making Gideon approach for a piece of paper.

Gideon came slowly, flexing his torn nostrils, trying not to catch the man's air. The eyes had life, but there was a glaze akin to cataracts. His skin was mottled. Spider veins stained his neck, and a large bruise covered the side of his head. On the paper was the address of a farm and directions on how to get there. "What happens after that?" said Gideon.

"You wait," said the second revenant, who turned and disappeared between the two houses, stopping only to retrieve the rat-man's heart. Gideon Walker knew better than to follow.

CHAPTER 62

1846

The first thing Gideon did after cleaning up was head to the address on the paper. Trips back and forth from Pennsylvania were neither short nor leisurely, and he had to economize. He had to trust that the women back home were running the show to his standards, but if they weren't, they would pay dearly.

The address on the paper was not located in Salem but in a village nearby called Beverly Farms. A man sat waiting in the window as Gideon arrived. The man was still alive, as best as he could tell. "Welcome, Mr. Walker," he said.

"Many thanks. May I ask your name since you know mine? Then we'll have a look around."

"I'm not here to show you around, Mr. Walker. I'm here to hand you the keys. I work for them, and so do you. I'm also here to help you move your things from Pennsylvania and move them quietly. I suggest you unpack your horse and get some sleep. We leave early. Call me Fenerty." With that, the man turned and disappeared into the house.

Gideon didn't enjoy taking orders. He would relent for now, but things would change as soon as he got his hands on the Book of Shadows. He looked around before bunking. It was a small farm with a nearby guest house and a medium-sized barn. There was also a shed across the property near the edge of the woods. There were no fields for crops, but there was a small patch of land that might once have been a small garden.

The buildings were in disrepair, and Gideon suspected the farm was never anyone's pride and joy. It was a camp intended for dark things, much like his Pennsylvania compound, and used for retreats, training, and following orders. The revenants, or whatever they called themselves, had probably taken over this property ages ago, using it to traffic, hide, and erase people ever since. Gideon smiled. It already felt like home.

CHAPTER 63

1846

Gideon heard Fenerty moving around before the sun came up and dressed to join him. It would be a long week. To his surprise, a large, covered wagon sat in the driveway with a pair of horses ready to pull. It took eight days to get to Pennsylvania.

All six women greeted the wagon like servants as they pulled up, with no joy in their eyes and no hesitation in tending to what needed doing. Fenerty looked around, took a headcount, borrowed Gideon's horse, and left for the night. Gideon wondered if it was a test. *Move thirteen people to Massachusetts by yourself, and you can read the Book of Shadows.* But he was wrong.

At two o'clock in the morning, he heard Fenerty return, this time with a different covered wagon, leading Gideon's horse behind it. "Let's go, Walker. Load it up. Get everybody moving. Nobody can see this wagon in broad daylight." Gideon realized what Fenerty had done and woke the women. They loaded one wagon with goods, woke the children, and herded them into the second.

Fenerty would not allow Gideon to put his property up for sale, and he even threatened to cancel the deal if Gideon did so. This trip was only to get the compound moved, safe and unseen. Gideon gritted his teeth but kept it to himself. Fenerty had a much scarier employer to answer to. Gideon didn't know it, but he would never see Pennsylvania again.

CHAPTER 64

Beverly Farms, Massachusetts
1846

They arrived in Beverly Farms ten days later, well after dark. When the horses stopped, Fenerty got off the wagon, murmured about some business he had to do, and then disappeared into the forest. Gideon watched him go, assuring himself he was here for a reason and all his questions would be answered eventually. The women set to work unloading the wagons, feeding the horses, and directing the children. They hadn't heard one of Gideon's sermons in weeks, so he decided to write one after mixing himself a tea.

Finding his bedroom on the second floor of their new farm, he sat down at a desk to write by candlelight. When he was halfway down the page, there was a sound outside the window. A white face outside caught him off guard, startling him badly, and he nearly dropped his candle.

Staring in through the glass was a revenant, clinging to the side of the house, suspended nearly twenty feet over the lawn below. His eyes met Gideon's, and his head gesture commanded that Gideon open the window. Gideon jumped back, heart in his chest. Even though he had defeated the rat-man if it had gone a second longer, it would have been his heart in the bushes, and he knew it.

Knowing that the window was no protection, Gideon let the beast in, and the stench filled the room. Gideon backed away, heart racing as the dead man crawled in.

"I want to read the Book of Shadows," he exclaimed, hoping to steer the conversation.

"I know," said the being.

"Who are you?"

"My name is Lyman Helms."

"Are you the boss? I want to speak to the person in charge."

Lyman Helms nodded his head, disturbing a half-dozen flies.

"I suppose I am."

"How many of you are there?" asked Gideon.

"Enough to haunt your dreams. We'll tell you if we decide you fit in. Are there any other trivial questions before I tell you how things will proceed?"

Gideon thought briefly about what to ask but was too distracted by Helms' indifference. Finally, he repeated his original question: "How can I see the Book?"

But the dead man changed the subject. "Walker, this sort of situation doesn't happen all the time. Maybe every once a millennium, for a guess. You caught our collective eye early on. When someone studies the occult, we know it. Whether it's here or as far away as Louisiana, word travels. And when someone starts a cult, we pay attention, but until you came along, to the best of my knowledge, no human has ever killed a revenant one-on-one. Mobs have banded together to do it, but never one man, head-to-head. You're special but don't count your chickens. You'll die in less than a minute if we disagree tonight."

Gideon swallowed hard. "I'm listening."

"Two dozen, over ten years. Any more risks unwanted attention."

"Two dozen what?"

"Two dozen people, of course. Five upfront. Nineteen more over the next ten years. To use as we like, which means we use them for parts."

As disgusting as that was, Gideon didn't blink and began to do the math. He would have to recruit two new souls yearly, but he was already surpassing that pace. If recruiting in Massachusetts was anything like Pennsylvania, he should have no problem.

"So, you do need bodies. I knew it. The rat-man said you didn't need my services. What will you do with them?"

"Almost the same thing you do, except we don't keep them alive. We can put the parts to good use and show you how over time, pending your progress. Recipes, if you will, from the Book of Shadows."

"Why not just take what I have and kill me?"

"We could. The fact that nobody knows you're here would make it very easy. We choose to be discrete. We don't need the townspeople hunting us with pitchforks."

"What are you? You seem too advanced for revenants. You're not hell-bent on revenge."

Helms smiled. "We're no strangers to revenge, but we are revenants. Better put, revenants evolved. Claude Allemand arrived here from Europe four hundred years ago with his Book of Shadows. He had devoted his entire life to collecting all things occult: Spells, talismans, runes, symbols, and that sort of thing, traveling the world for decades, putting his theories together, and translating them. When he had gathered all the information he needed, Allemand transitioned from a living being to an immortal so he could continue his studies forever.

Instead of a beast driven by vengeance, the original definition of a revenant, he used spells and procedures that enhanced himself and those that followed. He is gone now but left behind a race of ever-evolving beings adept in magick. Not parlor tricks, not rabbit-out-of-a-hat magic that ends with the letter *c*. I'm talking about real magick that ends with the letter *k*."

Gideon was more than intrigued. "What happened to Allemand?"

"As a group, we got greedy, dipping our pen once too often. The townspeople waited for us one night, and a mob ambushed Allemand. He killed nine before he fell, but they'll never forget the incident, or us, unfortunately. That's the reason we moved out of Salem. Allemand's death was fifty years ago. Things haven't been the same since."

"What do you mean?"

"Turnover and recruitment. Without Allemand's leadership, we became weaker as a group. However, we made a rule after his death to be stealthier. We focused on missing persons instead of smashing and grabbing. We put a cap on our population to help avoid detection. And we're learning. Allemand would have never recruited Sandberg, the revenant you killed. He had an eye for talent and was an even better teacher. We won't make the same mistake with you."

"So, you won't kill me and take my followers because you want me to join?"

"It's too early to say, but we see the potential. I may still kill you and take your following, but we have a vacancy because Sandberg is dead. Your total commitment is imperative. If you waver, then we will disappear. If you step out of line in any way, we will kill you. You seem the sort of man who likes giving orders, right?"

Gideon nodded.

"Put it out of your mind. Here, the race comes before the individual. Our evolution is ongoing. We grow together. Am I clear?"

Gideon nodded but wanted to hear more about Claude Allemand, a man after his own heart. Helms had him pegged correctly. Gideon was a leader like Allemand. His life had been about taking things over, and putting that on hold would be almost impossible.

"Don't let it get to your head, but some considered your victory over Sandberg an omen. You have potential. But I won't let that sway my decision. What's important is what happens from now on."

"Will I live forever?" Gideon asked excitedly.

"The odds are against it, especially considering your inherent nature to harm others. Sooner or later, these things catch up with you. Don't forget, Allemand is gone. For the most part, it's up to you, but immortality is deceptive. Many come to believe they are indestructible."

"Where will I live?"

"You will live here for a minimum of ten years as a mortal. After that, if things go well, we will finish the process. I have said what I came to say. Now I need your answer." Gideon didn't have to think about his response. There was only one answer.

"My answer is yes! Has anyone ever said no?"

CHAPTER 65

1846

The meeting ended with Gideon's acceptance of the deal. As soon as the word "yes" left his lips, Lyman Helms turned and climbed down the side of the building. Flies buzzed Gideon's head as the odor subsided.

Gideon delivered a distracted sermon that evening. He had accepted his wait-list position but couldn't share that this was the first of ten more years of lukewarm sermons because his heart was no longer in it. Helms had waved magick under his nose, and the old gig of collecting lost souls was a job Gideon no longer wanted. He knew, however, that he would be killed if he didn't live up to his end of the bargain. Gideon went to bed perplexed.

Three hours later, he woke to the sound of screaming. Gideon rose, burdened by unimportant problems, even though his life depended on fixing them for ten more years. Martha, the woman in the next room, made the racket. He entered the room as she stood there, staring out the window, shrieking into the night.

Marcus, her boy, was missing, and Gideon immediately knew why, although he was surprised by the speed of the transaction. He did his best to comfort her, pretending not to understand why. As he calmed her, he realized that more screaming was coming from other parts of the house.

Shrill, desperate voices filled the air, and he understood that Helms had come early, exercising his rights. He stole the first five souls before the townspeople of Beverly Farms even knew they existed. Intelligent and safe. The upstairs was howling with people who had lost family members, taken in the dead of night.

What surprised Gideon, but shouldn't have, was that all five were children. While he didn't have the Book of Shadows, he had read other books on the occult. The blood of an innocent was worth more than the blood of a sinner.

He also knew that nothing would go to waste. They would use every bit: blood, marrow, organs, brain, skin, fat, eyes, and tendons, every piece, used somehow, some way. Even ashes had value in some rites. *Of course, of course, of course.*

There was no rest that night. Gideon was handed a mess, a tough test for a new hopeful. He grabbed his rifle and headed into the woods, alone, under the guise of getting the children back, and as soon as he was deep in the trees, he pulled the blanket he had stashed under his coat and made camp. The kids were gone for good. He might as well get some sleep.

Tomorrow would be a long day getting the women back in line, and it would take more than a few herbs, teas, and punishments to calm them down. As Gideon pulled the blanket up, he criticized himself for not nailing the deal's specifics.

A warning would have been nice, as well as his input on how to stagger the abductions and make them look like accidents. He would likely have to get physical with them to calm their emotions. He did a headcount. Five children missing meant only two were left on the farm, but he wasn't sure yet which two.

CHAPTER 66

1846

The following day, Alice hugged Mary tight. Her eldest daughter, Sarah, had been one of the five children taken. Mary was all she had left in the world, but Gideon Walker searched in the forest to find the missing kids, and the six women awaited his return.

The wailing continued. Four of the six women were now childless. Only Mary and Cora's son, Edward, remained. Cora and Alice did the only thing they could do: hug their children, but the rest of the four women were inconsolable.

Quiet Mary, now almost ten years old, cried for her missing sister. Sarah had always done the talking, as she was the person who understood Mary's introversion best. Mary picked up Millie, her well-worn rag doll, and hugged her tight. The now twice-broken family was down to two. Mary had not accepted Gideon Walker as a father figure, nor would she. She knew he would return empty-handed from the woods.

CHAPTER 67

1846

Near mid-morning, Gideon emerged from the woods. And the six grieving mothers were crestfallen. The odds of ever finding the missing children had fallen exponentially. "I'm sorry. I'm afraid they're gone."

Margaret, one of the mothers who had lost her daughter, Anna, ran at him and began beating his chest. "Why, *why*? They were terrible! They smelled of death! Get a dog! Surely, they can be tracked! I will never forget their scent!"

Gideon wrapped his hands around her tiny arms and pushed her away. When she came at him again, he sent her to the grass with a powerful slap. "Tell me about them," he said. "Tell me what happened."

"I didn't see a thing!" said Clara, who had lost her son Robert. "I was dreaming about a dead deer we found in the forest and how bad it smelled. When I woke up, the window was open, and Robert was gone!"

"I felt George pulled from my arms in a dream. I smelled them, too. I thought it was a nightmare. I wish it were only a nightmare, and now—" Rose burst into tears and could not finish.

"I was awake when they opened the window," said Martha. I only believed I was dreaming. I thought it was from the herbs you're feeding us, things I didn't care about before because we had a roof over our heads, but now Marcus is gone, and you didn't protect him! Why did I let you into our lives? I don't want to be here anymore! You're terrible!"

"Enough!" Gideon bellowed. Martha knew he was keeping them docile. She would have to be filtered out. Her independent thinking was a threat to his livelihood. Gideon turned to Cora, Edward's mother. The revenants had spared Edward, and Cora hugged him tightly. She was the only mother not to lose a child, and the other mothers envied her.

Lastly, Gideon turned to Alice, the first sheep in the flock. Alice had lost Sarah, leaving her with Mary, the quiet one. Gideon frowned. He would have preferred if Mary had been taken. She was hard to read, and he never knew what she was thinking. Was she slow or just quiet? He would have to address this with Helms at his next opportunity. *Check with me first. Let me pick the names.*

Alice sat despondent while Mary clutched her doll, her sunken eyes hidden behind stringy hair. "I didn't see anything," said Alice. "I was on the floor across the room, and Mary and Sarah were in bed. The first thing I heard was Martha screaming in the other room, and then I smelled them. It was horrible, like a dead animal or a dog that rolls on one."

Disappointed, Gideon turned to Mary. "Mary, what did you see?" The gaunt-faced girl rocked back and forth but did not look up. As expected, she said nothing.

"Mary! What did you see? You were lying next to your sister."

Alice pulled Mary close and wrapped her in a hug. "Did you see anything, sweetheart?" she whispered. Mary locked eyes with her mother, shaking her head no. Gideon wondered if his herbs had any effect on her. Undoubtedly, the Book of Shadows would have more potent remedies. Perhaps Helms could share.

CHAPTER 68

1846

As the days passed, Gideon Walker suffered through damage control. Jarred by the abductions, his flock lost focus. "Where is Martha?" He asked. Martha, the thorn in his side, was missing. He checked the horses, and one was missing. Rage made his temples pulse. No one had ever left without permission. Hackles up, he prepared for visitors.

When law enforcement arrived, the women gravitated to them. Here, after all, was hope for their lost children. Martha rode in with the authorities, defiant. Gideon glared but let the women ask their questions, helping to fill in the gaps when their stories stumbled, playing the helpful and caring custodian.

As soon as the marshal heard the term, *dead men*, he nodded as if he had heard the term before and wrote faster. Gideon couldn't tell whether the man knew of Helms and his group or because they were so close to Salem. The marshal stayed for over three hours, touring the property and asking questions. Thankfully, Helms had not left any evidence that he or his kind were ever there, and the marshal and crew came up empty-handed.

Anxious, Gideon sweated Martha's performance. If anyone would sell him out or mention the word *cult*, it would be her, yet until now, she had depended on him for her general well-being. Luckily, she didn't cross that line. Later in the day, he even heard her complimenting him like a battered wife, describing him to the marshal as "father-like." After the interviews and a failed search of the woods, enthusiasm amongst the women waned, and they retired to their rooms, heartbroken.

When the last of them had left the living room, Gideon spoke: "Marshal, I'm sorry you were called to our farm today. Now that we're alone, I can explain everything. Gideon described the farm as a religious retreat and made up a story that his specialty was caring for women who had lost their children and never got over it. The poor souls were cursed to relive the episode in perpetuity.

"Have you heard of the Hoernerstown Tragedy? Four years ago?" asked Gideon.

"No, I'm afraid I haven't," said the marshal.

Gideon acted as if it pained him to retell the yarn. "Ah, well. Bad news does not always travel fast, and sometimes that's good. Four years back, two brothers got it into their sick minds to take over a schoolhouse in Hoernerstown, Pennsylvania. They carried knives and guns, barricaded doors, and took the children hostage. They held the authorities off for more than a week, and the children never made it out alive.

"Soon after, the church hired me as a caretaker because my wife had passed away. In desperate need of human interaction, I offered my assistance. I promised God to see these ladies live into their golden years and keep them at peace. The Lord knows they've already seen enough pain and suffering. Marshal, what I'm telling you is the children were never here. The clothing, shoes, and toys you see are nothing but souvenirs. Sad, but true."

The marshal nodded, horrified. "That's the saddest thing I've heard in quite some time."

"Poor Martha is not well, and they are all of this mindset. They usually relive their nightmares individually, but as you have witnessed, it can also be communally. Panic runs amok, and the only thing I can do is ride it out. If it is any consolation, your visit is a sort of closure. They will return to normal much faster, for the time being, anyway."

The marshal studied Gideon for several seconds. "Mr. Walker, as much as I sympathize, I do not have the time or the resources for false alarms. Please ensure your horses are locked up properly."

"I will, marshal. My apologies to you and your crew, and thank you for coming out."

The marshal and his men saddled up and left. As soon as they were out of sight, Gideon returned to the house. It was time to fix his Martha problem.

CHAPTER 69

1846

Mary lay next to her mother, who had just cried herself to sleep. It wouldn't be long before she woke again, so for a few moments, Mary had the sounds of the house to herself. She missed Sarah badly, and the bed, while still cramped, seemed empty without her. Mary was angry more than sad; she knew Sarah was gone for all the wrong reasons and that someone was at fault.

Mary blamed Gideon, but she didn't know why. It was nothing she could prove, but he was a poor substitute for her beloved father, and she never liked him. When he moved them here, bad things happened. Agitated but not daring to wake her mother, she stared at the ceiling with a brain full of spiders.

Suddenly, she heard a noise through the wall: several rapid thumps followed by someone heavy walking the floorboards. It was Gideon's gait; she knew it anywhere, and he was in Martha's room. Minutes later, the house fell quiet. An hour later, Mary fell asleep.

CHAPTER 70

1846

The following day, Gideon made an announcement. Martha had left camp again, and one of the horses was missing. She would not be invited back this time. Gideon spent the next few minutes feigning rage, throwing things and punching walls. When he had everyone's attention, he prayed for her safe return. Margaret and Clara were crying again. There had been so much turmoil on top of their fatigue and malnutrition they couldn't help themselves.

Mary wasn't having any of it. The things Gideon threw were cheap and unbreakable. None of the walls he punched were damaged. The horse Martha supposedly stole was the one with the gimp.

If her mother couldn't think outside the box, she would have to. Mary already knew the food was weak and that her mother was in worse shape than she was. Deep down, she knew this farm situation was wrong. In the wake of Gideon's spectacle, she decided to investigate.

It was easier to check out the buildings on the property during daylight hours. They slept in the main building, but there was a two-story barn next to the main house, a guest house, and a shed in the far corner. Gideon liked to poke around out there, and usually alone. She could ask her mother, but Alice was no longer in her right mind.

One afternoon, Mary decided to explore. When no one was looking, she bolted through the shin-high grass and looked back. *Did anyone see? No.* A padlock secured the door. Mary shook it, but it was locked tight. With no recourse, she walked the perimeter of the building and, with the shed between her and the farm, started into the woods. The forest beckoned. There was no fear, only the call of freedom. The urge to escape through the trees was strong, and inspiration struck. If not now, then soon.

But she could not leave her mother. A mother should never lose a child, never mind two. After one last look into the trees, she returned to the shed. Mary pressed her ear to the clapboards and heard nothing. Not a bird nor a squirrel disturbed the silence. With no way in, she searched the clapboards for a hidden key, but the search proved fruitless. *It would have been too good to be true*, she thought. Out of time, she ran back to her chores before she was missed.

CHAPTER 71

1846

Mary spent the next three days combing the farm for the key to the shed. There must be something important in there, and the key, unless he kept it on his person, had to be somewhere. Near the end of the third day, after she had checked almost everywhere, Mary walked straight into Gideon's bedroom and searched it.

There weren't many things to move or look under. The desk consisted of a fountain pen and two sheets of blank paper. There was one set of clothes, for he only owned two, the one in the closet and the one on his body. Just as she was about to leave and abandon the search, she closed the bedroom door.

There was a nail on the wall, and hanging from it was a key.

CHAPTER 72

1846

Mary did not take the key and sprint to the shed but instead left it and ran to the barn, where she knew of an old key rusting away in a padlock sitting on a shelf. Pulling the key from the old lock, she looked it over and judged it too worn to sit in for Gideon's. Mary buffed and shined the key with a horse blanket and lamp oil for six days. It was still not an exact match when she was finished, but it was close enough.

At four o'clock in the afternoon, Mary saw her first opportunity as she witnessed Gideon speaking with little Edward. Cora, his mother, wasn't doing her job controlling him, so they both had the pleasure of spending the afternoon under Gideon's tutelage.

Mary rushed out to the shed and tried the key. Thankfully, the lock popped, and the door swung open. Mary stepped in and closed it so no one from the house would know. Slowly, the room revealed itself to her as her eyes adjusted.

Shelves were stocked with food not found in the house: dried cod and dried beef, proteins she hadn't seen in as long as she could remember. There was a small stove, and some meat was sitting on top, rehydrating for Gideon's private dinner that evening. There were fresh pumpkins and dried corn, nothing resembling the mush the flock ate like zombies as soon as it hit the table. Mary left the beef soaking because Gideon would notice the short portion but went through the rest of the supplies, skimming small quantities he would never miss, filling her pockets.

Across the room was a bench, and on it was a cache of the dried herbs that went into her food every night. There were also some pretty rocks, sticks, feathers, candles, an assortment of beads, and some bottled liquids. Next to the bench, in the darkest part of the room, was an altar, similar to the one in the living room of the main farmhouse, and in the center of the altar was a thin book.

No words were on the cover, no author's name, and no table of contents. She picked it up, and it was warmer than the room itself. Immediately, she knew this was what Gideon was doing out here, even more important than the food he was hiding. Mary opened it and turned to the first page, which was the only page. On it was handwritten what looked like a poem, recipe, or hybrid.

In the margins were handwritten symbols, and the text was written in a different language. Mary could make out some words, but not many. The single page was not a leaflet tossed into a folder but a dedicated page sewn into the binding. *Why make a book for a single page?* She wondered.

Mary sensed time running out and closed the book. She couldn't squander this gold mine by getting greedy, so she placed the book where she found it and scanned the floor for stray kernels. When she was done, she locked up, jogged along the tree line to the house, emptied her pockets into a burlap sack, and hid it under the bed. Mary managed a smirk. This food would restore her health.

CHAPTER 73

1846

Mary skipped visiting the shed on the second and third days as she worked off what she had stolen, bite by secret bite. As she did so, she continued to observe Gideon and his patterns. Now that they shared an interest in the shed, she wanted to ensure they didn't cross paths. Gideon barely ever slept, and that made him dangerous.

Alice had been sleeping better recently so Mary could sneak out of bed and sit in the living room window, where she watched Gideon leave for the shed and remain there until dawn. When she saw the lamp go out, it was time to sneak back to bed before he began rousing everyone.

Once her supplies ran out, Mary snuck back into the shed just after noon. Everything was the same as on the first day, so she unfolded her burlap bag and skimmed an imperceptible amount from each bin. As she finished, she revisited the altar, wondering why Gideon spent so much time out here with the lights on.

Mary picked up the warm book and opened it again, but this time, to her surprise, there were two pages. Were they stuck together before? She counted twice to ensure both were sewn into the binding as if they had been there forever. Suddenly, a noise from outside the shed pierced the silence.

"Baaa!"

Mary nearly dropped her burlap bag. A kid goat had followed her to the shed. The plan she had for her mother, to one day walk into the woods and never look back, was in jeopardy because of this noise. Freedom, health, and a return to everyday life were at stake.

Mary grabbed a long knife from Gideon's bench and stepped outside. With two quick jabs, the kid dropped, and she scooped him up before he could leave a big red clue. Working fast, Mary rounded the shed and continued into the forest. While tiny, the kid goat weighed heavy before fifty yards had passed. Concerned he would bleed on her dress, Mary dropped the goat and slit him up the belly, letting the guts spill onto the forest floor. The blood was everywhere, and it wouldn't be long until the coyotes found him.

Blood was on her shoes, which she wiped away with some leaves. There was some staining but nothing bright red she couldn't explain away. There was also blood along the hem of her dress, and she cut it off with the knife. They were all wearing rags. No one would notice. Mary wiped the blade on the animal's coat, then ran to the barn and rinsed her bloody parts in the water trough. Finally, she slipped into the house, swapped keys on the back of Gideon's door, and smiled.

Gideon noticed the missing goat but did not suspect anything. It was not uncommon to lose an animal to a predator. He commented under his breath about getting another goat the next time he went into the city in two weeks.

Mary, eavesdropping, heard his mutterings and made plans.

CHAPTER 74

1846

It seemed like it took forever for Gideon to leave for Salem. Mary counted the days, budgeting the contents of her burlap sack. She wanted to share the food with her mother, but Alice was too mentally weak to be trusted. Mary wondered if she might even turn her in if she knew what was happening. If they were to escape Gideon's hell, it would have to be Mary's job to get it done.

Gideon left that morning, and Mary, who planned on raiding the shed, could not shake her mother's gaze, so she waited until her mother fell asleep. A thorough inspection was first on her list, followed by a snack and a decent night's sleep, the first in weeks. It was a quiet night, weather-wise. She enjoyed her walk across the lawn and the breeze blowing in from the forest.

The cabin was dark as she approached. It was the first time the interior had been unlit at this time of night in at least a month. Despite her positive mood, Mary, cautious as ever, considered for a second that this was a setup and that Gideon was in the shed waiting. Perhaps he knew everything: the key, the food skimming, the dead goat, and that she'd touched the book that seemed to grow pages. Her paranoia was talking, but she marched on.

The lock opened, and she was inside in an instant. Over the window, she hung her mother's black dress and, once ready, struck a match and lit the lamp. It was time to turn the place upside down. She started with the book, which now contained four pages but was still illegible. Starting at the beginning, she read one aloud.

"*Vinculum coniuro te nomine nel margine superiore nomen....*" The text rambled, and she gave up. She put the book down to eat, but as she was about to dig in, she noticed three tiny wooden cubes on the bench with strange writing on them. Mary picked them up and rolled them around in her palm, surprised they were even warmer than the book. Next to the cubes was what looked like a medicine bottle, but she left that alone.

Hungry, Mary couldn't wait any longer. She'd become so accustomed to extra rations that she feared she might start looking too healthy, but she could never give them up. Her mind had sharpened, and clear thinking was the gateway to freedom. Mary opened Gideon's dried beef container, disappointed to see only three strips left. He must have taken the rest with him.

She put the lid back on and tried the salted fish instead. Usually, this protein was soaked in water for hours to bring the salinity down to an edible level, but Mary didn't have the luxury of time. Three bites in, she had to quit. It took two carrots before she could taste anything.

After eating all she dared, Mary wondered what to do next. The other visits had been rushed due to the danger of being caught. She yawned, tired too soon. If Gideon were here, she would be dying to trade places. What a pity to run out of things to do so soon. Uncertain, she stepped outside to think, and it wasn't long before her eyelids grew heavy. The cool breeze and two weeks of anticipation had taken their toll. Mary stepped back into the shed to snuff the lamp, but something flashed by her feet. She jumped back.

It was her clothing. The white, frayed rag she wore was gone, and in its place, a black farm dress. *Where did this come from?* Mary turned to the book and leafed through it. It was still only four pages. She turned to the third page, the one she last read. She had no idea what it all meant, but come to think of it, wasn't Gideon wearing new clothes the other day? Now she had a problem.

Her new dress would stand out, and it would get back to Gideon. He would know what she'd been up to if they were the only two in the compound with new clothing. Cleaning up after herself, Mary grabbed the wooden cubes, locked the shed, hid the black dress in the barn, and spent twenty minutes digging through the laundry basket in the farmhouse, looking for her dirty nightgown.

CHAPTER 75

1846

Gideon Walker tied his horse in the woods off Broad Street in Salem. Staying hidden, he waited patiently for the boy to come running by. After two days of observation, he was ready to work. The schoolhouse was letting out, and he followed the slow-moving loner. Most children had already left, excited to head home, but this boy always took his sweet time.

It was still year one of his contract with Helms, who had already taken his first five victims and would be looking for number six soon. Gideon didn't enjoy this part of the deal, but it wasn't because it bothered him morally; he just didn't like the risk of getting caught. The new pages in the Book of Shadows piqued his curiosity, and he wondered what would happen if he fulfilled the deal early. Would the book fill up overnight? Would all the spells be made available?

Initially, the Book of Shadows had appeared with just one page, and he read it to himself, wondering what the words meant, but nothing happened. Days went by, and it wasn't until he read it out loud that he looked at his writing desk and a small wooden die appeared. When he reread the spell aloud again, a second die appeared twenty minutes later. Gideon recognized the dice as *runes* from his time in New Orleans and jumped for joy. If everything were this straightforward, the sky was the limit.

The next night, a second page appeared. How or why, he didn't question, but it was as if both pages were sewn in when the book was created. Again, Gideon read the words out loud and closed his eyes, hoping he would not be disappointed. On the bench next to the three runes was a corked medicine bottle, an amber liquid filled to the neck. *Do I drink it?*

Elated, Gideon crossed the room and removed the cork. Cautiously, he sniffed the contents. Immediately, his vision went black. Gideon dropped to the floor, breaking the bottle and cutting his hand on the jagged glass. Four hours later, when the liquid had evaporated, he came to with a splitting headache and bloody palm.

Whatever this bottle was, he had never dreamed such a power existed. Even doctors were without such a drug. Hopeful, Gideon reread the spell and went to bed. The following day, he found a fresh bottle waiting for him, and this time, he didn't remove the cork.

The slow boy approached, and Gideon looked around. Nobody was watching. Gideon pulled the boy into the bushes and placed a rag soaked with the bottle's contents over his mouth and nose. The boy collapsed as if his bones were made of gelatin.

Gideon rolled the boy into a blanket and threw him over the back of the horse. For disguise, he placed his purchases and another blanket on top for camouflage. If the boy woke during the journey, Gideon would drug him again. Taking the boy over the Essex Bridge was too dangerous. Once on it, there was no escape route. Instead, he would go the long way through Danvers, which offered multiple options and the cover of trees.

CHAPTER 76

1846

Gideon skirted the Crane River and, as he'd hoped, practically had the road to himself to Beverly Farms. At dusk, still two hours from home, Gideon began to wonder where he was supposed to leave the boy. He had not been given instructions and couldn't contact Helms.

He couldn't ride onto the farm, either. The women were under his influence, but they would not tolerate an abducted child. He could say that the boy was sick. Suddenly, Gideon saw a man staring from the middle of the road. Most travelers were home by this hour. Gideon squinted, trying to see better, but he had an idea of who it might be.

Just then, the blanket behind him moved. The boy was waking up and, with arms pinned to his sides, was panicking. Gideon looked to the man waiting and, as he did so, smelled death on the wind. Gideon wrinkled his nose. *Just in time.*

CHAPTER 77

1846

When Gideon returned to the farm that evening, Mary took note. There would be no trip to the shed tonight, and she felt something she owned had been taken away. She didn't know it, but she was as addicted to the Book of Shadows as Gideon was. Gideon, of course, was glad to return. Wise beyond her years, Mary went straight to bed to wait her turn.

Gideon hung close to the barn the next day, delivering lessons, sermons, and one-on-ones, reminding everyone whose farm this was. His presence kept Mary away from the shed for another day. She went to bed hungry and didn't like it.

CHAPTER 78

1846

The following day, Gideon announced he would go on a turkey hunt. Mary couldn't recall even one time in either Beverly Farms or Pennsylvania when they had eaten turkey. It was out of character, and she was immediately suspicious. Was this a ploy to catch her in the shed?

She decided she couldn't wait and struck the moment he disappeared into the woods and was back at her chores before the goats had finished breakfast. Her first stop was the dried beef, and she polished off two slabs, pocketing a third for the afternoon. Then, she read the book, surprised to note that there were now six pages. With her estimated time running out, Mary read the fourth page aloud:

In hoc carmine non poterit legere librum. Tantum phrase iterare: ego dominus, et non sunt locuti estis ad me sollicitat.

Nothing happened, or at least, nothing she noticed. Deflated, she shut the book and locked up, thankful for the nutritious protein digesting in her stomach, strengthening her body, mind, and spirit.

CHAPTER 79

1846

Gideon, of course, returned empty-handed from the turkey hunt, and Mary still wondered what he'd been up to. She went to bed with her mother, Alice, with the Book of Shadows on her mind. What did I read this morning? What did any of the pages mean? One page had changed her clothes. What did the rest do? There were no answers that evening, so she let it go in the name of sleep. Better sleep now meant clearer thinking later.

CHAPTER 80

1846

Morning came, and the women rose for work. Mary, always watching for Gideon's whereabouts, couldn't find him. Twenty minutes later, someone in the house screamed. Mary emerged from the barn to see the commotion and saw Rose, the mother of missing George, crying hysterically.

"She's gone! Clara is gone! I thought she went to look for grapes, but her shoes are still in her bedroom!" Rose and Clara had become close since the loss of their children. Now Rose had lost not only her son but her friend.

Gideon burst from the shed, awakened from a nap. Helms' schedule infuriated him. If it were up to him, Gideon would trade the entire compound for an early ticket to the afterlife. He already knew Clara would go missing. The previous day, Gideon had walked into the forest searching for the meeting, and Helms appeared out of nowhere.

"Helms, how can I speed up this process? Ten years is too long. I can give you the entire group today if you like." Gideon had once again underestimated the odor and the buzzing flies.

Helms frowned. "The process will kill you if you're not seasoned. Why do you think we only give you a page at a time? You aren't even putting in the time. You're doing what Gideon wants to do."

Gideon dropped his eyes, frustrated. Helms was right. He'd always been impatient. There was no way around this ten-year chore. The dead men were watching, and they knew he wasn't doing his homework.

"Can it be under ten years, or is that set in stone?"

"It might be, but no one ever has. Ten years is a heartbeat to us, and that's what you should expect. It might even take longer."

Gideon grasped at straws. "We have two children left. Edward and Mary. What about them? They could count towards my tally."

Helms gritted his teeth. "Are you deaf? You wouldn't be ready if you produced all nineteen today."

Gideon wasn't finished. "The boy from Salem was too risky. Eighteen more over ten years is near impossible without getting caught. Take Mary and Edward."

"You're in danger of losing control of your followers as it is, Walker. You think you're almost done and can neglect your duties, but you can't. More chaos will break up your little farmstead, and you'll be in jail if the women talk. If that happens, our deal is off."

"I'll kill them first. No one leaves."

"And what if the marshal decides to pay you an unannounced check-back? It might happen, you know."

"Perhaps you could step in and protect your investment."

Helms laughed. "Ha! What makes you think you're so special?"

Gideon simmered. "I have given you six. You need eighteen more. Odds are, the marshal will catch me. You've put me in a no-win situation. Take Mary and Edward. That leaves sixteen."

The dead man hesitated, knowing Mary had been to the shed even though Gideon didn't. "No deal. Mary and Edward need each other. The women need them, too, and you need the women. Pretend you're already dead, and time will pass."

"But I'm not dead. I'm at risk, and you hold all the cards," said Gideon.

Helms approached, bringing the flies with him. The aura filled Gideon's sinuses, and he gagged. His bravery had put his life in danger, but if given the chance to cross over, he could set them all straight and bend them to his will.

Helms stepped into Gideon's face. "Would you like to die right now?"

Gideon backed away, stunned. When there were seven feet between them, he stopped. "I'll do what you ask," he said.

Helms scratched his chin, thinking. "There is someone you didn't mention we could use: Clara. She is not the mother of the boy we took. That boy was her brother. She's a virgin."

"How do you know?" asked Gideon.

Helms' eyes narrowed. "You mean you haven't read the book?"

Gideon, embarrassed, mumbled under his breath. "Take her."

CHAPTER 81

1846

"She's gone! Clara is gone! I thought she went to look for grapes, but her shoes are still in her bedroom!" Gideon would rather take his eyes out than deal with Clara's abduction, but he was one-eighteenth closer to his goal, and these were the consequences. Like a hangover, there was a price. Rose continued to rant.

"Where were you? Why are you always in that shed? Clara is gone. She's gone! Another one of us, taken! We aren't safe here. We aren't s…" Gideon clamped his palm over Rose's mouth. A hush fell over the barnyard.

"Clara is not gone! Get to work, Rose! You attack me, and I haven't had a chance to piss! I'm working on this, do you understand? Does everyone understand?"

A murmur rippled through the women.

"I'm going to find her. Alice, there is a shotgun in my closet. Take it and guard yourselves. Everyone, wait in the house until I return."

Gideon disappeared into the forest, and the women moved like sheep to the house. A half-mile into the forest, he sat at the base of an oak tree and put his face in his hands, imagining what he would say when he came home empty-handed. Suddenly, he remembered the Book. There must be an answer in its pages. Circling, he approached the shed from the far side. He needed time to read.

Gideon lunged for the Book as soon as he was in and was surprised to find seven pages. What should have been relief was dread. He would need even more time now, reading gibberish, trying to guess which spell did what. It had taken him hours to this point, not counting the time spent unconscious after sniffing the bottle.

As much as he craved the book, it was a puzzle, and Gideon hated puzzles. It would be a long ten years if he had to read things he didn't understand and piece clues together. Page One, he knew, was about the wooden runes. Page Two was about the medicine bottle. Page Three, he hadn't read yet.

Gideon read from the beginning again and searched his surroundings. As always, it seemed nothing had happened. His blood pressure climbed. *Damn it,* he turned the page. Again, it was gibberish from top to bottom, but something happened as he finished bottom of page four. The text became English.

"This spell, when read, will enable the believer to see the ancient writings as though written in their native tongue." The text continued, but the first sentence said it all. *Eureka,* Gideon thought. *I can read it all now.*

He flipped back to page three, the spell that didn't seem to do anything, and read again:

"The one who reads this spell aloud will have the power to change their attire. This basic skill has proven most valuable in such instances as shaking followers and deceiving victims. The dead also use it on the occasion they outlast their clothing. User taste in clothing comes with time."

When he finished the page, his clothes changed before his eyes, startling him. His usual dark shirt, pants, and coat had become something a typical Salemite wore. Gideon hated the frilly jabot around the neck and tore it off.

Now, he understood the first four pages. *Why the hell do they put the instructions on the fourth page?* It was a test. Everything was a test. With that, he turned to page five.

"Whichever believer chants this text shall come to know which of those around him are unclean in spirit." Again, the text was followed by more Latin, Olde English, Wiccan, or whatever. Helms had mentioned this in the meeting in the woods the day before they took Clara. Gideon felt like a fool. He turned to the sixth page and read.

"It may become necessary to sap the motivations of human workers or enslaved people from time to time. For this purpose, speak the names of those you wish to compel followed by: In the name of Allemand, repose thy mind."

Gideon sat back in his chair and breathed a sigh of relief. The effects of this one would be a delight. He could return to the house to a crew of submissives. After reciting the names, he put the book down to check.

CHAPTER 82

1846

Mary witnessed Gideon's spell wash over the household and knew something was amiss. Her mother stood guard in the window with Gideon's gun, waiting dutifully. Mary, who was used to her freedom, was agitated by the droning in her head but at least had an idea of what caused it. She also knew that Gideon wasn't in the woods looking for Clara. He was in the shed with the Book.

Mary struggled against the spell, but it had full hold on the others. Rose stopped crying. Alice put the gun down. They looked like sleepy dogs after a big dinner. Gideon walked through the front door and smirked when he saw Rose's eyes. Mary witnessed his reaction and promised to get to the shed as soon as possible.

"Rose. Come here," said Gideon. Rose got up dutifully and approached him as if nothing had happened.

"Yes, sir. What can I do for you? And, if I may ask, was there any sign of Clara in the forest?"

"Rose, I first want to say how sorry I am for having to discipline you this morning. It was a stressful situation. And, to answer your question, sadly, no. I could not find our beloved Clara. It was as if the forest swallowed her up."

"I know you did your best," said Rose.

"Things will return to normal in no time. I'll make sure of it."

No one thought to question him, including Mary, the last to succumb.

CHAPTER 83

1846

Mary woke before dawn and couldn't recall the details of the previous evening, only that Gideon had a new spell, Clara was missing, and he wasn't doing anything about it. She was almost certain Gideon was still in the shed, probably getting ready to leave. She strongly considered leaving the bed, sneaking into the forest, and entering after he left, but realized he had the key.

Just after mid-day, Mary saw Gideon speaking with Rose in her bedroom. Biting her lip, Mary snuck into his bedroom, swapped keys, and headed straight for the shed to catch up on her reading. To her amazement, the book had seven pages, but what surprised her even more was that she understood every word. *The last page she'd read, the fourth one that didn't seem to do anything initially, was the key to understanding them all.*

Mary hurried, making the best use of her limited time. Perhaps she could learn something to put it all together, like making the wooden beads on page one. *They must come in handy, but I don't know why.*

Page two: *Knock-out medicine sounds dangerous.*

Page three: *The changing of clothes.* She remembered that one.

Page four: *The ability to read the language in which the book was written.*

Page five: *How to tell if someone is a virgin or not, whatever that means.*

Page six: *The ability to make people obedient.* That was the spell that turned the women into submissives.

Page seven: *Immunity. A-ha. In the name of Allemand, leave_____ impervious to the weave of enchantments.*

Mary read the seventh spell aloud and added her name. Before leaving, she reread the sixth page and said Gideon's name in case he wasn't caught up with his reading. Short on time, she closed the book, put it back, locked the shed, and ran through the trees until she emerged at the back of the house.

Gideon was in the kitchen looking more tired than she had ever seen him. Testing, Mary asked him if he needed anything and stared into his eyes. He shook his head no. "The goat's pen hasn't been raked yet," said Mary.

"All right. I'll be back." Gideon went straight to the barn, fetched the rake, and went to work. Mary smiled for the first time in years, wondering what the women would say if they saw him raking. Feeling victorious, Mary returned the key to the nail behind his bedroom door, took out her last strip of dried beef, and enjoyed the chore-free afternoon, wondering who Allemand was and where the book came from.

CHAPTER 84

1846

Weeks passed, and the next time Mary tried the obedience spell, it didn't work. *He'd caught up on his reading.* Having exempted herself, Mary played along, busier than ever, spending most of her time caring for Alice and the others as they suffered Gideon's manipulations. Mary was concerned. Alice looked as if she had aged twenty years in a matter of weeks.

Mary stole away to the shed whenever possible. She reread the first page with the wooden beads and made almost twenty more. With no idea what they were for, Mary found a spot by the corner of the house and buried them until she learned their purpose. She rechecked the book for answers, but only one new page had appeared, and it had nothing to do with beads.

Spell number eight was the ability to kill something and make it decompose immediately, but Mary saw no need for it. *Who needs that?* Then she remembered the noisy goat she had to kill and understood.

One afternoon, Mary tried it on a chicken. Only sixteen were on the property, so this would be her only chance. She scooped the bird by the feet, flapping and squawking, and sprinted to the forest side of the shed. Along the way, feathers flew, leaving a trail to her exact location. Angry, Mary pointed at the bird and tried the spell, but it didn't go well. Decomposition was spotty at best.

The bird was cooked in some spots and untouched in others. Maggots filled the eye sockets, and the carcass stunk. Reading a page was not like checking a box. Quality mattered, and practice made perfect. Hurriedly, Mary scooped up the mess and disposed of it in the woods. When she returned, she cleaned up every feather.

Two days later, nobody seemed to miss the chicken, so, with ice in her veins, she selected another. This time, she didn't bother taking it behind the shed but forced her will on it in front of the barn. The second bird dropped silently, its head slumped as if pressed by an invisible hand. Like the first chicken, the decaying process began before her eyes. It seemed to deflate but stopped halfway. Suddenly, little Edward, Cora's son, appeared.

"What's wrong with her?" he asked.

"It's a disease," she replied. "You'd better run." Edward was afraid of Mary, so he did. Angry, Mary grabbed the mess and threw it in the woods, where a chattering squirrel scaled a tree and paused to watch. Still simmering, Mary, staring intently, focused her ire and made it fall to the ground dead. Once over the carcass, she continued to concentrate, reducing the squirrel to a tail and a skull.

Savoring the crumb of satisfaction, Mary sat on a fallen log, exhausted. It wouldn't have worked if she had tried this on anything larger than a squirrel. Mary knew she had to return soon, but she needed a minute. Head dizzy, she wondered, *what next?*

This skill would be hard to perfect. It would be nice to melt Gideon's face, but she would need to practice on a herd of cattle to become that proficient. He was much too big and could probably turn around and do the same to her with better results. Head pounding, Mary decided to shelve the decomposition spell for now.

CHAPTER 85

1847

Fall turned to winter, and footprints in the snow made trips to the shed tricky. Luckily, it was not a harsh winter, and the ground was a bed of dead grass for long stretches. The turf was frozen, too, meaning Mary would not leave impressions, which was even better. Springtime would be a different story if they stayed that long. She would have to make the most of her opportunities now. Six additional pages appeared in the book before Gideon caught her.

The ninth spell was fun. Mary learned to create sounds and distractions. The first time she tried, it was on her mother, a simple crash in the kitchen as she was told to get ready for bed. The best was scaring little Edward with horse whinnies when no one else was around. She pretended not to hear the horse and convinced him he was crazy.

The tenth spell was the ability to detect a weapon on a person. The eleventh spell was the ability to call something to your hand as long as you knew its location. The first time, Mary tried it out in the privacy of her bedroom while her mother was outside. First, she set a button on her bureau, then, standing five feet away, called to it with her hand, and it rolled itself from between her fingers.

The button did not fly through the air but appeared like a sleight of hand trick. Mary tried it with success several times. Either it was an easy spell, or she was good at it because there was never a drop or a fumble. Mary watched closely for the exact moment the button entered her hand, but it was impossible. It happened as she moved. *Fascinating.*

From there, she experimented with distance. Mary placed the button a hundred yards in the forest, remembered where it was, and returned to her bedroom. When she moved her wrist, it worked. For the next several days, she tormented poor Edward by repeatedly leaving his teddy bear in front of the barn where it could be trampled. Cora scolded him twice, and

Edward protested, scratching his head, swearing he had never taken the bear from the bedroom. On the third day, however, Alice asked Mary if she was the one stealing the bear and thus ended the pranking.

Mary was not done with the spell, however. It worked with anything: A stick, a comb, a nail, and even a pumpkin. It took extra concentration, but she learned to call them one after the other, and as she practiced, her speed increased. Mary liked it so much she stole a long kitchen knife from the kitchen and brought it into the woods. At the base of a large oak, she stuck the knife into the ground and, with her shoe, pushed the weapon into the forest floor, blade, handle, and all.

Mary read two more spells she never got to experiment with because she ran out of time. The twelfth spell was the ability to make a dead body look like it had died from natural causes, but she wasn't sure she understood. *Does that mean the body is mangled?* It was hard to imagine a scenario where it could be used.

The thirteenth spell was the ability to shut the body down for long periods to hibernate. It wasn't clear how long, but Mary sensed it could be for years.

CHAPTER 86

1847

On a cold night in February, Mary snuck out of her bedroom again, as always, being careful not to wake Alice. Gideon was in Salem selling brooms again, and Mary was hungry. All day, she'd looked forward to the beef strips and whatever new information awaited her in the Book. Hopefully, there would be a fourteenth chapter.

Mary, now twelve years old, was in good health, as was her magick. She knew that Gideon enjoyed the benefits of the Book, too, but she would have the element of surprise when the time came. She would practice to perfection and, when the moment arrived, stab him between the ribs with the blade she'd hidden in the forest.

Mary unlocked the shed, let herself in, covered the window with the black farm dress, and helped herself to two beef strips. She savored the taste, so good compared to the mush the rest of the camp survived on. Guilty with the thought, she put the last bite on the bench and picked up the Book. To her excitement, there were three new pages.

Mary began to read and realized a third of the way down the page that there was a fatal problem. She would have to escape tonight, whether prepared or not. Her heart sank. The fourteenth spell allowed the reader to identify a mortal involved in the study of magick. As soon as Gideon obtained this information, he would know Mary was practicing.

Does Gideon already know? Of course not. If he had, he wouldn't be in Salem, she rationalized. She decided to rip the page out of the book to be safe, but first, she finished reading. Upon completing the last word, Mary heard a gentle *ping* inside her head. Instinctively, she looked around. Mary had brought the lamp to the bench to read by, leaving the back of the room dark.

There, on the floor, poking into the light were the tips of two riding boots.

Gideon sat in the back corner, watching her every move. He must have caught up with his reading and figured her out. Most likely, he knew more than she did now.

"That's a useful spell, isn't it, Mary? Don't you wish you'd read it first? I didn't realize you had been undermining me, but I can't say I'm surprised. We never really liked each other, did we?"

Mary, heart pounding, said nothing.

"There are some new pages you won't get to read—good, powerful stuff. You won't read them, but you'll feel them. Some of it looks painful, too, and you'll be my guinea pig."

Mary realized things would never be the same. *How will he hurt me without Mother knowing? Will he kill her too?* With her last free thought, Mary decided to fight. Gideon stepped forward to grab her, and the knife appeared in her right hand. She stabbed, connecting with his bicep. Gideon howled as he lunged and swatted the knife away before crashing on top of her. Mary couldn't move her arms.

With Mary immobilized underneath him, Gideon fumbled for something on the bench above. In rapid-fire, a stick, a hammer, and a pair of scissors all found her hand but fell to the floor as he crushed her wrist, causing her to cry out. "Mary, you've been busy! How long have you known?"

Incapacitated, Mary paused her struggle to focus on Gideon's face, attempting the decomposition spell, but he felt it right away and slapped her hard.

"I don't like people I can't read. You're a cold fish, little Mary." With that, Gideon scooped the runes from the top of the bench, rolled them in his hands, and pressed them hard into her face. One fell to the floor, but Mary felt the effects immediately. There was great pain as the cubes indented her skin. She tried to turn, but Gideon's arms, even the one she stabbed, overpowered her frail neck.

Defeated, Mary's last act of defiance before passing out was to send the kitchen knife back to its home in the woods. Hopefully, she would get another chance to use it.

When it was over, Gideon picked up the runes and returned them to the bench. Mary lay on the floor as if sleeping, and there were no burns or welts as he had suspected there might. It was fortuitous to have a test subject. Tonight would be the first of many such nights.

Gideon opened the dried beef and took a bite. He hated to waste even a scrap of it on the girl, but to make things look right, he placed the uneaten half-strip in her hand and grabbed the Book of Shadows. After reading the sixteenth spell to heal his arm, Gideon flipped back a page and made Mary forget everything that had happened.

"In the name of Allemand, turn the clock back ten minutes." Finally, he hid the book under a floorboard and left.

Mary woke up cold on the shed floor, wondering how she had gotten there. She pocketed the strip in her hand to dispose of it later. Her head was dizzy, but she felt better when she patted her dress pocket and felt the key.

What was he up to? The only thing out here was a stash of food he wasn't sharing with his flock. She couldn't remember passing out, which was very dangerous. He had to have laced the food. She would never touch it again. Tragically, Mary never knew that Gideon caught her.

CHAPTER 87

1847

The following day, Gideon was curious to see Mary's reaction. He'd watched her leave the shed and sneak back into the house, so he knew where she was, but what was on her mind? Would she remember anything? Or would she remember everything and cause a scene?

He chose a chair in the den with a clear view of the staircase and waited. Alice descended the stairs at a few minutes past four, followed by Mary. When Mary's foot hit the second stair, Gideon heard a gentle pinging sound. He had forgotten the fourteenth spell, the ability to detect a human practicing magick. They could detect each other.

"Mother, what's that noise?"

"What noise, Mary?"

Gideon got up and went outside. It was such an odd skill to have. Why the hell had they invented it? Under these circumstances, it was a nuisance. He would have to avoid Mary during the day. And what about at night? He would have to restrain her before she figured out he was why she heard the tones, then erase her memory after every meeting, a tedious, if not risky, endeavor.

CHAPTER 88

1850

Three years went by as Gideon experimented on Mary almost nightly. It was easier than expected to abduct her before she realized what the ping was. *It even distracted her from the attack*, he thought. On nights he was away in town, he would hide everything of value and leave her to discover a worthless shed.

Despite Gideon's dislike of her, it wasn't long before familiarity softened her looks, and he began to want her. Gideon, unhappy with seven more years to wait for immortality, took his frustrations out on Mary, now fourteen. She wasn't pretty, but she would do. Now, he had someone to take out his frustrations on. The best part was he didn't even have to fetch her.

Mary's body shrank back to its malnourished state. Her ribs began to show, her eyes sank into their sockets, and her hair became stringy. Alice, empty-headed, thought she was looking at Margaret one day as she crossed the yard. Alice called out to ask if the sick woman was feeling better, as she had been suffering from pneumonia. When the woman turned, however, it wasn't Margaret at all. It was her daughter. As much as she wanted to forget what she saw, Alice couldn't put it out of her mind.

CHAPTER 89

1851

That night, Mary set out for the shed, unaware of the waiting danger. Gideon's memory wipes worked flawlessly, and although she had been to the shed a thousand times, she had no idea.

Mary hugged the tree line amongst the shadows, practically tiptoeing, eyes glued to the shed door, ready to duck into the forest at a moment's notice. When she smelled something rotten, she kept moving, not seeing the revenant before he clamped his hand over her mouth and pulled her into the woods.

A half-mile in, Helms and two more revenants waited in a small clearing. The two helpers each took one of Mary's arms while the kidnapping revenant kept his hand over her mouth. Helms held his copy of the Book of Shadows. Mary couldn't see in the darkness and was naturally terrified. The smell was terrible.

"Hello, Mary, my private precaution. Don't worry, we'll be quick." Helms opened the book and read aloud. His words made no sense. *Is that a foreign language?* When he was done, he erased five minutes from her memory and left.

Mary woke in the barnyard, worried she had passed out on her way to the shed. If Gideon had found her, it would have been disastrous. Shaken, she ran back to the house, unsure what time it was. Rattled, she snuck back into bed and tried to sleep.

CHAPTER 90

1851

Gideon waited in the shed, but Mary didn't show. The next day, he found her alone in the kitchen, peeling a potato.

"What's that noise?" she said.

"Never mind that. What are you doing?"

"Peeling a potato," she answered.

He stared, formulating his next question. It didn't matter what he asked; Mary was alone, and he could easily erase her memory again.

"Where were you last night?"

"In bed with my mother. Where was I supposed to be?" Gideon ignored her and left the house, wondering what had happened, but he would have to wait. He couldn't tell if their little routine was truly broken until tomorrow.

CHAPTER 91

1851

Alice, too weak-minded to plan an escape, did nothing to help Mary for two years when, one crisp autumn afternoon, she saw Mary exit the shed. What's she doing? She shouldn't be in there. Mary walked with her head low, similar to when Alice had mistaken her for sickly Margaret. Was she wiping away tears?

"Mary! Are all you all right? What are you doing in there?" Alice dropped her rake, rushed to Mary, and hugged her.

Mary stared straight through her.

"Mary, are you sick?"

Mary shook her head, and suddenly, the shed door opened. Gideon emerged, adjusting his belt, and his eyes met Alice's. All at once, the haze clouding Alice's mind evaporated. Her only daughter was in danger.

CHAPTER 92

1851

Mary was like a zombie, and Alice, even weaker, couldn't bear it. She was in no position to play rescuer. For Alice, the past forty-eight hours had been about planning, and the stress was overwhelming. Before bed, she confronted Mary. "You're not leaving for the shed tonight, darling. I've made plans."

Mary's stare was vacant. She'd gone numb, and Alice blamed herself.

"At midnight, we'll walk out to the main road. I've arranged for the hay man to take us to Lowell. He knows people there who can help us." Mary didn't react.

Alice put her daughter to bed and shut the door. She felt ill and started a coughing fit. More than anything, Alice was worried about nodding off and missing the pickup. She would have to stay awake, which was nearly impossible in her state. Six years of malnutrition, the death of her eldest daughter, and Mary's bombshell had taken their toll.

Mary heard her mother's directions and stayed awake, knowing Alice was in no shape. The minutes crept by as she stared at the wall, nervous. A half-hour to go, and they were leaving for good.

Just then, Alice began to cough hard, and Mary sat up. *Was it enough to wake Gideon? Would he hear the hay man's horse?* Since they were both awake, they might as well leave now. Suddenly, Alice stopped coughing. Mary poked her, but Alice didn't move. Mary poked again, but nothing. Quietly, she put her ear to her mother's mouth. Ten seconds, twenty, thirty.

Alice was gone. Mary had planned to unlock and explore Gideon's shed while he slept, but her mother had surprised her with a plan that stirred real hope. Now, Alice was dead and would have to be left behind.

Mary would have to find the hay man without her. Goodbye tears poured down her face as Mary gathered her things. Finally, she kissed her mother on the forehead, mouthed *I love you*, and slipped out.

CHAPTER 93

1851

Helms waited by the end of the driveway, and Desjardins signaled that the girl was moving for the road instead of the shed. Helms perked up. Was she escaping? That was a surprise, but it would fit his plan perfectly. The straw poll was 6 to 5 in Gideon's favor, so he was still on track for immortality, but Helms' was one of the five dissenters. He wanted a secret weapon in case Gideon became dangerous, and someone who hated him like Mary did was the perfect fit.

As Mary passed his hiding place on the way to find the hay man, Helms leaped out, grabbed her by the neck. Mary stifled her scream, knowing only Gideon Walker would come running, and she didn't want his help.

"Don't fight. Listen carefully." Helms recited the spell, wiped five minutes from her memory, and disappeared into the woods. Mary ran down the road as if Helms had never been there.

CHAPTER 94

1851

Mary cried until the hay wagon entered Middleton. The hay man heard her sobs, and his heart went out to her. As soon as they hit North Andover, she fell silent. *She must finally be sleeping,* he thought.

Mary fumed all the way to Lowell, grieving for her mother and sister. This was not a time to be weak. She would never forgive Gideon Walker, who had taken everything from her. Perhaps one day, they would meet again under different circumstances.

The hay man left Mary at a street market with two well-worn Liberty quarters donated in sympathy. Looking to erase any possibility of Gideon following her, the next thing Mary did was find another farmer.

This one was from New Hampshire, selling wool to the textile mill. With only the two quarters to offer, she persuaded him to take her with him. Because the farmer didn't want anyone in his hometown to see him with a young woman, he left her off in the small town of Sanborn.

The first thing she did was search for steeples. Mary spent the entire first day visiting the only two churches in town, looking for shelter and help in general. When they asked for her surname, she used Clara's so that Gideon could not track her. She pondered using Sarah or Alice for her Christian name but decided against it.

After deliberating, she found the perfect name, going all the way back to her family's farm in Pennsylvania. It was the last place they'd all been together: Elmer, Alice, Sarah, Mary—and her doll, Millie.

CHAPTER 95

1851

Mary escaped, and Gideon Walker was beside himself. If she went to the marshal, he was in trouble, and he would have to work his way out of another jam or risk the wrath of Helms. It would be tricky, but no crimes could be proven. Thanks to the memory wipes, there were no witnesses to anything.

Alice was gone, taken by Helms, and disposed of. If Mary returned, he would deny her claims and memory wipe everyone on-scene, including the marshal. As far as the authorities were concerned, the remaining followers were devotees, here on their own accord.

The rapes, well, they hadn't occurred as long as the memory spell worked in perpetuity. But if it didn't, it was Gideon's word against hers. The six souls abducted by Helms as part of their original deal never existed, at least not in Massachusetts. Maybe Pennsylvania, but the police were not set up for interstate investigations. Gideon would pass inspection, but avoiding it would be better.

He considered hunting Mary and consulted Helms, who told him he would look around and keep him abreast of the situation. Perhaps there was no reason to worry. Still, the loose end bothered him. No one had ever left.

CHAPTER 96

1852

Mildred Wells began her new life by helping her foster parents run their farm, and in the evenings, she homeschooled. William and Claudia Downing were concerned that Mildred was abnormally gaunt and had gone through something traumatic, but the girl wouldn't discuss it. For the longest time, she would barely leave her bedroom. The night terrors were horrific.

Mildred blocked out her past to the point that she forgot her old name. Mary was gone, and in her place, Mildred. Mildred shut the door on Mary's past until she was in better shape, mentally. It was all too painful. Everyone she cared about was dead.

When Mildred regained some weight, the Downings began to take her into town and socialize, slowly introducing her to the townspeople. By April of 1852, Mildred had opened up considerably. Winter was over, and the change of seasons boosted her spirits. The nightmares were, for the most part, gone. The alter ego had protected little Mary and helped her heal. The confidence that she was under the care of a loving family began paying dividends, too.

One day, on one of her trips into town with her foster father, Mildred noticed a tall gentleman in the baking aisle of Philbrick & Mull. Five minutes later, they not-so-coincidentally bumped into each other and struck up a conversation. His name was Thomas Pike.

Thomas was the son of Herman and Charlotte Pike, who owned the local sawmill. He attended the Sanborn School and was sure to inherit his father's fortune when the time came. For the first time, Mildred knew she wanted to start a family.

Thomas swept her off her feet and vice versa. Mildred, now healthy and sporting girl-next-door looks, turned on the charm. Her adoptive parents were overjoyed. Their depressed little girl had a lighter, funnier side.

The girls in competition for Thomas's affections quickly fell by the wayside. By September, he asked Mildred for her hand in marriage. Sixteen was young, but the girl knew what she wanted, and her powers of persuasion were almost supernatural.

CHAPTER 97

1854

Mildred gave birth to a son, whom they named Elmer, after her father. To her shock, however, she felt disappointment—but having a boy was not the end of the world, she told herself. They could try again. Thomas, Mildred, and Elmer lived with Thomas' parents while Thomas finished school, and Mildred spent most of her time attempting to bond with little Elmer.

The plan was that after Thomas graduated, he would work in the sawmill and learn the trade. While he worked, they would save for a place of their own. Life slowed after the whirlwind courtship and wedding. Motherhood was hard work, and the mother-son duo struggled. Mildred hoped a little girl in the mix would be just the trick.

They tried, but nothing happened, and Mildred's spirits took a nosedive. She skipped meals, and the circles under her eyes, last seen on Gideon Walker's farm, returned. Claudia Downing became concerned about her foster daughter, who was not acting like the Mildred she had worked so hard to fix. The mood swings were hard on the whole family.

One night, after another tedious day, Mildred had a dream. In it, a bearded man was on top of her as she tried to free her arms to scratch at his eyes, but he was too strong and heavy.

Mildred woke screaming, adding to the troubled Pike family's woes. Even Elmer heard her from his bedroom. No one slept the rest of the night. Unlike most dreams, this one never faded, even into the next day. Mildred picked at it like a mental scab. The scene seemed real, like déjà vu. She could still see the details in the ceiling over the man's head.

Adding to Thomas' discontent, Mildred withdrew even more, and it was hard to get more than a dozen words out of her on any given day.

As the months passed, Mildred had more dreams, and Thomas moved to the guest bedroom so at least one of them would be rested. Despite his designs, however, he heard her through the wall, not only the startled awakenings but the hours of pacing that followed. He begged her to try sleeping pills, but she shrugged him off, growing paler and more gaunt as the memories she'd buried trickled back.

CHAPTER 98

1855

In early December, Thomas woke in the middle of the night to Mildred standing in his bedroom doorway.

"What's wrong, love? Can't sleep again?" Thomas' heart skipped a beat. It was the first time Mildred bothered him. Thomas noted that she was fully dressed. "Have you slept?" Something by her waist glimmered in the ambient light, and Thomas couldn't make it out. Mildred said nothing but stared, her eye sockets deeper and darker than he remembered.

Thomas sat up, worried. "Mildred, you need sleep. Nothing is good without sleep. Please, let me call the doctor, and he can help you." The thing by her waist moved, and he saw that she was holding a kitchen knife so large he knew it didn't belong to them. Thomas felt his heart rise into his throat. Mildred was not well. "What's that you have there, love?"

Mildred tucked the knife behind her back.

Thomas threw the covers back and approached with caution, never taking his eyes from the blade. "Give me the knife, Mildred, before you hurt yourself. Please, let me help you." Thomas grabbed her arms and pulled them from behind her back, but her hands were empty. When he didn't find the knife, he spun her around, expecting to find it tucked into her apron string, but it wasn't there. "Where is it, Mildred?"

"Where is what, Thomas?" said Mildred.

"The knife. Whose is it, and where did you get it?"

"I don't know what you're talking about." He patted her down one more time, and Mildred didn't flinch.

Was the light playing tricks on him? Thomas couldn't be sure. It was late, and they were all sleep-deprived. "I thought I saw you holding something. Are you all right, darling? Would you like to come to bed with me?"

"I wouldn't want to disturb you. I had another nightmare, that's all— same old thing. I just wanted to look in on you."

"You wouldn't be disturbing me, Millie, really—anything to help you get the rest you need. We're happy when you're happy. You know that, right?"

"I know that Thomas. I think I can sleep now. Kiss me, and I'll leave."

"You don't have to go, you know," said Thomas.

"I might wake up screaming again."

"All right then, love. Go and rest."

"I will. Thank you, Thomas."

"Good night, my love," said Thomas, shaken.

Mildred returned to her room, overwhelmed. Tonight's nightmare was the worst yet, and, in her panic, she'd awakened to find a knife in her hand. The dam had broken, and she remembered everything. The magick, the shed, the Book … and Gideon Walker.

CHAPTER 99

1856

Ten years crept by for Gideon Walker, along with eighteen risky abductions. He planned them out at two per year on a map to make them appear unrelated. Salem was crossed off the list for good because he had already stolen from that community. The Georgetown abduction got messy when the child's parents saw him in their barn, and he had to kill them. That wasn't good. It was big news and relatively close to home.

Gideon had to take a roundabout way home to minimize the odds of getting caught. As he rode, he cursed Lyman Helms. The Book of Shadows had stopped growing, and he wondered if it was because they were changing the deal. When he asked about it, he was given a vague answer:

"Much of the book has to do with your afterlife," Helms had told him.

Still, he practiced, mastering the pages he'd been given, and it became boring. A child could do them, as he had witnessed. "I have delivered sixteen children, with only eight more to go over five years. I have mastered what portion of the book you've shared with me. Why must I wait? I have more than proven myself."

"Because impatience kills. It even got Allemand killed, and he was the man who wrote the Book. We don't care about your agenda. Many skills we haven't shared focus on removing bloodlust. When you get there, you will understand. You wouldn't let a newcomer get you killed because he was too eager, would you?"

CHAPTER 100

1859

At Christmastime in 1859, Herman and Charlotte Pike gifted Thomas and Mildred a twenty-three-acre parcel of undeveloped land. In the coming spring, Herman would send employees from the sawmill to build the home and plant a timber grove. For the first time in forever, Mildred seemed to cheer up. Quietly, everyone was relieved.

Winter came and went. Supplies were ordered, and plans were made. Little Elmer was six years old, no longer the needy baby that had been so hard on his mother. Still, the two seemed at odds.

Ground broke on the house during the last week of March while the earth was still thawing. Construction went swiftly with the help of the mill employees, and they raised the barn in late April. Mildred grinned for the first time in forever as things began to take shape. She hadn't lived in a house like this since her childhood in Pennsylvania.

While the men worked on the framing, she helped plant seeds for the grove. She took Elmer to the pond and watched him try to catch bullfrogs. Thomas saw them together and came home the next evening with a brand-new rowboat to encourage more of the same. By mid-June of 1860, they moved in, with the interior only half finished.

June was a great month, as were July, August, and September, but in October 1860, there were rumors that a war might begin should Abraham Lincoln be elected president. Mildred's opinion was that Thomas paid too much attention to the newspapers. He began to speak of things like patriotism and the abolishment of slavery as if they had any effect on the people of Sanborn.

Her recall of the lost Gideon years had put her through hell, and Mildred could empathize with the enslaved but she couldn't help but think selfishly. She didn't want anything to jeopardize the freedom she had now, and she worried about Thomas. His commentary turned passionate, and she pushed back. He was a husband and father with, hopefully, more children to come. She implored him to stay focused on the family.

To Mildred's displeasure, Lincoln was elected, states began seceding, and Thomas became more vocal. Some of the men who had helped them build their home were of color and lifelong employees of his father's mill. Wesley and Abel were friends, practically family.

By February, word spread that the Union Army was organizing, and two of the sawmill employees who helped build the house were talking about signing up. Mildred continued to hope for a second pregnancy. At the same time, Thomas stopped talking about the tension between the North and South, and Mildred wondered if he was hiding it from her.

On April 23, 1861, Thomas came home late from the sawmill, looking guilty, and Mildred knew. "Did you do it?"

Thomas scowled, searching for words.

"You damn well did, didn't you! You volunteered! Look at me, Thomas Pike. Look at me!"

Thomas met her eyes. "Slavery is wrong, Mildred, they—"

"Slavery. What about your family? Is it right to abandon us so you can feel good about yourself? I can't do this."

Thomas tried to respond, but she wasn't listening. He saw her face and knew there were no more words, and then suddenly, she had his hatchet. For a moment, Thomas thought someone would get hurt, but instead, she left the kitchen as Elmer bounded down the stairs. Thomas heard the front door slam and went to the window.

Mildred crossed the driveway and down the front lawn, headed for the pond. Within moments, she snagged two Canada geese with her bare hands and slaughtered them messily on the stone wall. When she was done, Mildred picked up the bodies and returned to the house, stopping in front of the kitchen window, the headless birds still flapping.

When Mildred saw Thomas in the window, she dropped the hatchet and raised the geese high, spraying herself crimson. In the horror, Thomas had forgotten about Elmer, who stood under his right arm.

"Why is she doing that? She looks scary!" Thomas shielded Elmer's eyes and pulled him from the window. Mildred's mental condition was worse than he'd feared, and he began to regret his enlistment.

As the wings of the geese pumped, Mildred, soaked in blood, put both birds in one hand and picked up the hatchet. As she approached the porch door, Thomas took Elmer's arm and went in the opposite direction toward the side door.

"Elmer, come outside with me. We'll get you upstairs to clean up for dinner. While you're doing that, I want to talk to Mommy for a few minutes, okay?" Elmer did as he was told and followed his father outside, around the front of the house and where Mildred was, and through the front door nearest the road. Thomas ensured Elmer was upstairs before turning to face Mildred in the kitchen.

"Mildred, what are you doing?" The kitchen walls were splattered as the birds' death spasms faded. Mildred stood, her back to him, cutting something. A pot came to a bubble on the stove. When Mildred didn't respond, Thomas pressed. "Mildred, talk to me. Are you ill? You're scaring Elmer. Hold it together for his sake, please!" His eyes searched the kitchen, and the hatchet was missing. "Do you need help?"

Mildred stopped chopping and turned, speaking in a voice Thomas barely recognized. "What have I done, Thomas? Cooked dinner?"

"It's not that, Mildred. It's the way—"

"Don't worry about us, Thomas. We'll be fine. You're free to die in the war."

"It's only for three months, and then I'll be back. It's for Wesley and Abel. I've known them my entire life."

"You won't be back," she replied.

Thomas felt a knot in his stomach, worried for his son. Perhaps his parents could keep a close watch. He would be back. Mildred turned her back and began plucking feathers. It was nearly eight o'clock. Thomas knew slaughtering the geese in front of him was not about dinner, but he quit the argument and backed out of the room.

CHAPTER 101

1861

Mildred didn't speak to Thomas for two days, but he was scheduled to report for training in Concord the following day, and there had to be closure. When Herman and Charlotte showed up to wish him luck, Mildred put on a show that embarrassed everyone.

Mildred exaggerated her persona, three times more extroverted than Thomas had ever seen her. She dominated the conversation, which was off-balance at best. Nearing the end of the farewell, she cried for all to see. The worst part, however, was when Mildred burst out the front door, attempting to block his horse, running beside him, tugging his sleeve for the length of the lawn.

As Thomas rode, his last words were pleas to his parents. "Please help Mildred with Elmer."

Mildred finished the episode by collapsing at the end of the driveway as he rode away. When he was gone, she picked herself up and walked into the house as if it was just another day.

CHAPTER 102

1861

Gideon Walker delivered the twenty-fourth innocent to Helms four months shy of the ten-year mark, but still, they made him wait. Nervous, he found things to occupy his time rather than ponder his glorious day fast approaching. Still, paranoia whispered in his ear. *What if they pass me over?*

Helms would surely make him wait longer if he asked again, so Gideon kept his mouth shut. When the anniversary arrived, Gideon woke before dawn, walked to the forest's edge, and peered in as far as he could see. All was quiet. *It's going to be a long day. Find something to do.*

Noon came and went, and Gideon checked his watch for the thousandth time. At one point, he imagined it was all a scam and envisioned Helms laughing at his expense. If so, they would pay. *Somehow,* he would make them pay. Anguished, Gideon retired to the shed.

When it came time to feed the women, Gideon skipped his customary sermon and left the table, surprising the compound. After telling them to finish and clean up, he put on his coat and took another walk along the tree line, desperate for a sign the revenants would honor their agreement.

At last, a twig snapped behind him, and he whirled. A revenant he had never seen stepped out of the woods and began following him. Gideon stopped. "Where's Helms?" The revenant pointed into the woods, and Gideon followed. *It was finally happening.*

Visibility was good this time of year because the leaves had fallen, but the sun was setting, and it would soon be dark. If this weren't his long-awaited ceremony, it would be his end. *Either way, I die,* he mused.

The revenants appeared, almost as parts of the forest, ten in number, with an eleventh behind him. *I make them an even dozen,* he thought. *This is it.* He kept silent so as not to spoil anything.

"Good evening, Walker. What brings you here?" said Helms, and some of the revenants chuckled.

"Hello, Helms. Hello, everyone. I've been waiting a long time. Not just today, I mean, but—" he stumbled on his words, shaking. He was, after all, supposed to die if all went well.

Helms spoke: "Ten years can be a long wait for the living, but time means nothing to the dead. We've all been in your shoes, Walker. Tonight is the end of your wait, but I have bad news for you."

Gideon's stomach sank. *Don't do this, Helms.*

"We voted, and you did not pass muster." Helms stared, eyes piercing.

Gideon didn't have time to get angry. The surrounding revenants shifted, and the woods went still. He stepped back, unsure if Helms was done talking. "What are you saying? I delivered! I gave you the twenty-four! I waited for ten years!" No one moved, and Gideon saw a blade shimmer in the dying light.

They sprang at once, covering the distance between them in an instant. Helms got to him first, nose to nose, and Gideon felt his blade beneath his sternum travel up. Gideon gasped, eyes bulging, and the air escaped his lungs as the others joined in. Knives flashed, and everyone took their cut. Gideon Walker was dead within a minute.

Gideon opened his eyes, and they filled with dirt. He was immobile, pressed from all sides, and a twinge of claustrophobia struck him as he attempted to breathe—yet he wasn't suffocating. His mind drifted, reawakening, and Gideon recalled what had happened: the betrayal. Like waking from a nightmare, it took a moment to discern what was real and what was not, and a moment later, he realized. His induction ceremony did not go as expected.

But he was a revenant now. He'd still be dead if he weren't. Their knives had perforated him, stabbing every vital organ except his heart. Despite this, he felt no pain, and the threat of claustrophobia subsided. They murdered him, then buried him, as promised. It was all a hazing prank, and he had become one of them. Now, his climb to power could begin. The first step was to dig himself out.

Gideon wiggled his thumb, then his hand. His arms were more powerful than they had been as a human. The left arm broke the surface as the right arm worked to catch up. The legs kicked, and at last, he stood, dirt clods falling from his clothing. The whole process took two days, and when he was out, he checked his wounds, pleased to find only scars. Finally, a voice called out:

"Welcome back," said Helms.

Gideon turned his head, managing a smile. "Any more surprises?"

"Did you enjoy it? We thought we'd bring you over in style."

"I'm sure you enjoyed it more than I did. I can't say I've been the butt of many jokes."

"It was your rite of passage. Webb stuck you through the temple before you could feel anything."

Gideon rubbed his temple and felt the scar. "How long was I dead?" he asked.

"Two days," said Helms.

CHAPTER 103

1861

Now that he was one of them, Gideon was invited to a cave in the middle of the forest. The entrance was small and discreet, but the inside opened wide. There was nothing to light the space, yet he could see perfectly.

"Is this our headquarters?" he asked.

"Yes and no," said Helms. "We've been here forty-nine years. After Allemand died, they came for us. We used to live in a house on the outskirts of Salem."

They were downgraded, thought Gideon. *They live like wild animals.* "Do all eleven of you live here?"

"Of course not. We don't sleep, so no one needs a room unless you take an extended break. Your body will require downtime now and again. It will deteriorate if you do not. Coordinated breaks are recommended, but sleep is no longer daily." Helms ducked under a threshold and led him into a larger room. Jars, baskets, and canisters were everywhere, filled with bones sorted by type—leftovers of missing humans.

"We waste nothing. The blood and the organs decompose, so we use them first. Bones last forever. Some spells call for bones. When we need them, we come here."

"Where is the original Book of Shadows?" asked Gideon.

Helms looked at him sideways. "I was about to show you," then led Gideon into the next room. Only two items were there: the Book and the table it sat on.

It doesn't look extraordinary, Gideon thought. "Is this the whole thing? All of the pages?" He opened it and began skimming. "Thirty or so?"

"Those thirty pages are four centuries of work, Walker. If you think you can add something of value, then take your shot. Allemand himself put together all but three of the spells. Crafting is a lengthy and tedious process."

Gideon expected more. *They're primitive*, he thought, *still cave dwellers.* "I waited ten years for this?"

Helms grabbed his arm. "We're well aware you waited ten damned years. We did, too. Some waited longer. Two hours from the grave, and you're already complaining."

Gideon picked Helms' hand off his arm and pushed back. "Don't touch me, Helms."

Even though Gideon towered over him, Helms held his ground. *"Occlusis oculis,"* he chanted, dropping Gideon to his knees.

"I'm blind!" Gideon cried out.

"As I was saying, Gideon, there is much to learn. I have read the entire book, which you have judged by its cover. I've been practicing the spells in it for one hundred and thirty-four years. The difference is remarkable, wouldn't you agree? *Conversus in oculis vestris.*"

As soon as the spell was out of Helms' mouth, Gideon's sight returned. Humbled, he said nothing. Helms could have killed him right then. His grand plan would take longer than he realized.

CHAPTER 104

1863

Even after his death, Elmer was troublesome. He had a habit of attacking her fledgling relationships at their most vulnerable moment. First had been the Chief, then the editor, and then the lawyer. Elmer seemed to leave the casual ones alone, knowing they would never last, but as soon as one seemed to stick, his ghost would appear. He would never forgive her for that day at the pond.

She should never have placed both headstones at once. Now that Elmer was dead, he seemed to know everything. Mildred woke one night to his familiar dripping sound and left the bed, preparing to scold him, but as she entered the hallway, he'd already left, leaving another twenty-foot puddle soaking the floorboards.

Mildred followed, cursing. *Where did he go? Back to the cellar to bang his drum?* She would burn the damn thing as soon as the sun came up. As she reached the kitchen, the footsteps did not go down the cellar stairs but up to the turret. "Stay out of there! You'll soak the ceiling!" Mildred climbed after him, splashing on every stair, calling his name.

But Elmer wasn't in the turret. He was gone, and the desk had caught fire. Mildred grabbed a book and beat the flame out. The burning paper was her most recent Will with new instructions regarding her funeral and where she was to be buried.

"Stay out of my papers! Why on Earth are you messing with—" Mildred straightened up as she realized.

Thomas?

CHAPTER 105

1863

Mildred piled the last rocks atop the pine boards and brushed the dirt from her hands. *Any more weight and the planks will sway*, she thought. With one last look around, Mildred threw the tools into the grave and crawled in after them.

She couldn't ask anyone for help. Leaving a Will for Thomas to sabotage was a risk she couldn't take, and there was no magick she'd learned that could solve her problems. As soon as she was dead, they would be on a level playing field. No more chasing Elmer and begging for forgiveness. After death, she could guard their bones for an eternity. Mildred's heart raced as she closed her eyes and lit the match.

Hours later, after the grave collapsed, Mildred awakened, trapped beneath the stones and dirt. *Oh, God, no.* Had she buried herself alive? The weight caused no pain, but it forced her to think. She lay there, claustrophobic, and yet, she didn't need oxygen. *Was she alive or dead?*

As the hours passed, it was evident she had expired. No living person could survive this long. There was nothing to do but dig. With plenty of time to think, the questions mounted. Did Elmer have to dig out, too? *No.* His grave was undisturbed.

Two days later, Mildred's wiggling fingers became tunneling arms, onward and upward until finally, she broke the surface. She emerged from the grave bloated and ripe, and the flies found her in minutes. Free of her death bed, all thoughts went to Elmer. They were equals now, two ghosts with nothing but time to sort out their differences.

CHAPTER 106

1863

Lyman Helms trudged through the forest to check on Bardelli, his hibernating friend. The leaves had fallen, and visibility through the trees was good. Snow would fall soon, and he had to ensure Bardelli's resting place was still secure. It would be a quick trip, as Bardelli excelled at long sleeps.

Eight years ago, Bardelli had chosen the perfect spot between a maple tree and a stone wall for its impassibility and dug himself a proper pit. Before lying down, he planted seedlings near the head and foot to make his bed more difficult to walk over.

Helms heard something and stopped to listen. The only beings out this far were animals, revenants, and hunters. Hidden, he waited, and a minute later, a ragged figure rushed between the trees headed in his direction. *Desjardins*. After making sure Desjardins was not followed, Helms stood. "What are you doing?"

Desjardins stopped dead. "Where have you been? Have you checked your runes?"

Helms touched his pocket and felt the heat. Digging out the wooden cubes, he rolled them in his palm and began to count. Two revenants were sleeping, and eleven were up and around. *Thirteen?* At first, he was suspicious. Gideon Walker had been unnaturally quiet in the two years since their confrontation. But then, Helms remembered little Mary and the night she escaped Gideon's farm. "Poor girl," said Helms. "That was twelve years ago. She's already dead?"

Desjardins nodded. "Roughly thirty years old? Well, those problems are over. I imagine she's bewildered right about now. How long until she figures things out?"

"I don't know, but don't say a word. If you see Pratt or Sterritt, remind them, too. Bardelli's still sleeping. When the others find out, they'll have questions. Play dumb. Half of us voted Walker in."

"Do you know where she is?" asked Desjardins.

Helms shook his head. "No idea."

Word of the thirteenth revenant spread quickly. Nearly every one of the conscious revenants reported back except for McKenna, who was somewhere in Maine. Even Gideon Walker made his way back, wondering what it all meant. Gideon dropped his eyes as he addressed Helms. "What does this mean?"

"I don't know, but it has happened before. It is probably one of two things: somebody has the Book and converted a mortal without our authorization, or it is someone from overseas."

"Overseas?"

"Allemand came from Europe. He left several bastards, and they show up once a century or so. The runes can't read the whole world. The magick is not without limits."

"Who would convert someone? Would they be punished?"

"We keep our group to twelve, but there are rogues. I hope it's a European, but if so, I want to know why they're here. Keep a lookout."

CHAPTER 107

1865

Mildred spent most of her time hunting Elmer, but the boy continued to elude her even though they were both dead. He disappeared whenever he wanted, something she had yet to figure out, so she tracked his patterns. Every fifth day, Elmer would repeat himself, so every fifth day, she would know where to expect him. Mildred tried ambushing, but she still couldn't corner him. Perhaps this was her punishment. Maybe there was a higher power, and she had gotten it all wrong.

When Elmer's schedule became frustrating, Mildred developed one of her own. To relive the only happy years of her life, she created a mental calendar for things she had fond memories of.

One of those happy times was the barn raising. They were about to build the first house she could call her own back then. In her re-creation, she could even hear the hammering again as if it were 1860.

It was hard not to slip into darker thoughts. Every time she saw Gideon Walker's shape in her mind, she went hunting for Elmer. Her past could not be fixed. She had no control over it, but if she could fix her relationship with Elmer, maybe that would keep evil thoughts away.

Time passed, and rest eluded her. Elmer eluded her, too. Thomas was gone, probably resting in peace, which was a tough pill to swallow. Mildred wandered the woods, disheartened, wondering what came next. Suicide was no longer an option. Finally, one day, losing hope, Mildred dropped to her knees, curled into the fetal position, and listened to the forest. Oddly, she felt tired, which made no sense. She wished her body would dissolve into the aether.

Her mind foggy, Mildred rose and searched for a better place to lie down. It didn't have to be fancy. A bear cave. A coyote den. The grove. *Yes, the grove.* Beautiful and mysterious, she had always enjoyed the grove's dark magnificence. Letting the Christmas trees go wild was one of the best decisions she had ever made. The grove matched her mood almost every time. It was a hiding spot, a private perfection, and it would always be a part of her.

Mildred imagined the spade in the back of the barn and called it to her hand. It would be nice to dig a comfortable bed and lie down. Within ten minutes, she found a spot between four densely packed spruces and began the excavation. When she reached a comfortable depth, she gathered piles of fallen branches, creating a thick mound over the shallow hole. Over the deadwood, she threw bushels of natural mulch: leaves, sticks, briars, and stones.

When her task was complete, Mildred tunneled under the porous pile and lay down, pulling the earth over her, burying herself for the second time. At peace in her earthly cocoon, she closed her eyes and let her mind drift before slipping into deep sleep.

CHAPTER 108

1865

Helms checked his runes and saw that there were now three revenants hibernating. Was the third one Mary? Already? It had only been two years since her death. Aimless, he guessed. *She has no idea what's happened to her.*

For a moment, Helms felt guilty for the turmoil he'd inflicted on her, but then he justified it. *We might still need her. Trust your instincts. Walker is a man of ambition.*

Just then, Desjardins walked into the cave. "Did you see?"

Helms nodded. "Are we sure it's her? Did anyone else decide to take a break?"

Desjardins shook his head. "No. It's her. She must be lost. Probably depressed, laid down, and accidentally fell asleep. I wouldn't want to be in her shoes."

CHAPTER 109

1865-1875

While curious, Gideon was often seen studying after learning of the mysterious thirteenth revenant. Helms noticed that he seemed calmer than he used to be. Perhaps Gideon had matured, but Helms didn't think so. Two years later, after the excitement of the thirteenth sleeping walker faded, he began to disappear again.

In Helms' opinion, a revenant leader was no longer needed. The community was fluid and evolving. They were freelancers who sometimes joined forces. Helms, however, still suspected that Gideon might attempt to take control one day.

Helms voted against Gideon's inclusion, something the big man would probably find out sooner or later, but in the end, Helms and four others had been outvoted. Gideon Walker's potential, drive, and physical presence had swayed the other six to vote him in, but what bothered Helms the most was that Gideon's lust for power would set the group back fifty years. His ambitions, wherever they led the group, would change everything.

Helms shook the rune beads in his palm. It was October 1875, and he figured Gideon had been sleeping for two years. Two others, Bardelli and Thayer, were also sleeping. The remaining ten, including Mary, the thirteenth revenant, were awake, although their whereabouts were unknown.

Bardelli had been sleeping for eleven years, the victim of an experiment gone wrong. He was the most scientific of the group, often sacrificing health for the advancement of the race. He argued that time meant nothing and that testing new ideas was his calling. Allemand himself, after all, had taken extended absences for the same reason.

Bardelli had been working on a method to reverse decay, potentially paving the way to blending with the human population. With the offending odor neutralized, they would be nearly undetectable. Unfortunately for Bardelli, his spell had done the opposite, thus requiring the long rest. He would suspend the decay by shutting down, and in time, the healing would overcome the mistake.

Thayer had been asleep since Gideon was voted in but only required routine maintenance. Thayer was a reluctant revenant, still longing for the life he'd lived nearly two hundred years before. He took more breaks than the others, enjoying hibernation's escape. Thayer's whereabouts were unknown.

Gideon Walker had taken five rests in fourteen years, an unprecedented number. The first was after his first complete year, perhaps trying the spell on, but after that, he'd been asleep for five of the last six years. When the third sleeping revenant (Mary) showed in the runes as awakened, Helms sent word, and when Gideon caught wind, returned to meet with the group.

"Have you been busy, Walker? Working on your magick?"

"Yes, Helms. I'm working on something you'll all like. I'm doing wonderful things with blood. I've tried many things with the other organs, but for me, it's about the blood and the heart. I think I'm onto something."

"Tell me what it is, and we can help. We're a brotherhood, after all."

"Would it be improper to save it as a surprise? I want credit for this. I want to create a spell that belongs beside Allemand's."

"There is nothing to gain by claiming credit, Gideon. Allemand got the ball rolling, but he's dead now, and we move forward as a group. There's no money and no rights, only community."

Gideon did his best to stifle disappointment, then continued. "As you know, I've been hibernating. I believe I am on my way to refining Bardelli's work. If we can heal our flesh, we'll lose the damned flies. If we lose the flies, we can buy property and live in houses again. I've been working hard, and I'm close. Ten years away, maybe fewer."

Helms grinned. "Ten years? How ironic. Remember when ten years seemed like a lifetime to you?"

Gideon smiled, pretending to enjoy Helms' joke. "Touché, Helms. You were so right."

"How can we help? You've got me dreaming of living in a house again."

"You've caught me unprepared," said Gideon. "But I suppose I could use more blood if you want to collect some. The pure kind, of course. While you do that, I'll review my notes, and we can assign the work properly."

"How much blood are you looking for?"

"It's an ongoing process, so I'll always need more. I was about to fetch some myself, safely, of course. There's a schoolhouse in Boxford in a wooded area with lots of hiding spots. The children leave in all directions when school lets out. I'll tell you where it is."

Helms considered. "All right, give me the address. I'll be back in four days, so be ready. Sometimes, they die of shock, as you know."

Helms found the schoolhouse Gideon told him about and spent two days observing. After noting the lack of police and weak adult presence, he finalized plans. On the third day, just before school ended, Helms took a position in the woods a quarter mile down the least traveled road. One child walked this way, her home only a hundred yards past his position.

When the school bell rang, Helms waited in the bushes. Five minutes passed, but still nothing. Then, from the direction of the girl's house came a commotion, the whinny of a horse. Helms peered left but saw nothing. Suddenly, three horses burst from the end of the driveway in full gallop.

Helms ducked, still believing the horses were not there for him, but he soon realized his error. The trio stopped dead and reared up in front of his hiding place, and the men dismounted, holding rifles and swords. Helms knew he'd been betrayed and ran.

He thundered through the woods as two shots rang out, followed by a third a few seconds later. One bullet struck him in the back, turning two vertebrae into bone chips. The second bullet shattered his left shoulder blade just over the heart. The third bullet missed altogether, whistling past his left ear, and embedded itself in an oak tree as he passed it. A human would have died on the spot, but Helms kept running.

Going for the heart, he realized. He wondered how Gideon had coordinated everything, working with humans. How does a rotting dead man team up with parents and police? Perhaps an anonymous note blaming him for years of abductions would do the trick.

Be ready. Helms is after your children.

It didn't matter how Gideon did it. It was done, but Helms couldn't help himself. How could Gideon know which child he would select? Perhaps Gideon had bet on the most likely. Or might he have been watching? Helms stopped and looked back, feeling the hole in his shoulder blade. *That project of his.*

If Gideon had spied on Helms for an entire day undetected, then Gideon Walker might now be the most powerful being on earth. Helms ran for four more miles and stopped in a clearing. The broken bones in his back did not hurt, but he could sense the damage in his posture. The muscles and sinew held things in place, but they were damaged. His upper body wobbled, and it would only get worse. He needed to repair himself.

Helms' instincts told him he was in trouble. Gideon had betrayed him and would be looking to finish him off. On top of that, Gideon had new magick that made him invisible to other revenants, the limits of which he couldn't imagine. Sensing danger, Helms ran again, this time north, away from Beverly Farms. He ran for nearly a day, further damaging his shattered spine and extending his required recovery time.

But the further he got from Beverly Farms, the safer he felt. He walked for nearly two months, one day smelling the Pacific Ocean and realizing he'd reached the continent's end. Helms dug his healing bed in a dense forest under an overhanging rock and had one final thought before he closed his eyes. *Where was Mary?*

CHAPTER 110

1875

Gideon Walker stood over the body of Fenerty. The poor sap had hoped to become a revenant, but never made the cut. Fenerty's blood pooled on the kitchen floor as Gideon's rage died, leaving him with a mess to explain. He'd lost his temper and would have to cover it up.

It was Fenerty who informed the Boxford authorities on Helms, going so far as to pin ten years of abductions on him. Everything went according to plan until Fenerty caught his foot in his stirrup and fired too late. Even more pathetic, he had been the first horse to arrive, blocking the Boxford officers from better shots.

Now Helms was missing, no doubt aware he'd been betrayed. Gideon read his runes. Ten revenants were walking, which meant Helms was awake, although he could not tell where. Fenerty saw at least one shot hit its mark. Helms would heal up, then return for revenge, but when was anybody's guess. The idea of watching his back for a century left Gideon unsettled.

He didn't have the political support to hunt Helms down. The other revenants would never go for it. Helms, until now, had been their unofficial leader and was well-liked. Revenants killing revenants was simply not done.

But Fenerty was dead, and Gideon could blame his death on Helms. In the meantime, he would use his new spell to listen in on what they were saying. The new magick had worked on Helms, dulling his senses and leaving Gideon undetected. And none of them knew anything about it.

Gideon stayed away from camp for three weeks and then returned to the cave. Webb, standing guard, welcomed him.

"You haven't been around, have you?" said Webb.

"No, I haven't. I've been working on a way to stop our decay. Perhaps someday soon, we won't have to hibernate to heal."

Webb changed the subject. "Have you checked your runes? Helms is missing. Fenerty is dead. Newspapers say the police were after a child abductor, and shots were fired. The townspeople are restless. Helms is awake, but we don't know where."

"Who killed Fenerty? Helms?"

"Either that or the police. No one knows."

"Did they shoot Helms?"

"They think so, but no one can be sure."

Two months later, Gideon pulled out his runes and checked: one extra sleeper, probably Helms.

"Pleasant dreams." Gideon breathed easy for the first time since the betrayal. He'd been looking over his shoulder ever since Fenerty's murder. At least now, there was confirmation that Helms was hurt and was probably a two-month walk away. Gideon figured he had a year to get things the way he wanted them.

CHAPTER 111

1952

Helms opened his eyes and flexed his back, checking for damage. It sounded like a bag of broken glass the last time, but this time was much better. Hearing no grinding, he began to dig out, and as he rose from the pit, he looked around. The trees were much taller than when he went to sleep. *How long was he sleeping?* Helms dug in his pocket and took a reading.

What he saw troubled him. He counted again: thirteen walking and four sleeping. *Shit. Seventeen.* He shook the runes again. He'd been asleep seventy-seven years, and Gideon Walker was probably in charge, scrapping the old rules and growing the population. More population meant less control. Sooner or later, the revenants would clash with the humans, who outnumbered them. Attention was the last thing they needed.

What else had happened while he was out? There was always something new after a long sleep, especially one that lasted seventy-seven years. Perhaps Bardelli had fixed the decay problem. Helms might even support the expansion if revenants were able to blend with the human population.

Helms looked again at the runes and wondered if one of the little dots was still Mary. Was she alive? Had she found the rest of them? Probably not. She hated Gideon Walker. Helms had two choices: remain on the lam or crawl back and face the music. If he continued on his own, he would forever be visible, and the odds of a hunt would increase, especially if Gideon had revenants to spare. The more he thought about it, the more he knew that the only path was back to Beverly Farms.

CHAPTER 112

1952

Gideon rechecked his runes. He was proud his community was growing, and he was on his way to greatness, but two of the revenants in the readings were not part of his flock. Although many of his recruits were out searching, Gideon could not rest until their mysteries were solved.

Two of the newer revenants were recruited for their minds. One was a doctor, and the other a scientist. Both had been hard at work attempting to improve Allemand's spells but were reassigned to work on finding Helms, even though that's not what they were told. Their task was to engineer a spell to improve the runes and understand where everyone was at all times. Two other recruits were test subjects—their only purpose was to rotate in and out of healing sleep.

Gideon blinked twice, surprised that one of the sleepers was missing. *Helms is awake.* The man who used to tell him what to do, who had threatened to kill him on more than one occasion, was healthy and on the move. Gideon had spent the last seventy-seven years waiting for this moment. He wouldn't be caught unprepared. The clan's newest member was a giant named Saltz, who was recruited as his bodyguard and was even more physically intimidating than Gideon.

Two months later, Bergin came into camp with news. Helms had surprised him in a nearby orchard and given him a message. He wanted to talk. Gideon was surprised. This meeting could be a good thing. At least it was better than a blade in his chest when he least expected it. Helms had insisted on the Salem Willows Park at noon on Friday. Gideon agreed to attend.

CHAPTER 113

1952

Helms waited at Salem Willows, prepared to die. He didn't fear death, but he also didn't wish for it. Mary, his shot-in-the-dark, the person who hated Walker more than any other, hadn't come through, which was disappointing but no surprise. Thankfully, Gideon was never aware of his plan, and with the balance of power shifted in the cult leader's favor, it was time to kneel.

Helms prepared his excuse, which was easy because it was a partial truth. He ran because he was attacked and fled for his life. Depending upon how the conversation went, Helms would explain that he understood why Gideon wanted him dead, but it was time to wipe the slate clean. All Helms wanted was to live out his days without being hunted. He would pledge his loyalty to Gideon, and hopefully, that would be it.

The sun was high over the park as a large man approached. Helms had chosen a spot away from the crowds, near the rocky coast, so the breeze would mask the stench. The weather was cool enough to minimize the flies. With ten yards between them, the big man stopped.

"Where's Gideon?" asked Helms.

Saltz said nothing. Helms wondered momentarily if this was a distraction, an ambush, or a test to see how he would react. In doubt, he did nothing. Finally, fifty yards in the distance came the unmistakable gait of Gideon Walker.

"Gideon! I return in peace. As you know, I was ambushed near the schoolhouse, shot twice in the back, and wasn't sure who was after me. It could have been anyone. It could have been you for all I knew. When you're a leader, there are many reasons why you might be a target, but I'm not here to point fingers.

"I realize things have changed, and I don't intend to challenge you. If you're the leader, then so be it. I don't want to be hunted and don't want you to think I'm doing the same."

"You threatened my life," said Gideon. You blinded me and proclaimed your superiority after I became a revenant. Helms, you don't respect me, and that is a problem."

"You're talking about things any father would teach his son. Of course, I threatened your life, but that was when you were human. I even *took* your life, remember? You asked me to." Helms gestured at Saltz. "You didn't let this big one walk in without vetting him, right?"

Gideon let his shoulders fall, grabbed Helms, and pulled him close. "If you tell the rest of the clan this, we'll do great things together."

CHAPTER 114

1964

For the first time in ninety-nine years, Mildred opened her eyes, waking under the soil to painful memories. She felt rested physically, but dark recollections of Elmer and Gideon Walker were already working to sap her strength. Everything was dark, like the aftermath of her suicide. Her body was immobile, held fast by the soil. The mound above had fully settled as seasons had come and gone, turning the pile of brush and leaves into a rich layer of soil. The air pockets had been pressed out by decomposition and the weight of hundreds of feet of snow. The leaves that fell annually had rotted and sifted into the mix, making her part of the forest floor.

She worked her left arm. Thirty minutes later, she broke through the last layer of moss. The suicide burial of 1863 had taken her two days to dig out, but this time was different. Mildred had instinctively created a perfect shallow-grave revenant nest.

As soon as she sat up, she saw him. Elmer was twenty yards ahead, watching her dig out. Their eyes locked, but the boy didn't move. He hadn't changed a bit and was still every bit the eight-year-old she remembered. Chasing him had never worked, so she relaxed, half stuck in the earth for another minute. Mildred beckoned, and the boy stepped toward her. She thought he might approach her, but he stopped.

In what appeared to be a change of heart, he spun and ran off, disappearing in the foliage. Mildred's heart sank. Only minutes after opening her eyes, the loneliness came rushing back. Mildred felt the specter of hopelessness begin to creep into her thoughts, but she pushed it away. Nothing had changed, yet something must. At least now she had the energy to try and do something about it.

It didn't take long to learn that Henry and Annette Smith now owned her house. At least while Elmer was hiding from her, she could spy on them for something to do.

PART THREE:
DEAD WOMAN SCORNED

CHAPTER 115

May 1, 1971

Mildred wandered the property in the hours after Elmer and Thomas disappeared, wondering what happened. *Where's Thomas? Where's Elmer?* Confusion reigned. Mildred burst out of the forest and onto the driveway, but Tim and Holly wouldn't be home now. Tim, who Thomas stabbed with a bayonet, was no longer in her grave. Was he alive? If so, he would be at the hospital. Paranoia nibbled at the corners of her thoughts. She didn't want to believe her worst fears. Everyone disappeared as if it had been rehearsed. An hour later, she came to terms with the betrayal. She'd been played.

Thomas and Elmer had crossed over, yet she was still here. Thomas knew how to pull it off, and she didn't. *Why?* Did Tim and Holly help Thomas? Mildred sat down on the front steps, scheming. Thomas and Elmer were gone, but Tim wasn't going anywhere. Mildred had read his papers. He needed the money too much to leave.

CHAPTER 116

May 1, 1971

As soon as Mildred realized Elmer's bones were gone, she broke into the Sanborn Public Library, hell-bent on learning why she couldn't do the things Elmer and Thomas could. She knew magick, after all, and they did not. It took several hours in the occult section, but in the end, she understood.

She was not a ghost, and she should have known. If she were a ghost, she could have followed Thomas and Elmer. Thomas did, however, know this somehow. Despite her need for extended rest and inability to catch Elmer, she didn't see it coming. Mildred read from the library book:

Rev-e-nant

/ ˈrevə ˌnäN,-nənt/

(noun)

A reanimated corpse that has come back from the dead for the sole purpose of revenge. From the French verb revenir meaning "to come back."

No wonder flies followed her wherever she went. It made perfect sense. The smelly mystery man who cast a spell on her was a revenant, too. Perhaps she should return to Beverly Farms to learn the whole truth.

Mary read on, cracking every book she could find on the subject. Revenants supposedly drank blood, but that wasn't true for her, at least thus far. Mildred had no desire to eat whatsoever. Revenants could be most easily killed by attacking the heart or decapitation. Mildred took note. Revenants were single-minded creatures, hell-bent on revenge. That part seemed somewhat true.

Remembering Gideon's compound made her hair stand up. Memories washed over her like a filthy river. Her sister, her mother. The food, the sermons. The three revenants that had pulled her into the woods and the one that cursed her into becoming one of his own. She would never forget.

Mildred left the library book on the table and walked out the front door. It was still dark, but dawn was coming. As she walked, her mind spun, but it wasn't easy to think logically. There was too much emotion. Her life had always been chaotic, one disaster after another. *Hell hath no fury like a woman scorned* rang true, but even that didn't seem strong enough.

Another thought occurred to her: Was Gideon still in Beverly Farms? He should be dead, but picturing him as a revenant was a probability. Gideon Walker, the murderer. Gideon Walker, the cult leader. Gideon Walker, the predator. He would be dangerous as a revenant.

Mildred made up her mind. If Gideon was still there, he should be her priority. Tim and Holly could wait. Let them restore her farmhouse while she tended to business. If they thought she was gone for good, even better. Mildred looked to the stars with dawn about to break and plotted her course.

CHAPTER 117

May 2, 1971

Mildred walked through wooded areas whenever possible, for unwanted attention would slow her down. As she walked, she plotted, her thoughts jumping between where things went wrong and how she could make them right. At one point, Mildred's dress caught on a snag, tearing the old rag off entirely. Naked, Mildred stood over the discarded fabric and pondered her predicament. A nude corpse would be noticeable to everyone, even from a distance.

Mildred's swarm of flies took advantage of new landing places as she picked up the dress. To her frustration, the clothing spell from ages ago in Gideon's shed eluded her. Perhaps she could find a clothesline along the way. The walk from Sanborn to Beverly Farms was almost ninety miles. She would have to break into a house if she couldn't find anything.

With her mind set on finding a neighborhood, she took three steps and felt the comfort of cloth brushing against her legs again. Mildred looked down to see a full-length farm dress. It wasn't necessary to apply the spell whenever she needed new clothes. Reading it just once, a century ago, was enough. Some spells had faded, but some had not—something to watch out for.

CHAPTER 118

Hampstead, New Hampshire
May 2, 1971

Eric Enrico was twelve years old and grounded by his parents. He was not supposed to play outside after school or converse with friends, but Eric's mother didn't get home from work until after 6:30 pm, and what she didn't know wouldn't hurt her.

The first thing he did was phone his buddy Mark Gottlieb to tell him to meet at the stone wall in fifteen minutes. Eric and Mark were neighbors. Mark owned a BB gun, and the two of them had been caught shooting at streetlights in front of their houses. Eric's parents had grounded him, and Mark's had laughed it off.

Eric met Mark at the arranged location with the BB gun. The two would head into the woods this time and shoot stuff out there. Eric's brother Kevin had shot a red squirrel two years ago with a .30-30 rifle, and it blew a hole large enough to see inside the body cavity. Kevin said he watched the heartbeat for over a minute before it stopped. The two boys hoped to see something so incredible.

Spring had come early, and the forest was blooming. On a cold winter day, one could see a quarter mile through the woods, but with the new leaves, the visibility was less than ten feet in some areas, depending on how many low-hanging branches there were. Some paths resembled leafy tunnels.

At 4:00 pm sharp, the two boys stepped into the woods and headed for the Birchwood Farm cornfield about a half-mile through. Eric brought his father's spare watch so he could keep a close eye on the time. Despite their best hunter impersonations, the boys were as loud as a drumming of woodpeckers, and all the squirrels knew it.

Mark started things off by stepping on a rotten log and cracking it in half. Eric, notoriously loud, forewarned everything in a quarter-mile radius with his voice. With no squirrels in sight, boredom set in, and the boys began shooting at random objects.

Fifteen minutes later, on Eric's turn with the BB gun, he vowed to make his next shot count. A fat gray squirrel chattered above but remained out of sight. Another rustled through the bushes, mocking them. Finally, another crunched through the leaves on the other side of some oaks, moving toward them.

Most everything they had ever shot at had been running away. This one didn't know he was headed into a trap. Eric decided the best position was in front of a clearing. Hopefully, the squirrel would hit the open patch and run across, giving Eric more than a fair chance at shooting him. When the crunching grew louder, Eric wondered if it was a squirrel. It sounded bigger, like a dog or a coyote, but suddenly the noise stopped.

A woman's face emerged from between two bushes, head high and six feet off the ground. The whiteness of the face startled Eric, and the BB gun went off. At first, he thought he had hit the owner of Birchwood Farm, but the face didn't flinch. And then she disappeared into the trees.

Eric looked at Mark, whose face confirmed they had seen the same thing. One of the woman's eyes seemed unnaturally low as if the capsule surrounding the eyeball had failed. And she was as white as a ghost. A human would be howling mad if conscious.

Suddenly, the crunching started again, closer than last time, and Eric pumped the BB gun as if it could protect them. Bravely, he raised it as Mildred parted the saplings and stepped into their hiding place. It *was* a ghoul, thought Eric. Her face was milk white, riddled with scars like skin peeling from a birch tree, and along with the crunching footsteps came a buzzing of flies. They swarmed her, hundreds in all.

Eric fired again, and the BB smacked into her cheek. The woman did not flinch but lifted her hand to touch the spot. There was no blood. She left the wound alone and let her arm fall to her side, then raised it again, this time holding a knife.

Panicked, Mark and Eric scrambled. Eric ran toward home but lost Mark immediately and wondered if his friend had opted for the safety of Birchwood Farm. Weaponless, Eric turned back and ran as fast as he could through the bushes and trees, looking for Mark. When he reached an open area, he stopped, panting, listening.

The forest was quiet. Eric couldn't hear Mark or much of anything. Perhaps Mark had stopped, too. Most unsettling was he couldn't hear the woman either. With a sloping hill at his back, he sat behind a maple to catch his breath. *What happens now?* He couldn't leave Mark behind. A minute later, he realized he had to urinate.

There was little to no view from this spot. Even when he ducked to see around a leafy branch, there was another behind it to block his line of sight. Very quietly, he aimed for a small tuft of moss near his feet and relieved himself. He looked at his watch; it was 5:15 pm, and his mother would be home in an hour.

Eric found a baseball-sized stone and headed down the hill, but twenty yards later, he heard Mark scream. Eric bolted back up the hill, collecting a second stone on the way. The final twenty feet were the toughest, with a lip at the top like the edge of a golf bunker. Eric had no idea what to expect when he cleared the crest but had to imagine she knew he was there.

Mark cried out again, much closer this time. Eric pumped his legs and cocked his arm, ready to throw. Mark was twenty yards away, strapped to an oak tree by a length of barbed wire. It had him around the neck, and he was choking. He flailed at the wire with one hand, which was also bleeding. The other was held close to his side, clearly broken.

Eric rushed to his friend and circled the tree at full speed, looking for the tail end of the wire. As he rounded the trunk, he bumped into something behind the tree and bounced backward, stumbling. It was the woman, holding both ends of the wire, pulling hard, choking the life out of Mark.

As shocked as Eric was, there was no time for fear. One of them might die, if not both. Recovering from the collision with the woman, Eric picked up one of the rocks he dropped and hurled the stone before diving at her midsection.

Mildred ignored the rock, never taking her eyes off the boy. After it hit her, she dropped the barbed wire, called her knife, and sank it between his ribs. The boy she was strangling watched her pull the knife from his friend's body and fled. Mildred let him run. These boys were not worth chasing, but the anger felt good. She could only imagine how good it would feel against her enemies.

Mark Gottlieb ran all the way home, cradling his broken arm against his body. When his mother saw the blood and the holes made by the barbed wire, she screamed, but that wasn't the worst thing. Mark's mother called the police, and soon after, they recovered the body of his friend

Eric Enrico. Mark told the authorities that a woman covered in flies had broken his arm, strangled him with barbed wire, and stabbed his friend to death.

The Hampstead Police put out an all-points bulletin for a woman with a pale complexion wearing a full-length farm dress. At the request of Mark's parents, the press was not told the woman hadn't bled when shot with a BB gun or that she was covered in flies. The boy must be in shock.

CHAPTER 119

Sanborn, New Hampshire
May 3, 1971

Robert Simmons of Lancaster Hill Road went to the IGA grocery store to stock up for today's ball game. Mike Nagy, his favorite player, would pitch for the Red Sox, and the game started at one o'clock. Robert grabbed chips, beer, hot dogs, and peanuts for an authentic experience. It was too much food for one person, and the Chief had been on him about losing some weight, but he had nothing else to look forward to, so he decided to put his diet off for one more day.

Bob had slipped right back into the ugly side of bachelorhood. There was no wife (anymore), no children, and the house was a mess. His diet was that of a fifteen-year-old: processed meats and tons of sugar. On top of everything, he drank too much.

On his way to the checkout, Simmons passed the newspaper stand. He wasn't much of a "paper" guy, but the headline grabbed his attention: ONE BOY DEAD IN FOREST SLAYING. The story called to him. Bob put his groceries down and picked up the journal, forgetting about the Red Sox, the beer, and the store around him.

One boy was dead, and one survived. The police were looking for 'a pale woman in a long black farm dress.' He almost dropped his handbasket. Hampstead was an hour away, so why did the headline catch his attention? Was it her?

Robert was raised hearing how two of the Simmons clan were murdered by the neighbor up the road. The first Simmons casualty was his great-grandaunt Elizabeth, a gossip who had gone so far as to create a scrapbook featuring the life and times of her rival, Mildred Wells.

The second casualty was Elizabeth's daughter, Emma, who went missing shortly after. Robert never knew either of them, but the stories had been engraved into his soul and every other family member since.

Robert, now a Sanborn cop, placed the newspaper into his basket and paid, trying to get his mind back on the Sox, but the effort was futile. Mike Nagy gave up six runs in the first inning, and the game was over early. With hot dogs still boiling on the stove, Simmons shut off the television and reread the article.

CHAPTER 120

May 4, 1971

By the following morning, Bob Simmons was thoroughly obsessed with the death of Eric Enrico. The cop quoted in the paper was the Chief of the Hampstead police, Kevin Luoma, and as soon as Bob arrived at work, he called him. He had no idea what the Chief would tell him, but what he hoped to hear was an excuse to forget the whole thing.

"Hello, Chief Luoma. I'm Sergeant Robert Simmons from the Sanborn Police Department. I saw the article in the *Monitor* yesterday, and it strikes a chord. I don't know if I can help, but the case seems familiar. Maybe you can jog my memory."

"Your input is welcome, Sergeant Simmons. I know your Chief Galluzzo up there. Did he ask you to call?"

"No sir, he didn't. I wasn't aware you knew each other. I'd put you through to say hello, but he's on the second shift today. There's only three of us, you know."

"I used to work in a small town like that. What do you have for me? It's an ugly scene down here. People are shaken and won't let their kids out of their yards."

"I was wondering about the Gottlieb boy, the one who survived. I heard the 'pale woman/long black dress' description, but did he estimate her age?"

"Well, not her age, but he did have some information we kept out of the paper. I don't want this to get out, though, Officer Simmons. It was crazy talk. The boy was traumatized. The parents and I thought it best to blame it on shock. I'll tell you only because you're a cop, and I know your boss."

"Of course. Official police business."

"The kid said she looked dead. He said she was covered in flies. She even smelled 'rotten.' What gets me is these are farm boys, so they know what a dead animal smells like. They said her dress was old fashioned, like, and I quote, 'the painting of the farmer and his wife with the pitchfork,' unquote.

"The Gottlieb kid shot her with his BB gun and pissed her off. The woman chased, and the kids got split up. She had the Gottlieb kid around the neck with some barbed wire when the Enrico kid found them. He threw a rock and took a run at her, and the next thing he knew, the Enrico kid got stabbed."

To Bob Simmons' disappointment, he hadn't heard enough to let it all go. Worse, the pit in his stomach had begun to churn. He shouldn't believe in the supernatural, but he did. Simmons pulled a pencil from his cup and drummed the eraser off his notebook. "He thinks she's a ghost? What's the kid like? Is he all there? Are the lights on, if you know what I mean?"

"Tough call, but I hear where you're coming from. At first, I thought the same thing, but Mark's a smart kid. My best guess is shock. People's minds play tricks in traumatic circumstances."

Simmons scratched his chin and scribbled some notes. "Do you think there was a woman at all?"

"I do, but we're looking for her and not having any luck. We're checking nearby farms, and we have the barbed wire she used, but there's no evidence left, like blood. There's no knife either."

"What about dogs?" Simmons asked about search and rescue canines. He had adopted an ex-police dog two years back, a German Shepherd named King.

"Yup. We had some down here from Manchester. There was a scent, and the dogs followed it about a mile to Big Island Pond, then lost it."

"Maybe she did that on purpose."

"Maybe. There are a bunch of cabins around there. We're asking around, seeing if anybody saw anything."

Simmons broke his pencil, more worked up now than when he picked up the phone. "Chief Luoma, do you mind if I look at the crime scene?"

"You're welcome to take a look around. I'll be out there this afternoon to shut it down. I think we've collected everything there is to collect. What time can you be here?"

"How does three o'clock sound?"

The two men finished the call and hung up. The dead-end Simmons was hoping for had become a two-lane highway. But he didn't expect to arrive at the crime scene and find something Luoma and his men had missed. He wanted to see what his instincts told him when he walked in the footsteps of the killer.

Simmons showed up at three o'clock with his dog, King, and Chief Luoma took them out into the woods, where they climbed the eroding incline Eric Enrico had and laid eyes on the tree where he died.

Most of the Gottlieb/Enrico evidence was packed up and taken away, but there was still a drop of blood on the ground and some scratches on the trunk from the barbed wire. The hair stood on the back of his neck, something Simmons hadn't felt in a long time. Someone had been murdered here, and another boy narrowly escaped. On top of everything, King was going nuts. He picked up her scent and took off through the trees.

King followed Mildred's trail to Big Island Pond, where the scent ended at the water between two cottages. Simmons wondered if she had walked right in or swam across. Either way, finding her exit point would be nearly impossible. Big Island Pond had miles of shoreline and was shaped like a giant "C" with countless inlets and peninsulas. Not only would it take forever to walk the entire shoreline, but much of it was on private land or clogged with vegetation.

Simmons pulled out a map of New England and drew a line from Sanborn to Hampstead and beyond. Salem, Massachusetts, was almost directly in line, and according to his great-grand-aunt's scrapbook, Mildred Wells was from Salem.

There wasn't much more Simmons could do. He could try to interview the Gottlieb boy, but the results would be painful for everyone. As an insurance policy, he called the *Salem Evening News* and purchased a subscription, which he agreed to drive to Salem weekly to pick up. If Mildred headed in that direction, she might make the news. In the meantime, Simmons would brush up on Elizabeth's scrapbook.

When Simmons got home, he went straight to the bookshelf in the extra bedroom. He'd bought the house from his family years back but never refurnished or redecorated. Many of the knickknacks had been there for generations. His ex-wife had tried to replace them, but he wouldn't allow it.

Simmons scanned the dusty bookshelf but couldn't find it. *It should stick out*, he thought. It was as ugly as it was unorganized, thick with a quilted cover, photos, and newspaper clippings poking out in every direction. He gave the shelf another pass, this time slower, binding by binding. *Still not there*. Where the hell was the Simmons family scrapbook?

CHAPTER 121

May 4, 1971

As Mildred walked into the town of Wenham, she began to recognize the terrain. She had never visited this town, but the style of the houses was familiar. Perhaps her senses were heightened, but she could smell the ocean, something she had never noticed when she was alive.

It must have been the daily grind of life with Gideon Walker that dulled her senses. An hour with him would suck the joy out of anything. Gideon would soon pay for every pleasure he had stolen, including moments like this, if he was still there.

She crossed into Beverly Farms two hours later. It was almost time to hunt. By evening, Mildred was one hill away from the old farm, wondering what it would look like one hundred and twenty years later. Would he be expecting her? The Book of Shadows was only so thick the last time she saw it, and she remembered that new pages appeared regularly. It was a certainty that he knew things she did not, so she stayed sharp. Mildred also remembered the mystery tone in her head every time Gideon was near, but there was no tone yet.

Reaching the bottom of the hill just after sundown, Mildred slowed her pace. For every twenty yards, she waited five minutes, anticipating ambush. Halfway up the hill, Mildred spotted a man standing watch. He might have been missed without her diligence, but she was in no hurry. Compared to chasing Elmer, this was easy.

An hour passed before the guard moved to the other side of the hill, and Mildred quickly reclaimed the spot he'd occupied. From there, she climbed a tree and lost herself in the leaves. An hour later, footsteps came. Listening carefully, she timed her jump, calling the knife halfway down as her boots crashed into the guard's head.

Challenged for the first time in a century, the guard dropped his weapon, and before he could recover, Mildred plunged the knife into his chest as the fingers of her opposite hand found his eyes. As he screamed, Mildred pulled the blade and sank it again, silencing him. In less than a minute, Desjardins was dead.

CHAPTER 122

Beverly Farms, Massachusetts
May 4, 1971

Gideon Walker sat in his shed with an apprentice named Lammi. Lammi, a troubled soul, was addicted to heroin and in danger of losing his opportunity at immortality. Gideon called him in to remind him that death by overdose was a dealbreaker but paused mid-sentence, sensing something was wrong. Gideon's hand went to the runes in his front pocket. Lammi was high and droned on, apologizing as Gideon wavered between killing him and giving him one more chance.

Sixteen revenants were awake, and two were sleeping. Someone was dead or missing, and he had never seen anything like this. "Lammi, get out. And before you leave, remember that I will kill you the next time you use that drug." Lammi apologized three more times before letting himself out.

Gideon focused on the runes. Someone was gone, either one of his flock or the mysterious "thirteenth revenant," as he had come to be known. Gideon stepped outside and crossed the barnyard to the main house. It made perfect sense to use the farmhouse as headquarters. A never-ending stream of people had passed through for years, and the house was registered to a trust, making it difficult to trace the owner.

Helms sat at the kitchen table, checking his runes. "I saw," he said.

"Who is it? What happened?" asked Gideon.

"I don't know. I was about to radio the guards but thought better of it. I hate these radios. They're too noisy. They give our positions away. I'll check myself. If one of us was killed, then we've been compromised. Be ready." Gideon didn't argue. A knight should always protect his king.

Despite his hatred of technology, Helms grabbed a walkie-talkie and hurried out. He would radio back only after everything was clear. *She's here*, Helms thought. His plan had worked, although not even close to what he imagined. She took too long, and things had changed. He couldn't imagine what Mary would be like. *Better the devil you know than the devil you don't* came to mind. The phrase had never had a more literal meaning.

Helms rushed through the forest, favoring speed over stealth. Reid was still at his post, and so was Reveley. Without stopping, he ran on. Durant and Desjardins were the other two sentries. Minutes later, he found Desjardins' body heaped beneath the maple tree with his heart and eyes torn out.

The camp is in jeopardy. What do I do? Pinching the bridge of his nose, trying to concentrate, Helms reckoned it would be best to kill her and avoid rocking Gideon's boat. She must be here for a reason, coming from who knows where to seek them out.

But Helms pondered too long. As soon as he moved, a spear impaled him under his rib cage and through, embedding itself in the ground before him. He turned in agony. Mary was at the other end, lifting the spear, keeping him off balance.

"Mary, we want the same thing! I know you! I gave you your powers. You can have your revenge."

Mildred raised the spear, lifting one of Helms' legs off the ground. "Where is he?" she asked.

"He's in the house, and he's armed. He knows you killed one of us, but he doesn't know who. He also knows there is a mystery revenant but doesn't know it's you."

"How does he know?" she asked.

Helms was surprised by her question, but it made perfect sense. Mary was unpracticed. Her exposure to the Book of Shadows consisted of whatever she had learned in Gideon's shed, perhaps a dozen or so pages. She had no doubt created her rune beads but didn't know what they were for.

"His runes. Gideon read his runes. The square beads. *Walkers and sleepers?* You don't know about this?"

Mildred let one hand fall to her side, the other still holding the spear high, keeping Helms off balance. The beads! She'd buried them at the corner of the house eons ago but never understood what they were for. Mildred flexed her hand, and her runes appeared in her palm. They were warm, and she could read them like English.

Helms continued. "I'll help you kill him. I know what he did. He tried to have me killed, and I've wanted to kill him ever since. We can do it tonight."

Mildred took her eyes off her runes and eyed Helms, letting the spear fall, and he dropped to the ground. Using both hands, he pulled the spear from his abdomen. He was in bad shape and would need to hibernate to heal the damage, but he could manage for now. Helms rose at her mercy. After his actions this evening, staying with Gideon would be tricky. Perhaps it was time to switch sides.

"Go ahead, then." Mildred pushed Helms to lead the way, reminding him with her spear that she was in control. Twenty minutes passed before he spotted Reveley, and he turned and pointed out the sentry's position.

Turning back toward Reveley, Helms planned his route. Another dead revenant would create an emergency, and Helms would be caught assisting the attack. Choosing a path, he fell to a crawl and inched forward. Reveley was thirty yards to his left, partially obscured by the new foliage. Five minutes later and a third of the way to safety, Helms looked back. Mary was gone.

Suddenly, a whisper broke the silence. "Helms!" Reveley had spotted him despite his best efforts.

"I ... I'm hurt. Pierced through the back," said Helms. "I didn't see who it was. Stay quiet!" Reveley saw the blood on Helms' shirt and raised his axe. "Help me up. I need to let Walker know."

"You're too slow, Helms. I can get to the house faster." Without hesitation, Reveley bolted, but at the last second, Helms grabbed his ankle.

Reveley looked back in surprise. "What are you—?"

Mildred appeared over the two men with Reveley's ax and brought it down four times, obliterating Reveley's rib cage. When she was finished, Mildred put her hand in her pocket and checked her runes, reading the same indicators Gideon would see. Reveley was nearly dead, and she watched his final seconds dim, then extinguish.

"He'll send everyone now," said Helms, "but they don't know what to look for. He might even come himself. There are still two more guards. Be ready."

Mildred lifted the ax again, and Helms wondered for a moment if he might have outlived his usefulness. Instead, Mildred threw it past him, lodging it high on a tree trunk, invisible to passers-by. Mildred picked up her spear and gestured for Helms to retake the point, and Helms did as he was told.

Desjardins and Reveley were gone forever. Reveley was a Walker recruit, but Desjardins had been a revenant for as long as Helms could remember. Helms' life, too, was in doubt. It seemed that Mary was just beginning. Everything had been so easy for her, like a hot knife through butter.

Fifteen revenants were too many, in Helms' opinion. Twelve was how it had always worked. A purge would do the clan a favor, but where would that leave them? Minutes later, Helms spotted Reid and Durant with weapons drawn, but Mildred was nowhere in sight.

"Helms!" said Reid. "What happened? Walker needs you! He wants an update!"

Helms looked for his walkie-talkie and realized it was gone. "I lost my radio. I'm hurt, but I think I hurt her too. You didn't see her?"

"Her? A woman?"

"It's Mary. Little Mary, the one who escaped way back. You wouldn't remember." Reid appeared puzzled. "Be ready. She snuck up on me, and that should tell you something. Tell Walker." Helms kept talking. "Desjardins and Reveley are dead."

Suddenly, Mildred's spear flew from the dark and struck Reid in the chest, dropping him to the ground. Durant, stunned, managed to raise his machete as Helms dropped to one knee, feigning further injury, still playing both sides of the fence.

When Mildred appeared twenty yards away, Durant held steady. With ten feet between them, Mildred paused, and Durant lunged—but before he could swing his machete, Mildred called the ax from its hiding place, met him mid-charge, and it was over in less than a minute.

Mildred reread her runes, enjoying the new tool, and turned to Helms. *Four down, eleven to go.* "How many are on property?"

"There's no way to tell where they are," said Helms. "The runes are designed so a revenant won't be attacked while hibernating. Plan on all eleven, just in case."

CHAPTER 123

May 4, 1971

Gideon threw his runes against the wall. "They're dropping like flies!" Saltz, the bodyguard, stood ready, knife drawn. "Get upstairs. We can watch from the windows. We'll barricade the doors and watch the front and back yards from the bedrooms. Four dead. It must be Helms. He's a part of this."

"Gideon, stay calm. Two of us together can take down ten."

"Who's left? It's either a coup or the mystery revenant. What do you think?" Gideon was near panic.

"Let's sit tight and let them come to us," said Saltz. "There were seven of us in the compound. Four are dead, and probably the junkie, too. That leaves three." After extinguishing the lights, each took a window on opposite sides of the upstairs. Gideon had collected his scattered runes and was checking them every minute.

CHAPTER 124

May 4, 1971

"It's Walker and Saltz, his enforcer. They're going to expect trouble," said Helms.

Mildred said nothing and turned in the direction of the house. With caution she approached the last knoll before the shed and the beginning of the property. Helms noticed Mildred staring at the shed, knowing what happened so many years ago. "Go look if you want," said Helms. "I'll stand watch."

Mildred stared at Helms and decided to trust him for the time being. The shed had been altered since the last time she was here. It now had an addition, although the original structure remained, and the new door was on the side facing the woods. Mildred twisted the knob until it broke and let herself in.

With the lights off, she stood in the original part of the building, recognizing the floorboards. Memories flooded back. She didn't remember everything that happened here, but she knew a lot had. It was time to right some wrongs. There was no food storage anymore because he no longer had to eat. The workbench along the wall was still there, and the Book was too. Mildred left it for the time being. It would be her reward for finishing the job.

Gideon had a bed in here now, and she didn't want to think about what might have happened there. Between the bed and the workbench were two doors. One was a closet piled high with gardening tools, a lawnmower, and a cobweb-covered gasoline can. The second door was more of the same: boxes stacked high. Mildred opened one of them and pulled out a small human skull.

It could be anyone, she thought. *But it could be Sarah.* Mildred took the box from the closet and set it on the bed. She lined them up in the window facing the house and assigned names. Sarah, Edward, Anna, Robert, and

George came to mind, but there were too many skulls, and she ran out of names, yet they all deserved to watch what she was about to do.

Because these were dead children, Mildred couldn't help but think of Elmer. She had acted callously that day at the pond, but the anger and the weight she carried at the time was born in this room. Before Mildred left the shed, she gathered some things. Halfway across the clearing, obscured by the dark, she noticed Gideon in the house's front window overlooking the yard. Her first sight of him in a century sent a shiver through her body, but it wasn't out of fear.

After filling a bucket in the barn, she left it by the back corner of the house, returned to the barn, and wrapped the horse blanket around her. When she was ready, she struck the match and lit the bottle.

CHAPTER 125

May 4, 1971

Gideon stood sentry in his upstairs window as a flaming bottle arced through the night and crashed through the kitchen window below. "They're trying to burn us! Where are they?"

Immediately, Saltz regretted their watchtower approach. He and Gideon were at a disadvantage with the house on fire and didn't know where the attack was coming from. Saltz left his lookout position in the back of the house and looked down the stairs. Flames raged in the kitchen.

"Gideon, don't give us away. The stairwell is ablaze. We'll have to jump or climb down."

Gideon left his post and looked down into the kitchen. He could smell the gasoline. "But we don't know where they are!"

"It's getting hot, Gideon. I think we should jump."

Gideon hated being on defense, but it was the best plan. They each grabbed their firearms and an ax and headed for the third bedroom. "Saltz launched himself through the window and landed hard on the back lawn. Gideon landed a second later to his right. The two men raised their weapons but found themselves alone. Suddenly, Helms came bursting through the trees.

"Walker, it's Mary! She's back. She's a revenant. She killed four of our men!" Helms coughed and dropped to one knee, pulling his hand away from his abdomen to show his wound. "She stabbed me. I lost her in the woods. Have you seen her?"

"Mary? Alice's girl?"

"Yes, Gideon. Mary, from your shed." Suddenly, a loud bang echoed through the woods. It was a gunshot, and Saltz looked down at his abdomen.

Helms, working quickly, pulled a knife and pounced on Saltz, finishing the kill.

Gideon stiffened. "It was you. You never got over the schoolhouse, even after I took you back."

Suddenly, the backyard was flooded with light as Mildred emerged from around the corner, fully ablaze, a plume of black smoke billowing from the wet blanket wrapping her head and torso. Dropping the smoldering garments, Mildred doused her burning parts with a bucket she'd hidden in the shadows, then called her rifle.

Gideon was stunned. Five revenants had been assassinated, more casualties than they had suffered in centuries. Suddenly, his rifle was ripped from his hands, and Mildred had two guns pointed at him. Gideon thought he was dead when she disappeared around the side of the house.

Believing Helms had a part in this, Gideon leaped, and the wounded revenant was too slow. The ax landed hard, sending Helms to the grass, and Gideon began punching holes in his chest.

Helms was dead in the grass as the second floor of the house collapsed. Gideon's kingdom was burning, and the cause of his ruin was somewhere near the barnyard. Mildred had fought and defeated his army on their home turf, but he wasn't going to go without a fight. Hefting his ax and holding the blade over his heart, Gideon strode into the barnyard, prepared to dominate her as he had when she stole his food.

Before he got to the barn, however, Mildred's second bottle smashed against his cheekbone, soaking him in liquid flame from the waist up. There would be no dousing bucket for Gideon. Mildred watched from the barn, letting the fire cook, but she would interfere if he attempted to roll the flames out.

Gideon spun wildly, seeking water. The house was ablaze. The shed was too far.

Mildred opened her hand and conjured his ax, but at the last moment, something caught her eye—a corn broom in the barn. It was one of Gideon's, or, at least, his name brand—the same brooms he schlepped in Salem and the surrounding towns.

Mildred dropped Gideon's ax and called the broom instead. Gideon was almost to her, but his end was a foregone conclusion. He was no longer the massive man who got his way, but he was still the man who had stolen her innocence hundreds of times in his sinful shed.

Gideon stumbled, as predicted, far too distracted with his burning flesh to take little Mary seriously. Mildred sidestepped and cracked him on the back of the head with the broom, and he fell all too easily. But hitting him with the broom was not why she chose it over the ax.

Gideon lay prone, cooking alive as he tried to rise and find water, but Mildred kicked him down. She waited a moment to let the fire do its job, but not so long it would steal her vengeance. As Gideon rose to all fours, she raised the broom and aimed carefully. An ax was far too fair for a bastard like Gideon Walker. Seeing him die like a marshmallow on a stick was far more satisfying.

CHAPTER 126

May 4, 1971

Mildred walked to the shed and stood outside, admiring the window lined with skulls that had just watched their tormentor fall. She raised her hand to show them Gideon's heart.

After their closure, Mildred entered the shed, tossed the heart in the corner, and piled the skulls in a box. Minutes later, she lit the shed on fire and let everything burn except the Book of Shadows, which she kept for herself. It was best to hide the truth from the humans. They wouldn't know what to do anyway. Mildred checked her runes: Eight awake, two asleep. The remaining revenants would come and investigate.

At the height of the blaze, some citizens of Beverly Farms noticed the glow in the sky and called the fire department. Soon, half the town was on the scene, watching the mysterious house burn. None of them had ever gotten this close to the farm, and most were seeing the property for the first time.

After the fire was out, the investigation began. *Who lived here, anyway?* When the casualties were revealed, the rumor mill began to grind. To some, it seemed a murder-suicide, while others thought the owners had died of smoke inhalation before they burned.

The investigators found bone fragments amongst the ashes from as many as five people, but who these bones belonged to was another matter. The house was part of a trust, and the beneficiary was a man named Fenerty, who died seventy-seven years prior. The *Salem Evening News* wrote a piece entitled *House of Mystery Burns*. Within three days, it was broadcast on all three Boston news stations, and from there, the Associated Press picked it up as a curiosity piece.

Mildred climbed a tree on the hill overlooking the farm and waited almost a week as police and press vehicles came and went. While she waited, she studied the Book and listened carefully to the forest below. On day four, the first of the wayward revenants returned. She heard him passing cautiously in the dark and finally saw him when he hid by the shed ten minutes later. He was undoubtedly shocked that the house was gone and appeared confused about what to do next.

Mildred approached, waving as if he should know who she was, counting the seconds before he reacted. It happened when they were ten feet apart. Mildred tossed her runes as if he should catch them, and when he lost focus on her, she called the ax. When his heart was in her hands, she decayed the body.

PART FOUR:
ANGER IS AN ACID

CHAPTER 127

May 8, 1971

Robert Simmons started his dinner before six o'clock in preparation for the evening's Red Sox game. He'd already drunk a beer and a half and was feeling the buzz, and for a minute, thought he should slow down. In disgust, he looked down into the pot of water. Hot dogs were always disappointing. Why did he always think they'd remind him of Fenway Park when he was in the grocery store?

As he re-centered the pot over the flame, the Channel Nine News out of Manchester came on. Toward the end of the broadcast, he saw the story about the house in Beverly Farms. The State Police were helping with the investigation, and the Director gave a brief interview on camera, confirming that everyone was baffled by the circumstances. Simmons put down his beer and turned the television up, but the segment ended.

The following day, Simmons woke early to drive the hour-and-a-half to Salem, Massachusetts, and pick up his newspapers. After flipping through the stack, he paid close attention to the one from three days ago: '*House of Mystery Burns.*' *Damn*, he thought. *Three days ago!* He wondered what he might have missed since. The scene would be corrupted by now, no doubt.

He had never been to Beverly Farms, so while he was still in Salem, he bought a road map, drove across the Essex Bridge, followed the coastline, and turned inland toward the address in the paper. Despite the map, he had to stop for directions twice, and in the end, the farm was not at the address it was supposed to be. *No wonder nobody knew them*, thought Simmons. *Most people didn't know the place existed.*

Simmons saw the mouth of a driveway and took it. A quarter mile later, he pulled into the barnyard and laid eyes on the ashes that were once Gideon Walker's headquarters. No one was there. The investigators had finished investigating, and the press had written their articles. The story was at a standstill until new information presented itself.

Simmons shut off the engine and stepped out of his cruiser. Grasshoppers chirped, and the sun beat down. He walked to the foundation and looked down. The ashes had been thoroughly raked and sifted, looking for bones. He didn't expect to find anything new.

Next, Simmons entered the guesthouse, which resembled a summer camp. The furnishings were minimal, with no rugs, curtains, or decoration. Like the house, the shed in the corner of the meadow had been burned to the ground, and the barn was—just a barn.

Simmons had always had a fascination for visiting places where bad things happened. As a kid, he visited the Ford Theater in Washington, DC, where Abraham Lincoln was assassinated, amazed to learn that the museum even had the pistol that took Lincoln's life.

Like the Ford Theater, something evil happened where he now stood. The hair stood on his arms, just like it did when he visited the tree in Hampstead where the Enrico boy was killed and the homemade memorial on Lancaster Hill Road where his great-grandaunt's remains were found.

Simmons looked at his watch. He still had plenty of time before he had to work, so he returned to his Sanborn cruiser, sat on the bumper, and meditated. When the sensation wouldn't subside, he stood, trying to look through the woods, but it was like looking at a green wall. Coming up empty, Simmons combed the hill behind the burned-down shed—and there it was.

Something dark was in the tallest tree, much too big to be a squirrel's nest or a rabid fisher cat. Simmons stood up and squinted but still couldn't make it out. *It might be a bear,* he thought. *But it could be a person, too. It could be her. There's something against the trunk, no doubt about it.*

Simmons walked toward the woods, never taking his eyes off it. Twenty feet, forty feet, fifty, he was almost to the shed but couldn't see the top of the tree anymore. Now, he had to decide whether to enter the woods or quit and drive back to Sanborn.

Simmons turned and returned to his cruiser, but before getting in, he found the tree on the hill again, and the shape was gone. Nervous, he popped the snap on his holster. Five minutes passed, and nothing happened, so he decided to call it a day.

A New Hampshire cop firing his weapon in Massachusetts would be grounds for termination, and he couldn't afford to lose his job. Massachusetts' gun laws were strict, cop or not. Simmons touched his stomach. That thing in the tree had his guts twisting. He had to leave, but it would be impossible to forget this moment. If only he could make himself believe that the shape in the tree was not Mildred Wells.

Mildred knew the red-headed policeman saw her, but she didn't care. He didn't get a good look, but she did. She noticed the hair, the belly, how he walked, and the word *Sanborn* on the side of the vehicle. *Could it be? Oh, yes, it could, another busybody Simmons.*

CHAPTER 128

May 16, 1971

Tim banged his palm against the steering wheel. He'd forgotten his wallet and wondered for a second if he really needed it between now and tomorrow, then saw the gas gauge. The truck was nearly empty, and there wasn't even enough gas to make it to Laconia. Tim stepped on the brake, pulled over to turn around, and hesitated.

It shouldn't be a problem to walk into the house and retrieve the wallet, but it was, even though their struggles with Mildred were over. She'd been gone for weeks, but he couldn't relax even so.

I'm going back in, he thought, as he postponed thoughts of the beer waiting for him at the convenience store a mile down the road. *It's best to hit and run.* He stepped on the gas and made the turn, never taking his eyes off of the house and, more specifically, the turret where he'd left his wallet.

Tim pulled around to the side of the house, then backed up and parked in front of the porch, facing the road. Now, he had the shortest path. Tim jogged to the door and inserted the key, his actions the exact opposite of how he described his days to Holly. She worried about him as he worked alone, and he tried to persuade her that the house was a "totally different place now." Mildred was gone, and "it seemed as if she'd never been there."

None of that really mattered, however, because Holly didn't believe a word, anyway. She hated the house. It would never be right for her, no matter what he said or did to disguise it.

Tim was on the front porch in seconds, opening the front door, pretending there was nothing to fear. Once inside, he noticed that the kitchen seemed too dark. Tim looked out of the kitchen window. *Strange.* His truck was gone. In a panic, he spun for the porch, with the sinking feeling that forgetting his wallet had been the greatest mistake of his life.

And then the smell hit him. He looked back, and the porch door was closed and locked, even though he'd left it open. Tim grabbed the knob and twisted it when three flies landed on his wrist. *No.*

Tim turned around, and Mildred was staring at him from the corner. She knew he'd forgotten the wallet. She knew he'd be back. *She knew everything.* Tim gave up on the porch door and bolted through the kitchen but stopped dead as he rounded the breakfast bar. What had once been a sliding glass door to the carriage house was nothing but bricks. *How could this be? She was supposed to be gone!*

Mildred Wells moved from the dining room to the kitchen, driving him to the bricked-off dead end, and the flies followed. Her smell filled his nostrils, reminding him of the night he was in bed with his daughters and she was outside his bedroom door. Suddenly, the hatchet appeared in her right hand.

Was Mildred smiling under all that dead skin? There was nothing left to do but fight. Tim charged, screaming in fear for his life.

"*Tim, Tim!*" Mildred screamed—except it sounded more like Holly's. "Wake up, Tim! You're dreaming again!"

Tim opened his eyes, realizing he'd ruined all efforts to convince Holly that he believed Mildred was gone for good.

Halfway through the day, Tim noticed he was whistling to himself, so despite his nightmare, when Holly called at lunchtime, he told her how much work he and Johnny were getting done. "I'm so much more relaxed. I really think she's gone. Sorry for the scare this morning."

"Please tell me you check the field every five minutes!" said Holly, not yet ready to believe it.

"Absolutely. Johnny's watching, too, but I'm telling you, she's not coming. Thomas could have killed me, but he didn't. Those two anniversaries that were supposed to happen this month didn't either. I'm whistling! If anyone is in the field, it will be Snow White."

Johnny, opening his lunch box, laughed.

Holly heard Johnny and commented. "Don't encourage him, Johnny! He's not funny. Don't let him think he is."

Tim held the receiver so they could hear each other. "Funny? That's not one of the seven dwarfs. All I see is Dopey," said Johnny.

"Keep working, Sleepy," said Tim as he returned the phone to his ear.

"What time is quitting time?" Holly asked.

"Eight o'clock. I will be at your place by 8:30."

"I can wait for 8:30, but I'll be starving. I want payment for my sacrifice."

"How would you like payment?" Tim asked. Holly made him guess.

CHAPTER 129

May 17, 1971

Johnny left for Massachusetts that night, and the following day, Tim arrived at the house again, his eyes involuntarily sweeping the field. A few weeks ago, he would check the entire house before starting work. This was progress, but it was much less nerve-wracking yesterday with Johnny around.

Most of the house was a dusty mess. The bulk of the work thus far had been gutting the old walls, modernizing and re-insulating, and none of the rooms were finished. The turret was the cleanest room in the house, so Tim made it his office. The room included a desk, a folding chair, and two boxes of files: one for his business and the other for personal papers.

He came to look at his bank book. While the Mildred Wells episode had only taken two weeks, he had fallen behind on a plan that left no room for error. Buying, fixing, and selling this house was crucial, and his money situation was tighter than planned, with more than a year to go before completion.

He opened the passbook and saw the number: $3,422.83. He would have to subtract construction materials and living expenses from this amount. There would be odd money trickling in from Johnny's jobs back home, but probably little more than was needed to keep Johnny on the payroll. He could freelance in the Lakes Region if need be, but that would take time away from the house.

Tim promised himself he would not skimp on his love life either. He and Holly were in their honeymoon phase, and worrying about money was not sexy. Their dinners out did add up, but at twelve to fifteen dollars a pop, it was worth the investment. He and Sheila never realized that, and their divorce cost more than dinners ever would have, not to mention the emotional turmoil for the girls.

That afternoon, the phone rang in the living room. Holly had already called, so chances were, it was either garbage or bad news. Tim wished there was a machine that answered phone calls so he could respond whenever he wanted. Tim picked up on the third ring, and to his frustration, Sheila's voice was on the other end.

"I was calling about the pick-up tomorrow night," said Sheila. "The girls have a birthday party after school, so they'll be at Mindy Stevens' house, and she's on Route 110. The party's from 5:00 pm to 7:00 pm, so you can get them at 7:00."

The regular pick-up was any time between 6-6:30 pm, as written in their Permanent Stipulations document, but Sheila loved to test the limits and piss him off. This time, however, the extra hour worked in his favor.

"You know, Sheila, one of these times, I'm not going to be able to go along with your special instructions, and you'll have to keep them the extra night."

"That's fine, Tim. If you don't want to see your children, I'll happily keep them."

"That's not what I said, and you know it. See you tomorrow." Tim ended the phone call before she could get the last word.

The next day, Tim arrived at the Stevens' house at 7:00 pm, but the girls didn't come out until 7:30, and when they did, they begged to stay longer. Sheila's change of plans had made him the bad guy, even though she was not supposed to schedule activities during his visitation time. After a twenty-mile grudge, Vivian spoke:

"Are you going to let us play outside this time, Dad?"

"Yes, you can play outside. I know the house better now. Just be careful in the hayloft. And around the pond. And out in the grove. And ..."

"Daaaaa-aaad!"

"I was kidding! But watch out for nails lying around."

Arriving at the house, they pulled around to the side of the house and parked in front of the barn. Thankfully, no lights were on in the turret, no boats were in the pond, and no one was walking through his field.

Six minutes later, Holly pulled in. She didn't like being the first to arrive at the house, and he didn't blame her. After the previous visitation weekend, Tim and Holly told the girls they were dating. It was soon, but it felt right, and it wasn't like they were moving in together. Not yet, anyway.

The only problem was that Sheila knew, and when Tim was happy, she did her best to sabotage his plans, using the girls to mess with his schedule. Tim did not doubt that the holidays would be a nightmare when they came around, too.

"Hey, Holly's here," said Tim.

"Yay!" said Vivian. Olivia wasn't quite as excited, but Tim chalked it up to her eight year old attitude.

"Hi, guys!" said Holly, holding two pizza boxes. "How's it going?" Vivian grabbed her hand and began to tell her about the birthday party as Olivia and Tim followed. After they entered the breakfast area, Holly stepped aside, eyeballing Tim. Tim caught the signal, stepped ahead of the bunch, and rushed through the house, clicking on lights as he went.

"Dad, where are you going?" asked Olivia.

Tim jogged up the stairs to the bedrooms, head on a swivel, even though he wanted to believe Mildred was gone. A minute later, he returned to the kitchen. "I couldn't remember if I made your bed, so I had to check. You're all set." The girls looked at him sideways. Relieved, Holly pulled a bottle of wine out of her bag and winked at Tim, smiling for the first time and finally feeling the relaxation of Friday night.

Olivia changed the subject. "Dad, you're not going to change our nightgowns again, are you? Mom was mad you never returned our other ones."

Tim grimaced. "No, I'm not going to do that. Let's forget it ever happened."

"Hey, Holly, Daddy says he's not going to freak out this weekend when we go outside," said Vivian.

"Well, that's good news." Holly looked at him, wondering what his exact words had been.

"Yeah. Farms can be dangerous, and I'm still going to worry, but I promise to be better." Olivia rolled her eyes as cheese dripped from her chin.

"I don't like the geese," said Vivian. "One hissed at us last time. And the little boy wouldn't talk." Tim stopped chewing. Holly gagged on her wine.

"Well, I think the little boy moved away, but the geese still show up."

"Are you sleeping over, Holly?" asked Vivian.

Holly blushed and turned to Tim. "Well, yes, I was thinking about it. And then tomorrow, I'll show you how to make my favorite breakfast, *waffles*. I even brought my waffle iron. It's out in the car."

"Yay!" Both girls cheered.

CHAPTER 130

May 22, 1971

Holly heard the girls wake early. They had the sunniest room in the house, and she wondered if Tim had thought that one through. Two more bedrooms were at the back of the house but were plastered with construction dust.

Tim got up and dressed as the girls whispered their way downstairs, followed by the sound of the porch door opening and closing. A minute later, she heard him follow them outside. The house went quiet, and Holly realized she was too afraid to fall back asleep.

But she also didn't want to get up. It felt safer to listen to the house rather than vice versa. Walking down the hall would set off creaky floorboards. A toothbrush made a racket and might cover up things she would want to hear. Holly realized that she was trapped.

If she had to, she could bolt down the stairs and exit through the front door, but then what? Find Tim, still in her pajamas, and ask him to come back in so she could pee? Suddenly, inside the bedroom, a housefly buzzed.

Holly leaped like a cat, dressed, ran downstairs, and was on the lawn barefoot in less than a minute. She used to hate spiders, but the common housefly, the mother of the maggot and harbinger of Mildred Wells, had taken over as Holly's worst household pest.

In need of human contact, Holly walked to the corner of the house and peered around. Thankfully, Tim stood in front of the barn, barking reminders to the girls who had climbed up to the hayloft and were in the doorway above the driveway.

"No, I won't throw it up to you. You're scaring me. Get away from the doorway. I don't want you to fall!"

Vivian had somehow dropped her shoe. "Back up, back up, back up!"

"Dad, you're boring!" cried Olivia.

"Olivia, I'm *this close* to going back to Boring Dad. There's plenty to do around here that isn't fifteen feet in the air." With all the fun of throwing things down to the driveway taken away, the girls climbed down, disappointed.

"I knew you'd be boring," exclaimed Olivia.

Tim looked at his watch. "7:52 am on Saturday, and you're already bored. That must be a world record."

"Is it safe in the front yard?" Olivia quizzed.

"Yes!" answered Tim.

"Is it safe in the field?"

"Yes!"

"Is it safe in the grove?"

This time, Tim hesitated. "Uh, no." She'd caught him off guard. "Not alone because I can't see you out there. Do you want to go? I'll take you out there right now."

"Dad, you have to trust us! We can't even climb those trees!"

Tim looked to Holly for help, but Holly let him be the bad guy. "Fifteen minutes. If you're not back, I'm coming to get you, and I won't be happy."

"Yay!" they said in unison, and both girls bolted for the trail at the bend in the driveway.

When they were gone, Holly spoke. "I thought you were sure Mildred is gone."

"I—*am*. I work here alone, and I'm telling you, it's different. It's just that the grove and the pond are still a little scary."

Holly was skeptical, too, but Tim might be right. There was evidence things had changed. They had used Annette's journals and Holly's calendars to piece the month of May together. May 12 was the day Thomas died, and May 14 was his funeral. Annette had seen and heard things happen on her watch, but none of that came to pass in 1971. It was a sign that Mildred was gone, but it wasn't proof. "Let's spy on them for fifteen minutes. I'm not going inside alone."

Fourteen minutes later, Tim and Holly exited the woods undetected by the girls and acted as if they'd been in the house the entire time.

"Hi, Dad, you can relax. Is it time to make the waffles?" said Olivia.

"Yes, it is. How was the grove? Did you get it out of your system?"

"Creepy!" said Vivian. Vivian liked spooky things like Halloween and *Casper the Friendly Ghost*. She also enjoyed a new cartoon called *Scooby-Doo*.

"You like creepy stuff, don't you, Viv?" *Oh, if she only knew.*

"Yup!" she retorted.

"Somebody was planting a garden or something. The forest is all dug up in the last row," added Olivia.

"Girls, what do you think of your waffles?" asked Holly, wanting to change the subject.

"They're great!" said Vivian.

"You sound like Tony the Tiger," said Olivia. Both girls giggled. "These are better than Frosted Flakes."

"I like how the dimples catch the syrup," said Holly.

"Me too!" said Vivian.

"I don't know if I'm supposed to say something, but your dad and I have a surprise for you." Holly looked at Tim, who exaggerated the excitement by bulging his eyeballs.

"What is it?" asked Olivia.

"Well, it's been a month since we've been there, so we thought you might like to go to—well, maybe I shouldn't say."

"What! Come on! You have to tell us now! It's not fair!" complained Vivian.

"Okay, I'll tell you. We're going … to … Funspot!" Holly referred to the arcade with go-karts, video games, and other fun stuff. The adults needed a break from Lancaster Hill Road, and it was only Saturday morning.

The patchwork family enjoyed their day away, stopping for Chinese food on the way home, and all was well. Holly drove up the driveway, and the adults checked the turret, pond, and field on their way to parking in front of the barn. Holly breathed a sigh of relief. It was a lovely house as long as the previous owners left you alone.

They went to bed that evening without incident, and Holly felt she was getting to know Tim's kids for the first time. She listened carefully to their stories and found herself forgetting about April. Sunday morning came, and the kids woke early again. Holly was surprised when Tim lifted his head and let them leave, then rolled over and massaged her.

"Did you hear them leave? I'm not sure I—"

Holly protested, but Tim held a finger to his lips. "They're outside. Let's take advantage of the opportunity."

Holly smiled. Tim really was confident they were safe here. They ran to the bathroom without wasting more time, brushed their teeth, and jumped back in bed.

CHAPTER 131

Hampstead, New Hampshire
June 8, 1971

Diane Enrico, the mother of the boy murdered in the Hampstead woods, was angry with the authorities. In her opinion, things were moving too slowly, and the trail was growing cold. She checked with the police daily, and they had begun to shun her, sure signs nothing was being done, which was unacceptable.

After three sleepless nights, she decided that she could do better, and with that in mind, Mrs. Enrico went to the local printer and had a thousand full-color flyers made and mailed to every news agency she could find. She posted the rest of the flyers on every telephone pole in a ten-mile radius, and eventually, the *Salem Evening News* picked up her story.

Robert Simmons read the article and slept on it. He thought about the line he had drawn on the map that clearly intersected Sanborn, Hampstead, and Beverly Farms. He also thought about the Gottlieb boy's description of the woman and the shape he saw in the tree.

When he woke the following day, he picked up the phone and dialed Diane Enrico anonymously. During the phone call, he recanted his version of the "legend" of Mildred Wells (as he put it) and her Sanborn history. Before he hung up, Simmons was sure to mention he believed Mildred Wells was responsible for the death of her son and that he might have seen her recently at the farm that burned down in Beverly Farms.

Diane Enrico, already angry, went straight to the press with the information. From there, the news went in several different directions. First, the press once again swarmed the burned-down house in Beverly Farms. On the second day, everyone spent their time gathering information on the new suspect but discarded the theory when they discovered Mildred had been dead since 1863. After that, the press dropped Diane Enrico like a hot potato.

Simmons didn't care that he'd made a fool of Mrs. Enrico or that the story made no sense to the public. It would take time for people to accept a ghost story. Diane Enrico was an introduction. In the end, everyone would see.

CHAPTER 132

June 10, 1971

Neither Tim nor Holly watched the Channel Nine broadcast featuring the update on the Enrico boy, but Robert Simmons did and was highly pleased. Things couldn't have gone any better. Before putting on his shoes, he cracked another beer to sustain his courage. Tonight would be the first time a Simmons set foot on Mildred Wells' property in a long time.

Minutes later, Simmons drove up Tim's driveway and parked in front of the porch. The police cruiser would make a formidable backdrop. He wore street clothes, which was appropriate. He was only doing his neighbor a favor. As he parked, he grabbed the empty ring in the six-pack, gently swinging the five remaining beers as he knocked on the door.

A saw buzzed from inside, so he waited until it stopped before knocking again. Tim Russell came to the door, apparently working alone in the kitchen.

"Hello … officer? Can I help you?"

"Mr. Russell, my name is Robert Simmons, and I'm your neighbor. I live about a mile down—"

Tim smiled, recognizing the name. "I know who you are. The cruiser had me confused for a minute. Nice to meet you. It looks like you came bringing gifts. Come in!"

Robert Simmons hesitated, lost in the moment. To his knowledge, none of his ancestors had ever set foot inside the Wells house. "Uh, sure, that'd be great. I stopped by to welcome you to the neighborhood, but I'm about a month or so late."

"Better late than never, Bob. Come on in. I just made my last cut, and it's time to clean up. Want to talk while I do that?"

Simmons nodded nervously and stepped into the house. "Wow. I've lived on this road my whole life and never set foot on this property. I'm a little overwhelmed."

Tim looked at him sideways but knew Simmons and his family history. "Aw, it's just a house. Hey, listen, I'd offer you a seat, but I don't have much furniture."

Simmons handed Tim a beer, and Tim cracked it and took a long sip.

"That hits the spot. Want to see the place?"

Simmons couldn't say no. Along the tour, he imagined Mildred Wells roaming the hallways, the crazy, murdering bitch she was, living free when she should be burning in hell. The house was looking good, and the work-in-progress was terrific. The two men made small talk along the way: neighborhood talk, the Sanborn Police, and the Red Sox. Finally, the tour ended, and they were back in the breakfast area.

"Do you know about the history of this house?" Simmons asked.

"Uh, I know a little bit about the house, I guess," said Tim. "The last family here was the Smiths. It was empty for three years …"

Simmons cut him off. "No, before that. Like, way back. The people who built it and so forth."

"Well, I'm not sure. What do you want to know?" said Tim.

"My family has a history with the Pikes, the Wellses, or whatever you want to call them. Some of the people in my family never got over it. Two of my ancestors were killed, and many in my family think it happened on this property. I don't mean to get all gory on you, but I feel like, in a way, I'm helping my family. Thanks for letting me see the place."

"Well, I can't say I know how I've helped, but you're welcome," said Tim, drying his palms on his pants. *Please, Bob, don't be the guy that wouldn't leave.*

"My great-grandmother Elizabeth, or great-aunt, maybe, I can't remember her actual relation to me, was alive in the 1800s, and what was left of her was found just across the street. My family always believed it was at the hands of the woman who built this house, Mildred Wells, a.k.a. Mildred Pike. My other ancestor, Elizabeth's daughter, Emma, went missing and was never found, but they always suspected the Wells woman of that one, too.

"I admit my family had a bit of a reputation. They were nosy, and everyone knew they didn't like Ms. Wells. Some townspeople thought they got what they asked for. All this information is creepy. I apologize." Simmons slurred his last sentence badly.

"Hey, no problem," said Tim. "I'm sorry about your ancestors. That sounds like some grim stuff that happened here." Tim shifted from one foot to the other, trying to get comfortable, then leaned back against the counter, which seemed to work.

"She killed her kid, you know," said Simmons. "In the pond. Did they tell you before you bought the place?"

"Yes, Officer, I know some things that happened, but I try not to dwell on it. I hope to erase that past by restoring this property."

"Please, Tim, call me Bob. We're neighbors. Did you read the news about the kid they found in Hampstead last week?"

Tim had not but braced for another boring story. "No. All I do is work on this place with a little radio in the corner playing Top 40. Bob, why are we talking about murders? Are you the Welcome Wagon or the Meat Wagon?" Tim tried to crack a joke, but Simmons stared back, straight-faced.

"I don't drive an ambulance," Simmons stated in a monotone.

Tim didn't understand. "What?"

"You called me the Meat Wagon. That's an ambulance." Simmons was feeling no pain. The last sentence sounded like *thatch an ambulanch.*

"Oh, right, sorry, I meant a hearse. Forget it. The point is, I work alone in this place from dawn 'til dark. I don't want to think of dead people."

"Are you superstitious?"

"Not particularly, but I get startled when somebody knocks late in the evening."

"Sorry about that. I could never do what you're doing. I am a superstitious man. I can't even watch a horror movie."

Fascinating, thought Tim. *Why don't you go home and watch a comedy then?*

"I believe in ghosts, do you?" Simmons continued.

"No. I don't believe in ghosts, Bob."

"You haven't seen the news. You were busy fixing this cursed house."

"Cursed? What news, Bob?"

"It was on Channel Nine about a half-hour ago. I came here to warn you if you believe in this sort of thing, but you don't, so I'll tell you anyway as a neighborly courtesy. First, there was a kid killed in Hampstead. Then there was a house fire in Beverly Farms with bones found in the ashes."

Tim wasn't sure he wanted to hear the rest. "Bones, dead people. Beverly Farms? A hundred miles away? Where are you going with this?"

"Mr. Russell, you've been here since April. Have you seen anything?"

"Bob, is this official police business?"

"No, this is not official police business. I'm talking about ghosts. I'm sticking my neck out. The name 'Mildred Wells' was mentioned on the Channel Nine news tonight, and she's been dead for a long time. What do you know about her?"

"I don't know what you're talking about, Bob," said Tim, attempting to laugh it off.

Simmons stared, and Tim dropped his eyes. "Bullshit."

Tim put his beer down and stared at the floor, wondering if he should do what he was about to do. Mind made up, he walked through the kitchen and climbed the turret stairs. Bob Simmons wondered for a drunk second if Tim might be fetching a gun, so he rested his hand on his holster. Tim returned fifteen seconds later with the Simmons Family Scrapbook. Bob's eyes bugged, and he gasped. "How the fuck did you get that?"

Tim wished Holly was here to help. Tim didn't know Officer Bob Simmons at all, yet somehow, they had become neighborly. Due to his empty stomach, the beer went straight to his head. Perhaps giving Simmons the scrapbook was premature, but the cat was out of the bag.

"How the hell did you get that?" asked Simmons.

"It was here when we moved in. I saw the name Simmons in it and put it aside. I planned on dropping it off. Sorry, I haven't had a chance to get out much. I didn't know it was a big deal."

Simmons cradled the book as if he'd found a baby on the railroad tracks. "I've been staring at this book on my bookshelf for as long as I can remember, even recently, I think. There's no way Annette Smith had it, she would have told me." Trying to recall the last time he'd seen the scrapbook, Simmons pulled out his map. "This is weird, too. Check this out." Simmons showed Tim his hand-drawn hundred-mile line through Sanborn, Hampstead, and Beverly Farms.

"So, you're saying you think a ghost has something to do with the death in Hampstead and the fire in Beverly?" said Tim.

"Beverly Farms, to be more specific. I saw the Hampstead story in the newspaper, which set off alarms. I told you, I'm superstitious. Then I drew the line, thinking she was headed for Salem, Massachusetts. Mildred Wells was from Salem."

"You know that the Salem Witch Trials were not about witches, right?" said Tim. "Those were innocent people that were hanged."

"Yeah, but tell that to the crazies that want Halloween to be three hundred and sixty-five days a year. It's way more than witches down there now. There's a dark underbelly of devil worshippers, the occult, Ouija Boards, the whole thing."

Tim grew up in Ipswich, not far from Salem. "Oh, come on, Bob, I don't agree with that."

"Yeah? Look me in the eyes and tell me you don't think there's a chance she's back." Caught off guard, Tim hesitated just enough to fail the test. "Tim, it was on Channel Nine. They're looking into it. They said the name, Mildred Wells!"

"You're saying that Channel Nine reported that police are on the hunt for Sanborn's Mildred Wells? A ghost?"

"No, I didn't say that. They looked her up. They know she's dead."

The phone rang. *Oh no.* Fifty-fifty chance it was Sheila. "Excuse me, Bob." Tim walked to the living room to answer the phone, and thankfully, it was Holly. "Oh, good. I thought you might be you-know-who. I'll be on my way soon. My neighbor is here. Bob Simmons. He brought me a beer."

Holly sounded upset. "Lucky you. I know why he's there, though, and you won't like it."

"I think I know what you mean."

"Channel Nine just mentioned Mildred Wells in connection with a murder in Hampstead and a fire in Beverly, even though she's been dead since the 1800s."

"Yeah. I heard the same thing." Tim stretched the telephone cord to see into the kitchen. "Why?"

"It was the boy's mother in Hampstead, Diane Enrico. An anonymous caller told her that it was Mildred, but whoever it was didn't mention she was dead. As embarrassed as the mother is, she's still pissed at the police. She doesn't think they're doing enough and took the opportunity to embarrass them on TV."

"What has she told about Mildred?" Tim winced as the words tumbled from his lips. No doubt Simmons heard.

"I have no idea. Mildred was never convicted of anything. They couldn't even prove she drowned Elmer. Nobody knows who Mildred Wells is except maybe the three of us: you, me, and Simmons. I've lived in Laconia my entire life and had never heard the name."

"That's weird," was all Tim could say, still regretting his slip-up. "Hold on. Hey Bob, you saw the Channel Nine story, right? What do you know about Diane Enrico, the lady from Hampstead who mentioned Mildred?"

Bob Simmons entered the living room so that Holly could hear him. "I don't know anything about her. Hampstead is a half-hour away from here."

Holly whispered in Tim's ear. "Is it safe to talk about this right now, Tim?" Holly was right. It was time to end the evening and get to Holly's house.

"All right, honey, I'm almost done here. Cleaning up. I'll be over soon."

"Alright, see you," she said, and they hung up. "This is a lot to process, Bob. What do you think the market for a haunted house will be in about a year?"

"I wouldn't worry about the house so much as your safety," he replied. "And if you know what Mildred is capable of, I'm betting you agree."

Very clever, Simmons, Tim thought. *But I'm done giving you information.* "Bob, I appreciate you coming over and getting to know you. I don't know what you're talking about, and I'm late for a date in Laconia. Why don't we continue this conversation some other time?"

"Sounds good. Name the time."

"You know where I'll be."

"I'm anxious to hear more," said Simmons.

"Sure. Hey, are you okay to drive? I can run you back if you like."

"It's only a mile. I don't think I'll get pulled over." Simmons smiled.

Sanborn's Finest, Tim thought. "All right, take care, Bob, Thanks again."

Simmons drove out, backing over a portion of the lawn before straightening the car. Tim closed the porch door and got ready to leave for the night.

CHAPTER 133

June 10, 1971

Back in Laconia, Holly was beside herself. "What the hell was the Bob Simmons visit about? Exhuming bodies and moving the bones is illegal to the best of my knowledge. We have to be careful around him. He might be a loon like his ancestors. And what the fuck, Thomas Pike? He was supposed to take Mildred with him! I hate everything. I hate Thomas Pike, I hate Bob Simmons, and I hate your house."

"Hey, you sold me that house," said Tim. Holly rolled her eyes. *Not funny.* Tim continued, "Simmons heard me ask you about Mildred. That proves we know who she is. I need to sell this place. Who the hell is this woman from Hampstead anyway?"

"I don't know, but I can't get past Thomas Pike. He used us! Tim, I don't want to stay at your place until we're sure she's gone. Maybe this Diane Enrico is wrong, but until we know different, I'm sleeping in Laconia."

Tim sighed. Holly still didn't know everything. "Honey, Simmons showed me something that bothered me." Tim went to his truck, fetched a map, and brought it inside. Using a book as a straightedge, he drew a line between Sanborn, Hampstead, and Beverly Farms. "Simmons says the farm in Beverly used to be a cult, and Mildred might have been a part of it. It's the next town over from Salem."

"So—she walked there? She didn't even use the road. Wonderful. Did she walk through that pond? Tim, if she's back, she's pissed at us."

Tim didn't know what to say, and they finished dinner in silence. Before bed, Holly made Tim drag the dining room table in front of the door for added security. Despite their fatigue, they couldn't sleep and stayed up to watch the eleven o'clock news for a replay of Diane Enrico's piece. When it came on, they couldn't believe their ears. It was as bad as Bob Simmons said.

CHAPTER 134

June 11, 1971

Tim woke early after a miserable night's sleep. Not surprisingly, they had not made love after the news broadcast. Tim ran out to the gas station to get them both coffees and as he pulled out his wallet, he glanced at the newspaper rack.

The *Manchester Union Leader* was there, and Diane Enrico was the headline. MOTHER BLAMES GHOST FOR DEATH OF SON. It was a misleading headline, seeing as the woman wasn't told Mildred was dead, but it would sell newspapers. Tim picked up a copy and paid, then rushed back to Holly's house.

The fact that Mildred Wells was a front-page story in the state's biggest newspaper was a bad sign. The writer touched on Mildred's history, but only that she had lived in Sanborn and was a widow. It listed her death as 1863 but made no mention of her son Elmer or his death.

From there, the story went to Diane Enrico and why she named a dead person as a murder suspect. Diane told the reporter the details of the anonymous phone call and that the person told her convincingly that Eric's death and the fire in Beverly Farms were related.

"That's got Bob Simmons' fingerprints all over it," said Holly. "Like I said last night, nobody, not even the locals, has ever heard of Mildred Wells."

The following day, Tim returned to work, and it wasn't long before Bob Simmons' police cruiser came up the driveway. Simmons stepped out of the vehicle wearing the same clothes he had the previous evening. "Good morning, neighbor," he said.

"Hi, Bob," Tim replied.

"Hey, I know you're starting your day, but I'd like to show you something if you have a minute. You busy?"

"I have a minute. What do you need?"

"Walk with me." Simmons went to the road and crossed. "Watch out for that, that's Poison Ivy." Simmons gestured to a patch of shiny-leaved plants.

"Thanks, uh, where are we headed?" But Tim knew.

"Well, I wanted to show you something dear to the Simmons family, and that's where they found Elizabeth. I come here twice a year to lay flowers."

Not far into the woods and just across the street from Tim's house, a modest cross made of welded metal pipes stuck out of the ground, anchored in a cement foundation. A metal dinner platter was bolted to it with a hand-engraved epitaph.

Elizabeth Simmons
1835-1862
Vengeance is mine, sayeth the Lord

The Bible quote seemed oddly inappropriate, yet so on brand for a Simmons. Tim looked back. The June foliage had filled things in, but if he looked hard enough, he could see white paint through the trees. It was his house and, more specifically, his bedroom.

"Can you believe she got away with this? It's not technically her property, but give me a break. That was probably her bedroom right there, and she got up every morning and flipped the bird at my great-aunt. It's a damned disgrace she was never brought to justice."

"Wasn't her husband a cop? How did he let this go?"

"You know a lot, don't you, Russell?" Simmons smiled.

"Call me Tim."

"Tell me about your April, Tim. How was the move-in? Did you see her?"

Tim looked away. It was an odd feeling being in the woods and talking to a man with a gun. "Bob, I hate to ruin your theory, but I haven't had any problems. All I want to do is fix this place and resell it, and your Mildred Wells story doesn't do me any favors. I want it to go away."

"Well, that's up to her, isn't it?"

"You're talking about a dead woman, Bob. The Enrico woman got a crank phone call. Did you see the newspaper this morning?"

Simmons had not but didn't care. "No, I didn't see that."

"Mrs. Enrico says she received an anonymous tip. Somebody called Mrs. Enrico, gave her Mildred's name, and never told her she was dead."

"And you think it was me?"

Tim felt a drop of sweat run down his back. He didn't want to be alone in the woods with Simmons anymore.

"Where are you going?" said Simmons.

"I'm going back to work."

"I'm just interested in some family justice, Tim. They only found parts of Elizabeth, you know. The coyotes took the rest. My other relative, Emma Simmons, is still missing. The Gottlieb kid saw her. Mildred Wells, in the flesh. The boys said they saw a woman in a black farm dress. They said the dress reminded them of that old painting with the farm couple holding the pitchfork. So, I did a little investigating. I took my dog to Hampstead, the place where the kid was killed. He used to be a cadaver dog. He went nuts when he caught a whiff of her. I practically had to chase him to a pond, and the trail ended there."

"So, you—"

"I'm not finished. Then I went to Beverly Farms, where that cult farm burned, and saw something."

"What did you see?" said Tim, hating that he had to know.

"Before I tell you, Russell, I just want to say I know you're full of shit. You've seen her. The fact you know her name is enough to give it away."

"Bob, I don't want to get into a shouting match, so I will excuse myself. And stay off my property. I don't want to hear any more ghost stories."

"When I went to Beverly Farms, I saw her up in a tree, watching. It was just her and me. The firefighters were gone. The press had left. It was like she was waiting for me. You know when the hair stands up on the back of your neck? I pulled my pistol and walked to the forest's edge but lost sight of her. I got spooked. Pistol or not, I got the hell out of there. Do you know what I mean?" Simmons stared. "I'd bet my house you do."

Tim kept a straight face even though Simmons had rightfully called him out. "Bob, I wish you luck, but we're talking in circles. I'm going to leave now. I'm late for work."

CHAPTER 135

June 11, 1971

Five more revenants snuck into Beverly Farms after checking their runes and seeing their population dwindle. One by one, they came, and one by one, Mildred killed them, always aiming for the heart. Only three remained: one awake and two asleep. Mildred suspected the conscious one was hanging back for fear of getting ambushed, but the sleepers wouldn't know anything was amiss.

Mildred stood in the tree overlooking the farm, patiently waiting, unable to stop thinking about the Simmons cop from Sanborn. She recalled the snowless December when she caught a different Simmons on her property, chased her across the street, and killed her in the woods.

Committing murder was complicated back then because she was still mortal. Mildred couldn't move the body, so she covered it with leaves as best she could and went back inside. It was plain luck that it took them so long to find her body. There were days when Mildred could see body parts strewn by coyotes from her bedroom window. Even Elizabeth's father, George, a police captain, didn't search the land across the street.

Emma Simmons, too, was quite a story. Mildred caught Emma in the grove, which made things easy. Emma's screams went unheard, and when it was over, all Mildred had to do was dig a hole and dump her in it. Who would have thought that a hundred years later, she would get to kill another nosy Simmons?

CHAPTER 136

June 12, 1971

Tim sat at Holly's table and told her all about his encounter with Bob Simmons. The forecast for their future as neighbors was cloudy at best, not to mention the possibility Mildred had never left. Tim talked about buying more weapons and safeguards to protect himself during workdays.

"With what money? said Holly.

"I'm not sure I even believe this guy, but do I have a choice?" he asked, and Holly couldn't argue.

"If you go out and buy stuff, have a plan. Don't blow a bunch of money without a budget."

"It will start getting dark earlier in a month or two, so I'll need floodlights. Eventually, half my workday will be in the freaking dark. That takes time to set up. I can't wait until November. Also, I think I'll need a rifle, some extra machetes, and either barbed wire or an electric fence. Maybe just around the main building while I'm working."

"If Bob Simmons sees any of that, he'll know who it's for."

"Yeah, well, Bob Simmons isn't allowed on my property. I'll tell him it's for him! I should rope off the entrance to the driveway. He'll need a warrant."

"He has no cause for a warrant."

"Even if he did, we already moved Elmer's bones, and I tilled the spot. There's no evidence to uncover."

Tim's words comforted Holly. Somehow, their lives had gone haywire, and hiding graves was the good news. Smiling, she asked him to turn off the light.

CHAPTER 137

June 12, 1971

Sheila Palmer (formerly Sheila Russell) looked at her kitchen calendar. Her friend Sylvia had just called to let her know she had an extra ticket for the Johnny Cash concert in Portland, but it fell on a Friday night, which was Tim's visitation time, so Sheila bit her lip and invented a story. Tim called every Monday evening before dinner to speak with the girls. Sure enough, at 5:30 pm, the phone rang.

"Olivia, get the phone! It's probably your father!" barked Sheila.

"Coming, Mom!" Olivia picked up the receiver. "Hello?"

"Hello, Liv! It's Dad. What's going on? Getting ready for dinner?"

"Hi, Daddy! Yeah."

"What are you having? Do you know?"

"Mom, what are we having for dinner?"

"No, never mind, Liv, you don't have to—"

"Chicken and corn."

"So, what are you up to? How was school? How's your boyfriend Brian?"

"You know I don't have a boyfriend, Dad. There's only one Brian in my class, and I hate him. He pulled my hair when we were in second grade!"

"I'm teasing. I'm just checking in to see what's up. I'm looking forward to Friday. We'll have fun."

"Oh, okay. Hey, Dad, do you want to talk to Vivian?"

"Uh, sure. Have a good week, Liv, I love you!"

"I love you too!" Olivia yelled the last sentence as the phone changed hands.

"Hello?" It was Vivian.

"Hi, Viv! How was school?"

"Good. Um, Dad, Mommy wants to talk to you."

"Wait, you just picked up the—"

Sheila took the phone from Vivian. "Go take a bath, honey. Dinner will be ready in a little bit. No, no. What? Because I said so, now start the water, I'll be right up. Because. Because I have to talk to your father for a minute. He can call you after dinner. Or tomorrow. And you'll see him this weekend. Go. *Go!*" Sheila waited until Vivian was gone before dropping the bomb on Tim.

"Hi, Tim. I wanted to touch base with you about Friday's pickup."

"I told you, Sheila, don't schedule anything for the girls during my visitation."

Sheila ignored him and continued. "My parents are watching the kids on Friday, so they're going to be in Kennebunk."

"You expect me to drive to Maine? No way, Sheila. You test our written agreement every time you get a chance, and I'm sick of it!"

"Oh, relax, Tim. It only adds twenty minutes to your commute, and the girls want to see their grandparents. If you want to see them this weekend, you'll have to pick them up in Kennebunk." Sheila smirked but was getting bored. Tim was so easy to manipulate. *Just shut up and do it.*

"We spent a ton of money on the lawyers, and you don't even follow the agreement," said Tim. "Do you know what agreement means? It means you don't sign the paper if you disagree. Otherwise, it's bad faith."

"Sorry, Tim. It's the only time that worked for everyone. You're self-employed and make your own schedule. You can see the children any time you want, but for some reason, you choose to do so only every two weeks."

"That's written into the agreement, too. You act like it was my choice. Where the hell will you be on Friday?" he asked.

"I have business to attend to," she spat. "Life happens, Tim. A five-page agreement can't possibly cover every scenario. Will you be there, or should I tell my folks they have the girls overnight?"

"Tell them I'll be there at 6:00 pm. But one day, Sheila, we're going to get this habit of yours fixed, no matter how much money it costs."

It was a rough night for Tim. He managed to maintain conversation for the most part, but there was a dark cloud over his head. The problems had come simultaneously: Bob Simmons, Sheila's torment, and the possibility that Mildred was back. All three beat his brain like a drum as he tried to fall asleep.

As he stared at the ceiling, Tim sorted through his issues. The Mildred possibility was by far the worst and the one that wouldn't let him sleep. Tim imagined her sneaking up on him as he worked and knew he needed to be safe, which would cost money. Tim fell asleep after 2:00 am.

CHAPTER 138

June 13, 1971

Tim kept the machete close the following day and set up two nuisance barricades: the desk from the turret and the telephone table from the living room. Both were tilted on two legs against different doors and would make noise if anyone tried sneaking up on him.

Rather than eat lunch, he drove twenty minutes to Concord, parted with one hundred fifty dollars, and bought a double-barreled shotgun. Back at the house, he leaned it in the corner and returned to work. For practice, he grabbed the gun and pointed it at the kitchen doorway as if Mildred were approaching. Four trial runs later, he decided it was too bulky. Taking his saw, Tim cut most of the buttstock off, making the grip pistol-like.

Still unsatisfied that he had to use both hands, Tim took the next step. Sawing the barrel off would make the gun illegal, so he would have to make sure Bob Simmons didn't see it. Once most of the barrel was gone, he practiced a few more times and found it to his liking.

Tim returned to Laconia that evening exhausted but happy that Mildred Wells hadn't shown up. Perhaps Bob's story was gossip, after all. Bob Simmons hadn't shown up either. Tim was so full of good news he conveniently forgot to tell Holly about the sawed-off shotgun.

"How was your day?" he asked.

"I called the Chief of police in Hampstead," she said.

Tim put down his beer, stunned. "You did?"

"Yeah. I didn't learn much, though. I think I'll try the Gottlieb kid next."

Tim was at a loss for words. "How do you plan on doing that?"

"Picking a traumatized kid's brain is not my idea of a relaxing evening. I'll be honest, I suppose. I'll say I saw Mildred, too, and I want to compare notes. I can't think of any other way to go about it."

"You are tenacious," he said, trying to lighten her mood, but his attempt at levity fell flat.

"Can you think of any questions you want to ask?" Together, they wrote down everything that came to mind, and when they were finished, Holly picked up the phone.

"Hello, Mrs. Gottlieb? I'm sorry to bother you at dinnertime. My name is Holly Burns, and I live in Sanborn. I've been following your story thanks to a police officer named Robert Simmons. It's complex, and I apologize, but Officer Simmons said your son saw a woman who may have owned my boyfriend's house long ago. I was wondering if we could compare notes?"

Marcy Gottlieb sounded skeptical. "A policeman told you this? I'm sorry. I'm just not following."

"You probably don't know him. Sorry for the confusion. Officer Simmons is familiar with the woman your son saw."

"Does this have anything to do with that dead woman bullshit? Because I don't have time for this."

"Absolutely not, ma'am. I'm talking about a woman I saw on my boyfriend's property."

"How come I don't know about this? Chief Luoma never mentioned anything about new leads!"

Holly knew she was walking the razor's edge. "I'm not sure, but I can direct you to Officer Simmons if you like." Tim looked at Holly in disbelief, most likely upset that she'd just given Simmons a reason to be in his driveway again. "You can also talk to my boyfriend, Tim Russell. I want to see this woman put away." Holly was careful not to use any words concerning the supernatural.

"Mark has not been well since his friend died. I hesitate to put him through this," said Mrs. Gottlieb.

"I would be concerned too if I were in your shoes," said Holly. "Perhaps I should tell you what I know, and you can think it over. I want to be sure we're talking about the same woman. My boyfriend bought his house in April. Officer Simmons lives about a mile down the road and claims to have a history with the woman. He also says the fire in Beverly Farms is related to the Hampstead incident."

Tim grabbed his hair and pretended to pull it out, and Holly turned away so he wouldn't ruin her concentration. "Every so often, we saw a woman walking through our field, wearing a long black farm dress."

"Did your boyfriend buy the house from her?"

"No, the bank owned it at the time. This woman was a previous owner." Tim seemed to relax as his faith in Holly's story grew. "Anyway, one day by our pond, we saw her, and she—I apologize for what I'm about to say, but she killed two geese as if she still owned the property."

"Did you call the police?" asked Mrs. Gottlieb.

"No. The woman seemed deranged, and Tim told her to get off his property. She took the geese and left. That's why I'm reaching out. I hoped we could compare notes."

There was silence on the other end of the phone. "Mark, honey, can you come here for a minute? Just for a minute." Mrs. Gottlieb put her mouth to the phone again. "I must warn you, Holly, I think he's still in shock. His description differs somewhat, but I think you might help him. It's been so hard on us. Your police references won me over. You can be sure I will look into this."

"Thank you, Mrs. Gottlieb."

"Thank you for calling. Now, here comes Mark. If you could use discretion, I'd appreciate it."

"I certainly will, Mrs. Gottlieb, thank you." Holly heard the phone handoff between the boy and his mother.

"Hello?"

"Hi, Mark. My name is Holly Burns. I told your Mom I think I've seen the same woman you did, but I want to be sure. I know this is painful, but can you tell me what she looked like?"

"Yeah, she had a farm dress like the lady in the *American Gothic* painting."

"Was it just the dress, or did her face look like it too?"

"Not the face. Her face was terrible. I made her mad when I shot her with a BB gun. She had a knife and started to chase us. She choked me with barbed wire around a tree."

"I heard that, and I'm so sorry. Are you feeling better?"

"I'm going to have a scar."

"I'm sorry to hear that. Mark, what else can you tell me about her face?"

"It was white, really white. And scary. Sometimes, I wake up in the middle of the night because I dream about it. Mom got me some pills, though."

"Mark, we're trying to find her. Is there anything else you can tell me about the woman?"

"Yeah, she killed my friend Eric. I didn't see it, but I heard it. I heard the air come out of his lungs."

It sounded as if Mark might start to cry, and Holly realized her time was running out. "Oh my gosh, that's horrible. How did you—"

Mark cut her off. "She smelled terrible, like she was dead, and she was covered in flies! And nobody believes me!"

Mrs. Gottlieb took the phone away. "I'm sorry. He's upset. We have to go. I have to calm him down." The call disconnected, and Holly couldn't take her eyes off the receiver. Mildred Wells had never left.

CHAPTER 139

June 14, 1971

It didn't take long before Bob Simmons' cruiser came up the driveway. Tim shrugged his shoulders and went outside to meet him on the lawn.

"I just got my ass chewed out by Chief Luoma of the Hampstead Police," said Simmons.

"Why is that?" asked Tim.

"Don't play dumb with me, Russell. You and your girlfriend called the Gottlieb woman and talked to her son. Now Mrs. Gottlieb is up Chief Luoma's ass. He doesn't appreciate that, and neither do I."

Tim kicked the grass as if fixing a divot. "Mrs. Gottlieb was on Channel Nine. My girlfriend called to ask about the woman who her son saw, that's all. It has nothing to do with you or Chief Luoma."

Simmons stiffened. "I thought you said you didn't know who Mildred Wells was? You told Mrs. Gottlieb you saw Mildred as if she were a living person, and now she's expecting Luoma to find her."

Tim remained calm, prepared for this moment. "Your family scrapbook told me the name Mildred Wells. You did, too. All I know is we have a woman trespassing on our property, and we're trying to figure out if the boy's murderer is the same woman. I'm sorry for doing your job, but someone has to."

Fire raged behind Simmons' eyes, and his face turned red. "You told me you never saw her, Russell."

"I don't know who Mildred Wells is, Bob. All I know is I have someone trespassing from time to time."

"I try to do you a favor, maybe save your life, and you stab me in the back."

"You aren't helping anyone but yourself, Bob. You want revenge at my expense. Get off my property. Next time, I call your Chief."

Bob Simmons spent the rest of the morning in full uniform, on his own time, driving to Hampstead to share what he knew with Mrs. Gottlieb. Chief Galluzzo, embarrassed, made him do it. When Simmons arrived, he denied everything, saying Holly Burns had lied. "Maybe Holly and her boyfriend were the ones who called Mrs. Enrico, too, Mrs. Gottlieb. Don't worry, the police will investigate them."

When he finished with Mrs. Gottlieb in Hampstead, he had to drive back to Sanborn and work his shift. He knew in his heart he was right about Mildred Wells. He just needed more information. Tim Russell was lying.

When his shift ended at 11, he headed home, passing the Russell house on the way. All the lights were out. Russell didn't appear to be there most nights. A mile later, Simmons pulled onto his family cul-de-sac and parked in front of his house, and King was there to greet him. Heart pounding, Simmons went inside, fed King, changed his clothes to all black, and grabbed his flashlight and Kodak Instamatic camera.

Fifteen hundred yards up the road, he could see the Russell house. Just in case he was mistaken and Russell was indeed home, he cut up by the property line where the woods ended and the field started. The bugs were terrible, and he wished he'd brought repellent.

The other night, he'd had his first time inside the Pike house, and tonight was his first time exploring the land. It was not lost on him that his ancestors had died doing the same thing. It was hard to keep his breathing under control.

As soon as he'd crossed the field and was into the forest, he turned to get a look at the house. When he couldn't see it, he clicked on his flashlight. A mosquito bit him good behind the ear, and he slapped it away too late. It itched immediately.

Simmons wasn't sure what he was looking for, but he imagined Elizabeth and Emma hadn't been either. What were they all looking for? He should have grabbed the scrapbook and studied before coming out, but it was too late. He pulled his pistol to move branches aside as he searched for a trail.

But all of a sudden, there were no more branches. Five yards from Simmons was a row of overgrown spruce, their lowest boughs several feet above his head. He shined his light to the left and realized he was looking down a corridor: the old Christmas tree farm. Simmons, already superstitious, felt the creep-meter climb. To be here was almost too much, and he nearly turned back. Darkness was in both directions. The flashlight was not powerful enough to reach either end.

Hefting his pistol, Simmons began counting the rows and lost count in the thirties when something flew over his head. He didn't know if it was a bat or an owl, but it whooshed past his ear. Mosquitos feasted on his flesh as both hands were occupied. Finally, he began to see imperfections in the perfect rows. Wild trees sprouted of different species and different heights. Finally, the grove ended, and the forest's darkness continued into the night. Simmons shined his light on a patch of ground and noticed something out of place.

The natural carpet of spruce needles was missing, and the soil sank under his weight when he stepped on it. The patch was rectangular, bordered by briars on three sides. Someone had trimmed the thorns to turn the soil. It looked like a garden, but nothing grew. *What have you been doing out here, Tim Russell?*

Simmons pulled out the Kodak, took a few flash pictures, and moved on. Afterward, he jogged through the other rows, looking for similar projects. Minutes later, he considered checking the barn but figured he might be pushing his luck. It was a long shot, but someone might be home. He looked at his watch, and it was past midnight. He still had plenty of time to sleep in.

Inspired by his find, Simmons ran home, grabbed a lantern and shovel, returned, and dug until 3:30 am. He uncovered bits of burned wood, some feathers, and pieces of fabric.

CHAPTER 140

June 19, 1971

Tim bought a map of Southern Maine and drove through unfamiliar towns like Alton, New Durham, and Lebanon. During the ride, he cursed Sheila but tucked his anger away when he pulled into her parents' driveway. The Palmers had always been fair with him, but Tim wondered what they had been told about the divorce. No doubt Sheila had blamed him for everything.

The handoff of the children went smoothly. In the back of his mind, he wished all the pickups could be so easy. Perhaps the kids should visit Grandma and Grandpa more often. The extra driving would be worth it. He and the kids sang songs on the radio together all the way home.

Tim stopped for the Chinese food, and Holly, as customary, showed up minutes after they'd arrived. Their Friday night was enjoyable. They ate their pu pu platter, played board games, and went to bed. Tim made sure he had several hidden weapons ready.

The following day, while making scrambled eggs, Holly opened a drawer and, instead of a spatula, found a long object wrapped in a blue dishtowel. Holly flipped open the towel and quickly covered it up again before anyone saw it. Later, she pulled Tim aside.

"Tim, what's with the shotgun in the kitchen drawer? Dear God, you're going to hurt someone!"

Tim sighed. "Oh, my God, I forgot to move that. It makes me feel better when I'm working. I'll hide it better."

"Obviously! You don't want your daughters to find that, do you?"

Other than Holly's discovery, the day went smoothly. After another quick trip to the Sears store in Concord, Tim and Holly worked on the porch, which meant the adults were doing something productive toward the house, and the kids were free to play in the yard.

The stress returned, however, the following morning. Holly nudged Tim at 8:30 am, and Tim jumped out of bed and ran across the hall. The girls were already up. Tim grabbed a shirt and ran down the hallway. After quickly checking the yard and the barn, Tim began calling their names. As soon as Holly made it outside, Tim appeared with the girls at the trail at the bend in the driveway.

"Didn't you hear me calling?" asked Tim.

"I don't get it," said Olivia. "Last time we went to the grove, you said it was okay. This time, we're in trouble."

Tim's face was pale. "You're right. We haven't been consistent, so here's a new rule: no grove from now on because you can't hear us from out there. Oh, and another rule: wake me up before you leave the house."

"We didn't have to do this when you lived at mom's house," said Vivian.

"Honey, this isn't Mom's house. I'm going to tell you a story. It's a true story, and it's scary, but you need to hear it so we can understand each other. You see that pond over there? Well, a little boy drowned in it because his parents weren't watching. Let's pretend my yard is this little front yard and the barn. I'll let you play in the barn but not the loft. And I will check on you occasionally. That's your new yard."

Olivia turned away, rolling her eyes, while Vivian dropped to the ground, throwing a tantrum. "No fair!"

CHAPTER 141

June 28, 1971

Bob Simmons left the Photosmith store, got into his car, and opened the package of snapshots. He'd expended the entire roll, snapping away before and after the digging. They weren't perfect pictures, but they were enough. These photographs, the Enrico boy incident, and the Beverly Farms fire might be enough to get people talking. Maybe when that happened, Russell would have to join in.

Simmons went home and added the photos to the presentation he'd been working on. Much of his source material was newspaper clippings and notes from Elizabeth's scrapbook, but he tied everything in with the most recent happenings. All he needed was a little help from the media.

It took about a week, but he finally got through to a popular DJ on a rock station in Boston who called himself Orfeo, named after a vampire in Romania. Simmons could pick up the show all the way up in Sanborn on clear summer nights. Orfeo, whose real name was Scott Carson, spent his shift spinning cutting-edge rock 'n roll intermingled with ghost stories.

Simmons hand-delivered his package to the radio station's front desk to be sure it didn't get lost in the mail, the name "ORFEO" written in magic marker underlined twice. Simmons listened every night for two weeks before he heard the payoff.

"Ladies and gentlemen, that was 'Sweet Leaf,' I'm guessing it has nothing to do with marijuana, but don't ask me. We've got more brand-new rock 'n roll comin' at ya in a few minutes, but first, gather 'round. It's time for a *storryyy* …"

"A mysterious package was delivered to the station a couple of weeks ago, and it took us this long to get it on the air because we had to fact-check it. We're not even sure who dropped it off. I asked around, but Brinko, my intern and personal assistant, the man who accepted the envelope in his own grubby hands, couldn't seem to remember **cough**

dumbass! *cough* who left the package … But I digress." Brinko was intentionally left off-mic and served as Orfeo's lightning rod.

"Did you folks hear about the boy who was murdered in the woods up in New Hampshire two or three months ago? Brinko, did you? No? Oh, right, you can't read. Brinko, the intern, everybody! Let's give him a hand!" Orfeo stopped the show and clapped for the humiliated Brinko, complete with canned applause.

"Alright, well, for those of you who read as much as Brinko does, I'll recap. Two or three months ago, in Hampstead, New Hampshire, two boys went out into the woods to shoot some squirrels. You know, a typical Saturday night in Cow Hampshire, I mean, *New* Hampshire. Sorry about that, New Hampshire, if you can even hear me. We're a fifty thousand watt station, and we know most of you probably went to bed when the sun went down anyway.

"Where was I? Oh! These two boys saw a mysterious—hold on, I want to quote the official police document on official police paper with the name cut off. Does this mean a cop dropped off the packet, right Brinko? Thinking he might get fired if he puts the department's name in the package? Did he look like a cop?

"Dammit, Brinko! If you weren't free, I'd fire your ass. Anyway, these two boys saw 'A white-faced woman who looked like she was dead and had flies all over her.' Hmm, I might have dated this woman. I'm kidding. I'll repeat that. *Dead, with flies all over her.* Think about that for a second, folks.

"According to the boy, this white-faced woman with flies all over her begins to choke one of the kids after he shoots her with his BB gun. Then the second kid comes over to help and ends up knifed to death. If I understand correctly, the shooter-kid escaped, and I'm not going to give out the kids' names, but everything I'm saying was in the *Derry News* newspaper. I have a clipping of it right here.

"No wonder you didn't hear about it. Brinko, you're off the hook. You canceled your subscription to the *Derry News*, am I right? Sorry, everybody, we're supposed to be getting scared, and I'm cracking jokes.

"A short while after the kid gets killed in the woods, there is a housefire in Beverly, no, sorry, more specifically, Beverly *Farms*. For those falling asleep, look alive. We're getting closer to Boston now. According to our source, nobody knows who lived at this farm, and I mean, like, the last town records are from the nineteenth century. An entire century and nobody knows their freakin' neighbors. How does that happen in Massachusetts? This place has a trust listed as the owner or something. I'm no lawyer, so I'm not sure how that all works.

"Well, the mystery person who delivered this package did some research, and it seems that the farm was some sort of cult that didn't want anyone in their business. According to the modern-day witches from Salem—yes, they do exist, ladies and gentlemen—these modern-day witches are saying off the record that the people on this farm worked for an 'army of the dead.' Beverly Farms is right outside of Salem, folks, not too far from any of us. And this story gets worse, so bear with me.

"This unknown, unnamed source tells me that they went to Beverly Farms after the fire and after everyone left, and saw a quote, 'white-faced lady in a dress,' unquote, and got the hell out of there.

"However, the key to the story is that this woman has roots in the past. My source tells me that they know who the fly-covered lady is, but the police aren't allowed to believe this kind of thing, so nothing's going to get done. Watch yourselves out there, people, especially if you live in the Beverly Farms area."

Orfeo lowered his voice and got serious, preparing for his horror punchline. "Here's the kicker that ties it all together. Here's the reveal of who this dark bitch is. Shut up, Brinko. You're breaking the tension. I can say 'bitch' on the air. Sorry, everyone. The kicker is that this woman comes from a little town called Sanborn, New Hampshire. I pass this place on my way up to Loon Mountain when I go skiing, Exit 20 off 93. Sorry. Her name, write this down, is Mildred Wells.

"It says here that back in the 1860s, Mildred Wells drowned her son in a pond. Then, she killed as many as four people, but nothing was ever proven. The rumor is that Mildred even buried the bodies on her property and then disappeared. I even have some snapshots of—something.

"Man, these pictures are dark. I see trees, maybe a grove. Do you know what these are, Brinko? Is that a grave? I don't see a coffin or anything, but I guess that's where the bodies were. Not very clear. Anyway, years later, in 1968, an elderly widow named Annette Smith was found dead in the very same house. She'd been there for weeks before anyone discovered the body. Her husband, Henry, was also found dead on the property a few years earlier. Man, that's creepy as hell! How come I've never heard of this?

"Brinko, I want to know what happened between 1860-whatever and 1971. Who woke this ghost up? I don't know about you, but when I don't like the lady to wake up, I've got mad moves to get out of there. I'm like the wind, you know what I mean? I'd even chew my arm off if I had to, right?

"Ladies and gentlemen, if you want more information on—let's call this, 'The Legennnnd of Milllldred Welllllls,' don't call me. Call the *Derry News*.

Or call the *Salem Evening News!* It was even reported on WMUR Channel Nine in Manchester. That's it for story time, ladies and gentlemen. Coming up after the break is more of the new rock 'n roll you want to hear. First up: The Doors and 'L.A. Woman'!"

CHAPTER 142

July 12, 1971

Bob Simmons was ecstatic about the radio broadcast. His hard work had paid off, and when he heard Orfeo's show opener, he pressed the record button on his shoebox tape recorder, holding the microphone by the speaker. When the segment was over, he popped the cassette and called his friend from high school, Chuck Garlington, who had since become a private investigator.

Garlington, accustomed to catching philandering spouses, took the case at a ten percent discount to help his friend. He didn't believe in ghosts but knew Bob Simmons' family history. So be it if his buddy wanted to fork out good money for garbage. The job required a day, maybe two.

Simmons asked Garlington to knock on Russell's door and provide a copy of the radio show but not disclose who his client was. Garlington was also requested to send copies of the radio show to the Beverly and Hampstead Police because they might show interest in the Sanborn connection.

CHAPTER 143

July 12, 1971

What Bob Simmons didn't know was that the national television program *Only If You Dare* was in Boston filming an episode about Albert DeSalvo, the notorious Boston Strangler. *Only If You Dare* covered a different subject each week, everything from Bigfoot to Lizzy Borden to UFOs.

The producer of the show, Nate Hoginski, needed fresh ideas. The Bigfoot episode had performed poorly in the ratings, and upcoming shows included equally well-worn subjects such as the Loch Ness Monster and the search for Jimmy Hoffa. Luckily, he turned the radio on as Orfeo's story segment ran.

Immediately, Hoginski scrapped the expensive Scotland trip. This New Hampshire story was nearby, current, and best of all, cheap. The nature of *Only If You Dare* was to present open-ended topics, so there was no urgency to solve the mystery. The better the mystery, the better the ratings. This show would be an *Only If You Dare* original.

CHAPTER 144

July 17, 1971

There were three visitation weekends in July, and the girls obeyed Tim's "no pond, no grove" rules for the first, but midway through the second, Olivia got bored.

"Let's go to the grove," said Olivia.

"No, Dad said we can't," answered Vivian.

"He always works on the house on Sunday afternoons. We aren't going to Funspot, and we aren't going out to eat. I saw a chicken in the refrigerator, and I know Holly will cook it. This place is so boring. Follow me to the barn."

Vivian stood, pretty bored herself. "Yeah, there's nothing to do."

"Follow me. I have an idea." Olivia led the way to the bend in the driveway and, when they got there, turned right and bounded up the path.

Vivian followed her, protesting. "We're not supposed to!"

Olivia stopped and turned to face her sister. "Shh! It's only for a second." Vivian took her hand, and it turned into forty minutes of top-notch hide-and-seek.

CHAPTER 145

July 19, 1971

As time passed without incident, Tim began to get sloppy. The sawed-off shotgun was still wrapped in the blue towel but hadn't left its hiding place since Holly made him move it. There was not even a hint of Mildred in their lives. Was the Hampstead episode over? Like every news story, the Enrico boy's death faded.

In the meantime, Tim's restoration progressed at an unprecedented pace, akin to his original plan. The kitchen and dining rooms were complete, and they looked great. Holly started to get excited. It was her first time seeing the outcome of Tim's professional talents, and she began to dream of an Open House. Tim's next focus was the turret, ripping out old boards, and installing a hardwood floor. One day, however, came a knock.

Tim turned down his radio and stood up to look outside. A tie-wearing man he had never seen was at the porch door with a folder under his arm. *A salesman*, thought Tim. He put down his tools and marched downstairs.

"Good afternoon. Are you Mr. Timothy Russell?"

"Yes, I am. What can I do for you?"

"Mr. Russell, my name is Charles Garlington, and I'm a private investigator. I represent a client who is looking into the death of a young boy named Eric Enrico. I believe you're familiar with that case?"

"Yes, I heard about that. That happened in Hampstead." Tim had suspicions but didn't want to mention any names.

"Well, sir, a radio show in Boston broadcast the story the other night, and they got into detail about the Hampstead death, the fire in Beverly Farms, and Sanborn. I've brought you a recording of it right here." Garlington pulled a cassette tape out of his folder.

"Alright, well, spare me the time and tell me what it says," said Tim.

"In a nutshell, Mr. Russell, the radio show ties the Enrico murder to the fire in Beverly Farms and to a woman in Sanborn named Mildred Wells, who used to live in your house. What can you tell me about her?"

"Mr. Garlington, were you hired by a man named Bob Simmons?"

"I'm not at liberty to say, but I can tell you that many people are interested in solving this case, including the Hampstead and Beverly Police."

Tim was finished. If it was Bob Simmons behind this, he was insane. "If you can't tell me who sent you, I will have to decline."

Tim spent the next hour building two sawhorses, which he placed at the end of the driveway, blocking the entrance.

Two weeks passed, and Tim continued his progress on the house but figured he was still a year away from finishing. However, Simmons was always in the back of his mind, consuming his thoughts. In the first week of August, Tim started on the roof and heard another knock on his door.

"May I help you?" said Tim. It was two police officers from different jurisdictions: Chief Galluzzo of the Sanborn Police and another cop named Vendasi with a patch on his sleeve indicating Hampstead. Chief Galluzzo's cruiser was parked on the road behind the sawhorses.

"Good morning, Mr. Russell," said Galluzzo. "This is Sargent Vendasi of the Hampstead Police Department."

"Hello Chief. What can I do for you gentlemen?"

"Sargent Vendasi is here on behalf of Diane Enrico, and he's investigating the death of her son, Eric. We recently received some information from a Mr. Charles Garlington potentially linking your property to the crime."

"Do you mean Charles Garlington, who was hired by Officer Bob Simmons?"

"Mr. Garlington did not want to disclose who he was working for, yet he presented information relevant to the investigation."

"Is this about the line Officer Simmons drew on his map?"

"Partially," said Sargent Vendasi. "We'd like to know if there is any evidence that—"

Tim interrupted. "Sargent, forgive me, but Officer Simmons is harassing me, and I don't have time for this. His family didn't get along with the woman who lived here, and somehow, that's my problem. Do you realize the person he's looking for died in 1863?"

"All we're doing is looking for the woman who killed Eric Enrico, investigating every lead. Someone called Marcy Gottlieb and told her they'd seen a woman in a black dress. Her name is Holly Burns. I understand you two are familiar. Anything you could do to help the investigation would be appreciated."

"Just because the three towns line up on a map?"

"Yes, but also because of your conversations with Officer Simmons and Holly Burns' conversation with Mrs. Gottlieb."

A lump formed in Tim's throat. He had never admitted anything outright to Simmons, but he had said the name Mildred in his presence. Tim's mind raced. He knew nothing about the law. Would he be obstructing justice if he said no? Should he make them get a warrant? These were questions for a lawyer, and lawyers cost money. Tim bit his lip and doubled down. "I'm sorry. I want to discuss this with some people first."

"Mr. Russell, what can you tell me about these?" Sargent Vendasi produced a picture from his back pocket: The graves, with freshly turned soil and a spade stuck in the dirt. The photo was taken with a flashbulb in the dark.

Tim froze, knowing damn well who had taken it. Immediately, he understood how Mildred Wells must have felt when Elizabeth and Emma Simmons did the same thing. But what was the penalty for illegally moving a grave?

"Do you condone your police officers trespassing on private property, Chief?"

"Those pictures were sent anonymously, Russell. We don't know that Officer Simmons is responsible."

"So, the guy with a hard-on for Mildred Wells didn't take those? And you aren't sure that he hired Mr. Garlington, either? Give me a break. As I said, I want to speak with some people before we proceed."

CHAPTER 146

August 3, 1971

Nathan Hoginski, producer of *Only If You Dare*, put his best employee on the show's first original story with the working title *The Legend of Mildred Wells*. David Bonnette, Hoginski's apprentice, yearned to be a player in Hollywood, but at only twenty-four years old, he had yet to catch a break. Eager to climb the ladder, he threw himself into any task he was given.

Bonnette was bored with the Boston Strangler episode and welcomed the chance to create a story from scratch. Embellishment was crucial to a TV show like his, and there was already too much info on Albert DeSalvo to find any wiggle room.

It was effortless to get the materials from the Boston radio station. All he had to do was slip a fifty dollar bill to a disgruntled employee named Brinko, and in an hour, he was handed photocopies of everything in the folder. Fifteen minutes later, he was driving up Interstate 93 to Sanborn.

Bonnette stopped for gas off the Sanborn exit and asked the attendant if he knew anything about Mildred Wells, the local legend who drowned her child and murdered some others back in the 1800s. The man looked at him like he had two heads, and "nope" was all he said.

From there, Bonnette went to the Town Hall and searched for Thomas Pike, not Mildred Wells, as Thomas was originally from Sanborn. The newspaper clippings from Brinko's folder narrowed the search considerably, but all the Pike records were irreparably smudged. *Creepy*, he thought, snapping a few pictures and continuing.

While there, Bonnette also looked up the Simmons family and was intrigued to learn they had lived just down the road from Mildred. He didn't know if the Simmons information would lead to anything, but getting the lay of the land helped. Now, he could concoct better embellishments and put things in the order he wanted for broadcast.

When he had found all the paperwork and properly photographed everything (to be used for slow panning shots), Bonnette drove out to the house. On the way, he passed a mailbox with the name Simmons on it. *Well, I'll be damned*, he thought. *Could it be this easy?* Driving on, he made a mental note to check back.

A minute later, after driving past a meadow, the house appeared on the right, unimposing but on a nice piece of land. Bonnette passed the house the first time in case the owner was outside, but on his second pass, he saw the pond on the other side of the stone wall. *There's the murder spot*, he thought.

Not yet ready to knock, he drove for a half-mile, parked on the side of the road, and got out. Using almost the same path Bob Simmons had when he took the photographs, Bonnette snuck through the woods, snapping pictures of the field, the pond, and the house in the distance. Like everyone who had ever entered the grove, he was taken aback by its sudden appearance.

In the last row, he found the supposed grave left by Bob Simmons. Bits of charred wood were in the dirt pile, but there were no headstones. It was impossible to tell if it had ever been a grave, and the overall vibe was disappointing. Simmons' nighttime photos gave it more of an edge. Perhaps he would sneak back tonight with a portable video camera and well-placed props to spice things up.

CHAPTER 147

August 3, 1971

The previous night had been an exceptionally dull shift, and Officer Bob Simmons had even fallen asleep in his cruiser. Luckily, the radio crackle woke him up just before his shift ended. The thought of being caught sleeping by the Chief was unimaginable.

Exhausted, Simmons slept in but was awakened at 10:00 am by a knock on his door. King, of course, went crazy, barking up a storm.

"Hold on, I'm coming!" Simmons gave a quick look in the mirror and patted his hair down. Looking around the floor, he found yesterday's pre-shift sweatpants and put them on. His tank top undershirt with the pepperoni stain would have to do. Finally, he put on his holster and locked King in the bedroom.

Simmons pulled the curtain aside and found himself staring at a man he had never seen before. *Good*, he thought. *Maybe just a salesman.* He opened the door a crack. "I don't want to buy anything," he said, disinterested.

Bonnette looked Simmons over. *Holster. Belly. Sweatpants. Stains.* "Excuse me, but are you Officer Simmons?"

The man had undoubtedly seen the black and white Plymouth Fury parked not ten feet away. Simmons looked him over, especially his hands, which were in plain sight. He didn't appear to have a weapon. "That's me. Who are you?"

"My name is David Bonnette, and I am the production assistant for the TV show *Only If You Dare*. Have you heard of it?"

Simmons couldn't believe his ears. "Yeah, I love that show." He opened the door wide. "How can I help you?"

"Officer Simmons, I'm doing the legwork on a potential show. The working title is *The Legend of Mildred Wells*. Are you familiar with that name?"

Again, Bob Simmons was floored. "Did Chuck Garlington send you?" If he had, Simmons owed his buddy a couple of beers.

"No, I'm afraid I don't know the man."

Simmons made a mental note to tell Garlington his services were no longer needed. "Ah, no problem. You want to come in?"

Bonnette cringed, reminding himself it was part of his job. "That would be great, thank you." The house was as filthy as he imagined. "As I was saying, Officer, I'm researching a show on Mildred Wells, and a couple of Simmons are already in the story. Do you know who Elizabeth and Emma Simmons were?

"You're damn right, I do. Elizabeth and Emma are my ancestors, and I know a shit-ton about Mildred Wells. She killed Elizabeth and Emma and a lot of other people, too. You came to the right place. How'd you hear about her?" Simmons asked, already three-quarters sure of the answer.

"We heard it on a Boston radio station. A DJ named Orfeo talked about it on-air. It captured our attention."

Simmons mentally patted himself on the back. "Great. This Mildred Wells thing was a great injustice to my family and several others in the Sanborn area. She killed as many as six people, including her son."

"Six? Who were they?"

"Well, there's her son, who, rumor has it, she stuffed like a taxidermist. Also, the Chief of Police Abner Wallace, Henry and Annette Smith, um, Emma, Elizabeth—how many is that?"

"Six. That's quite the body count. And the police couldn't prove she killed Chief Wallace?"

"Guess not," said Simmons. "He fell off a ladder when they were allegedly dating."

Bonnette liked what he heard so far. "You're saying she stuffed her son and kept him in the house?" Even if it turned out to be inaccurate, "local sources say" was an excellent line for television.

"That's what I was told. My family has always been a little gossipy, though. You might want to fact-check." Suddenly, Bob Simmons was so excited he began to worry that Bonnette would discover that he alone was the keeper of the Mildred Wells flame.

"Officer Simmons, what would be the first place you would look if you were me?"

"I'd want to look around that property, not just the house, the whole thing. I'd treat it like a crime scene and look for bones. I'd get dogs in there and check basements, crawl spaces, attics, etc. I'd look in the woods, too.

See if there are any unmarked graves or any graves that have been moved."

"Do you think the current owner would let us look around?"

Simmons frowned. "No, he won't. Tim Russell is all about fixing it up and reselling. It's all about profit for him, while some of us still search for loved ones."

Bonnette loved the drama. "So, it's possible Russell is afraid of someone finding something?"

"Yes, I think so. And I think the boy who died in Hampstead is related to this whole thing, but Russell won't cooperate, and there's not much I can do about it."

"Officer Simmons, can I ask you a personal question?"

"Go ahead."

"Was it you who sent the packet to the radio station?"

Bob Simmons hesitated, then came clean. "Yes." He winced, waiting for Bonnette's reaction.

"That's fine. The fact that you're a cop lends this story credence, but we'll keep that little tidbit quiet. You'll look good on camera. We'll use you for the authoritative shots. Do you have any more materials you could share with me? Like the stuff you gave the radio station?"

Simmons breathed a sigh of relief. His story was alive. This Bonnette kid didn't care where the information came from. He just wanted *juice*. Simmons stood up and left the room briefly, returning with the scrapbook. "There's a lot of stuff in here, the whole 'Legend,' if you will. I bet you'll be able to spin this thing pretty well. If you have any questions, here's my phone number. I work the third shift most nights. What's your plan?"

"I will try to film some B-roll. I looked around in the daylight, and it wasn't creepy enough. In the meantime, I'll read this scrapbook and start fleshing out a show. We might even have more than one with all this material, but that depends on the ratings the first show gets."

More than one show, thought Simmons. "You're going to sneak on his property, film it, and use the footage?"

"Officer, I don't think you want to know exactly everything about my job, am I right? You do your job, and I'll worry about mine. When I'm done here, we'll build a replica set in Hollywood."

"That's smart," said Simmons. "I won't ask you what you're doing."

"Exactly, Bob. I think we understand each other. Now, let's make a TV show."

"Let's do it," said Simmons.

CHAPTER 148

August 4, 1971

Tim stared at the phone before gathering the strength to pick it up. A year and a half of bad memories came rushing back when he heard the voice at the other end.

"Timmy Russell! What's up? Are you keeping it in your pants? Or are you calling because you're ready to say goodbye to the latest Mrs. Russell? Just kidding, buddy, what can I do for you? How's New Hampshire?" It was Frank Turnbull, his divorce lawyer.

"Hey Frank, no lady problems, yet anyway. You're not just a divorce lawyer, correct? And you're licensed in New Hampshire?"

"That's right, I do it all: personal injury, real estate, whatever you need. I am licensed in New Hampshire. You have to be, so close to the state line. You caught me at the perfect time. My secretary's on lunch break."

"Thanks. I'm not sure if you heard about the boy who was killed in Hampstead or not, but the Hampstead cops came knocking on my door yesterday, and they asked if they could take a look around."

There was dead silence on the other end. "Maybe we should meet face-to-face. You never know nowadays, I—"

Tim cut him off. "I didn't kill the kid or anything like that. It's a long story, and I can't drive to Amesbury. They want to search my property for signs the killer was here, but the problem is, I did a little digging in the woods recently, and I don't want them to know."

"What the hell are you talking about?" said Frank, for once not trying to crack a joke.

"I found two headstones on my property and moved them, along with some bones. I think my neighbor snuck on my property and took some pictures. The cop knocked on my door, and he had pictures of the spot I rototilled in the woods. I'm afraid it will make the newspapers."

"Trespassing? I can get it thrown out. What are the pictures of, exactly? The spot you dug up? Or the entire surrounding area?"

"The spot I dug up. The pictures were taken at night. He snuck onto my property and went digging, looking for bones."

"Tim, I'm going to make your life easy. Go to a bookstore and buy yourself a book called *Forest Gardening*, then burn the receipt. My sister-in-law is a real hippie who does this sort of thing. She says it's good for the environment and all that crap. The forest is self-fertilizing, blah, blah, blah.

"After you buy the book, take your tiller back into the woods and rototill five times the land you already turned over. And rototill the grave site again to make it look like the rest. Then go to a greenhouse, buy some of the seeds they use in the book, plant 'em, and there's your excuse. What are you afraid of?"

"Desecration, maybe? That, and all of the negative attention it would bring. I need to sell this place in about a year."

"Well, don't worry yourself too much, Timmy. I'll have to brush up on my exhumation laws, but it sounds to me that even if you were found guilty, you'd pay a fine. They don't have any evidence, correct? No bones, etc.? I bet they're more afraid that you will sue them."

A measure of relief washed over Tim. Maybe this wasn't the debacle he'd made it out to be.

Tim jumped in his truck and drove to Franklin, where he rented the rototiller. Tim's next stop was Abbott's greenhouse, where he filled his pickup bed with vegetable seedlings. *Unexpected expenses,* he thought. *Hopefully, it will save on groceries.*

CHAPTER 149

August 6, 1971

David Bonnette entered the woods just after midnight along with the on-screen host of *Only If You Dare*, Simone Infante. They lugged the video camera, a spade, a flashlight, a bouquet, and Simone's on-camera blazer between them. The props were reference pieces for the set designers back in Hollywood. That bunch didn't know their ass from their elbow about directing, and Bonnette had to spell everything out. They built exactly what they saw in the reference video, no more or less.

Simone was unhappy with this week's assignment but was paid well, so she shut her mouth. Branches brushed her cheek as Bonnette forged ahead, holding their only flashlight. They had done night shoots before, but this was the first time they had to sneak onto a property or trudge through the woods. Bonnette promised a short twenty-minute shoot.

To Bonnette's delight, the woods were much creepier at night, and the fear factor doubled when the grove opened up before their eyes. Because they were trespassing, talking was minimal, and Bonnette pointed them toward the back corner. The only sound was the soft crunch of spruce needles beneath their feet. The bugs were terrible, and at one point, a moth found the side of Simone's face, buzzing like a helicopter until she dropped the flashlight.

"What happened?" Bonnette whispered.

"A bug flew into my ear!" she replied, picking up everything she'd dropped.

Bonnette, too, felt the anxiety. He asked for the flashlight back, and she yielded. One by one, they cut through the rows. Bonnette knew he'd reached the last one when the beam began to pick up green leaves. They took a right and followed the corridor to the end, but something was different. Bonnette wondered for a moment if they were in the wrong spot. "What the hell?"

"What?" asked Simone.

"It wasn't like this today." It looked like a garden. There were even plant stakes in the ground labeled lettuce, spinach, and turnips.

"It doesn't look like a grave," said Simone.

Bonnette clenched his teeth. "It's not anymore, Simone, but thanks." Simone was beautiful but stiff on camera, and the ratings hadn't popped as they'd hoped. Perhaps tonight was the beginning of the end for her. Just then, a mosquito bit his neck, and he slapped it. *Gardens aren't scary.* Pissed, Bonnette snapped a few pictures. He'd have to drag the set designers through the mud to get things the way he wanted. "Let's get the hell out of here. The shoot is over."

CHAPTER 150

August 7, 1971

Tim finished the cut and shut off the saw. Progress had suffered due to the full day of forest gardening, and the roof was still unfinished. It had been four months since they'd seen Mildred, and his daily concerns centered more around police visits. Just in case, he kept the sawhorses at the end of the driveway. If someone wanted to visit, they would have to park on the street. He wondered what had happened to the Hampstead Police. Bob Simmons had disappeared, too, and the silence, while not quite deafening, was in the back of his mind.

Tim heard someone knocking and realized it was coming from the front door by the road. On his way through the house, Tim looked through the living room window and saw two strangers on the front steps. The first was a distractingly beautiful woman, clearly overdressed for rural New Hampshire. The other was a man, roughly the same age, but dressed casually.

Tim opened the door. "May I help you?"

"Hello," said the woman. "Are you Mr. Tim Russell?"

Tim wondered for a second if they were Jehovah's Witnesses but didn't see any pamphlets. "Yes, I am."

"Mr. Russell, my name is Simone Infante, and my colleague David and I are from the TV show *Only If You Dare*. Do you mind if I ask you a few questions?"

"You're from a TV show? Are you from Channel Nine?"

Simone smiled proudly, imagining she was about to blow Tim's mind. "We're not out of Manchester, Mr. Russell. We're nationally syndicated and have over a million viewers each week. You've never heard of *Only If You Dare?*"

Bonnette cut off Simone. "Mr. Russell, my name is David Bonnette, and I help produce the show. We were in the area and happened upon a story about a woman from these parts with a dark history. We researched and tracked her back to your property, which used to be her house. Her name was Mildred Wells. Were you aware?"

Butterflies erupted in Tim's stomach as he imagined his situation broadcast nationwide. A million viewers was more than the population of New Hampshire. His house was on the brink of infamy. "Uh, no, I don't believe in that sort of stuff. I'm just trying to get this place fixed."

"You don't believe in what sort of stuff, Mr. Russell?" asked Bonnette.

"Mysteries and conspiracies, I guess. I've seen your show. How did you get my name?"

"Well, part of our research was spending time in the town hall looking up records. So, you're fixing this place up, huh?" Bonnette asked. "So, how's it going?"

"I hate to be rude, Mr. Bonnette, but I'm way behind."

"Mr. Russell, our show could help you sell this place. You'd be surprised what the attention of two million eyes can buy. You might even make a tidy profit before finishing it. Take the money and run."

Tim paused. Bonnette's idea sounded terrific if it were true. "What do you want, Mr. Bonnette? Do you want to film on my property and put it on your TV show? Set up cameras everywhere and record every shadow? How can I be sure this will help me?"

Simone Infante's head bobbed back and forth as if watching a tennis match.

"Yes, I'd love to film on your property," said Bonnette. "It would make a much better program. Rumor is she drowned her son in that pond, so that would be a major set-piece. We'll talk about the death of the Police Chief too, and of course, Thomas Pike."

As soon as Bonnette mentioned 'Police Chief,' Tim knew he'd seen Bob Simmons' scrapbook. Tim also knew there was little to be found in the town hall, meaning Bob Simmons might as well be the executive producer of this garbage TV show. "I'm going to pass, Mr. Bonnette. I'm not sure your show will help me. Thanks for asking first, though."

On their way back to the car, David Bonnette spit into a patch of poison ivy on the side of the road. He wasn't discouraged. This was the essence of his job. There was more than one way to skin a cat.

CHAPTER 151

Durham, New Hampshire
September 14, 1971

Andrew Vaughn strolled through the University of New Hampshire campus, looking like any other student. On his way across the quad, he tapped both front pockets to make sure he had everything. He'd been so clumsy lately, so forgetful, as he always was when he was using.

It was a miracle he'd ever been accepted to UNH. If it weren't for his mother's persistence, he might be living in the street. As tenacious as she was, however, she'd missed several key opportunities over the years to be supportive, and Andrew, a tormented soul, was convinced he was alone.

Colleen and Markus Vaughn owned a funeral home in Sugar Hill, New Hampshire, and Andrew and his sister Rebecca grew up helping as needed. To have a hearse in the driveway was no big deal. To see the coffins was a routine occurrence, but one day, at the age of seven, Andrew was playing alone in the cellar and found where they kept the dead bodies.

What looked like a potential hiding place was a refrigeration unit behind the hearse. Andrew grabbed the latch and pulled, feeling the cold air hit him in the face. But someone had already found his new hiding place, and they appeared to be taking a nap. At a loss, Andrew's hand fell off the latch, and he stared at the dead man, but it didn't end there. The corpse stirred and turned its head.

"Where am I?" The man's skin was whiter than anything Andrew had ever seen, and Andrew's bladder let go. "Don't just stand there! What am I doing here? What are you d—"

Andrew slammed the cooler and ran upstairs, looking for someone to help him. The first person he found was his sister. "Rebecca! There's a man in the box behind the hearse! He's dead, and I think he wants to get out of there!"

Rebecca laughed. "What are you doing in the basement, dumb dumb?" Still only fourteen, Rebecca did chores around the funeral home as part of her allowance.

"Where's Mom? Where's Dad?" said Andrew, in complete panic.

"Mom is still at the hospital, you know that. And Dad is talking to a family. Do not interrupt."

"The guy is going to escape! What if he comes upstairs?"

"Dead people don't talk, Andrew. Your mind is playing tricks on you."

No one, his parents included, believed Andrew, which began a slow and festering disconnect. First, Andrew refused to set foot in the funeral home, which rubbed Colleen the wrong way. "Your father has built a wonderful business for you and your sister to inherit. How will you take over if you don't learn how it works?"

"I hate the funeral home. I don't want to work there, ever!" Soon after, Andrew's grades began slipping, and he started hanging out with the dregs of Sugar Hill. At the age of eleven, Colleen caught him drinking, and the overprotective mother she was marinated in frustration.

Eventually, Andrew succumbed to the pressure from his family and helped where he was needed. Rebecca, however, opened old wounds when she played a prank on the now fourteen year old, locking him inside the funeral home, where he saw his second ghost.

"You did not see a ghost, Andrew. You just can't take a joke!" said Rebecca, playing defense.

"Nobody believes me!"

"Andrew, are you going to start this again? Rebecca said she was sorry, and we need you to work!" said Colleen. What had been a disconnect became a wedge, and Andrew embraced his role as the family black sheep. He returned to the funeral home and did his chores, but only after sneaking drinks from the liquor cabinet.

In 1968, Andrew was accepted to UNH through his mother's efforts and his desire to escape Sugar Hill. At least, that was his plan. Andrew checked his pockets a third time, paranoid he'd lost a bag at the last stop on his way to Engelhardt Hall and the next customer. Andrew still looked like a student, but his health was fading. In his mind, he could hear the clock ticking. His family would find out, and they'd put him back in rehab. For now, though, it was one day at a time. Andrew sold drugs to support his habit, and that's all that mattered.

When Andrew saw the police car turn onto Quad Way, Andrew changed course and turned right toward Hunter Hall. It was best to be safe. If he could enter the building, he could get lost inside and exit from any number of doors. But another cruiser appeared around the corner, and the cop got out.

"You in the plaid shirt, stop!" Andrew pretended he didn't hear. There were dozens of students around. He could play dumb for forty more feet and then disappear.

"Andrew Vaughn, halt."

In a panic, Andrew ran, but they were ready for him. That was the moment Andrew realized he'd lost his freedom, and for the first time in three years, he felt real fear. *Back to reality,* he thought.

CHAPTER 152

October 5, 1971

After a five-month wait, Mildred heard the last of Gideon's followers crunching through the forest. Bardelli, the scientist, had spent much of his time hibernating to fix self-inflicted wounds. The penultimate revenant had returned, but years of self-experimentation had left him handicapped, and his death was too easy, like shooting fish in a barrel.

Bardelli had barely enough time to be surprised. He looked Mildred in the face like an old man returning from a walk, nearly disinterested. In seconds, she was the last revenant. There was some satisfaction as the goal was achieved, and it felt good. Mildred had destroyed Gideon Walker and his legacy. The farm was gone. The abductions were no more. She meditated for a moment over the memory of her mother and sister, the closest thing to a spiritual moment in as long as she could remember.

Mildred crossed into Northfield, New Hampshire, just after midnight. The coyotes were out. She had seen three in the last two hours. Most predators left her alone once they got a good sniff, but forty minutes outside of Sanborn, she stumbled upon a rabid male near death.

The other coyotes had abandoned the area, waiting for him to die. Suddenly, the poor animal emerged from his hidden entrance and tried to bite Mildred across the wrist, but instead, she dropped the Book of Shadows and put the beast down. After returning the blade, she crouched between the boulders he came from and peered in.

It was a shallow cave with just enough shelter for a mother and pups. The rabid coyote had come here to die, and Mildred helped him. Now, the cave was hers. Mildred placed the book at the back where it wouldn't get wet and rolled a large stone over the entrance to keep it safe.

CHAPTER 153

October 6, 1971

The Simmons compound was made up of three houses on a hundred foot driveway. Decades back, the family had nailed a homemade sign to the tree at the end of the driveway that read *Simmons Road*. The driveway had never been declared an official road by the town, nor did it show on a map.

Mildred saw that the nearest house had a police car in front and decided to save it for last. Despite having lived down the road, she'd never been here because they always seemed to come to her.

Simmons Road was a dump. The house on the left had an old toilet and a rusted-out automobile in the backyard. Ugly, unkempt lawn ornaments cluttered all three lawns, and a toppled birdbath lay smashed in the driveway.

The dwelling on the left stood in complete darkness, seemingly on the verge of collapse. The house at the far end of the driveway had a glowing blue light coming from the living room. Mildred peered into the window unseen. She wondered if the man inside was a Simmons from birth or had married one, then decided she didn't care.

The man in the house on the right with the cruiser parked outside was watching television alone. *He was the man at Beverly Farms,* she thought. *Nosy like his ancestors. He must think he knows something about me.*

The windows in her old house were dark, and Russell's truck was gone. It was all hers for the first time in as long as she could remember. Mildred walked up the driveway, trying to imagine what it looked like in 1860, but the memory was lost, along with her happiness.

There was a newness to the outside. Russell had been busy preparing for winter during the summer months. It looked good, she had to admit.

Mildred tried the doors, being careful not to break them. When she couldn't find an unlocked entry point, she scaled the building and tried the turret windows. When she found one unlocked, she let herself in.

Mildred had no illusions that Elmer would appear. Russell had ruined the soul of the building, but she wasn't after sentiment. The key to her happiness was not rooted in the past.

Mildred found the sawed-off shotgun in the kitchen drawer but left it there, memorizing its location. After that, she climbed the stairs to the turret and opened Tim's box of files.

CHAPTER 154

October 7, 1971

Tim moved his work back inside after the roof was complete and winter weather was on the way. There was nothing but finish work inside left, but there was a ton of it to do. Choosing his next project, Tim went to the room closest to the road and began work on the floor.

Hours later, Tim shut the saw off and listened. He thought he'd heard Holly's Volkswagen in the driveway. Holly left work most days at 5:00 pm, and Tim worked until eight. In recent weeks, she'd begun showing up more, perhaps a sign that she, too, believed the haunting was over.

Tim opened the front door. "Whoa, it's still warm out! Are we having a second summer?" The sky was dark, but the temperature was seventy-four degrees, a near heatwave for October.

"I love it! We're supposed to get colder next week, so enjoy it. I heard it on the radio."

"How was your day?"

"Average, but I'll take it. Things could always be worse. What about you? Almost done with the floor?" Holly entered the house and took a peek. "Oh, nice. You got a lot done today. Where do you want me?"

Tim stared, smirking.

"Nice try, but that's later," said Holly. "Put me to work. I'm getting hungry, and if I sit down, I won't want to get back up."

Tim set Holly up with painting materials across the hall in the living room. In between saw cuts, they conversed. "Whatever happened with the Hampstead Police? Did they give up?" said Holly.

"Frank said I don't need to worry. He thinks they're afraid I'll sue them for trespassing. If they had any evidence, they would use it."

"What about that TV show? Anything from them?"

"What, The *Bob Simmons* Show?" said Tim. "Nothing. I hope they realized it would be a boring story and gave up."

Holly grabbed a screwdriver and began prying the lid off a paint can. "I can't imagine knocking on someone's door asking to film their house. Who wants the whole country looking into their living room?"

"Can you imagine Sheila checking this place out? She'd be so jealous she'd make my life a living hell."

Holly stirred the paint and, without fail, drizzled three drops over her jeans. "Dammit! You're right. Sheila wouldn't let the girls come anymore. She'd say the girls were afraid of ghosts. If they put Bob Simmons on camera, she'd track him down to compare notes. Speaking of the girls, has Sheila changed your pick-up for this Friday?"

"Not yet, it's only Wednesday. Remember, she likes to throw her monkey wrenches at the last minute."

"Hey, I have an idea," said Holly. "Let's shut down early, and I'll take you out to dinner. We'll have some wine and go to bed early, and you can get a fresh start tomorrow morning." She winked from across the hall and noticed that Tim looked tired. Almost six months of twelve-hour days, along with Sheila's stress, was taking its toll. "Come on, you haven't taken a day off since the girls were here last Saturday. Call it a sexual spa day."

Tim's eyes widened. "Wow, you should be a salesperson."

"I guess I missed my calling," said Holly.

Tim crossed the hall and hugged her. "Let's lock up and go." The house creaked on their way through the kitchen, but they ignored it. All eyes were on the side door and getting out of there. They missed the flies in the window over the sink, too. Luckily, Holly decided not to pee in the bathroom off the kitchen, or she would have heard many more buzzing in the turret.

CHAPTER 155

October, 1971

The good news following Andrew's arrest was that his lawyer, hired by his parents, kept him out of jail. The bad news, however, was that Colleen and Markus were beside themselves. Andrew had not attended any of his classes all semester and, in effect, had quit school. One of his addict friends had died, and Andrew never mentioned it. Worst of all, he had track marks on both arms and had lost thirty pounds. They put him in Wanderley Hills Recovery Center in St. Johnsbury, Vermont.

Thirty days later, after his release, Andrew seldom left his bedroom, claiming depression. He had no desire to participate in the business's day-to-day operations and hated comforting grieving families. Andrew hated the wakes, too. He hated that his whole family had been on call twenty-four hours a day his entire life to pick up dead bodies in the middle of the night. But the rigors of the job were not the real dealbreakers.

Andrew was afraid of the Foggy Orchard Funeral Home. He was worried every time a child died. And he was scared of car accidents and the restorations that followed. He'd witnessed pacemaker and artificial hip removals before cremations. He hated *setting the features*, which meant massaging the dead person's face into a look of serenity. Most of all, he hated sewing mouths shut and inserting spiky eye caps under eyelids to keep them from opening.

The Foggy Orchard building had always been ominous and intimidating: a nearly eleven thousand square foot Victorian mansion with a tower protruding from it. One particular incident still gave him nightmares.

Andrew had been about to assist his father with an embalmment when the elder had to take a phone call. The deceased, an eighty-four-year-old man, lay on the table stark naked. Suddenly, the corpse began to gurgle. Panicking, Andrew witnessed the body rise to a sitting position, a guttural groan filling the room. Andrew screamed as one of the man's eyes opened, and the lifeless orb rolled to find him. Just as the corpse was about to stand, Andrew wondered if his father was already dead.

Suddenly, Markus Vaughn returned, laughing. "Oh no, Mr. Fenton, lie back down. We'll take good care of you. Rest in peace." Andrew's father laid his weight across the corpse and leveled the body out. A cacophony of gas and gurgling bubbles echoed in the tiled room.

Andrew couldn't believe his eyes, and his father turned with a huge grin, laughing maniacally. "Welcome back to Foggy Orchard, Andrew! Bad timing on that phone call, I suppose. It's okay! It's rigor mortis. They sit up if you aren't careful. Your sister's going to get a kick out of this." Andrew failed to see the humor.

CHAPTER 156

October 7, 1971

Bob Simmons pulled into his driveway after an uneventful eleven-to-seven shift. He'd counted sixteen cars over eight long hours. To make matters worse, they all drove by before midnight or after 5:00 am. Between those hours, he may as well have been on the moon.

As Simmons was about to open the door to his house, his eyes passed over his father's junkyard: faded plastic flamingos, stolen milk crates, and his last recliner littered what used to be a lawn, and he'd have to be the one to clean it all up someday. But something didn't belong. She stood as still as a statue between a rotting wood pile and an Adirondack chair: the pale white face, the long hair, and the black farm dress, exactly as the Gottlieb boy had described. Mildred Wells was in his backyard.

"Freeze!" Simmons screamed as he drew his pistol. Instinctively, he ran to the front of the cruiser and knelt, gun raised, but she'd moved, so Simmons circled, hoping to find her again, but she was gone. Panting, Simmons ran to his father's house. Thankfully, the elder Simmons was in his recliner, sleeping. Frantic, Bob checked the yard through the windows in all directions with no luck. Sweating, he ran back to check his house, and King was missing.

How? There was no sign of an incident, and the door had been locked. Panicked, Simmons spent the rest of the day hunting a ghost. Hours later, he went to bed but didn't sleep a wink.

"Tell David Bonnette I need him to call me back. It's urgent!" Simmons hung up the phone and paced, high-strung and bleary-eyed. Work was going to suck tonight. He hadn't slept a wink in thirty hours. Finally, at 6:00 pm, after bouncing from window to window all day, the phone rang, startling him.

"Bonnette, what the hell? I called you hours ago!"

"Relax, I'm busy out here. I'm working on three shows at once, scouting for one, shooting another, and editing a third. What's so important?"

"I saw her! She was in my yard, waiting for me! I saw Mildred Wells!"

"Say that again?"

"Are you ready to take this seriously? She was in my yard, then she disappeared. My dog is missing, and I think she got him. Get a camera out here. I told you!"

Bonnette pinched the bridge of his nose. Producing a show that featured ghosts in it once in a while was one thing, but dealing with the kooks that believed in them was another. The dog probably found something to hump. Paying a cameraperson to fly to New Hampshire was not in the budget, but maybe he could move some things around.

"Did you get a picture of her? I need proof. I can't just send somebody, Bob. Everybody's busy." *The Legend of Mildred Wells* needed a shot in the arm, and a missing dog wasn't enough. If this country bumpkin could snap a picture of a shadow, or a shape, at least they'd have something to show on television.

"No, I didn't get a picture! I wasn't expecting her, I—"

"Hold on, Bob, I have an idea. Everything's closed out there now, right? Give me a day, and I'll call you at 10:00 am your time tomorrow morning."

Upset and overtired, Bob Simmons brought a wind-up alarm clock with him in his cruiser, setting it every twenty minutes, and every time it went off, he reset it again, but even so, he didn't really need it. Though he kept the doors locked, he couldn't relax, imagining the horror of waking to a dark figure standing outside his window.

After barricading the front door and pulling the curtains, Bob Simmons sat on the edge of his bed, shaking from fatigue, yet still, he could not settle. He'd been awake so long he was beginning to hallucinate. Would barricades be enough to warn him if Mildred showed up again?

Every shadow, every curtain, and every*thing* was starting to look like a woman in a dress. Simmons asked his father across the way if he'd seen anything, but the old man was quasi-catatonic, as always. Fearing for his health, Simmons grabbed a three-year-old bottle of Nyquil from the medicine cabinet and chugged half of it. Two hours later, the telephone rang. Simmons jumped groggily and answered on the second ring. It was Bonnette.

"I rented a video camera for you, but you have to go pick it up. It's in Manchester."

"Manchester? Why not Concord?"

"The Concord camera store didn't have what I wanted. Be grateful it wasn't Boston. Here's the deal: getting a shot of whatever you think you saw will be gold. I don't care if it's long-distance bullshit like Bigfoot, get something.

"I want to stretch this into two shows, but we might be talking four episodes if you can get even a three-second shot of her. If you get a video like that, we can run it ten times an episode. We slow it down, zoom in on it, slow pan, you know what I mean. And you'll get credit for the photo. You know you get paid for that, right?"

It wasn't the help Simmons was hoping for. He wanted a cameraperson, if only to have someone to take shifts with. "Right." He rubbed his eyes, head still spinning. "What time will it be ready?"

"It's ready to be picked up now. Don't miss that shot! If you film her, I'll send someone to help."

"Right," Simmons said again. They hung up, and he dressed for the drive to Manchester.

CHAPTER 157

October 8, 1971

Holly helped Tim with the interior painting, freeing Tim up for the more technical projects on the house. Thursday night after clean-up was rejuvenating, and she rolled out the red carpet when they were alone together. The night was capped off by eight hours of sleep, and he awoke the following day refreshed.

Miraculously, the Friday daughter pickup went without incident, and Tim and the girls were on their way to Sanford just after 6:00 pm. Tim breathed easy and felt a wave of happiness wash over him. All he needed now was a glass of wine, a nice dinner, and maybe some laughs around a board game with the kids. Sitting at a table and talking with family was always the best medicine.

Mildred read Tim's papers in the turret as they enjoyed their board game downstairs. Holly came to the kitchen once to get more wine, but it was a cold day, and the flies were minimal.

Tim and Holly took the kids out on Saturday, and Mildred went through the girls' overnight bag: more hideous nightgowns with ugly designs. She despised the mother's taste in clothing, but more than that, she was disappointed they weren't spending more time on the property.

Mildred watched from the hayloft as the Russells returned just after 4:00 pm with what appeared to be groceries. The girls had balloons and oversized stuffed animals. Vivian was eating an apple on a stick. As Mildred stared, she felt contempt. Why should these people enjoy a healthy relationship with their children when hers was stolen away? It would be so easy to swoop down and even the score were it not for the audience.

Olivia's eyes opened just before 7:00 am, and she nudged her sister. Sunday was what they had come to call Exploration Day. Quietly, both girls rose and changed out of their nightgowns, tiptoeing through the house to the side door because it made the least amount of noise.

Exploration Day would have been called Grove Day if they hadn't known that the word *grove* upset their father. Asking them to stay away from a playground like the grove while he worked on the house was unfair. Tim had mellowed somewhat recently, but they didn't want his limitations to return.

Olivia figured they had roughly an hour before Tim and Holly woke up. They would play for an hour and then rush back to make it look like they had been playing near the barn all along. They'd have breakfast together, and then Tim and Holly would pull out the tools and paintbrushes—another boring Sunday.

That afternoon, the weekend was down to its last few hours before two weeks of school, soccer practice, and homework. Tim and Holly hadn't checked on them in hours, so Olivia grabbed Vivian's arm and pulled her up the trail. "Go, hide, quick! I'll count first. One, two, three …" Vivian sprinted ahead and disappeared, but Olivia found her almost immediately. Vivian's favorite move was to try to hide behind a tree and then step back into the row Olivia had just left, but it never worked.

"Found you. Hey, where did you get that?" said Olivia. Vivian was eating a slice of apple.

"By Dad's garden. He left us a note. I guess he knows we come out here."

"Show me," said Olivia. Vivian walked her to the last row and showed her the plate sitting on the ground with several more apple slices. Underneath the apples was a handwritten note in block letters:
FOUND YOU.

"Good, now we don't have to sneak. Your turn to count!"

But Vivian wasn't ready to play. "Who's that?" she said.

Olivia spun. A woman stood at the end of the row. "I don't know," said Olivia. The woman raised a hand and waved, then turned and left. The girls didn't have a chance to wave back. Olivia looked at the plate of apples and put down the slice she was eating. "Don't tell Dad."

CHAPTER 158

October 11, 1971

Bob Simmons crashed hard after his Friday night shift, even though he knew sleep was life-threatening. He'd slept two of the last fifty (or sixty?) hours and was so tired he couldn't even do the math. When he woke after midnight on Sunday, he cursed at his watch. His sleep schedule was upside down.

12:37 am was a bad time to wake up. Simmons didn't dare turn on the lights for fear of being visible from outside. The bulky video camera was close by as he peered out the window into the blackness. He ate cold food out of a can and tried to go back to sleep, even drinking the rest of the expired Nyquil. *Damn you, Mildred Wells.*

Simmons wondered how it would all play out. Was he doomed? Desperate, he unlocked his gun safe and pulled out a twelve-gauge shotgun. It would stop a bear in its tracks but probably wouldn't work on a ghost. Dubious, Simmons loaded it anyway and stood it in the corner. He was tired of being scared.

Simmons passed out before dawn and slept another nine hours, waking at 4:00 pm. After getting up, he searched the family compound again, holding the shoulder-mount camera. As he returned to his house, Simmons saw Russell's truck speeding down Lancaster Hill Road.

Three heads bobbed as the vehicle bounced down the dirt road toward the highway. *Kids. He must be bringing them home.* Four seconds later, a green VW Beetle followed behind. *Must be the girlfriend*, he thought. Right then, Bob Simmons had his best idea of the weekend.

Simmons walked fast up Lancaster Hill Road and crossed the gully into Russell's meadow. The pond lay ahead, and then the house. He lugged the heavy camera on his shoulder, hoping to find something Bonnette would like, preferably from a distance.

Mildred watched Simmons lumber through the meadow from her spot in the woods. What was he carrying? Simmons pushed it against his eye and aimed it like a rifle. Was he trying to photograph something? No doubt she spooked him the other day. And if Robert Simmons were like the women in his family, he wouldn't be able to let it go.

Simmons pointed the gadget through the house windows for another twenty minutes before touring the barn and grove. It would have been too easy to kill him.

The phone rang an hour and fifteen minutes after Simmons closed his eyes. He rose irritated, painfully overtired. "Hello?"

"Simmons, it's David Bonnette. Did you get her?"

Simmons immediately woke up. "No. I even searched the property while they were gone."

"You searched the property? Did you get in there? The house?"

"No, not inside. I'd lose my job if I broke in. I'm a cop, remember?"

"How'd you know they were gone?" said Bonnette.

"I saw them pass my road and knew the house was empty. He was returning his kids to their mother. He leaves the house every evening, too. I think he works there then sleeps at his girlfriend's."

"Do you think you could get in there and film the interior? It would help my set designers."

"What did I just say? I'm not doing that, David."

Bonnette quit asking. "Our little project is hurting, and we need something to tickle the head honcho's interest. I need you to get something on film, or *The Legend of Mildred Wells* will die on the vine."

CHAPTER 159

November, 1971

As much as Mildred wanted to hurt Tim and Holly, something held her back. Olivia and Vivian were *fun*. Mildred even made corn dolls for the next time they saw each other, but the divorce documents indicated Tim had visitation every two weeks, so the girls would not be coming this weekend.

Surprisingly, divorce was commonplace in 1971. Tim's documents were cold and impersonal, devoid of the love that united the two people in the first place. Even the names were omitted. Russell and his ex-wife Sheila were most often referred to as *petitioner* and *respondent*. For a moment, Mildred wondered why Tim and Sheila had parted ways.

CHAPTER 160

November 7, 1971

Bob Simmon's phone rang at 9:00 am, waking him prematurely. "Who is it?" he mumbled, opening the curtain.

"Simmons, it's Bonnette. I've got good news. We got approval for a second episode, but it comes with a stipulation."

Simmons smiled. "That's good news. What do you need?"

"I know we've been over this, but the Big Guy won't budge. I need you to get inside and film. We need to build sets, and I need the layout. Get the barn, too, if you can."

Simmons frowned. "I told you, I can't do that, Dave. My job is all I have, and how do I know this will turn into money for me? What happens when Russell sees shots of everything he owns on TV? I need some reassurance."

"Bob, this is a team effort. The better the show, the more sponsors we attract, and the more money we have to work with. We're on the west coast, and you're next door. It's your turn. Now, take the camera and get in there."

"And get fired? No chance. Write me a check."

Bonnette swore under his breath. "I guess we'll just have to work around you then, Bob."

Bonnette's plane touched down at Logan Airport in Boston two days later. *If you want a job done right, you've got to do it yourself.* He'd spent six hours in the air stewing on the Bob Simmons situation and how to motivate the lazy bastard short of writing a check.

Bonnette drove an hour and a half to Sanborn, parked at the beginning of Lancaster Hill Road, and set out through the woods, lugging a movie camera. When Bonnette reached the forest garden, he gave it his middle finger. *Forest garden, my ass.* Russell was up to something.

It was 4:14 pm, and sunset was fifteen minutes away. Hopefully, Russell would quit work early, and he could get in and out. Looking for an excellent place to wait, Bonnette walked the path to the driveway and hid in the trees thirty yards from Tim's truck. It had been a long day already. Sleepy, Bonnette laid back and closed his eyes.

Bonnette woke to an acorn landing next to his head. The sun was down, and the sky was nearly dark. Bonnette looked at his watch: 6:17 pm, *Wow. How did that happen?* He hadn't napped since grade school, never mind in the woods. Russell's truck was gone, and the house was dark. Mystified, he shook it off. It was time for work.

Bonnette grabbed the movie camera and crossed the driveway with the barn and the turret looming over him. He'd never believed in ghosts, but, like everyone, he'd been a child once and remembered what that fear felt like.

He found his entrance in the backyard, one of the unlocked windows into the carriage house. Bonnette crawled through and looked around. The room was unheated and unfurnished, clearly not part of the main house, and there was nothing worth filming. From there, he opened the sliding glass door to the breakfast area and let himself in.

Bonnette felt the heat as he stepped into the main living area. Mounting the camera on his shoulder, he turned it on. The eyecup was in his face, and it was hard to peer around, giving him no choice but to look through it. The body of the camera blocked peripheral vision to his right.

Flustered, he pushed the record button, and the filming light illuminated the room, temporarily blinding him. *Thank God there are no immediate neighbors,* he thought. *Otherwise, they'd be calling the police.* An old radiator rattled in the kitchen as the furnace under his feet burned, and it was as loud. *Thank God I live in California,* he thought. He'd been here for two minutes and already wanted to leave.

Bonnette swept the kitchen area with the camera and continued into the dining room. He planned to pass through each room once, spin around, and be gone. From there, the studio could rebuild the home interior on a soundstage. The assholes in set design could slow the film down if they had to.

As he passed through the kitchen, Bonnette wondered when was the last time Russell had taken out the trash, but the garbage can was not visible. *Is it under the sink?* From the kitchen, Bonnette climbed the stairs into the turret, temporarily pausing the camera so the light bulb would go out and the turret wouldn't resemble a lighthouse from the outside—*nothing much up here but an old desk and a few boxes of papers*. Back down the stairs, he paused outside the cellar door and tried the knob.

Hairs stood on the back of his neck, and Bonnette was disappointed in himself. *It's only a house.* Bonnette opened the cellar door, which squealed louder than anticipated. *It's a good thing nobody's seeing this, right? Now point the camera and be done with it.* Bonnette didn't take more than a step down for fear the door would close behind him and panned the camera a bit too fast. *It's tiny, anyway. Maybe we won't build that set.* Closing the cellar door, Bonnette crossed through the empty dining room and into the living room.

The smell was worse in here. Stepping into the empty den at the back of the house, he did a quick 360 and returned to the living room. He'd seen everything except the bedrooms and hated himself for having to get up the nerve to approach the stairs.

Bonnette recalled some of Simmons' stories, and the smell dovetailed with all of them. *Bullshit*, he told himself, but alone with the lights out, it was hard to play the logical adult. His head commanded, but his legs wouldn't budge. He didn't even want to peek around the corner, but he did. The smell was even more pungent here. He would have thought this a prank, but nobody knew he was coming.

Maybe Russell worked all day in the kitchen and didn't come to this side of the house. It's probably yesterday's lunch in a trash can. Bonnette couldn't wait to lug the camera into the studio and replay the footage, but that wouldn't happen until it was shot. With that, he started up the stairs. Three steps from the top, Bonnette had the horrible feeling he'd gone too far.

Mildred watched from the balcony behind him, her body blocking the hall window and most of its light. Anxious, Bonnette reached the top stair and spun, feeling vulnerable between the two back bedrooms. When the recording light found Mildred, Bonnette screamed like never before. Her pale skin illuminated the balcony, and Bonnette dropped the camera but stumbled on the top step, landing on the floor in front of the bathroom.

Like a cat, Mildred leaped as Bonnette attempted to throw himself down the stairs. He would gladly trade broken bones for his life. The woman was the smell. Flies buzzed in his ears, tasting something warm for a change. With a flick of her wrist, the blade appeared, and she plunged it into his chest. Bonnette sucked for air in short breaths as if wading into a frigid sea. He turned his head, determined to make his last thought about something else, but all he saw was the pattern on the wallpaper as Mildred found his heart.

CHAPTER 161

November 10, 1971

Bob Simmons woke up unrested at 3:00 pm. Sleep had been terrible ever since he'd seen her, so he'd started leaving booby traps to see if she had gotten inside, like baby powder on the floor to check for footprints and tape on doorjambs, but was it even possible to tell?

He spent his day on the couch watching television, dozing intermittently. His breakfast was a box of macaroni and cheese. He felt miserable, so he drank two beers to help him nap. The sun set two hours after he woke up. It was vampire season, as he liked to call it. He would see very little sunshine between now and April.

Feeling antsy, Simmons dressed for work early, deciding to spend some time at the station before another night in the cruiser. Rubbing his eyes, he stepped onto his rickety porch and descended the stairs, pulling out his keys and missing a significant detail. Eyes still blurry, he found the right key, opened the car door, dropped his two hundred and forty pounds into the driver's seat, and screamed.

David Bonnette's face stared through the windshield, inches away, eyes open, body splayed on the hood face down. Simmons leaped from the car, drew his gun, and scanned the property. On the ground was a movie camera identical to the one in his living room. Bonnette must have come for some filming of his own. There was no blood.

Simmons pulled Bonnette's wallet from his back pocket and went through it. Inside, he found three David Bonnette business cards. Simmons took one and put the wallet back, then grabbed the movie camera and put it inside the house. After that, he did the only thing he could: call it in.

CHAPTER 162

November 10, 1971

Tim slowed his truck as he passed the Simmons house. Three county police cruisers lined the road, and yellow tape was strung across the driveway. He slowed to a crawl, trying to get a look at whatever the commotion was. When he couldn't tell, he pulled over and walked up.

"Crime scene. Sorry, you can't pass through here, sir."

"I'm Tim Russell. I live in the house up the road." Tim pointed. "Is Bob Simmons okay?"

"He is, sir. But I can't let you pass. It's a crime scene."

"I don't want to pass. I just wanted to see if my neighbor was all right. What happened?"

"I'm not at liberty to tell you everything, but a body was found on the premises. The ambulance left a half-hour ago. It will be in the newspaper, I'm sure. I'm afraid we don't have any more information to share right now."

Bob Simmons was nowhere in sight, so Tim returned to his truck and drove to the house. The first thing he did was call Holly.

CHAPTER 163

November 11, 1971

Bob Simmons told the police the truth, except for keeping Bonnette's movie camera. When the police left, he paid his father a visit. Eighty-nine-year-old John Simmons lay sleeping in his recliner as always. *Good*, Bob thought. *There's less explaining to do.* Quietly, he snuck down the hallway and removed the fake electrical outlet that served as a hidden safe. Not knowing how much he would need, he took three hundred dollars and left.

Simmons drove to Boston and paid to have the 16mm film developed while he waited. Three hours and two hundred and twenty-five dollars later, it was finished, and Simmons threw in an extra fifty bucks to watch it in a private back room, and what he saw surprised him. *Son of a bitch, that would have been me.*

He could tell that Bonnette's last moments were nervous moments. The camera was all over the place, and he could hear Bonnette breathing. During the final steps up the stairs, Simmons heard a faint sniff. Was Bonnette crying?

Suddenly, the camera fell, continuing to film sideways, recording mostly shadows and the horrific soundtrack of a man dying. Simmons rewound the tape and slowed it for a second viewing. When finished, he hit the rewind and played it again. *Oh my God.*

When he got home, he pulled out Bonnette's business card and called the office number.

CHAPTER 164

November 18, 1971

Nothing much was reported in the days following David Bonnette's death. All the public learned was that the dead man was from California, and Bob Simmons was not charged with anything. As much as he wanted to know what happened, Tim didn't feel like asking Simmons, so he let it go.

Holly, wanting to know what happened, asked around. It took a week of poking around before she could piece things together.

"The dead person at Bob Simmons' house was the TV show producer who knocked on your door."

"What?" said Tim. "So, 'California man' was David Whatshisname?"

"David Bonnette. They said it was a heart attack."

Tim stood up from the dinner table, suddenly anxious. "A young guy like that had a heart attack? Hard to believe." Tim picked up his wine glass, took a drink, and sat back down. "Bastards. Serves them right. He should have stayed in California."

"Yeah, no wonder Bob Simmons fell off the face of the Earth. His gravy train derailed."

CHAPTER 165

November 19, 1971

According to Tim's visitation schedule, the girls were coming to visit, and if that were true, they might try to sneak off to the grove. It was still too early for a formal introduction, so she left the corn husk dolls where she'd left the apples. When the girls found the dolls, Mildred waved to them from a distance before circling to watch from another angle. Her face tightened as she walked, and it took her a minute to realize it was because she was smiling.

It was an uplifting Sunday for Mildred. Despite the rapidly cooling mid-autumn temperatures, everyone seemed to have had a good time. No one got bored. They played games and played with dolls, and both girls were remarkably polite despite their magickally altered awareness.

For sure, the girls might have been afraid without the spell. Or shy. Worse, they might have shunned Mildred like Elmer used to, which would have been unbearable. But as it was, Olivia and Vivian seemed just as happy as Mildred to be friends, and the afternoon surpassed her greatest expectations, confirming that it must have been Elmer's fault that they never got along.

The one caveat to the afternoon was the father. Tim Russell ran into the grove yelling, and when he did, Mildred prepared herself but thought better of it, sending the knife back to Beverly Farms at the last minute.

Unfortunately, they didn't get a chance to say a proper goodbye.

CHAPTER 166

November 29, 1971

In mid-November, after what seemed to be a successful stay at the Wanderley Hills Recovery Center, Andrew suffered a relapse and went straight back. Two weeks later, his parents were passing through Franconia Notch when headlights from the opposite direction swerved into their lane. Colleen died instantly, but Markus held on. Left alone to decide, Rebecca chose not to tell Andrew while he was in recovery.

Sensing something was wrong, Andrew insisted on calling his family. When Rebecca told him the news, he was livid. "Dad is still in the hospital? How's he doing?"

"Andrew, it's day to day," said Rebecca.

"Get me out of here. I want to see him. If he dies before I get there, I'll never forgive you!"

Andrew was granted temporary release with the condition that he return within three days. Markus didn't last that long. "Dad, oh, my God. Are you in pain?"

Markus nodded his head. "Pretty ... bad."

"I'm so sorry, Dad. I'm sorry for everything. I'm sorry that I'm in rehab. I'm sorry I've been the black sheep my entire life!"

"Andrew." The word left Markus's lips like a whisper.

"Oh no. Don't die, Dad. Should I call a nurse?"

"No. Listen."

"What is it, Dad?"

"Find ... George."

"Who is George?"

But Markus was gone.

Their Will left everything in a trust with Rebecca as the executor, stipulating that Andrew would always have a job at the Foggy Orchard Funeral Home, but that didn't sit well. Andrew was angry. The Will was a travesty. The business would set both children up handsomely if sold, but Andrew had no say. He tried talking it out with Rebecca, but she wouldn't hear it. She had plans to marry her boyfriend, who would join them on staff. Andrew returned to rehab angry.

The last two weeks at Wanderley Hills were a nightmare for Andrew. His parents were dead, and he missed them but was angry with how they had left things. His only options were to work in the funeral home or quit and start over from scratch, and he wasn't fond of either. Naturally, Rebecca bore the brunt of it.

The loss of Markus and Colleen also meant they were two high-quality employees short, so Andrew, Rebecca, and her useless boyfriend, Chris, would be busy. Andrew had gone from college dropout to drug rehab to funeral home administrator in a matter of months, trapped in a building he feared. He was pigeonholed, and the pressure to stay clean was immense.

One day, he left work unannounced. When Rebecca saw his desk, she knew he'd dropped everything. She searched the property and made two desperate phone calls with no success. *Don't do this, Andrew. I need you.*

Andrew spent the night in a bar three towns away, drinking alone until he met a stranger who seemed willing to listen: an anonymous sounding board to vent his frustrations. The man's name was Jeremy Clary, and although he didn't tell Andrew, he'd been recently released from the Concord State Prison.

Jeremy bought Andrew two shots of whiskey to keep the stories flowing, interested in Andrew's family and the funeral home business in general. *Foggy Orchard? Yeah, I know that place. What's it like to work on a dead body? What kind of hours do you have to put in for a career like that? Is there any money in it? Hey. Sorry about your parents, man. At least you have your sister. I'm sure you'll find some help.*

When Andrew lost his train of thought, Jeremy reminded him where he'd left off. Andrew even began to cry once, and Jeremy gave him a few friendly pats on the back. They drank until closing and then parted ways. Andrew drove home so drunk he wouldn't remember.

Rebecca was still awake in her office, finishing what Andrew had not. She saw him pull in and park his car crooked. He'd been crying and was nearly incoherent, so despite her disappointment, Rebecca had no choice but to save the lecture for later. She put him to bed, knowing he would be no help in the morning.

CHAPTER 167

December 5, 1971

Two weeks later, the girls returned, but December had turned cold.

"Dad, come on! We're bored!"

"No, honey. It's twenty degrees out there, it's windy, and your mother didn't pack anything. I always tell you to check your suitcase before you leave! You don't have hats, mittens, or boots. It snowed this week! You'd be frozen in fifteen minutes."

Mildred waited in the grove, but the girls didn't show. It was a cold day, and there was snow on the ground. Mildred walked down the aisle, feeling sorry for herself. She'd never missed Elmer like this, at least while they were alive.

Deer tracks crossed her path, and she followed them. Then, she turned and noticed her own footsteps scarring the snow. The girls didn't come, and maybe that was better. The father might see her footprints and the fun would be over. Winter was almost here, and outdoor playtime would be reduced. Perhaps Mildred would have to find other ways to occupy her time.

CHAPTER 168

December 9, 1971

Simmons woke seven hours after a restless sleep, and after a quick check out the windows, he went to the bathroom and peed. The garbage had to be taken out. He couldn't remember the last time he'd been to the dump. After reluctantly tying the bags and putting them outside, he returned to make breakfast. Without bothering to wash his hands, Simmons opened the freezer, took out a frozen bagel, and cut it in half.

As soon as the bagel ejected, he cursed, burning his fingers. When multiple tablespoons of cream cheese were spread over the first half, he made it into a sandwich, sat at his tiny kitchen table, and bit in, squirting cream cheese in all directions. Two globs landed on his plate, and another hung on his chin. As he stood up to get a paper towel, he saw it. Sitting on the far counter across the kitchen was a long bone.

He wasn't quite sure what kind of bone it was or whether or not it was human, but he knew beyond a shadow of a doubt that he had never seen it before. His heart pounded as his mind made excuses. Was it one of King's old chew bones? *No, it sure as hell isn't.* As much as he wanted to justify it, Simmons knew this femur (?) should not be there.

Simmons spat out the bagel, threw the rest in the trash, and then checked the yard for the thousandth time. She was wearing him down, and he could do nothing about it, beyond tired and on the verge of surrender.

After some deliberation, Simmons decided not to report the bone. Chief Galluzzo had been on his ass ever since the Bonnette incident, and he didn't need any more headaches. Once the written warnings started, they usually came in threes, and then you were gone. Luckily, he had no idea Bonnette was in town the night he was killed, and he was allowed to keep his job for the time being.

It was also good that nobody knew about Bonnette's movie camera. That little baby could be his saving grace; maybe he could afford to quit his job and leave this haunted town.

CHAPTER 169

December 31, 1971

Tim was surprised the holiday visitation season went smoothly. Sheila hadn't thrown any monkey wrenches. She had the girls for Thanksgiving break, so Tim and Holly enjoyed a cozy and romantic long weekend together.

Christmas Eve was also Sheila's, but Christmas Day was Tim's. Thankfully, both went off without a hitch. The biggest holidays of the year were history, and it was on to January. Unfortunately, it wasn't long until Sheila ruined all that good faith.

The issue involved the terminology of the phrase *New Year's*. Tim hopped into his truck on the morning of December 31, intending to pick up the kids at 9:00 am, but Holly required some extra attention, and he was running late. As the only parent driving (Sheila had refused ever since Tim's move to New Hampshire), delays were bound to happen occasionally.

In a defensive move, he took the Londonderry exit to find a payphone so Sheila couldn't say he hadn't reached out. "Sheila, it's Tim. I'm going to be about ten minutes late. Sorry, but I'm coming. Don't go anywhere."

"Uh, Tim, it's not your year. I have plans with the girls."

"What do you mean, it's not my year? It says in the agreement that I get the kids for New Year's every odd year, and this is an odd-numbered year." Tim felt the heat rising through his temples. *Here comes the sabotage.*

"Tim, New Year's Day will be in 1972, an even year. We've made plans. We're leaving for them as we speak." She'd exploited a technicality, even though it wouldn't fly in court.

The phrase "you get them in even years, and I take them in odd years" worked for thousands of other couples who could act like adults for the children's sake. Lawyers worked off of templates, didn't they? "Dammit, Sheila, what about tonight? Tonight is my night!" He kicked himself for attempting to explain to someone who didn't want to reason. Then, the line went dead.

Tim slammed the receiver into the phone booth three times, cracking it. She said she was leaving *right now*. If he showed up and she was home, she would call the police. *Maybe that would be a good thing in the long run. Let's let it play out.*

It started to rain, and Tim yanked the handset hard, breaking the telephone. Blood dripped down his palm, and he dropped the handset on the ground. He paced for minutes, trying to decide what to do. He couldn't call Holly, at least not from this phone.

In the end, he decided not to go to Amesbury. He was not financially strong enough to take her back to court yet. Shaking, he got back in his truck and drove back to Sanborn. *Maybe I'll just fucking work all day.*

Mildred was about to leave the woods when she heard Tim's truck. It was best to keep him in the dark about her existence. He was young, and she could wait forever, so there was no hurry, but she looked forward to seeing the surprise on his face one day.

Mildred watched Tim's truck pull into the driveway and was disappointed to see he was alone. According to his divorce agreement, he should have them. Mildred wondered what happened. Even though cold weather had hampered their meetings in the grove, she still enjoyed listening in on their conversations.

Tim slammed the door on his truck, and she could tell he was angry. He ran to the side door, opened it, and ran inside. Something had happened. Mildred snuck through the woods around the back of the barn and climbed to the roof. Carefully, she made her way to the turret and let herself in. Flies were not a problem this time of year. She heard him on the telephone, heated. Sheila had 'stolen his visitation time.'

"It's frustrating. What if Sheila does this on a major holiday like Christmas? I'd have to take her to court. She's daring me to spend the money. She knows she can get away with anything as long as I'm strapped!"

"You're right, Tim, but I have some money. I could lend you some if need be. If she does it again, that's what we'll do. New Year's isn't worth fighting for, but look at the bright side. Why don't you work on the house for a few hours, and I'll finish shopping.

"Instead of family pizza night, we'll have a romantic dinner, followed by some TV and 'spa' time. What do you feel like? Sirloins? Baked potatoes? A nice bottle of red? There's always a silver lining."

"You're right. I need to pick my battles. You're the best. If I were alone right now, I mean, like, not dating you, I'd be punching holes in the walls. I love you."

CHAPTER 170

March 31, 1972

It was almost quitting time on Friday afternoon at Depot Realty, and Holly, bored, flipped the calendar on her bulletin board. The first thing she saw was Easter, which would happen this Sunday, April 2. For a second, she forgot to breathe. A year had passed since she figured out how Annette Smith's journals worked. Well, almost a year.

April 1971 was a month she would just as soon forget. Sure, she and Tim had started dating, which was nice, but April 1971 was also the year they met Mildred Wells, and Mildred had filled their second half of April with a flurry of nightmares.

Would the anniversaries start again? Would Mildred be back? Holly opened her file cabinet and pulled out her calendar project. She drew a blank April 1972 calendar and began filling in the dates. Almost immediately, she noticed that April 1972 was the same as April 1967, both starting on a Saturday. Now, all they had to do was follow the happenings of 1967 to know if the anniversaries were still happening.

But they would have to wait for the 17th for their first clue. That was the day Tim heard someone banging on the roof. Or was that Thomas? Everything was so confusing. When was the first time that they saw Mildred celebrating an anniversary? Not just walking through the field but performing a one-woman play? Holly took a breath. It was April 27 last year, meaning April 25 this year. It was the day Mildred slaughtered the geese.

April flew by, but it was an anxious time the closer they got to the 17th. Tim woke and started his truck, which he had already parked at the end of the driveway, ready to flee. They stood at the bend in the driveway listening, but nothing happened. "Are you sure it happened this early, Tim?" asked Holly.

"Yeah, it woke me up. Anyway, I didn't see Mildred that day. I thought it was Thomas, to be honest, and we know he's long gone."

Holly frowned. April 25th was still eight days away.

Holly didn't sleep all week, and Tim didn't get much, either. She wished they could set up a movie camera and film the yard, but neither had the funds for such equipment if it existed. Holly wanted to be off property all day and avoid it entirely, but to prove that Mildred was back or vice versa, they had to bear witness.

"Okay, but we're not going inside. You said you saw Mildred in the kitchen," said Holly.

"Yes, but Annette saw her kill the geese down by the pond. Where do you want to be?" said Tim.

"How about Florida?"

"Ha-ha."

"I don't know!"

"How about the turret? We can hear the kitchen from there and see the pond," said Tim.

"Are you crazy? We'd be trapped up there!"

"We could escape out the window. I'll set up a ladder on the back of the house. If she follows, we climb down and knock the ladder over."

"Oh, I can't stand this!"

They waited four nervous hours in silence, but Mildred never showed. Holly couldn't remember a time she'd ever felt such relief.

CHAPTER 171

May 4, 1972

As May arrived, Mildred looked forward to the girls' return. She'd spent the winter listening when she could but missed their private time together. The three of them had been on to something last fall, something that made her feel good.

"Can we please, please, please, please play in the grove, Daddy? We can plant seeds in your garden for you. You've lived here for over a year, and we've never hurt ourselves!" Olivia attempted to negotiate with Tim, who was having a good morning. The house was coming along nicely, and he and Holly had begun to talk about her open house.

Tim was proud of every nail and cut. When the public got their first look, people would talk. Thankfully, everyone had left him alone: Bob Simmons was quiet, the police didn't want to look around, and the TV show disappeared. Most importantly, Thomas Pike might have kept his end of the bargain. *No more anniversaries!*

But the Gottlieb boy's story still ate at him: *a white-faced woman with flies all over her.* That was eleven months ago. Elmer was gone. Maybe Mildred left, too. "Go ahead. Go play," said Tim.

Olivia reached the grove first, and their friend was already waiting at the end of the row. Olivia slowed as a fog rolled over her mind. Not far behind, Vivian caught up, and the same thing happened. The two girls walked the final forty yards as the woman stared past them. *She must be watching for Daddy*, Olivia thought.

The flies swarmed, but Olivia didn't care. There was an odor, too, but it was far from unpleasant.

Vivian, excited, spoke the first words. "I missed you! What's your name?"

After an afternoon of—*what was it?* Corn dolls, for sure, but then there were dice and magic tricks. Yes, lots of magic tricks. Olivia couldn't remember everything, but it was more fun than hide and seek. Vivian, too, enjoyed the day.

"What should we tell Dad about today?" asked Olivia.

"I don't want him to get nervous again and make us play on the lawn," said Vivian.

"Me either. I'd rather stay at Mom's house. At least she gets all the TV channels. Don't say anything about Mildred."

"I won't."

CHAPTER 172

June 4, 1972

Rebecca Vaughn worried about Andrew. The loss of Colleen and Markus was devastating on many levels, especially in the parenting department. Andrew's recent setback seemed to be smoothing itself out, however. At least he hadn't gone back to hard drugs. Every drug is dangerous around an addict, but something about Andrew and heroin was a match made in Hell.

Since the rough patch, he had shown up for all his shifts, but Rebecca realized his heart wasn't in his work, and he was hard to read. Perhaps she could afford to buy him out one day, which would be best for both of them. Whatever Andrew chose, Rebecca wished him the best. "How's Jeremy?"

"He's good. I like listening to him. He's been through some tough times, too."

"What's his last name? How come I've never met him?"

"Clary is his last name. I'm not sure where he's from."

Rebecca scowled. Andrew had a poor track record of choosing friends, and his lack of questions allowed it to happen.

The following day, as she was leaving her office, she collided with a thin, thirty-ish man with a mustache and baseball hat. Andrew was right behind him.

"Oh! Excuse me—"

"I'm so sorry, Ma'am," said Jeremy.

Andrew began his sales pitch. "Rebecca, I'd like you to meet Jeremy Clary. Jeremy, this is my sister Rebecca. She runs the place now that, uh, well, you know the whole story."

"Yeah, I know the story, and I'm sorry about your parents. Hello Rebecca, nice to meet you. I've heard a whole lot about you. Andrew speaks well of you." Jeremy reached out and shook Rebecca's hand.

"Nice to meet you too, Jeremy. Andrew says you've helped him through some difficult times." Rebecca disliked Jeremy immediately. He reminded her of a weasel, such a smooth talker. He also didn't have the good sense to take his hat off inside the funeral home.

"Jeremy can start tomorrow. I was giving him the tour. Jeremy used to manage a restaurant."

Rebecca couldn't believe her ears. "Uh, you've hired him?"

"Well, you were asking about him, and you've been saying we need more people. He's used to dealing with customers and employees. Plus, he's a handyman." Discussing business in Jeremy's presence was wrong, but Andrew had no idea. Not surprisingly, Jeremy didn't seem to care either and stood there with a big smile as if he were used to asking for things he didn't deserve.

"Ms. Vaughn, I used to manage the Howard Johnson's in Darien, Connecticut," said Jeremy, taking over for Andrew. "That location was number four in the company, pulling in nearly fifteen thousand dollars weekly. We had a staff of nearly fifty employees, and I oversaw training. We also had the lowest turnover in the company. I won't let you down. I'll be the first person to work and the last person to leave. I'm an extremely hard worker."

"Do you have a resumé, Jeremy? Usually, we make some phone calls before hiring a new person. Andrew is a brand-new employee himself."

Andrew frowned.

Jeremy reached into his back pocket and pulled out an off-white envelope with a perfectly typed resumé. The paper was quality: cotton, or linen perhaps, and had a nice weight. There was a six-month gap between his last job and today's date.

"Are you currently employed, Jeremy?" Rebecca was still angry that this meet and greet had become a job interview.

"No, ma'am. I'm unemployed. My wife wanted to move us to Northumberland to care for her mother. I had to leave HoJo's as there aren't any up here. Family first, I guess. I've been looking for employment since."

"All right, if you'll excuse us, Jeremy, I'd like to take a closer look at your resumé, and I'll be in touch with you tomorrow." Rebecca glared at Andrew, who was also angry. Jeremy thanked her and left. Neither said a word as Rebecca took the resumé into the office and sat down to call the Howard Johnson's in Darien.

Jeremy Clary earned a lukewarm recommendation from the manager of the Darien HoJo's. Patrick Lallo said that Clary had worked there for one year and two months but had to leave for family reasons, but nothing more.

Rebecca picked up the phone again and called Lum's Restaurant in South Portland, Maine. Clary had put his dates of employment as April 1963-June 1970, seven years. *Not bad*, she thought. *They must have liked him if they kept him for so long.* Unfortunately, three shrill beeps sounded from the handset, and she pulled the phone away from her head. Their phone had been disconnected. Rebecca left Jeremy's resume on her desk and went to find Andrew.

"You've got to discuss things like this with me. You can't hire someone without talking first. I would extend you the same courtesy." Andrew sat at his desk, brooding. "You're barely twenty-two years old, Andrew. I've been doing this for five years. I saw Mom and Dad run this place full time."

Andrew nodded, still licking his wounds. Deep down, he knew she was right. Rebecca continued: "He checked out, or mostly anyway. And we need people badly. Tell him he can start tomorrow, but we've got to get him going on his certifications immediately."

Andrew nodded and picked up the phone.

CHAPTER 173

September 8, 1972

After nearly a year and a half of construction, Tim and Holly were on the brink of putting the house on the market. On September 8, he quit work early, drove to the supermarket, and bought some salmon for the grill. While at it, he also purchased a special bottle of wine.

After dinner, he and Holly retired to the couch for television and more wine. Holly picked up the new copy of *TV Guide* and thumbed through it. New TV shows debuted in the fall, and this was only the second Friday of the month. Tonight's prime-time lineup was about to begin, and Holly read descriptions of each show out loud.

"*The Brady Bunch*," said Holly. It was the show's third year, and Tim hated it.

"Nope. Next!"

"*The Sonny and Cher Comedy Hour*. This is a new show."

"Comedy? They sing too, don't they? That sounds like a variety show."

Holly read on. "*Only If You Dare*. Those are the people that knocked on your door, right?" Holly read the description to herself and put her wine glass down.

"What is it?" said Tim.

Holly's face was as white as a ghost. "You're not going to like this. *The Legend of Mildred Wells. A ghostly woman haunts a sleepy New Hampshire town.*"

Tim spilled his wine as he lunged for the magazine. "Can I see that?" There it was in black and white: *Mildred Wells, New Hampshire town*—one short sentence that set his world on fire. Tim walked over to the television without a word, turned it on, and remained standing. Their relaxing evening was over.

"*Welcome, ladies and gentlemen. Tonight, on* Only If You Dare, *a small, sleepy town in New Hampshire is haunted by the ghost of a woman who allegedly drowned her child. Mildred Wells, born in 1836 and died in 1863, was the 'mother from Hell' to her young son, but even death couldn't stop her from terrorizing the small town of Sanborn for more than a century after that.*

"Welcome, folks, and thanks for watching Only If You Dare. *I'm your host, Simone Infante."*

Tim and Holly's hearts sank as the TV screen panned across the front of Tim's house. The camera appeared positioned in the middle of the field, but with the zoom lens, perhaps they were just over the property line. Tim was beside himself.

The show recapped Mildred's life, according to Elizabeth Simmons' scrapbook. They attempted to back it up with a cheesy-looking Hollywood set recreating the two graves. Then, the show burned an entire segment trying to tie in the Hampstead murder and the Beverly Farms fire. Tim's refusal to interview on the front steps was included, but his name was not mentioned, and his face was blurred out.

Only If You Dare dedicated an entire segment to David Bonnette's death and another interviewing Bob Simmons, who explained his family history. The show closed with Bonnette's footage of Mildred inside the house. They repeated the final scene no less than twelve times, slowing the poorly-lit, lightning-fast shot frame by frame, squeezing it for all it was worth.

"Did you see that?! That was real. Heart attack, my ass. That son of a bitch was in my house, and that was Mildred!"

CHAPTER 174

September 9, 1972

Bob Simmons woke at 3:00 pm with some extra pep in his step. The *Only If You Dare* show had aired the previous evening. The three thousand he was paid for his part felt good, too, so he bought himself an eighteen year old bottle of scotch.

Although he'd just woken up, he couldn't help but celebrate and drank a glass of the expensive stuff. He hadn't tasted scotch in ten years, and it was so good he poured another as he sat down and flipped on the television. An hour later, he fell asleep again.

He woke after 8:00 pm, and it was pitch-black outside; part of life working the vampire shift. An episode of *The Mod Squad* was playing on the television, so he shut it off. He had a headache and regretted the liquid breakfast. Now, he'd have a miserable night in the cruiser. Nauseous, Simmons headed to the kitchen, hoping something in his stomach would smooth things out.

He noticed a glow from the kitchen as he left the couch. Had he left a burner on? He saw the flame as he entered the room, but it wasn't the stove. It was a candle on the other side of the room and something else. *What the hell is that?* Simmons flicked the wall switch, and the kitchen came alight. Blinded, he squinted at the mystery candle. It was sitting on a skull, the eyes still packed with dirt.

Simmons charged into the living room, ripped his pistol from its holster, and turned back to the kitchen, ready to shoot someone who was long gone. Pointing the gun at the skull, he read the four letters finger-painted on the forehead.

E-M-M-A.

CHAPTER 175

September 8, 1972

The girls came for visitation that weekend but never saw the house on Lancaster Hill Road. They all stayed at Holly's home in Laconia, the excuse being Tim had just polyurethaned the floor, and it wasn't safe to breathe. Tim was less than a month away from completing the refurbishment, but the timing of the *Only If You Dare* program and proof that Mildred had returned made him nervous.

Mildred knew the schedule as well as anyone. The weather was good, and there should be no reason the girls weren't here unless Emma's skull was public knowledge. If that was the case, then so be it. It might be time to return to the original plan. It was easy to be angry when the girls weren't around.

CHAPTER 176

September 15, 1972

Only If You Dare's Nathan Hoginski flew into Boston, drooling at the story's potential. The ratings of the first show were good enough to warrant further episodes, and the executives loved it.

Bob Simmons had mixed emotions. The New Hampshire State Police were called in to examine the "Emma" skull but could only determine that it was female. Since he didn't feel safe, he moved to his father's house, where a mouse ran over his face the first night. Back in his own bed, defeated and afraid, his anger for Tim Russell grew. Russell knew things but hid them to protect his wallet.

Hopefully, because of the TV show, the asking price of Russell's house would drop like a stone. Now that the *Only If You Dare* crew was back in town to film another episode, he put his faith in karma. Simmons asked again about a chance of getting a warrant, and his lawyer friend laughed.

"A warrant for what? The dead guy and the bones were on your property, not his. And that video Bonnette took doesn't prove anything. Your only ticket onto Russell's property is the Open House."

CHAPTER 177

September 22, 1972

Another Friday arrived, and Mildred waited to see if the girls were coming. Last time, they spent the weekend at Holly's house, and Mildred wasn't sure why. She missed the girls. Without them, her bitterness bubbled. Looking for information, she listened in on a phone call between Tim and Holly from the turret.

"Bring the girls right to your house," was said, and "lose a half-day of painting Sunday because we'll be in Laconia." Mildred balled her fist as flies bounced on the turret window. She would have to leave before more of the dirty creatures found her.

"… I … right. No, I don't know how I'm going to sell it. One day at a time, I guess. I'm still hoping it's not true, or—yeah. I know it's morally questionable, but that TV show brought out the crazies. I get at least one call per day asking if I want to sell. What? I don't care! They can have it! I can't save their lives if they knowingly buy—right. Okay. I have to leave soon to get the girls. I'll see you at around seven. Love you too."

Mildred heard Tim put down the phone, grab his keys, and leave.

The following Wednesday, Tim took a final look around. He had finally finished work on the house, and it was spectacular. Despite the accomplishment, the specter of Mildred Wells ate at him. He would have to be honest with prospective buyers. Whoever bought the house could be in danger. The house was not a novelty item. Most of the crap reported by *Only If You Dare* piqued curiosity in the wrong way.

Tim and Holly hadn't seen Mildred Wells in seventeen months, but the Bonnette recording seemed real. His speech to potential buyers would no doubt be a dealbreaker for some, but all he needed was one.

CHAPTER 178

September 30, 1972

During a funeral service in late September, Rebecca checked in with Andrew and Jeremy to ensure everything was ready at the cemetery. Jeremy had been very hands-on, and she was happy with his performance, yet she still didn't trust him.

The priest began his graveside sermon, and the Foggy Orchard Funeral Home employees took their places, watching the attendees and ready to assist. Jeremy had adopted the proper stance: feet shoulder-width apart, arms clasped at his beltline. Rebecca stood ten feet behind him, observing.

Something caught her eye under the cuff of Jeremy's jacket. He wore a watch, something she was pretty sure she had never seen him wear before. In the post-funeral staff meeting, she touched on everyone's performance (including the part-timers) and thanked them for an error-free ceremony. She also complimented the staff's appearance.

"I know you've all heard this before, but it bears repeating. A watch or a ring is fine, but no more than two. Jeremy here has the look we're looking for. Jeremy, I'm not trying to embarrass you, but his jacket is pressed, his shirt is starched, and he wears a modest watch. Nice watch, Jeremy, by the way."

Jeremy smiled. "It was my grandfather's. I don't know why I put it on today. I guess I just kinda threw it on."

Rebecca hoped it was true.

CHAPTER 179

October 7, 1972

Holly considered hosting open houses her strong suit, but this one was incredibly nerve-wracking. She recalled the conversation with Tim before their first date about the morality of selling a home that someone died in and wished it were so easy. This time, the dead person was probably still around.

They had to warn potential buyers. It couldn't be a blanket statement to an open house but a discreet rundown for qualified people placing serious bids. All bidders would get "the talk" before signing on the dotted line, regardless of whether they believed in ghosts. After that, adults could make up their own minds.

Because of this, the money worry remained, and Tim would be on edge until the minute the money was in the bank, but even after, he would worry whether or not the buyer understood what they were up against. The moment of truth was here. Tim's work was era-appropriate and beautiful, and the housing market was favorable. Pending the "talk," it seemed things might work out.

A good crowd arrived that Saturday, close to twenty people, but Holly was skeptical about how many were qualified buyers when she saw a policeman with Simmons on his name tag. *So that's Bob Simmons. Thank God sellers don't come to their open houses. Tim would erupt.* Bob Simmons could wander free without trespassing. Holly let it go but tried to keep tabs.

She had already shown the house privately twice, with both couples submitting bids even after hearing the talk. She'd even prepared a page that read like a warning:

You may have seen this house featured on the TV show Only If You Dare in an episode titled "The Legend of Mildred Wells." In it, a cameraman is allegedly killed in the upstairs of the house by the ghost of Mildred Wells. Let it be known that there is no proof the footage was filmed in the house. The owner granted no permission for any such filming, and the studio refuses to comment.

There is also the issue of a boy who was drowned in the pond in 1862 by his mother, Mildred Wells. Although Mildred was never officially accused, to our knowledge, it did happen. Like the property owner Tim Russell, I, Holly Burns, have seen Mildred Wells and believe her to be real. Before you decide to buy, I urge you to consider that you may see her too, and she may be dangerous.

Holly had initially included, "I believe she has the potential for violence," but decided her statement was strong enough without it. She also left out details about the bayonet and the geese. The bayonet was something Holly wrestled with—Tim had been stabbed. It was real and dangerous, but Thomas Pike was gone forever, so she no longer considered him a threat.

The kitchen splattered with goose blood seemed a thing of the past, too. Tim and Holly hadn't seen Mildred perform one of her anniversary routines in a year and a half. It was hard not to justify the right to sell now that the house was finished. Nearly everyone attending had seen the Bonnette tape on television.

Holly read the "talk" to each of the potentials with a straight face, and it was met with nervous laughter both times, but Holly remained sincere. The talk would do no good if it sounded like part of a gimmick to sell the house.

Holly didn't escort people to the pond or the grove anymore but instead hung back and pointed people in the right direction from the relative safety of the front lawn. The turret was also off-limits in her mind, but Tim had done such a fantastic job that it was almost easy to pretend it was another house. After the open house, there would be two more private showings, and after all was said and done, they would select the winner. Things were looking up, fingers crossed, but she couldn't wait for it to end so she could get the hell off the property forever.

Holly waited on the front lawn as the stragglers returned from the grove. She thought Bob Simmons had disappeared into the house but couldn't be sure. *Have you already seen the grove, Bob?* Of course, Holly already knew the answer. One couple returning from the field strolled past the stone wall where Mildred slaughtered the geese. When they arrived at her lemonade stand, Holly composed herself. "What do you think?"

"I love the property, and I love the turret. The owner did such a beautiful job."

"It's gorgeous, isn't it? What was your favorite part about the property?"

"We both liked the grove. Puts you in a mood."

"Absolutely. I'll never forget the grove."

"Is that a garden back there?"

"Yes, it is."

Just then, a woman tapped Holly on the shoulder. "Excuse me, Holly, was it? I have a question."

Holly turned. "Mrs. Wallace. Yes, how can I help you?"

"I don't recall a house on this road except at the beginning. How many neighbors are there?" she asked.

"The closest neighbors are Officer Simmons and his father. You can talk with him if you like. He's right over there. It's very private out here. Plenty of New Hampshire fresh air."

"And the meadow comes with the property? To the trees?"

"That's right. You get the meadow, the pond, the house, the barn, and a big chunk of woods, including the grove, twenty-three acres in all. You can even tap your maples to make homemade syrup."

"Well … who's that lady in the field? She's been staring at the house since we arrived. We said hello, but she ignored us. She smells bad, too. I don't think she's here for your open house. You might want to keep an eye on her."

CHAPTER 180

October 7, 1972

"It's her! It's Mildred Wells!" Bob Simmons went wild as Holly turned, a chill running down her spine. Mildred was staring from the meadow, her wild hair blowing in the wind. Holly couldn't distinguish her features, but the pale skin and black dress said it all.

In an instant, Holly was transported to Tim's first month on the property when Mildred sightings were as ordinary as blue jays. Had she never left? Before Holly could react, Bob Simmons shuffled past her on his way to the pond. Everyone at the Open House stopped what they were doing to see who the police officer was yelling at.

"What's happening?" said someone who hadn't heard the whole conversation. "Where's he going? Who is that?"

Holly's worst fears had come true. Bob Simmons ran past the pond and out into the meadow, then pulled his pistol. The crowd gasped.

Mildred stood firm, still a hundred yards from the lumbering Simmons. A moment later, she stepped into the woods. Holly heard Bob Simmons yell, "halt," and shook her head in disbelief.

"Ms. Burns, what is happening?" said a man whose name she didn't remember.

Holly, in the heat of the moment, improvised. "You know the show mentioned in the leaflet I gave each of you? *Only If You Dare?* Officer Simmons plays a big part in that."

"So, Mildred Wells is really haunting this place?" another woman asked in disbelief.

Holly almost rolled her eyes but stopped herself. "That TV show is trash! This is a prank. Somebody watched the show, and they're having fun. Something you'll have to get used to if you buy the place, I suppose."

"If you'll excuse me, ladies and gentlemen, I'd like to speak with Officer Simmons." Holly trudged down the lawn to intercept Simmons in the meadow. When Holly caught up to him, she spoke. "Did you have to pull your gun, Bob?"

Simmons talked tough even though he knew he was probably in trouble. "You and your boyfriend should be ashamed of yourselves. She's a killer, and you know it. You're hiding something."

"We're hiding something? This is an open house. You toured the property without supervision. You created this whole phenomenon, and you trespassed to do it."

"You moved her grave."

Holly could tell Simmons hadn't figured everything out. "What grave, Bob? I want you to leave the property, or I will call your boss. If you're lucky, we won't seek a restraining order."

Simmons bit his lip but did as he was told, cutting across the field to his cruiser. After starting the engine, he stepped on the gas, spraying gravel. Holly returned to the house, checking over her shoulder before arriving on the front lawn. Only one couple was left, and it looked like they were about to leave, too. "I'm sorry about that, folks. Did you have any questions?"

"Yes, Ms. Burns. We saw the TV show, and it's the main reason we're here." The woman's smile was ear-to-ear. "This is so exciting! We're real ghost story freaks, and that made our weekend! Was that the real Mildred Wells or a prank? I'm freaking out right now!"

Holly bit her lip. "Yup, another prankster. Somebody wants to be on TV."

"Tell me you're joking," said Tim.

Holly said nothing and dropped her head.

"You saw everything you just told me?"

Holly nodded.

"And it was her?"

Holly buried her face in her hands and began to cry.

CHAPTER 181

October 8, 1972

Bob Simmons was scared. Holly might report him to the chief, and unfortunately, she was in the right. His days as a Sanborn police officer were over. Mildred's taunts had him on edge, and seeing her staring at him was too much. Still, there might be a chance. He knew what he had to do. With nothing left to lose, it was time to double down.

At four minutes past midnight, he parked his cruiser north of the house and left it running with the parking lights on. From the trunk, he grabbed the movie camera, his hunting rifle, and his ax and fast-walked the half-mile to Russell's property. Russell was with Holly in Laconia, where he spent his nights. The house was dark.

Simmons' heart pounded as he considered perching in the hayloft but realized he couldn't see the front of the property. Entering the house was out of the question. He'd seen how quickly she killed Bonnette and wanted no part of a close-quarters confrontation. Simmons hoped to film her unaware.

To avoid being seen, he unscrewed the filming light. Hopefully, the moonlight would suffice. Simmons walked to the pond and camped under one of the willow trees. From this spot, he could see the house and the field. The hanging willow branches even provided camouflage.

Mildred watched Simmons search for his spot from the turret, back and forth from the barn to the lawn to the pond, overloaded with tools and equipment. After ten minutes of indecision, unaware he was being hunted, Simmons settled under one of the willows, and Mildred slipped out of the house.

It took ten minutes to slither through the cattails but only one to cross through the pond. Simmons was beneath the tree, his back to her, his head on a swivel, woods to house, house to woods. When she was ready, she exploded from the pond, quick like an alligator.

Simmons tried to look back over his shoulder, but Mildred was already on his back. She pushed the blade in. Simmons reached for one of his weapons but coughed a spray of blood. Recognizing defeat, Simmons made a last-ditch effort to turn around and take her with him, but Mildred pinned his head to the ground, and Simmons writhed as intense heat on the back of his head boiled the blood in his eyes. A moment later, he looked like he'd been dead for a month.

With no reason to disguise the body, Mildred left. She didn't want Tim Russell moving away just yet.

By Tuesday, Bob Simmons was reported missing, and Nathan Hoginski, producer of *Only If You Dare*, took note. He contacted his sources at the Associated Press and suggested they investigate Simmons' disappearance and compare notes with the remaining *Only If You Dare* team members. If nothing else, it was a boon to the ratings. The suggestion that a police officer's disappearance might be related to Mildred Wells would blow the ratings through the roof.

CHAPTER 182

October 10, 1972

With the work on the house completed, Tim drove daily to Massachusetts to help Johnny. When he called Holly at lunchtime, she told him the news. "Simmons is missing."

"Oh, my God, I'm going to go broke. *The Legend of Mildred Wells* has become a thing."

"Not yet, Tim. I'm still getting calls for showings. We have to make sure they're qualified. I'll find out if they're pre-approved for a mortgage first."

Tim went quiet on the other end.

"Tim? Are you there?"

"Holly, Bob Simmons is a homebody, and Elizabeth Simmons was found across the street."

Holly frowned. "Well, he's not at his house." Seconds passed as both Tim and Holly thought things through. "Tim, you're in Massachusetts. What are the chances the police are trying to call you? You might want to check in."

Holly was right, and Tim got nervous even though he had nothing left to hide. If Simmons was missing and the police thought Tim skipped town, it wouldn't look good. He thought of calling Frank Turnbull for a second but held off. "You're right. I'll call you when I get there."

Tim got in his truck and left for New Hampshire, praying Bob Simmons was nowhere near his property.

Tim entered Lancaster Hill Road with a lump in his throat. Something terrible was happening. He could feel it in his bones. Simmons Road was taped off as expected, but closer to Tim's house, a Belknap County Sheriff's cruiser had set up a roadblock just before the pond. Tim parked and got out. Several more vehicles were ahead, including three State Police in his driveway, two black sedans, and a team of official-looking people under one of the willow trees. His worst nightmare was coming true. Chief Galluzzo of the Sanborn Police noticed Tim arrive and intercepted him as he hopped the stone wall.

"Mr. Russell? Special Agent in Charge Whitlock of the FBI is here and wants to speak with you. Right this way, please."

"I don't need an escort Chief. Just point him out."

Galluzzo grunted and pointed to a large man with broad shoulders near the pond.

"Special Agent Whitlock? I'm Tim Russell. I live here."

"Mr. Russell, we've been waiting for you. Can you tell me where you were for the past twenty-four hours?"

Tim noted that Special Agent Whitlock had not mentioned Bob Simmons or the crowd by the pond. "Yes, I can. But can I ask if that is Bob Simmons? And if so, what's he doing on my property?"

"We're still confirming the details, Mr. Russell. We'd like to hear what you have to say first. In fact, we require it." Whitlock handed Tim a search warrant. *Galluzzo must have found him*, Tim thought. *He snuck on my property, too.*

"Yeah, you don't need a warrant. Please, look around all you want, I just didn't want Bob Simmons spreading lies about a ghost on my property, but it looks like he managed to draw negative attention anyway. I've been working on this place for a year-and-a-half, and now this."

"Do you want to talk in your house or at the Sanborn P.D.?" Tim agreed to the former, and the two men weaved between vehicles to the side door. They went inside, and Tim watched what was happening from the kitchen window.

"Where were you for the past twenty-four hours, Tim?"

"Twenty-four hours ago, I was working on a job in Newburyport with my co-worker Johnny Upson. The owner of the house, Sherry Pratt, was also there. Then, I drove back to Laconia from about 6:00 pm to 7:30 pm. From that time until 7:00 am, I was with my girlfriend, Holly Burns. Then I drove back to Newburyport and returned home as soon as Holly told me Bob Simmons was missing. I haven't been alone at all except for the drive-time."

"I'll have to corroborate this. Chief Galluzzo told me all about Bob Simmons and his family history. I saw the TV show, too. I also walked to the grove to look at your garden. Not planting anything this year?"

Tim paused momentarily, wondering if he should tell the truth, then thought better.

"No, I'm selling the place, so I skipped it this year."

Whitlock took some notes. "Any reason you wouldn't use the meadow to plant a garden?"

Tim left the room and returned a minute later with the "Forest Gardening" book Frank Turnbull had told him to purchase. "It's a great place to grow. My friend Frank told me about it. Who knew?"

Whitlock took the book from Tim and flipped through the pages. Tim hoped it looked used enough. "Interesting. So why not allow the Hampstead police to inspect your property? Galluzzo said he and a Hampstead officer asked for permission to investigate, but you turned them away."

Tim considered confessing to moving Elmer's bones but thought better of it. "Bob Simmons was hell-bent on promoting the Mildred Wells story, and I didn't want to entertain it. And they were snooping. Bob Simmons snuck onto my property and took pictures of my garden; Lord knows why. Now I'm guessing Galluzzo trespassed, too. It had to be him that found Bob Simmons."

"Galluzzo says the police received an anonymous tip," said Whitlock. "What can you tell me about two murders on this road in less than a year? And the human skull?"

Tim had to refresh his memory. "Human skull? David Bonnette died, and perhaps Bob Simmons, but what skull are you talking about?"

"Bob Simmons reported a skull he found on his property with the Word *Emma* written on it."

Tim felt the hair stand on the back of his neck. "Wow. I don't know anything about that. Emma was one of his relatives from years and years ago. He showed me where they found Elizabeth, but I didn't know about Emma."

"Did you say 'where they found' Elizabeth?" asked Whitlock.

Tim realized how screwed up the situation had become. "Yeah. Two Simmons ladies were killed before he was born. They were his descendants. They found Elizabeth across the street, and he showed me her memorial while we were still friendly. The last I heard, Emma was never found."

"I'd like to see this memorial before I leave."

"Sure. It happened in the 1800s, though," said Tim.

"Go on about the two deaths," said Whitlock.

Tim looked down at his feet and began crafting his story. He would have to be careful. Lying to an FBI agent was big trouble. "Well, they say Bonnette was killed in this house, but I can't be sure. Have you seen the film?"

"I have, and I have a team of people analyzing it frame by frame. We took some pictures of your hallway, and they're comparing them to the video. What's your take?"

Tim decided to tell the truth. "I think it happened here. But I wasn't here that night. Yet another trespasser, can you believe it? I haven't complained because I didn't want to harm the resale value."

"What about your ex-friend, Bob Simmons?"

"To be clear, we were neighbors but never friends. I—don't know what happened to Bob, but I do know that he believed in Mildred Wells or whoever is going around dressed like her. Maybe he went looking for trouble, and trouble found him."

"And what about you, Mr. Russell? What do you think about this person who has allegedly committed murder inside your house?"

"Are you asking if I believe in ghosts, Special Agent Whitlock?"

"Speak your mind, Tim."

Tim looked at his feet again, knowing he'd better not think too long. "I've seen a woman occasionally, usually way out in the field, passing through or staring at the house. The entire Open House saw her, too. For a few weeks, I thought she was stealing blueberries, but I always wondered where she lived. There aren't many houses on this road." Tim let his words tail off, omitting his closer encounters with Mildred.

"Would you agree with the Gottlieb boy's description of her? Pale skin, black dress, etcetera?"

"I would."

Whitlock took notes as Tim watched the men down at the pond through the bay window. The officials came up the lawn to their vehicles with a five-gallon bucket. What looked to be a long bone protruded over the rim.

"Is that his body?" said Tim.

The man in the hazmat suit was close enough that Tim could see what he was holding. The femur sat on top of a skull, with some hair and a host of shorter bones. It was as if Simmons had already decayed. Tim looked back at Whitlock, who suddenly regretted conducting his Q&A on the property.

"Come sit down, or we'll have to finish this at the station," said Whitlock. Tim turned and sat for the first time. "I was about to get your take on the body's condition. Bob Simmons was here for your open house three days ago, wasn't he? Why do you suppose his body is so decomposed? My first thought was lye, but first reports suggest no chemicals were used."

"He was here three days ago. I wasn't, of course, but there are several witnesses. Holly said he pulled his gun and went running across the field after someone in a dress."

Whitlock stopped writing and looked up. "Why was that not reported?"

"I don't know. Simmons is a cop! He should have reported it. We just want to sell this damned place. We don't want to be in the news."

Whitlock shook his head. "The officer pulled his gun over a copycat? Show me where it happened."

Tim took Whitlock outside and began to explain. "The woman came out of the woods in that corner of the field, and—wait, what the hell is that?" Tim saw a reflection under a tree across the meadow, just over the property line, where two people were holding something. Tim couldn't quite make it out. Whitlock saw them, too.

CHAPTER 183

October 10, 1972

Nathan Hoginski had already been to Boston and rented the best camera available when the police scanner squawked. Officer Bob Simmons, the hero of *The Legend of Mildred Wells*, was missing. *Chance favors the prepared mind*, thought Hoginski.

The police spoke cryptically, but the address was unmistakable: Lancaster Hill Road. Hoginski arrived on the scene just after Tim and parked off the road under cover of the woods, hidden from view. The camera was mounted on a tripod, and they began filming. The *Only If You Dare* crew captured hundreds of feet of mind-blowing footage, including a bone sticking out of a bucket and a skull being turned over in the gloved hands of an official.

"Oh shit!" Larry, the cameraman, swore and ducked down. They were the first two words either man had spoken since entering the woods.

"What is it?" Hoginski looked across the field and saw two men staring in their direction. One was wearing a trench coat. "Let's go. We can't lose this footage." They broke down the tripod in ten seconds and ran. If the footage was confiscated, the day was lost. Hoginski looked back to see the cops trying to navigate through the jam-packed driveway. Hoginski might have to contact the studio's legal department the way this story was developing.

He had enough new material for at least three more shows. The next step was to get it out of New Hampshire and edited and narrated as soon as possible. After their getaway, Hoginski found a payphone and called Hollywood.

The plan was to bump tonight's episode of *Only If You Dare (Stonehenge)* for a rerun of *The Legend of Mildred Wells*, except they would rename it *Part 1* for tonight's broadcast and have a dramatic voice-over promising breaking news, then bust ass all week cutting the new shows. They might get an entire season out of it the way things were developing. The ratings would be through the roof.

CHAPTER 184

October 7, 1972

During a funeral service in October, the Foggy Orchard Funeral Home facilitated the ceremony of a man named Gerald Nye. Jeremy was late to the hearse, so Rebecca went looking for him and finally found him in her office hanging up the phone.

"Sorry. I left a burner on my stove running. I had to let my wife know."

"Okay, let's go. They're waiting." Rebecca hated being behind schedule. Thankfully, the rest of the funeral went off without a hitch.

The next day, Rebecca made a follow-up phone call to the Nye widow as a professional courtesy. To Rebecca's horror, Mrs. Nye was upset, but not for the reason she had imagined.

"We were robbed while we were at the cemetery! Nothing was broken or trashed, but they must have known we would be away. I lost my jewelry. We had a little bit of cash. They even stole tools from the garage! How can people be so cruel?"

One week later, Jeremy Clary was in a celebratory mood. "One more, buddy, I'm buying."

Jeremy Clary waved to the bartender and paid for another beer. It had been a long day at the funeral home, and the boys needed to burn off some steam.

"Last one. We have to work tomorrow," said Andrew.

"Yes. Last one, but we deserve it! Do me a favor and pass the pretzels, would you?"

Andrew looked to his right. Just down the bar was an unattended bowl. Without hesitation, he got up, took a few steps, and retrieved it. While Andrew wasn't looking, Jeremy sprinkled something in his drink, a combination of Quaaludes and something else he couldn't remember. His brother swore that it worked.

"You're still hungry? Didn't you just eat a double cheeseburger?" said Andrew.

Jeremy took a handful to make it look good and raised his beer. "Yup, still hungry. Cheers, buddy."

CHAPTER 185

October 15, 1972

Where the hell is Andrew? Rebecca wondered. Jeremy was on time, early even. At least there was someone to help her greet the mourners. "Jeremy, hold the fort. I'll be right back." Rebecca ran across the parking lot to the house and found Andrew in bed, sleeping something off. His breathing was fine, but she couldn't wake him. "What time did you get home last night?" He didn't answer. *Pathetic*, she thought.

"Dammit, Andrew, we need you!" She shook him one more time with no success. Things could not continue this way. There were three more funerals this week. Frustrated, she left him and ran back to the funeral home. When she reentered the building, Jeremy was nowhere to be seen. Elderly mourners often arrived early, and having an employee as a greeter was a must. Rebecca checked the bathroom and sitting room with no luck. Finally, she looked in the office and found the petty cash drawer empty on top of the desk.

Sadly, she'd seen this coming. Jeremy was a street rat. She knew one when she saw one. *Had he set this up?* Thinking fast, she looked out the office window and saw Jeremy's Ford Pinto backed up to the loading bay. When she ran down to intercept, she caught Jeremy loading the last of the embalming fluid and anything else readily available in the back of his car. She'd heard stories that criminals were using the fluid to get high, and apparently, Jeremy had, too.

"What are you doing, Jeremy?"

Jeremy knew his time was over at the Foggy Orchard Funeral Home, and it was time to move on. He was nearly untraceable, with no address or phone number. The funeral business wasn't as lucrative as expected. There wasn't as much jewelry as he'd thought there would be. He'd sell the embalming fluid and the rest of the stuff on the street, then disappear.

Jeremy saw Rebecca but pretended he didn't until the last second. Just as Rebecca got close enough to grab him, he spun, lowered his shoulder, and lifted her under her rib cage. The hit knocked her off her feet, and Rebecca fell hard, hitting her head on the curb. Jeremy slammed the hatchback and sped away as Rebecca's blood pooled on the driveway.

There were no witnesses, but with Andrew's help, the police found him in Dover attempting to sell the embalming fluid on the street. Rebecca, unconscious, had emergency brain surgery and died nine days later.

CHAPTER 186

Amesbury, Massachusetts
October, 15, 1972

Sheila Palmer, formerly Sheila Russell, heard the phone ring in the living room. "Hello? Oh, hi, Judy."

"Sheila, turn your television to channel seven, quick!" It was five minutes past eight, and Olivia and Vivian were in bed. The TV wasn't on yet, so she pressed the button and waited for the old Zenith to warm up. Judy, bursting at the seams, took the opportunity to fill Sheila in.

"It's Tim's house! In New Hampshire! It's on TV!" Sheila felt a twinge of envy, thinking it was a news segment showcasing Tim's skills. She and Judy had driven by one weekend to snoop while he had the girls. They'd taken Judy's car to make it less conspicuous.

The two women could carve up just about anything, but neither could deny Tim's talent. Sheila went home wishing they'd stayed home. The new house was twice the size of hers and would be gorgeous when it was finished.

Finally, the picture focused, and Sheila turned the dial to channel seven. The first thing she saw was the house, with Tim's face blurred out, refusing to be interviewed. Over the next half hour, she learned the whole story: The drowning, the haunting, the fire in faraway Beverly Farms, and most shocking, the recent deaths of the Enrico boy and the TV show cameraman.

The found footage of the Bonnette death was especially creepy. Something about that scene struck Sheila, and after five minutes of venting to Judy, she hung up the phone and dialed Tim's number.

CHAPTER 187

October 15, 1972

Tim answered the phone, bracing for trouble, even though he had no idea *The Legend of Mildred Wells Part 1* had just been broadcast on national television.

"Tim? Have you been hiding something from me?"

"Sheila? What are you talking about?"

"I saw that TV show. Two people were murdered! You're putting our daughters' lives in danger!"

Tim's heart froze. Sheila, a problematic person on her best day, had finally seen *Only If You Dare*. His heart was in his throat, and she hadn't even heard about Simmons yet.

"Relax, it's a tabloid show! Pure garbage!"

"People died, Tim, and you have your daughters up there every two weeks like nothing ever happened. We question your parenting skills." Sheila had switched to *we* mode. *We* could mean Sheila and Judy Larson or Sheila and the whole world.

"You can't trust me? Weren't you the one bouncing from bed to bed while we were married? Give me a break, Sheila. I'll be there on Friday. Have a good night."

"I could get a restraining order if I wanted to, and I don't need a reason. Don't mess with me, Tim."

"I'll be there Friday, Sheila, and you'd better be there too unless you want to pay my legal fees!"

Sheila slammed the phone down, and it took all of Tim's willpower not to do the same. He swallowed hard as his heart pounded. How long would it be before he saw his girls again?

When the phone call ended, Mildred crawled from the turret window and disappeared into the woods.

CHAPTER 188

Amesbury, Massachusetts
October 17, 1972

Two days after slamming the phone down, Sheila's hand still hurt, but the kitchen garbage needed to be taken out. Scrunching her nose, Sheila flicked on the kitchen light, put on two yellow dish gloves, and pulled the bag out of the can.

The *Tim situation* still bothered her. Sheila pretended to call all the shots but privately worried about his next move. Denying visitation was serious business, and Tim would fight, but people had lost their lives on Lancaster Hill Road. Surely, the court would see things her way, wouldn't they? If only he would give up and go away like Judy's ex-husband, it would be much easier to label him a deadbeat.

As things stood, she would have to find something to do outside the house Friday evening so that when Tim showed up, if he showed up, the girls would not be home. Sheila stepped back into the living room to escape the garbage odor and take a sip of wine. She put her nose in the glass, savoring the bouquet, temporarily escaping the dirty chore. The smell returned immediately, however, when she pulled the glass away.

Okay, hold your nose, and let's get this over with. As Sheila stepped back into the kitchen, she stopped. *What happened to the lights?* Sheila tried the switch, and the light came on. To her horror, flies were everywhere, buzzing off the light and the cupboards and strafing her head. Sheila held her hands up to block the insects as she tried to make sense of things. *What? I was just here ...*

It was then that she noticed the figure just inside the pantry. Sheila stepped back and was about to scream when she stumbled over a chair and fell hard underneath the breakfast table. The woman was the source of the flies, and the stench was more than garbage.

It was the woman from the TV show. Her face was pale, her skin was mottled, and she was as quick as a cat. In less than a second, a rusty knife flashed, and the woman was in her face.

Mildred held the knife steady in Sheila's chest until she stopped breathing. When it was over, Mildred left the kitchen, and listened up the stairwell. *Did they hear? No. Good.* The girls slept through it. Now, she would hide the body so they wouldn't see, and they would leave together.

Mildred turned back to the kitchen when Vivian suddenly appeared in the upstairs hallway. Mildred intercepted her before she could descend. It wouldn't be good if the little girl saw her mother.

"Mildred! What are you doing here?" said Vivian. Mildred held a finger up to her lips. If Olivia remained sleeping, things would go smoother.

"Are you friends with my mom? Her name is Sheila." Mildred glided up the stairs, closing the distance between them. "Something smells terrible!" said Vivian. It would be the last words she uttered that night. With a quick finger tap on the little girl's forehead, Vivian stopped questioning.

Without breaking stride, Mildred stepped past Vivian and into the dark bedroom. Olivia was still sleeping, so Mildred shook her twice. As soon as Olivia's eyes opened, Mildred repeated the forehead tap, and both girls were under Mildred's spell, courtesy of the Book of Shadows.

Now, there would be no screams to wake the neighbors. All she had to do was get them through their Amesbury neighborhood and disappear into the woods. Mildred found shoes and coats for the girls and marched them through the living room and kitchen directly past Sheila's body. The girls didn't even turn to look.

Checking one last time, Mildred realized she had forgotten her knife in Sheila's chest. With a flick of her wrist, she called the knife to her hand and returned it to its spot in the woods of Beverly Farms, thirty miles away.

PART FIVE:
THE PATIENCE OF A DEAD MAN

CHAPTER 189

October 17, 1972

Andrew couldn't bear to take the responsibility of burying his sister and wisely hired another funeral home fifteen miles away. Aside from the funeral, he felt guilty for never suspecting Jeremy. Depressed, Andrew closed Foggy Orchard for three days while extended family returned for Rebecca's service. Nobody said anything to his face, but he heard them whispering. Only Aunt Jenny spent any quality time asking him how he was and how he was dealing.

Everyone except for Colleen's brother, Uncle Roy, left the day after the funeral. To say that Roy was disappointed was an understatement. Rebecca had always been his favorite niece, and to make matters worse, Andrew had, as a child, been caught going through Roy's wallet. Since then, even without the added guilt of Rebecca's death, it had always been a shaky relationship.

Being with Uncle Roy was uncomfortable but better than being alone. While Uncle Roy was in the bathroom upstairs, Andrew made breakfast for two. He returned, extra serious.

"Andrew, I have to know. What happened?" Uncle Roy looked tired, the dark circles under his eyes making him look angrier than usual.

Andrew shrugged his shoulders, having anticipated this talk. "I wish I could say, but I can't. We had a couple of beers, which I know I shouldn't have in my condition, and I blacked out." Andrew held his tears back as best he could.

Uncle Roy threw his coffee mug into the wall, and the pieces exploded everywhere.

Andrew dropped his spatula in shock.

"Damn you, Andrew." Roy put his face to his forearm, shedding tears of his own. "I can't believe I'm saying that, but you make me that mad. Your parents gave you everything, every opportunity, and all you did was piss on their hard work. I hope you feel one-tenth of what I feel. You're used to hanging out with scum, though, aren't you? You can't tell right from wrong anymore."

Andrew knew nothing he could say would make things right, but he tried. "I knew I didn't want to be a funeral director, and I didn't want to live in the country anymore, but I messed up and have no excuses. I'll regret Rebecca's death for as long as I live."

"And what do you plan to do now?"

"I don't know. Maybe I'll sell Foggy Orchard, live somewhere closer to Boston and find a job doing something else."

Uncle Roy went silent, put his face in his hands, then lifted his head and smiled as if he had a secret. "Andrew, you're not moving to Massachusetts, at least not with family money. The trust is set up to keep you kids on the right track. Your parents intended for the two of you to inherit this business, and they knew you would be a disaster.

"They even had a plan for you if Rebecca died. I come as the bearer of bad news, Andrew. I'm the trustee, and you're the beneficiary. That means I decide what happens. Your mother and I ..." he trailed off, emotional. "Your mother and I were very close.

"She told me to give you the funeral home and nothing more, but you can't sell it. You can work here as long as you like and take all the profits. You can even abandon it and let the business die, but that would be against her wishes. If you tank the business, the property will be sold, and the proceeds will be given to charity.

"There are no shortcuts to running a business like this. You earn every penny, and it builds character. It teaches you the right way to live. Your mother had faith that you would someday be that kind of man, someone she could be proud of. Today is not that day, but you have the rest of your life to get there."

CHAPTER 190

October 18, 1972

Nate Hoginski sat in his car two miles from Tim Russell's supposedly haunted farmhouse. Nate had been in the business long enough to know that when you had a good thing going, you rode it for all it was worth, even if law enforcement was involved. Money took care of everything, including legal bills. Careers were launched on gutsy stories like this one.

Hoginski couldn't give two shits about the dead cop Bob Simmons, but David Bonnette had shown promise as an up-and-coming television producer. Before this story ran its course, Hoginski would make him a legend. Because of Bonnette's death, they could now interview their own people and eat up countless minutes of airtime, saying what a great guy he was, a family man, etc.

Hoginski's CB radio crackled to life: "Bossman, this is Satellite. We have scanner activity, and it looks like big stuff. Russell's ex-wife is dead. Send the truck ASAP."

"Ten-Four. The truck is on the way," Hoginski almost spilled his coffee, scrambling out of his car to talk with the passenger van parked behind him. "Did you hear that? Get your ass down to Amesbury, and don't stop for anything, not even gas. If you have to piss, use a bottle. You have the address, right?"

"Got it, boss." The driver of the van started the engine and threw it into gear. The car in Amesbury didn't have a video camera, and Hoginski was nervous. The men had more than an hour's drive to Sheila Russell's house. He prayed they wouldn't miss any filming opportunities. A body on a stretcher would do wonders for the ratings.

Four hours later, Nate Hoginski combed his hair and prepped himself for an impromptu on-camera interview. It wasn't his forte, but this trip's on-camera talent was not in the budget, especially with possible legal battles with the Feds on the horizon. He'd have to ask the questions, and he was nervous. They'd blown so much money on international episodes that *The Legend of Mildred Wells* had to suffer. *No worries*, he thought. The beautiful people were pains in the asses anyway, and this might be his chance to shine.

Clearing his throat, Hoginski walked up Tim Russell's driveway and knocked on the front door. Russell had not taken too kindly to the last time *Only If You Dare* showed up, and there was no way he would appreciate this episode either. The cameraman hefted the camera onto his shoulder, and Tim came to the door.

"Oh, for crying out loud."

"Mr. Russell, sorry to bother you. I'm Nathan Hoginski from *Only If You Dare*. Would you have time for a few questions?"

"I'm afraid not. Goodnight."

"Mr. Russell, do you have any comments about what happened in Amesbury last night?"

Tim froze. "What are you talking about?"

Hoginski wasn't sure if Tim had heard the news, but now he knew. Nervous, Hoginski stammered. "Uh, your ex-wife was found dead this morning by one of her neighbors. We can't confirm, but it looks like a stabbing. Do you know where your daughters are?"

Tim grabbed the camera off the cameraman's shoulder and smashed it on the steps, and neither man challenged him. Tim turned to face Hoginski. "Tell me everything!"

"We heard it on the scanner. Some of it we had to piece together, but we saw a body taken out of the house. It sounded like they were looking for the girls. You might want to get down there." As Hoginski finished his sentence, a black sedan pulled up the driveway. Tim ran to the vehicle.

CHAPTER 191

October 18, 1972

FBI Special Agent Lamar Whitlock sat at Tim's dining room table. "The waitress and the clerk at the hardware store remember you. Your story checks out. We're interviewing Sheila's neighbors to see if anyone saw anything, but we need your help. So, my question to you, Tim, is, who do you think did this?"

Sheila was dead and the girls were missing. Tim was beside himself, and Holly sat close, her arm wrapped around his. The shock of hearing it from the damned television show was icing on the cake. His house was searched as well as Holly's. Both cars were checked for evidence and nothing out of the ordinary was uncovered.

"I just want my daughters back. How are you searching for them? How many men?"

"First, you need to tell me what you think and what you know. Everything you say will influence my plan of action."

Tim stared at the back of his hand like a zombie. Mildred Wells had his kids, but who would believe him? "Special Agent, Bob Simmons was obsessed with Mildred Wells, and it got him killed. I hate to say this so late in the game, but he was right."

Whitlock dropped his pen on the table. "You can't be serious."

Tim rubbed his eyes, tired of crying. "I haven't lied to you, Special Agent Whitlock, but I haven't been completely truthful. That forest garden was once a graveyard. Two graves, specifically. Elmer Pike and Mildred Wells. We dug up Elmer's bones and moved them."

"And you're suggesting what?"

Tim was in terrible emotional shape, so Holly interjected. "Tim is saying that a mass murderer is on the loose. Someone is angry that we destroyed the family plot."

"You're losing me," said Whitlock.

"The copycat, whomever it may be, knows we disturbed the graves and is after us."

"You mean like a relative of Mildred Wells? Who knew the graves were there?"

"We don't know, but as Tim told you, we saw a woman come and go occasionally. Way out by the tree line, crossing the field and moving toward the graves."

"Why did you move these bones?" asked Whitlock.

Holly hesitated, unsure what to say. Tim had painted them into a corner, and it was her job to get them out. "We discussed plans for this property. Maybe subdivide it and sell it in pieces. The graves were in the way. We knew we were breaking the law, and that's why we didn't want anyone searching the property."

Whitlock looked up from his note-taking. "Have you ever spoken with the person that you believe is after you?"

"No," said Holly. Tim was glad she had taken over answering questions.

"Then how do you know this person is angry?" said Whitlock.

"Because they won't go away."

"That's the only reason?"

"Yes."

"And you think this person drove to Amesbury, killed Sheila Palmer, and kidnapped the two girls?"

Holly considered the question before answering, and Tim interrupted.

"I think she walked."

Holly clenched her teeth.

"You think she walked from Sanborn, New Hampshire to Amesbury, Massachusetts?" asked Whitlock. "That's at least seventy miles. Who would do that?"

"Special Agent Whitlock," said Tim, "I want you to look for my girls where I think this person is, and I think she's in the woods because of the Enrico boy incident. He was killed in the woods in Hampstead, and that's only twenty miles from Amesbury. If you lump the kidnapping with Beverly Farms and the Enrico boy, you begin to believe that this person is deranged and probably doesn't have a home or a driver's license."

Whitlock put down his pen and rubbed his temples. "So, you think a recluse or a hermit … is the person we're looking for? Someone who walks back and forth between here and Beverly?"

"That's just how I put the pieces together," said Tim.

THE LEGEND OF MILDRED WELLS

"And how would this person know your daughters live in Amesbury?"

This one was easy to answer for Tim. "Because, like Bob Simmons, Chief Galluzzo, and David Bonnette, they've been in my house. They got into my papers and read about my whole life."

"Bob Simmons trespasses. David Bonnette trespasses. Chief Galluzzo trespasses. And the person you believe is responsible for kidnapping your daughter trespasses. Have you reported any of this?"

Tim squeezed the edge of the table until his fingers turned white. "I could never prove they were in my house, but I found an open window in the turret once. The Sanborn cops haven't been great neighbors, either, if you know what I mean. I just want my daughters back."

Whitlock sat back and ran his fingers through his hair. "At this point, a ghost story is more believable. You think a vagrant without a driver's license kidnapped your daughters and is walking them through the woods. To me, it makes a lot more sense that someone tossed them in a car and has them holed up in a house. What's their next move?"

"I think she's coming here to gloat," said Tim. "She wants to rub it in my face."

"And then what? Ransom? Worse? How do you think this ends, Russell?"

"I'm hoping your men and some dogs find them, and your men are armed. There won't be any sort of surrender."

"You have a lot of opinions on a person you've never spoken to, Russell. What are you not telling me?"

"It's guesswork, Agent Whitlock. I've been afraid of her since the first time I saw her, and now it seems she's killed at least three people."

Whitlock stared Tim in the eyes wondering if Tim Russell was in his right mind. "I don't have the manpower to search seventy miles of forest. And I still have my doubts about you, Russell."

"Where are your men now, Special Agent?"

"In Amesbury, getting nowhere."

"How many?"

"Four."

"Send two up here, then have the other two start in the Amesbury woods and head North toward Sanborn. See if you can pick up her trail. I'll start up here with the other two."

"No chance. We're thin enough as it is, coordinating with local and state police, and I'm not sold on your theory," said Whitlock.

"Okay," said Tim. "Then be ready for my call."

445

CHAPTER 192

October 18, 1972

Tim jogged to the grove, daring Mildred to show herself, but he couldn't shoot her if she were alone, or he may never find the girls. The daylight was almost gone. He jogged, breaking a sweat, looking down each hallway, praying to see a ghostly face staring back. The rows zipped past until he came to the last one, but there was nothing to see. Mildred wasn't here. Nobody was.

The sun finally set, and tiny bits of orange sky faded between the spruce boughs. Frustrated, Tim left the grove for the deep woods. "Olivia! Vivian! Yell, if you can hear me!" Frustration turned to desperation as Tim tripped on a root. While he was down, he screamed again.

"Olivia! Vivian!" Tim's anger boiled as he turned back for the house. Coming to his senses, he suddenly realized that visibility was near zero. His thoughts turned to Holly and how upset she would be that he was in the woods alone. Now, all he could imagine was what an easy target he had made himself.

Tim booked it down the trail to the driveway, out of breath, and as his shoes found the asphalt, he looked back. The trailhead was a yawning black hole in the trees. Thankfully, no one followed. It was not lost on him that he was standing in the exact spot where Annette Smith was killed. Shaking, Tim jogged to the side door and let himself in.

"She knows this place better than we do, Tim, that's why I hate staying here! Please, let's go to my place. Even though she probably knows where I live, I'll feel better."

"I can't, Holly. I need to wait for her. And I have to search. I told Whitlock I'd call for help if I saw her."

Holly nodded, unhappy. "You'll see her again, Tim. At least once, anyway. She wants revenge. That's what revenants do, remember?"

"I need to booby-trap this place. Set a trap, then let her up here again. A bear trap or ..."

"A bear trap? You don't think she'll see a bear trap in the middle of the floor? That's just going to piss her off."

"I mean something that could warn us. Something to make her fall down the stairs. A bag of marbles, I don't know ..."

Holly snickered. "How about a wire with a little bell on it?"

"Oh, you're hilarious."

"Wait, I was laughing at the marbles, but I'm serious about the bell. We'll set up one at the bottom of the turret stairs, one in front of the sliding glass door in the breakfast area, and one at the bottom of the bedroom stairs. We set it up every night. In the morning, we unhook it, so we're not tripping it ourselves."

Tim looked up at her. "Better than nothing. Like you said, we're gonna see her again. We have to. I hope you're right, but—" Tim balled his fist under his nose.

Holly saw he was getting emotional. "Honey, we're doing all we can."

"But if she's already done, if this is her revenge and she's never coming back, then I'll never see them again." Tim choked up, worried sick. Holly hugged him, holding back tears of her own.

Tim searched the woods for nearly two hours after Holly left for work, going so far that he came upon a farmhouse with a dilapidated barn. *Varney Road*, the sign said. He didn't realize it, but he had almost crossed the town line into Belmont.

When he was almost home, the sound of a Volkswagen engine broke the silence. Holly's car bounced down Lancaster Hill Road, and Tim checked his watch: 3:00 pm. *She's early*, he thought. It was nice to have Holly home, but he was itching to return to the woods, and she would protest. As the Beetle pulled up the driveway, he greeted her. She had a passenger.

"Who is this?" asked Tim.

"Honey, I want you to meet Neptune. Neptune, meet your new dad." A large German Shepherd stared at him, panting in the back seat. He was handsome and intimidating but had no issue with Tim's approach. The dog smelled his hand and let him pat his head.

"A dog? That's not a bad idea. Why didn't we think of that last night?"

"I did. I didn't say anything because I didn't want you to say no. Kind of like how you go into the woods without checking, you know? So, do you like him?"

"Yeah, my parents used to have dogs. I like dogs. I hope he ..." Tim trailed off. Holly followed his gaze to the field. Mildred was not there.

"Jeez, don't do that! 'I hope he' what?"

"I hope he doesn't get hurt."

Holly's smile faded, and Tim could tell she was already attached, so he changed the subject. "How did he get the name Neptune, anyway?"

"Previous owners, I guess. I didn't think to ask. He's handsome, isn't he? I needed this big boy. I didn't sleep last night."

"Do you want to show him around the property?"

"Yes. Bring your shotgun, though."

Neptune seemed to adore the property and took the opportunity to chase his first squirrel. Tim and Holly let him off the leash as they passed the pond. The poor dog had lived in a cage for nearly a year and was delighted with his newfound freedom. Halfway to the tree line, he stopped and perked his ears.

Holly called to him. "Neptune, come here, boy!" As she began to jog in his direction, the big Shepherd bolted for the woods and disappeared into the trees. Holly was near panic. "Oh my God, Tim!"

"Neptune!" Tim followed his bellow with a shrill whistle, but the dog didn't listen. Holly broke into a run, and Tim followed. "Neptune!" Tim called again. Just before they reached the trees, Neptune emerged from the woods with the body of a fat gray squirrel hanging from his jaws.

"That didn't take long," said Holly. "Come here, Neptune." The dog did as he was told but needed a few minutes of coaxing to give the squirrel up.

CHAPTER 193

October 19, 1972

As much as he hated the idea, Tim knew the right thing to do was attend Sheila's funeral. Olivia and Vivian loved Sheila's parents and the Palmers had loved Tim pre-divorce, but ever since, Tim sensed a distance whenever they bumped elbows. Privately, Tim wondered what they thought he did to break up the marriage. Obviously, they only heard Sheila's side of the story.

As Tim arrived at the funeral home, he caught Ted's glare from across the room, and when the service was over, he approached. "Hello, Linda, hello, Ted. I have no words except to say I'm sorry for your loss."

Linda interrupted. "We wanted to bury her even though the girls haven't been found. It's the Godly thing to do."

"I agree," said Tim.

Ted couldn't hold his tongue. "You know, I thought you did it. I wanted the police to nail you to the wall. I still hope they take a second look after all you put her through." Ted, seventy-five years old and in poor health, was shaking.

"Look, Ted … I don't know what you heard, but there's a good chance it was exaggerated. He said/she said stuff." Ted lifted his index finger to interject, but Tim cut him off. "But I'm not here to talk about that. We need to work together. Your granddaughters will want to be a part of your lives. You have my number if you want to talk."

Ted Palmer continued in a low whisper. "What's this malarkey about a ghost? And that TV show … they've got people talking!"

Tim shifted awkwardly. He'd hoped the Palmers had missed the media circus, but no such luck. "Yes. Pure garbage."

Linda nodded her head. "I haven't seen the TV show, but I know about the Enrico boy they found in the woods. They don't have a suspect, do they?"

"Not yet. I'm headed to Amesbury after this. I have a meeting with the police. I'll do anything I can. I promise."

Ted Palmer scowled.

Tim pulled into the driveway of Sheila's house and parked behind Whitlock's black sedan. A detective from the Amesbury police met Tim at the top of the porch stairs, the same place Tim had suffered countless confrontations with Sheila on so many stressful pick-ups and drop-offs. Things were different now, but they weren't any better.

"Good afternoon, Mr. Russell. Remember not to touch anything, as we discussed." Tim nodded, preparing for a nightmare. Everything was left as they found it, minus Sheila's body. One of the chairs surrounding the breakfast table was upended, and another was three feet from the table.

There was no chalk outline of Sheila's body as he had guessed there would be, but there was a beer-can-sized puddle of dried blood under the table where the far chair should be. Tim could easily picture how Sheila's death played out, and despite their heated history, it gave him no pleasure. Mildred had attacked from right to left, pushing Sheila to the floor, upending the chairs, and stabbing Sheila under the table.

Tim swallowed. His throat was dry. It was eerie in here. There were all sorts of reminders that the girls had called this place home, but the toys, the Barbie drinking glass, and the pile of laundry were meaningless without them.

Tim pulled out a Kleenex and wiped his eyes as he tip-toed around the murder scene, and Whitlock entered the kitchen. Everything was familiar yet different. Under Whitlock's supervision, Tim opened the hall closet and flipped through coats and rain slickers. Tim wasn't sure, but he thought Vivian's three-season jacket was missing. Looking down at the closet floor, he saw a pair of Sheila's hiking boots. There was no foul-weather footwear for the girls.

"There might be some coats and boots missing from this closet," he remarked.

"I'll make a note of it," said Whitlock.

Tim then went upstairs with Whitlock on his heels. Other than the girls' unmade beds, nothing seemed out of order. Tim dropped his chin and cried, keeping his back to the FBI agent.

"I have a daughter too, Russell. We'll find them."

Tim nodded thanks as he pulled another tissue from the box on Olivia's night table and swept the room one last time. A corn husk doll lay on Olivia's dresser. He remembered seeing the girls with them at his house some months back but, for whatever reason, never commented. He picked it up. The handiwork was unusually intricate. Had the girls made them? Tim wondered for a second if Mildred could have made the doll. He lifted it to his nose, smelling for death, but sensed nothing.

"Uh, don't touch, Russell," said Whitlock.

"Right," said Tim, and put the doll back. Just then, a fly bounced off the interior of the bedroom window and buzzed Tim's head. Panicked, he turned and sniffed the air.

"Are you all right?" said Whitlock.

"Of course not," said Tim.

CHAPTER 194

October 19, 1972

It had been two days since Uncle Roy's lecture, but Andrew hadn't learned his lesson. After a day at his desk, he pulled the bottle from the drawer and took a drink. He hadn't figured out how to get out of the irrevocable trust, but until he did, he would have to keep the business afloat.

Business aside, the dreary building alone was enough to drive him to drink, but there was too much work to do to leave at 5:00 pm. Andrew looked at the clock: 9:47 pm. He was getting tired, and the hallway outside the office seemed to be getting darker and darker. The thought of some dead soul waiting to speak with him in the hallway was unbearable. Andrew took two more pulls from the bottle, felt the sting in the back of his throat, and ran home.

The house, too, seemed extra empty since Uncle Roy had left. Even though they were at odds, Andrew hated to see him go. Andrew fixed himself a bowl of noodles and three more drinks, then collapsed on his bed upstairs. He feared bedtime. Sometimes, sleep didn't come.

On this night, however, Andrew passed out immediately, fully clothed, yet awakened in the middle of the night feeling nauseous. He'd overdone it with the whiskey, and tomorrow was halfway here. He could not afford to be sick at work.

Andrew went to the bathroom and forced himself to vomit, then downed two glasses of water and showered. After the shower, he closed his eyes but couldn't sleep. Soon, Andrew's bladder joined the reasons for being awake. The clock read 4:17 am.

The house was silent, and the room was cold, so he put on a T-shirt on his way to the bathroom, oblivious to the woman ascending the stairs. When finished, Andrew washed his hands and gulped water to hydrate his headache. Twilight had begun to leak through the bedroom curtains, so Andrew opened the bureau, took out another t-shirt to throw over his eyes, and crawled back into bed. Eyes covered, he couldn't help but listen to the house. Everything went silent when the furnace finished its next cycle, until someone whispered his name.

"Andrew."

Andrew threw off the eye mask and sat upright. In front of the glowing curtain was a dark figure. He screamed. "Who are you? What do you want?" Andrew looked to his nightstand for a weapon as the woman stepped closer. Andrew squinted but couldn't see her face.

Colleen Vaughn paused, waiting for Andrew to realize. What a disappointment he had been. After all the pain he had caused the family, getting mixed up with deadbeats and drug addicts, poor Rebecca paid with her life. Worse, he was still numbing his mind with substances. She could smell the whiskey.

Colleen was wrong about one thing, however. Andrew had always complained about seeing ghosts; now she knew he wasn't lying. *It's time to put that talent to work.* Colleen might be dead, but she wasn't finished raising her son.

"Mom?" Andrew thought he might be hallucinating. "I know you're angry. I know I let you down, but I wasn't there when she died. This guy Jeremy—" Suddenly, something to the left caught Andrew's eye. A stranger stood in the doorway. "Who is that?"

Two ghosts surrounded Andrew's bed. They loomed as his eyes darted right to left, and his heart pounded. The dead man was tall, bearded, and dressed in farming clothes. Despite the fear he felt, Andrew noticed his eyes were blue.

"It's time you helped someone," said Colleen, and as soon as she finished the words, she stepped into Andrew's closet and disappeared between the clothes. Alone with the tall man, Andrew wondered what came next.

Thomas Pike stared at the young man in the bed. Writing things in a book was one way to communicate with the living, but it was slow and tedious. According to his mother, this boy could speak directly with the dead.

Mildred's fuse was lit, and time was a factor. Thomas had to be at the right place at the right time to catch the pieces before they fell. Without mincing words, Thomas told Andrew go to the living room, then disappeared.

Andrew padded down the hallway and paused at the top of the stairs. His view of the living room was obscured, but voices were coming from the television. On edge, Andrew descended. The living room was empty, and as he reached to shut off the television, the news ended, and a promo for the next program began.

"Coming up next: A ghostly woman terrorizes a small New England town. Two young girls go missing, and their mother is murdered. Stay tuned. Only If You Dare *is next."* Andrew wanted the noise to stop, but someone squeezed his shoulder. Thomas Pike was behind him, his hand so cold it hurt.

"Tonight on Only If You Dare, *Murder in Massachusetts. Two girls are missing. At least four are dead. Is a sleepy New Hampshire town in the crosshairs of a murderous ghost? Don't turn that dial. You're watching* Only If You Dare!*"* The theme song for the TV show played, and Andrew turned to Thomas, who stared back, insisting Andrew paid attention.

"Mildred Wells. Remember that name, ladies and gentlemen. She's accused of kidnapping two girls and murdering as many as four people in New Hampshire and Massachusetts. Still, there's something undeniably odd about that: Mildred Wells has been dead for over one hundred years.

"The townspeople of Sanborn, New Hampshire, are haunted, but no one will admit it. This unassuming farmhouse was built in 1860 by a young couple named Thomas and Mildred Pike. They had it all, according to local historians, including a young son named Elmer. Everything seemed fine until Thomas felt the call of duty and signed up to fight for the Union Army."

The show went on to recap the entire *Legend of Mildred Wells*, including Thomas's death during training exercises, Elmer's drowning, and everything leading up to the kidnapping of Tim's girls. Andrew watched, relieved that the television was doing the talking.

When the show ended, Andrew turned to ask a question, but Thomas was gone, leaving a lingering chill on his shoulder. Andrew flicked the switch, watched the test pattern disappear, and listened to the house. Now that the ghost was gone, fatigue hit him hard.

His mother had dished him off to Thomas Pike. *'It's time you helped someone,'* she'd said. Besides running the funeral home, he now had a side project. How was he supposed to manage?

CHAPTER 195

October 19, 1972

Somewhere between Amesbury and Sanborn, Mildred Wells walked the forest in ever-widening circles, the girls safe in the coyote den that held the Book of Shadows. Mildred trudged through the dead leaves, pointing at every squirrel and bird she saw until nearly every living creature in a half-mile radius was dead.

Today was her third day on the beat, and nature was adapting. Fewer animals dared enter the circle of death. Still, there was enough meat on the ground to slow any dogs they might send, and if the bait didn't work, she could always take matters into her own hands. When finished, Mildred returned to the den and removed the logs blocking the entrance.

With the girls in her possession, Mildred's anger waned somewhat. Returning to Sanborn seemed more like an obsession than a passion. And somewhere in the mix was a whisper of guilt. Gideon Walker had altered her memory countless times, and she was doing the same thing to Olivia and Vivian. Happy to have a plan, Mildred forced the negative thoughts from her mind, for walking the Earth without one was madness. *The passion will return*, she promised herself.

CHAPTER 196

October 20, 1972

The next night, *Only If You Dare* aired an episode teasing the death of Sheila Russell. The big reveal didn't come until the half-hour mark because the first thirty minutes were devoted once again to the deaths of Bob Simmons, David Bonnette, the Enrico boy, and the fire in Beverly Farms. Anyone following the show from the beginning saw the same slow-panning photographs played to ominous music for the umpteenth time.

But almost no one changed the channel because it was teased ad nauseam that, coming up, 'two missing girls were most likely kidnapped by the ghost of Mildred Wells.' The cult of Mildred Wells had caught fire, and the show closed with the blurred-out face of Tim Russell being notified of his daughters' disappearance. Nate Hoginski was sure to mention that Tim had been cleared of any suspicion.

Tim got up and shut the television off. He wasn't happy, but at least the show mentioned that he wasn't a suspect.

"Maybe Hoginski isn't such a sleaze. I mean, at least for a tabloid journalist," said Holly.

Tim said nothing. He didn't know what to think anymore. His world was upside-down. Holly was the only bright spot. "I've never felt this helpless. I need sleep, and I can't even do that."

Holly cringed. She would rather be at her house, but Tim insisted on being at his house so he could speak with Mildred should the opportunity arise. As a result, Holly kept them up because she feared turning out the lights. Now, once again, it was bedtime, the worst part of the day. She reached down to pet Neptune, her new security blanket.

Tim left the bedroom to brush his teeth.

Neptune was tired, but his ears were alert, making her feel better. Holly could hear Tim's toothbrush as she tried to listen to the rest of the house. She wondered if Neptune was already doing so. Could he listen as far as the turret?

Nervous, Holly walked to the hallway to check on Tim and looked out the window to the lawn below. An eerie fog clung to the lawn, reminding her that every night on Lancaster Hill Road had a unique way of scaring her. Once across the hall in the guest bedroom, she looked through the window facing the turret. She couldn't hear that far, but she could see it. Mildred had broken in and read Tim's papers, or at least they thought so. What would stop her from doing it whenever she wanted?

The lights were out in the turret, and no one was on the roof, so Holly turned back to Neptune and rubbed his ears while waiting for Tim to finish in the bathroom. A thought crossed her mind. She should have brushed at the same time he did. She hated the bathroom at the top of the stairs. She would kill for a bathroom off the main bedroom.

Finally, Tim was ready for bed, and she envied that his turn was over. He seemed tired. *How can he sleep in a house like this?* Tim lay down, and Holly tiptoed down the hall. The railing along the balcony ran the depth of the house, and she couldn't help but measure each step as she approached the bathroom. She looked over the railing. It was dark downstairs, and Holly wondered if they shouldn't leave the lights on down there for safety.

Finally, Holly reached the bathroom, and with no immediate urge to pee, she skipped it, hoping she could last the night. Holly wanted nothing more than to get back to the bedroom. When she finished brushing, she had a decision to make. *Leave the light on in the bathroom, or turn it off?*

If she shut it off, she would be blind while her eyes adjusted. She could eyeball her path, flick the switch, run to the bedroom, or leave the light on all night. Standing at the top of the stairs, Holly looked down at the front door and the darkness on both sides of it and decided to leave it on.

She found Tim asleep. Neptune raised his head at her arrival and put it back down. *If they can do it, so can I*, Holly thought, and she crawled into bed and stared at the bathroom light leaking through the crack in the door.

Three hours later, the pressure in her bladder came back to haunt her. The house was quiet. Surely Neptune would hear what she couldn't? The fact that he was resting was a good sign. After five more minutes of procrastinating, Holly swung her legs over the dog and stepped out of bed.

Every board creaks in this house, she thought. Holly studied the floor, trying to recall which floorboards made the most racket. Before stepping, she watched the light under the door, ensuring it was uninterrupted. Slowly she turned the knob and peered around the doorjamb.

The light blazed in the bathroom, yet the bedroom to its right was dark. Worse, Holly couldn't see into the fourth bedroom because of her angle. With great hesitation, she padded down the hallway to do her business. When done, Holly bolted out of the bathroom past the dark bedrooms. Halfway home, she looked back to make sure she wasn't being followed.

From the safety of the main bedroom and with the bathroom illuminating the stairwell, Holly decided to recheck the turret and found it still dark. Somewhat relieved, she returned to join Tim and Neptune, but something outside caught her eye. Someone was walking through the field, out past the pond. Holly blinked to be sure it wasn't an illusion, and her fears were confirmed.

"Tim, get up! Get up! She's in the field!"

Tim sat up, scrambling for his pants. Neptune stood and watched, wondering what all the fuss was. Together, they huddled around the hall window. The figure was now parallel to the pond, heading toward the grove.

Tim looked at Holly in disbelief. "I have to go," he said. Holly blinked but didn't question as she moved for Neptune's leash. Tim rushed downstairs and fetched a flashlight and the shotgun. He was out the door first, but Holly and Neptune were close behind. Tim entered the pond area through the break in the stone wall as the shape disappeared into the trees. Sensing he might lose Mildred, Tim called out.

"Hey!"

The figure turned. Mildred had something slung over her shoulder, and as Tim closed the distance, he began to distinguish her features, the first being she was not wearing a farm dress. Tim raised the shotgun.

"Don't shoot! I'm here to help!" It was a man's voice.

Holly arrived at Tim's side, struggling with the big dog. "It's not Mildred!" she said. Neptune broke free as soon as the words were out, yanking the leash from Holly's grip. "Neptune, No!" But the dog didn't listen, and the trespassing man braced for teeth and fury, except Neptune ran straight past him and into the grove. "Neptune!" Holly continued to shout, but Tim's focus was on the stranger, now thirty yards away.

"Don't shoot! I'm sorry to alarm you. I thought you'd be asleep. I figured I'd grab a prime spot before everyone else arrived. I'm here to help. My name's Ed Bodwell. Wow, everything was so quiet, and all of a sudden I hear 'hey,' then …" The man was old and sported a bushy gray beard. He wore a red plaid flannel coat and dungarees. The cylindrical thing on his shoulder was a rolled-up tent.

Tim lowered his shotgun and tried to keep one eye on Neptune, but the big dog had disappeared in the darkness. "What are you doing here?" he asked.

"I'm here to help. I …"

"You already said that, Ed. What does that mean? Why are you here at 3:00 am marching across my property?

"There's a bunch of us coming. We want to help you get your kids back. You've got two beautiful girls, and we want to see their safe return."

Holly continued past the two men and yelled for Neptune to return.

"Who is 'we' Ed?" asked Tim, unsure if he should be angry or hopeful.

"A bunch of us at the Elks. And some of the Lions, too. And the Rotary. It's more than that even. We've been following the story on TV."

"You've been watching *Only If You Dare?*"

"That, and the local news. I live in Northfield. Many of us have discussed meeting up, especially after the last show. I guess I beat them here. I wanted to get a good spot. Do you mind? Can I pitch my tent behind the pond over there?"

"Tim, I don't know where the dog went," said Holly.

"I know. This dog is going to drive me crazy. One second. What's the big plan, Ed?"

"We want to call attention to your cause and help with whatever you need. You need help, am I right?"

Tim looked at Ed Bodwell sideways. "Do you believe in Mildred Wells, Ed?"

"Are you saying you don't? Tell me, is it nonsense or what? You'd know better than anyone. People are dying, even folks the TV show hasn't thought of, like Annette Smith. We locals remember that stuff. I wasn't supposed to spoil it, but the plan was to have a vigil until your daughters are rescued. I'm going to catch hell for blowing the surprise."

"You don't have a rifle wrapped in that tent, do you? I don't want any guns, Ed. Mildred Wells, or whoever it is, might know where my daughters are. If any of your friends get trigger-happy, the girls might not make it back."

"Nope, I don't have a rifle. We're here for support, prayer, and attention. And don't worry about the dog, miss. He looks like he can take care of himself."

"I'm not so sure, Mr. Bodwell. We just got him. He's a runner, and I don't feel like searching the woods right now," said Holly.

Tim wondered if more eyes on the property might put Holly at ease. "All right. If you help us get our dog back, you can stay. Where do you want to set up your tent?"

"Well, thank you, Tim. I thought I might set up over there by the pond. That way, she has less chance of sneaking up on me."

Holly left the conversation behind and walked toward the forest, listening for Neptune.

Tim didn't like her so close to the tree line. "Holly, you aren't going into the woods, are you? Give him a chance to come back."

Neptune ran through the woods, stealing a moment of freedom. He was an intelligent dog, smart enough to know that it was too early to commit to Holly and Tim unconditionally. He'd been returned to the shelter twice, once as a puppy and again at age two after a four-day tryout with a young family. No squirrels were awake yet, but there might be rabbits, so he kept his eyes and ears perked.

His nose was low to the ground as he cut through the grove. Something smelled good. Perhaps he would roll in it, wear it like a badge of honor, and then return to Holly and Tim to show it off. As Neptune broke through to the next row, he stopped dead, but the woman didn't flinch. As soon as he caught her scent, his bladder let go.

Mildred saw the dog when he left the house and retreated to avoid him, but he found her anyway. She called the knife just in case he came, but he didn't. The dog whined once, stepped back, and laid down, staring at her. She studied him, then stepped closer. He didn't move except to lower his head and twitch his tail.

Mildred had never had close contact with a pet except for Bob Simmons' dog, King, and that meeting ended differently. Satisfied this dog was no threat, she returned the rusty blade to where it came from and turned to walk away. It was the first time she'd decided to let something live in as long as she could remember.

After Neptune bounded out of the woods, Tim, Holly, and Ed Bodwell went to bed in their respective sleeping quarters. Holly surprised herself by sleeping until almost 9:00 am, attributing her relaxation to the extra eyes in the field. She and Tim weren't in this alone anymore. People were coming. She stretched, feeling better despite the early-morning interruption. The fact it was her best night's sleep in recent memory said it all. She and Tim were both running on fumes.

Tim was already up and out of the bedroom, unable to rest with his daughters missing. Holly rose and walked to the window to look at Ed Bodwell's tent and was astonished at what she saw. The green tent was there, but there were eight more next to it, some in the process of being assembled. Several cars were parked along Lancaster Hill Road. It was the beginning of a tent city, and she picked Tim out of the crowd, talking to some newcomers. Neptune was outside taking pats on the head from anyone and everyone. Holly wondered for a second if she had picked the wrong guard dog.

She dressed and made her way into the field, an unforced smile on her face and feeling a little choked up. It was an overwhelming display of community, led by good Samaritans. As Holly closed in on the heart of the little tent city, she noticed that the young man Tim was talking to was wearing camouflage pants and had a compound bow slung over his shoulder.

"... back from Vietnam. They gave me a Purple Heart because my leg's pretty messed up, but all that means is I can't run, but believe me, I won't need to run. I've been bow-hunting my whole life—"

Tim interrupted him. "Look, Corporal, I appreciate what you can do, but we can't kill the person who has my daughters, especially if she shows up alone. We can't have guns or bows ..."

Holly wished Tim would relax this rule, at least for this man. He was tall and strong and looked like he might give Mildred problems, especially with the bow. *What if he could stick one of those through her heart?* Holly knew that was wishful thinking. She interrupted to free Tim from the conversation.

"Good morning!" said Holly. "Wow, Mr. Bodwell was right. Looks like he called in the Cavalry!"

Tim introduced Holly to the folks he had already met, and they chatted with Ed Bodwell again. Many vigil-goers were already making themselves at home, combing the property, entering the woods and grove, and getting the lay of the land.

More cars pulled up to the stone wall, and people poured out of them carrying tents and coolers, stepping over the knee-high wall and into the meadow. Just then, a white van parked at the end of the row, and Nate Hoginski stepped out of the passenger side, looking sheepish. Holly's eyes met Tim's, and she saw how tired they looked. He most likely hadn't slept a wink. She jogged to catch up to him before things got ugly.

"You aren't allowed in, Hoginski. Take your TV show and get out of here," said Tim.

"Mr. Russell ... Tim, please hear me out. We can help you. Take a look behind you. These people are here because of the light we've shined on your problem. You want people to know what's happening. I promise we will not film you or your family again without your permission."

Tim was caught off guard. "You trespassed in my grove. David Bonnette was murdered in my house."

"Bonnette came here without our knowledge. I'll take responsibility, but I had no idea. If he broke in, it was of his own accord. I thought he was coming to check on Officer Simmons, who we did hire, but we didn't tell anyone to trespass. What I am responsible for and regret the most is filming your reaction to the news of your daughters. I haven't slept well since. I mean that sincerely."

Holly watched Tim's shoulders relax. "Tim, can I have a minute? Just a quick minute." Both men seemed grateful for the intermission as Holly walked Tim twenty feet into an open patch of meadow. "We could use the attention. We're both exhausted. We need help. The girls need help. Extra eyes and ears, at the very least."

Tim made Hoginski wait another minute and then marched back over. "Okay, Hoginski, but I have rules." Tim cleared his throat, turned, and yelled over the buzzing crowd. "Everyone, can I have your attention for a moment? Gather around, please!"

When everyone hushed, Tim began. "First, no guns. If we kill the kidnapper, we may never see the girls again. It is unlikely they would bring them along. Second, you can camp in the field, but not on the lawn by the house. We still need privacy. Does everyone understand?"

The crowd murmured as Tim returned to Nate Hoginski for a private conversation. "You can stay as long as you agree to rent three portable toilets and set them up by the road."

Hoginski held out his hand, and the two men shook. Hoginski then barked orders to his men, who quickly unloaded the van. Another car approached, and Tim noticed the lights on the roof. Chief Galluzzo of the Sanborn Police had come to check out the commotion. "What's all this?" he asked.

"We appreciate the company in this difficult time. It distracts from the reality of my girls being missing. And nobody can seem to figure out who took them anyway."

Galluzzo bristled. "No thanks to you, Russell. Bob Simmons was found under your willow tree, your ex-wife is dead, and your children are missing. We might have been able to help after the Enrico boy's death, but you turned us away."

"And you should be charged with trespassing, Chief! I know you're the one who found Simmons's body!" screamed Tim. "What the hell are you doing here, anyway? Whitlock's in charge!"

Holly grabbed Tim's arm and gave a tug. "Let's go inside, Tim. Chief Galluzzo isn't here to help."

CHAPTER 197

October 20, 1972

Hollywood executive Jordan Block landed at Boston's Logan Airport and drove a rented Mercedes an hour and a half to Wolfeboro, New Hampshire. He was newly single again and relieved to have his latest divorce over. It was time to celebrate.

Jordan Block came to New Hampshire every year. He was grateful to the Barrymores for introducing him to this peaceful part of the country. Who knew it was such a world-class vacation spot? Compared to Lake Tahoe or Palm Springs, New Hampshire was undiscovered, and for that, he loved it. Around here, all you had to do was put on a fishing hat when you bought your groceries, and you'd blend right in.

Block parked his car and pulled out his house key, anticipating the smell that always greeted him as he opened the door. Jordan Block was addicted to pine-stuffed pillows often found in gift shops and general stores, and he owned more than thirty of them. He found his first one in Moultonborough, and ever since he'd become a collector of the damned things.

Once inside, he inhaled, savoring the clean scent, then unpacked the groceries, including the handle of scotch he'd purchased at the state liquor store. After putting the food away, he took his rocks glass and the several newspapers he'd bought and sat in the chair next to the window overlooking the lake, losing himself in the first precious moments of his vacation.

Ten minutes later, the telephone rang. Almost no one knew where he was. *Wrong number, most likely*, thought Jordan as he sipped his scotch. The phone rang ten times before it stopped, and Jordan Block held his breath. If it rang again, he would have to answer it.

Brrrrrrring!

Shit. Jordan Block put down his scotch and rose, pissed off. The first day on the porch was always his favorite, and it was ruined. "Laurie? This better be good."

Laurie was Block's assistant, one of only four people with his Wolfeboro number. Laurie told Jordan that there had been a kidnapping of two young girls in Massachusetts, but the father was in Sanborn, less than an hour away. The townspeople had rallied around him and had organized a vigil. A supernatural being was believed by many to be responsible for the disappearances.

The best part was that a television show had gotten involved and was already cranking out shows. The name of the show was *Only If You Dare,* which was produced by CBS, a partner of Paramount Pictures, of which Jordan was CEO.

Paramount had recent success with *Rosemary's Baby,* of which Jordan was integral. Since then, he'd been asked countless times if he had anything else scary up his sleeve, a question he usually dismissed because nothing had struck his fancy.

After the phone call, Jordan downed the rest of his scotch. He felt goosebumps, and that was a good sign. His instincts were usually spot-on, so he picked up the phone. "Barry, it's Jordan. Yeah, I just got here and am settling in. What can you tell me about *Only If You Dare?* That's ours, right? Is it any good? Right. Who's show is it? Hoginski? Why does that name ring a bell? When does it air? Tuesdays? Hmm, three days from now. Listen, Barry, I need you to get me some tapes, like the last half-dozen episodes, and ship them here. Super 8 is fine. Good. Remember, express mail or whatever's fastest."

After another slug of scotch, Jordan Block went to the closet, fetched his fishing hat, and grabbed his keys. Before he touched the knob, he grabbed hold of a fist-sized pillow with an embroidered chickadee on it, put it to his nose, and took a long pull. *Home again,* he thought.

Once in his car, he popped open the glove box and thumbed through his maps to find the best road to Sanborn.

Tim sat in the turret paying bills, and it was the same old story: the well was almost dry. Johnny Upson had been kicking ass, but the inability to sell the house was crippling, and he began to wonder if he would have to look for local work. *Or maybe I'll just go bankrupt. I can't be far from the house as long as the girls are missing.*

Tim pushed away from the desk and stood to look at the circus now filling three-quarters of his meadow. It was not just hunters, Elks Club members, and soldiers of fortune but partiers, musicians, and hippies.

The mob was orderly, but Tim wondered how long it would last. Suddenly, he heard his name shouted, and Neptune barked once.

"Mr. Russell? Is that you up there?" Jordan Block stood on the front lawn looking up at the turret, dressed as a native New Englander.

Tim opened the turret window and called down to him. "That's me. What can I do for you?"

"I was wondering if you might show me your house. I'm up from Connecticut and looking to relocate. They tell me your house is for sale."

"My real estate agent is responsible for setting up the showings. Have you spoken to her?"

"I tried, but she wasn't available. I went to her office in Laconia, and she was out. I left a message, and since I had nothing to do, I thought I'd take a drive. Have I interrupted a party?" Jordan gestured to the mob in the meadow. "I can return later if this is not a good time."

Tim was surprised. Everything the man said sounded legitimate. Holly had a showing this morning and was out of the office. The man also knew that she worked in Laconia. So far, it seemed he'd gone through the proper channels.

Tim felt a glimmer of hope, but just as quickly, it melted away. He couldn't sell now. He had to be here when Mildred returned. Tim descended and met the man on the front lawn. Jordan Block offered his hand, and they shook. Neptune sniffed his pants leg and lay down in the grass. Tim watched the dog close his eyes and shook his head.

"My name's Jordan Banks. And my wife and I are looking for a change of pace. We were here this summer and fell in love with the area. We're only forty minutes outside the city, and it grinds on you after a while."

"Nice to meet you, Mr. Banks, but as much as I want to, I can't sell right now. This party isn't a party, or at least it shouldn't be. You haven't heard?"

Jordan Block pretended he didn't, and Tim told the story.

Block feigned shock. "I'm so sorry, Mr. Russell. This must be so tough on you. I wish I could help."

"It's been chaos around here."

Jordan looked at the house, noticed the new clapboards and gutters, and changed the subject. "How long have you lived here?"

"About a year and a half."

"Did you do this work?"

"I did. I own a small construction company in Massachusetts, and this was to be an investment property."

Jordan smiled. They were both members of the brotherhood of divorced husbands, except that Block wasn't ruined financially, and Tim was. "Mr. Russell, I own a place in Wolfeboro that could use some work. If it helps you get by, come work at my place for a few hours daily, then return and wait for your daughters."

"Wolfeboro? What's that, an hour away?"

"It took me about forty minutes. I don't need an answer today, but please consider it."

"Mr. Banks, if you're from Connecticut and already have a place in the Lakes Region, why are you looking in Sanborn?"

Block stumbled with his answer. "I forgot to mention that I'm looking for my folks. They're looking for a place to retire. Please call if you can help me out."

Tim nodded, confirming he would, and Jordan Block took another look at the crowd in the field. Two more cars had shown up since he'd arrived. There was something sticky about this story. People were turning out. Attention was where it's at in Hollywood, and attention meant money.

CHAPTER 198

October 20, 1972

Mildred cut off the squirrel's head and pulled until the skin peeled off clean, then slid the body onto a wooden skewer. There were three in total, which should be enough. The girls hadn't eaten in two days and would be hungry when they woke. As she put them over the fire, Mildred stirred the tea, which would get them over the hump. She stared into the pot, finding it impossible not to think of the man she had stolen the recipe from.

As much as she despised Gideon Walker, Mildred could admit he was right about some things. Even a broken clock was right twice a day. She had to keep the girls docile. It was that or live alone forever.

The squirrel meat was an upgrade over Gideon's meals. Mildred provided far more nutrition than he ever did. She recalled her hunger as a girl in the shed, now more than a century ago. Olivia and Vivian wouldn't suffer like that—if she decided to transition them to immortality.

Olivia called out as she slept, and Mildred perked up. The older girl was more aware of things than her younger sister. Suddenly, Olivia sat up. "Mommy!" she shouted, but her eyes were glazed.

Mildred gently grabbed her forehead and pushed her back to sleep, but Olivia shrugged her off. Thinking quickly, Mildred grabbed a squirrel off of the fire, ripped off some meat, and let it cool. She put it to Olivia's lips when it was safe to eat.

"Ew, I don't like it! I don't want it!'

Mildred tossed the meat into the fire, sending sparks into the night air. It was hard enough hiding two girls in the woods. Now, one of them was a picky eater. *Nothing's easy.* Mildred forced Olivia to sleep, and she closed her eyes when the girl was out. *Why do I crave rest?* There was so much work to be done. Motherhood was a full-time job.

CHAPTER 199

October 20, 1972

Tim had nothing to do but search and wait, but the waiting was getting old. Jordan left, and Tim wondered if he should have talked numbers. *What the hell was his last name?* Tim decided to refer to him as Jordan Almond before he forgot the first name. Feeling restless, he decided to take Neptune into the woods.

Neptune smelled the barbeque coming from the meadow and led Tim toward it. Tim didn't mind. He'd been sitting in the house too long, overthinking, and anything different was welcome. In need of friendly banter, he sought out Ed Bodwell.

Bodwell saw him approaching and announced it to the crowd. "Hey, here he is, the reason we're all here. Mr. Tim Russell, everybody!"

Tim was surprised by the amount of applause. Neptune found the closest dog lover to rub his ears.

When the crowd returned to their cookouts, Tim spoke with Ed Bodwell. "I'm going stir-crazy, Ed. This thing is eating me alive."

Ed Bodwell offered a brotherly hug. "That's why we're here, Tim. Be strong. We're taking shifts. Duncan and Hightower are out there searching for your girls. My shift is at four thirty. What do you say we start early, take a walk together, look for your girls, and burn off some of that negative energy? Bring Neptune."

Tim, Ed, Neptune, and two others went on the walk. Together, they were gone for three hours, canvassing a spot on the map chosen by Bodwell. By the end, Tim was spent. The mental exhaustion, coupled with the exercise, left him drained. As they exited the grove, Neptune followed Ed Bodwell toward the vigil, and Tim let him go. No doubt, Holly would fetch him when she got home.

Tim looked at his watch and it was 5:27 pm. Holly would be home soon, and it was better to be home when she arrived than out searching.

Tim stepped through the porch front door. Things seemed safe in the dining room, but the smell of something dead hit him in the face as soon as he stepped into the kitchen.

Mildred was standing in the breakfast area.

Tim dropped the flashlight, his heart in his throat. Although shocked, he had to seize this opportunity. Words gushed from his lips. "Mildred, I'm sorry. We're sorry. My girls are my everything. How can we make this right?"

Mildred didn't move, and her swarm was the only evidence that time had not stood still. Suddenly, the rumble of an engine pulled up the driveway, and Holly's Volkswagen drove past the picture window.

Tim took his eyes off Mildred as Holly parked in front of the barn. She would enter through the side door behind Mildred. He had to do something.

"Mildred, I know you saw Holly drive in. I can't let you hurt her. We want to make peace." Tim knew how fast Mildred was. To see Holly in her grasp would be too painful to bear, and Mildred did not respond.

When Holly opened the side door, Tim had no choice but to rush. He wound up and threw his best punch, but Mildred easily caught his arm. Tim felt her strength and knew he had no chance. Flies swarmed his head as she held him tight, her arms like iron bands. He couldn't move. Holly opened the sliding glass door, seeing Tim in big trouble. She screamed.

"Holly! Run …"

"Let him go," Holly commanded, her voice steady. "Where are the girls?"

Mildred eyed Holly and the rusty knife appeared.

Tim swallowed hard, fearing their time was up. He felt for Holly, who would have to witness him die first.

"Where are his daughters, Mildred?" Holly repeated.

Mildred ignored Holly, and with a flick of the wrist, the knife disappeared, and she shoved Tim to the floor. The three were now equidistant, and Mildred turned to Holly.

Holly backpedaled but persisted. "Where are Olivia and Vivian? You can talk. Don't kill them like you killed Elmer."

Mildred flexed her shoulders, and the knife reappeared. Holly regretted her words. There was nothing to do but turn and run.

With Holly gone, Mildred turned to Tim, who had yet to pick himself up. *Taking his girls is better than killing him,* Mildred reminded herself. Tim stared up from the floor, flies buzzing in all directions, then dug in his heels and pushed away.

Holly went to the barn, grabbed the first weapon she saw, then circled to the front of the house and entered through the porch. Mildred paused, staring at the pitchfork in her hands. Holly wondered if the pitchfork worried her. *Are you worried about your heart?*

Tim stood. Eight feet and a pitchfork separated them, and Holly spoke. "Where are the girls? Tell us where. We won't hunt you. We don't want to fight."

The vigil-goers in the meadow had no idea what was happening in the house, but an armed mob was a revenant's worst fear. Holly wished they had not implemented the no-guns policy. She also wished she had a police whistle. Perhaps if she screamed, they would hear.

Mildred pumped her arm once, and Holly's pitchfork was hers. Holly felt as helpless as the night they stole Elmer's bones. Mildred pointed the pitchfork, and they stepped back. Then, with a mighty thrust, she plunged the pitchfork into the kitchen floor and turned for the side exit.

Tim felt his opportunity slipping away. "Wait! Where are my daughters?"

Mildred left the building and crossed the driveway to the forest path. It was nearly dark, and visibility was less than a dozen yards. Tim barreled out of the house behind her and lowered his voice so the vigil-goers wouldn't interrupt. *"Mildred!"*

When she would stop, Tim lost his temper. He charged, and once more, she stopped him cold and pinned him to the ground. Holly, close behind, found him helpless as a fawn in the jaws of a mountain lion.

"No!" Holly screamed as Mildred's knife flashed, and she held it to Tim's throat, his two hands working at her vice-like grip. Mildred checked for any signs of the vigil, but no one approached. The fun was over, and she was almost finished. With Tim's undivided attention, Mildred leaned in until their noses touched. Her hair hung around his face, and he breathed her fetid air.

Mildred's vocal cords crackled as they worked for the first time in ages, her words as raspy as her knife. *"You took mine."* Mildred no longer breathed, yet her conviction pushed the air from her lungs and overpowered Tim's senses. A wave of hopelessness washed over him as he realized how powerless he was.

Mildred tapped the blade on Tim's Adam's apple and let go of his throat. She stood and stared at Holly, who had finally decided to shut her mouth. With the emotional damage done, Mildred turned and walked up the trail.

Holly rushed to Tim's side as he lay on the ground. He looked beaten, an Everest climber too exhausted to care. Holly could still smell Mildred on him. "Tim, let me help you up. Come on!" Tim raised his arm for Holly's assist, and together they got him to his feet. "Let's get you in the shower. Come on."

"Is everything alright?" Ed Bodwell was standing in the driveway with Neptune at his side.

Holly regrouped, still processing the nightmare. "We had some drinks, Ed. Bad day. I'm going to put him to bed. Thanks for checking."

Ed Bodwell watched Tim's drunk act and fell for it. "Call if you need anything, ma'am. I'll bring the dog back later."

Holly stayed in the bathroom as Tim bathed, trying to keep him thinking positively. They were lucky to be alive. As Tim dressed, Holly ran downstairs to pry the pitchfork from the kitchen floor. Tim didn't need to see it again. As Holly hid the pitchfork in the hall closet, she recalled how it had been taken from her, like a parlor trick. *What a terrifying skill*, Holly thought. *Weapons are useless*.

Tim came downstairs looking lost. Holly wanted to break down, too, but it was her turn to be the glue holding everything together.

"We made a big mistake helping Thomas Pike," said Tim. "I'd give anything to have Elmer running around here again. I have to call Whitlock."

Holly sat up straight. "And what will you tell him?"

"I don't know yet," said Tim.

CHAPTER 200

October 20, 1972

Special Agent Lamar Whitlock was handed a note to call Tim Russell and stuffed it in his pocket. Things were going nowhere in Amesbury, and he was in no mood to talk to a man he didn't trust. Russell wasn't a suspect, but he was odd. *Forest gardens and moving graves.* Something didn't add up.

But Russell had said something that stuck with him. *Be ready for my call.* If this was that call, Russell was right about the Mildred Wells impersonator returning. Whitlock waited ten minutes, hoping to forget the note in his pocket, but *be ready for my call* wouldn't go away.

"Russell, it's Whitlock. What's up."

"I was right. She's here."

"Who is? And where?"

"I don't know who it is, but I saw her by the barn. She stared as I pulled in, then pointed and ran into the woods."

"What about your daughters? Did you see them, too?"

"No. I think she's got them stashed somewhere—or at least, that's what I hope. I think it's time you moved your men up here."

Whitlock pinched the bridge of his nose, trying to think. He'd been running a three-day clusterfuck in Amesbury, and the only thing they found was a hundred dead squirrels. "I'll send someone, Russell, but as soon as he gets there, he's in charge."

"Only one person? I'm telling you, Whitlock, the person you're after is here."

"Yes, and my man will get to the bottom of it. I'll have him coordinate with Galluzzo. Do what he says, or I'll slap you with obstruction. Something tells me you're hiding something, and if I find out you are, you'll be in big trouble."

Tim heard a knock on the front door the following day. Neptune barked once.

"Mr. Russell, I'm Special Agent Souza. I need you to show me where you saw the Mildred Wells character."

Tim took Souza to the barn and invented a story that wasn't far from the truth. "What's with the party by the pond? There must be fifty people down there. Maybe it was one of them? I saw at least one wearing a farm dress."

"I told them to stop doing that. And they're not allowed on the lawn. Pond and field only."

"They're breaking the rules. Send them away. If the killer/kidnapper is in the area, they're a distraction."

"But they're extra eyes and ears," said Holly, coming out the side door.

"Sorry," said Souza. "They're a distraction, and possibly in danger. I can't have them getting in the way."

Tim and Holly exchanged glances. The vigil was over, and the nights would be longer and darker without the extra company.

"What about the TV show? They're at the pond, too. We got off to a rocky start, but they've been professional ever since," said Tim, already missing safety in numbers.

Souza drew his finger across his throat.

The last person to leave was Ed Bodwell, and he left the way he'd arrived, mysteriously and without a vehicle. As the last car pulled away, he slung his tent over his shoulder and strolled down Lancaster Hill Road toward town. After a quarter mile, however, he took a sharp left into the woods and doubled back toward Tim's property. Fifteen minutes later, he set up a well-camouflaged camp in the middle of the grove.

CHAPTER 201

October 21, 1972

Mildred pulled the Book of Shadows into her lap as the girls slept. She had only dabbled with it since the Beverly Farms fire. It was thicker now, most likely reflecting Walker's achievements. Her reading had paralleled his up to a point. They'd learned together, in a way, until her escape.

Thumbing through parts of the Book was nostalgic. She remembered creating her first runes even though she didn't know what they were for. Nowadays, they were obsolete because she'd killed everyone else. *Flip, flip, flip.*

Finally, she came to a page she had never seen but recognized nonetheless. She remembered Lyman Helms sneaking up behind her while escaping Gideon's cult. He whispered some words in her ear, and as soon as he was finished, she forgot he was ever there. She'd heard the words only once, yet reading them brought everything back. She could even recall them:

"Be quiet, or Walker will hear you, and you'll be right back upstairs. Listen carefully: Et ultimum carmen brevis ..."

Mildred stopped reading and checked on the girls. It was impossible not to dream, but it was too early to make a decision. It would be better to wait and let the girls decide for themselves. Honesty was the best policy, or at least she'd heard as much. *Daughters forever. Family: Take Two.* Mildred hovered over the page for another moment, then closed the book.

It took some time, but Mildred found some wild turkeys and killed two, just in case Olivia liked the taste. When she returned to the coyote den, the girls were practicing calling objects from across the room. Mildred knew it was spell #11, and she should start with spell #1, but they were only fooling around for now.

Each had a pile of acorns and attempted to snatch them from each other's hands. Olivia was stronger than Vivian to the point that she was stealing acorns both from Vivian's hand and the pile at her side.

"No fair!" said Vivian. "You're not allowed to do that!"

Olivia persisted and bounced two acorns off her sister's forehead.

"Stop it!" cried Vivian. Two more acorns flew, and one hit Vivian in the eye. "Ow!"

Vivian began to cry, and Mildred, who had yet to use her voice with the girls, spoke. "Stop."

Both girls turned, surprised. All was quiet as Mildred glared, and Olivia took the opportunity to launch one more acorn, catching Vivian in the teeth.

"Ow!"

Mildred clamped her hand around Olivia's cheeks and Olivia seemed scared. Mildred squeezed the little girl's face, too tired to deal with such stupidity. Vivian was the cute one. The one that took to her immediately. Olivia was bratty, an eight year old with a pre-teen mentality, yet the girls came as a pair. Mildred scattered their acorns, then stared into Olivia's eyes. "I said stop."

Despite doing the right thing, Mildred knew it was a no-win situation. In consolation, Mildred pulled a turkey leg from the fire, picked some meat from the bones, and tossed the chunks to Olivia, but the girl ignored them. Vivian ate to her fill, yet Olivia moped the rest of the night. The following day, Mildred saw that Olivia's turkey meat was gone.

CHAPTER 202

October 22, 1972

Jordan Block sipped his coffee when the damned phone rang again. Why did he have to waste a vacation working? "What is it, Laurie?"

"Mr. Block, this is Nathan Hoginski. I produce *Only If You Dare*."

At first, Jordan thought one of his suck-ups had gotten ahold of his New Hampshire number, but *Only If You Dare* struck a chord. "Who? *Only If*—Oh, wait, yes, I know who you are. What do you want?"

Hoginski was ecstatic that Jordan Block knew who he was. "I talked to Mr. Silverman, who talked to Mr. Wood, and they wanted me to tell you directly that we were kicked off the shoot this morning by the FBI."

"What? The FBI? Why?"

"They said it wasn't safe to be there, but they wouldn't say why."

"What's your take, Boginski?"

Hoginski cringed when Block got his name wrong. "It's Hoginski, sir, and I think they've got a person of interest in the area."

"You're not buying the ghost story you're selling, are you?"

"Of course not, sir. But I'd love to help you make this into a movie."

"First things first, Hoginski. Thanks for the info. Keep me posted." Block hung up and dumped the rest of his coffee in the sink. There was more than one way to skin a cat.

Jordan Block drove past the house twice before turning back for town. As soon as the black sedan left for any reason, he would make his move. At 1:00 pm, he got his chance. "Tim?"

Tim put down his binoculars and looked out the turret. He'd seen the Mercedes coming down the road but thought it continued past. Jordan Banks was on the lawn again. "Is that you, Mr. Banks?"

"Hi, Tim! Where's the crowd? The last time I was here, your field was a party."

"The FBI sent everyone home. They've taken control of the situation."

"Oh? What'd I miss?"

"They believe a woman impersonating Mildred Wells is in the vicinity. She might have my daughters."

"I don't mean to be insensitive, but wouldn't a kidnapper demand a ransom?"

"I don't pretend to know what sick people think," said Tim.

"Tim, I have a proposition for you. My folks really liked what I told them about your place. I'll give you ninety thousand dollars, sight unseen."

"I'm sorry, Jordan. I can't sell the house right now."

Block changed gears. "I understand. You want to be here for your daughters. I'll tell you what. You can stay rent-free for six months."

Tim flipped the binoculars over in his hands. "Your folks must be itching to move. I don't know. Ask me in a week. I promise you'll get the first shot. The FBI agent left for lunch. I have to stand guard."

Jordan Block kicked at a tuft of grass. "I apologize, Tim. I want to make this work for both of us. How does one hundred thousand sound, and you get to stay here for three years." It would take that long to prep the movie anyway.

Tim put the binoculars down on the sill. "One hundred thousand and three years? I'll do that."

"Hold on. You allow me full access even though you're still living here. And you give me a house tour and answer my questions. No bullshit."

"No bullshit? Who are you, Mr. Banks?"

"Do we have a deal?"

"Not yet." Tim left the turret and went downstairs to face the mystery man.

Block hated how the negotiation was going, but the FBI on the scene gave Russell the advantage. "My name is Jordan Block, and I produce films. I want to hear everything, and I want to hear it from the horse's mouth. I don't believe in ghosts, but I think you do. Either that or you're responsible for the murders. But why would you stay if you killed Bonnette, Simmons, and your ex-wife? The whole thing is strange, but it'll make a hell of a movie."

Jordan Block reached into one pocket and pulled out a checkbook with gold-plated trim on a leather cover. From the other, he pulled out a gold Cross pen.

Tim noticed the name "Jordan Block Paramount Pictures" in the upper left-hand corner of the checkbook. "Since you think I'm responsible, the price is one-fifty."

Block stopped writing. "Don't fuck with me."

"If you want the house, full access, and my story, it's one-fifty."

After a halfhearted stare-down, Block relented. "I'll write the check, but that's the last time I give in to you." As Tim examined the check, Block pulled out a California driver's license to prove his identity. "You can deposit that today. Are we square, or am I walking away?"

Tim stared at the check one more time before folding it. At least his money troubles were over. "Not yet. I want to get this in writing. I need to know how far you're going to crawl up my ass."

It took two days to iron things out, but Jordan Block wanted *Only If You Dare* to take up residence in Tim's house, and Special Agent Souza reminded everyone involved that the FBI was pursuing legal action against the TV show. Block dropped the stipulation but went ahead with the purchase of the house.

Jordan didn't care about losing the TV show. "That's fine. I'm more interested in making a movie. Now that we have a deal tell me what the hell is going on."

Holly wanted to hold her tongue but couldn't. "The truth is, Mildred Wells is real, but she's not a ghost."

Jordan Block tilted his head, dubious, and Tim was forced to start at the beginning. Jordan learned about Henry and Annette Smith, and Tim showed him the exact spots where they died. Tim also showed Jordan where the two headstones used to be in the last row of the grove. Together, the three of them parted the willow's branches down by the pond and witnessed the spot where Bob Simmons was found.

Block marveled at the hallway by the upstairs bathroom where David Bonnette was struck down. Finally, Tim took him to the kitchen and recanted a blow-by-blow account of Mildred's dominance not forty-eight hours before. Block was horrified but had to grin. One hundred and fifty thousand dollars for the rights to a story like this was a bargain.

"Did you tell the FBI all this?" he asked.

"They would never believe us, and we need them to find the girls," said Tim.

"I don't believe half of it either, but it's a hell of a story." Jordan laughed out loud, insulting everyone in the room. Everything Tim said conjured a dead woman covered in flies with superhuman strength in his mind. Jordan smelled a franchise in the making. Even if it was bullshit, he could sell the *Legend*. "I bet you didn't want to say goodbye to that mob in the field, am I right?"

"Right. But the FBI was right to send them away. They were chickens waiting for the fox."

"Has the FBI found anything?"

"Whitlock sent us Souza, who is pretty diligent. We take shifts walking through the woods; sometimes, he brings dogs. They're finding a ton of dead squirrels and birds, though."

"Everything's dead? That's eerie," said Jordan, taking notes on a pocket pad. "I'm going to get you a cameraman. A cameraman/bodyguard combo."

"Jordan, don't. Agent Souza won't like it, and whoever comes will be in danger. Don't forget, she can take a weapon from him in the blink of an eye."

Jordan smirked, pushing Tim's words aside. "You need sleep, and the guy I send will help with that. Plus, I want him to film things while I put the project together."

Holly liked the idea. "Tell him to be discreet, or Souza will kick him out."

CHAPTER 203

Sugar Hill, New Hampshire
October 22, 1972

Andrew woke to a rapping noise. He was still on top of the covers, exactly as he had crashed a few hours before. His sleep was good, but he needed more.

Andrew's head swooned as he stood up. Bracing himself on the bureau, he changed out of his pajamas and put on street clothes. It might be a customer at the door, some poor soul who lost a loved one in the middle of the night. Had he slept through a phone call?

A second thought crossed his mind. It could be Thomas Pike, but Thomas Pike wouldn't knock. He'd be standing over the bed, telling him what to do. Andrew went downstairs and peeked out of the sidelight. An older man stood staring at the door knocker. He was pale like a ghost, and a chill went down Andrew's spine.

Andrew jumped as the man rapped again, and he cracked the door, anxious to get the affair over. "May I help you?"

"Yes, Mr. Vaughn. My name is George Randall, and I just came up from Hell. I've come to apply for a job."

"What did you say?" Andrew looked behind the man. An old Cadillac with Massachusetts plates was in the driveway.

"My name is George Randall, and—"

"Where did you say you were from?"

"Hull."

"What?"

"Hull, Massachusetts. The South Shore."

Andrew exhaled. "I'm sorry. I thought I heard you say something else."

"No problem. I used to know your parents. We worked together for a time, your father and me. I was sorry to hear about your family."

"Thank you. So, you drove up from Hull for a job?"

"Yes. I was retired, but it's not as fun as it sounds. I miss the business, and I can start right away."

"Come in!" said Andrew, opening the door wide. "When did you know my parents? I think I remember them mentioning a George."

"Oh, it was decades ago, Mr. Vaughn. Is this the beginning of the job interview?"

Andrew's smile faded as he felt control of the conversation slip, but it was hard to trust anyone after the Jeremy Clary incident. "Well, yes. I like to chat and then check references, but if everything you say is true, and I have no reason to doubt it is, I can have you start on Saturday. How many years have you been in this line of work?"

"Mr. Vaughn, can I call you Andrew?"

"Sure."

"Andrew, I've already taken the position. I know you have someplace to be."

Andrew leaned forward in his chair. "What are you talking about, Mr. Randall?"

"Your mother told me everything."

Andrew paused, wondering who George Randall really was. "You mean while she was alive?"

"No, I mean after. I understand you and I share a talent—or curse."

"You saw her recently, then."

"Several times."

Andrew sat back in his chair, thinking about alcohol. Any alcohol. "Prove it."

George, too, sat back and exhaled. *Denial: It's not just a river in Egypt.* "Okay. How about the name Thomas Pike? You're a recovering heroin addict who drinks Jack Daniel's every night. You hired a man named Jeremy—"

"All right, that's enough. I believe you. Dear God, she told you everything."

George nodded.

"What about my father? Do you see him too?"

"I haven't. I assume your father rests in peace."

"My mother used to call me crazy when I told her I saw ghosts. Now I see *her.*"

"I know. But your mother told me to tell you it doesn't change a thing."

"Of course it does! Seeing ghosts pushed me over the edge!"

"She doesn't see it that way."

Andrew sat back in his chair, mind spinning. "What else do you know?"

"She told me that Thomas Pike wants you in Sanborn, and I'm going to watch the funeral home while you're gone. When you come back, if you come back, I will stay on."

"What do you mean *if* I come back?"

"I don't exactly know what she meant, but those were her words."

CHAPTER 204

October 22. 1072

The girls stretched their legs outside the den while Mildred cooked. Vivian struggled to grasp the eleventh spell, and Olivia attempted to help her.

"No, it's not like that, it's like this." Olivia flexed her wrist, and a pinecone appeared in her hand.

"I can't do it," said Vivian.

"You have to look where the pinecone is. If you know that, you think of it, and it appears in your hand."

"That's what I'm doing, but it doesn't work!"

"Yes, it does. You're just not doing it right."

"I'm never going to get it," said Vivian. Mildred took the turkey off the fire and set it aside, then went to Vivian and attempted to show her how it was done. She placed the pinecone six feet away, stepped back, and called it to her hand.

Vivian did her best to mimic the skill, but nothing happened.

Why can she call acorns and not pinecones? Thought Mildred. It made no sense.

CHAPTER 205

October 23, 1972

Holly wanted to leave the bed but didn't dare go to the kitchen alone. Things were different for her since the pitchfork incident, despite the comfort of Special Agent Souza down the hallway. Like Tim, her thoughts were hazy from lack of sleep.

Tim got up three times during the night to go to the bathroom, complete with security checks of the entire upstairs. Now, he slept, and as long as one of them was resting, it was better than no one. Quietly, she grabbed a magazine off her nightstand and tried to read it as she waited. It was 8:13 am.

It was the August edition of *Yankee Magazine*, not her cup of tea, but it was better than thinking of Mildred. Suddenly, she heard knocking downstairs and sat up, waking Tim, who pulled his pants on as he tripped to the bedroom window. Neptune lifted his head and barked one time. There was a strange car in the driveway.

"It's a car. Relax, I'll check it out. What time is it?"

"8:14. I'll be right down."

Wrapped in a robe, Souza met Tim at the top of the stairs, and together, they descended and headed for the porch door. Along the way, Tim looked out the living room window and saw a skinny young man who looked as tired as Tim felt. *Who is this?* Tim opened the front door, walked through the porch, and opened the outer door. Neptune stood in the kitchen doorway, wondering where his breakfast was.

"Can I help you?" said Tim.

"I hope so, Mr. Russell. I understand you know someone named Thomas Pike."

Tim looked back at Souza, who knew nothing about Thomas Pike. "I'll take care of this, Special Agent. Thank you." As Tim turned to the stranger in the doorway, Souza went back upstairs. "You know Thomas Pike? Excuse me, but who are you?"

"My name is Andrew Vaughn, and I'm here on behalf of Thomas Pike."

"What does that mean?" asked Tim, skeptical. Anything on television could bring out the crazies.

"Thomas Pike sent me, and I know how that sounds. I'll leave if you want, but I don't think he'll like it."

Tim took a step back and invited Andrew into the enclosed porch. "Come tell my girlfriend what you just told me."

Holly hit the bottom of the stairs and approached. "Holly, this is … I'm sorry. What did you say your name was?"

"Andrew Vaughn."

"Andrew, this is Holly. Andrew, please repeat what you just told me."

"I said the ghost of Thomas Pike sent me."

Tim and Holly looked at each other. Holly spoke first. "Tell me about Thomas Pike. What was your first impression?"

"He's got blue eyes and doesn't talk much."

Tim liked what he'd heard so far. "How does he communicate?"

"What do you mean?" said Andrew.

"You said he doesn't talk. So, how does he tell you things?"

Andrew blinked twice. "I said he doesn't talk *much*. He talks, though. I can promise you that."

"Yeah? Tell me something Thomas told you that only he would know," said Tim.

"He told me you dumped his bones in a lake. His son's bones, too. And the mother isn't happy about it. Her name is Margaret Wells."

Holly giggled. Andrew wasn't an *Only If You Dare* loony. "Close enough. For the record, her name is Mildred Wells."

"Oh, right. Mildred. My mistake."

"Why can you talk with Thomas and we can't?" asked Holly.

"I think I'm cursed. You wouldn't want to talk to ghosts, trust me."

Tim put his hand on Andrew's shoulder and invited him in. "You *look* cursed. Go lay down in one of the guestrooms. When you're rested, we'll compare notes."

Tim and Holly set Andrew up in the back bedroom across from Souza's, which wasn't so sunny. Andrew slept for three hours before his mother's ghost appeared over the bed and stared him awake, then disappeared into the closet.

Andrew heard voices downstairs and turned to descend, then realized where he was standing: the hall window was across the stairwell between the front bedrooms. The railing in his right hand ran the length of the hallway, then took a sharp left over the stairs. Andrew recognized the scene from the TV show. The worst scene, the one they repeated in slow motion so many damned times. The cameraman died here.

For a moment, Andrew's mind flashed to the TV show and the woman on the balcony. Andrew blinked twice to clear the image, then bounded down the stairs two at a time in need of human contact. He found Tim and Holly waiting for him at the kitchen counter.

"Oh! Here he is!" said Holly excitedly. "Are you hungry?"

"I feel a little better."

Tim couldn't hold back. "Do you have news for us? Please tell me you do."

"Yes, we need to talk. Where's the other guy?"

"Special Agent Souza? He's outside somewhere. He always takes the first shift."

"Agent? Is he FBI?"

"Yes."

"Wow. I guess things are really bad here. Uh—I don't have any breaking news about your girls, but Thomas wants you to keep looking. He's looking, too, if it makes you feel any better. I'm not exactly sure why I'm here, but I think part of it is to await instructions. Man, this place is creepy. I just saw the spot. Upstairs."

"What spot?" asked Holly.

"Where the woman murdered the cameraman."

Tim spoke. "Yeah, we weren't here for that."

Andrew's gaze went from Tim's face to Holly's. "Do you sleep here?"

Tim and Holly both nodded. "Yes," said Holly.

"I have to be available as long as she has my girls," said Tim. "I can't miss an opportunity."

"What's her problem?" asked Andrew.

"She's haunting us because we dumped their bones in the lake. The way we understood the deal, if we helped Thomas, he'd get rid of Mildred. Instead, he's left us high and dry. What else did Thomas say?"

Andrew sipped his drink, attempting to slow the questions down. Thomas had told him to keep some things from Tim, and he didn't want to slip. "He made me watch a TV show and told me I should come here."

"Why are you putting yourself in danger?" asked Tim.

"Because of my mother," said Andrew. "My parents were killed by a drunk driver. Then, I hired a guy who ended up murdering my sister. I've made many bad decisions, and my mother was never happy with me."

"Your mother is dead?"

"Yes, and somehow, she found Thomas Pike and volunteered my services."

Tim stared at Andrew, lost. "What happens if you disobey orders?"

"I'll never sleep again, and honestly, that's motivation enough. Does the FBI know they're after a dead person?"

Holly took a breath, completely riveted. Andrew was the brightest ray of hope they'd had in a year and a half. "No, the FBI does not know. They think they're after a mass murderer. Did Thomas tell you that Mildred is a revenant?"

"What's a revenant?" asked Andrew, pretending not to know. Thomas had told him, but he also said not to mention the Book of Shadows. To Andrew, the two seemed related.

"It's like a zombie, but not slow-moving or brain-dead. Revenants are, by definition, hell-bent on revenge, and we pissed her off." Tim gestured to the wall across the room. "She grabbed me right there two nights ago, and it was like being held by a gorilla. I couldn't budge her arm with both of mine, and she wasn't even trying. I didn't stand a chance, and the only reason she let me go was because holding my kids hostage is more satisfying."

Tim knocked his knuckles against the countertop, trying not to let his emotions get to him. "I don't see how I can win. I had a shred of hope when you showed up, but now you tell me that even Thomas doesn't know where she is."

Andrew turned his water glass, processing. "Well, I'm here. And I can talk to Thomas when he's available. That's all I can promise."

"So, you'll stay until you and Thomas figure things out?" asked Holly.

"I think that's the plan. I don't see Thomas much, though. Only twice, so far."

"Did you ask what his plan was? How are we supposed to deal with Mildred when we see her?"

"I asked a lot of things, but when I say we talk, I mean he talks, and I listen. I can't get a word in edgewise. I think we're on a need-to-know basis." Andrew felt sweat on his upper lip and wiped it away. He couldn't wait for the questions to be over.

"I'm skeptical that he wants to help us," said Tim. "But we're glad you're here. What do you want to know?"

"Can I get a tour? I want to know everything. It could mean life or death, right?"

Suddenly, there was another knock at the door, and all three heads turned. Tim got up and went to the window.

"It's a big guy. He has a mustache." Andrew peered at the man outside. He looked like a bodybuilder, holding a movie camera by his waist.

Tim went through the porch to let the man in. "Are you Jordan Block's man?"

"That's me. Mark Folsom, nice to meet you."

"Are you ready to protect us from a dead person?" said Tim.

"Mr. Block told me you'd say something like that," said Mark with a smile.

Andrew saw Holly frown. Had Jordan told his hired hand the whole truth?

"Come on in," said Tim. "Some of us don't sleep well, so your eyeballs will help. I'd like you to meet Holly, and this is Andrew."

When Souza saw the movie camera, he explicitly instructed Mark on what he could film and what he could not. In short, he was told not to interfere with Souza doing his job. After that, Tim and Holly took Andrew and Mark on a tour of the house and property, explaining where bad things had happened and could happen again.

"It's weird being here," said Andrew, walking through the grove. "My funeral home is a working apple orchard. People from Sugar Hill spend their lives coming each fall for apples, then return when they die to be buried. The apple trees are in symmetrical rows like these spruces. I get a tingle in my gut like someone's watching every time I'm there. I feel that here, too."

Mark Folsom, the only non-believer on the tour, shook his head in disbelief.

After the tour of the property, Tim and Holly spent the afternoon settling the two new guests into their rooms. Now they were five. Andrew stayed where he had napped, and Mark moved into the quarters at the front of the house across from Tim and Holly.

The house had little food, so Tim drove into town for pizzas and a salad. On the way home, he stopped at a convenience store for a case of beer and four bottles of wine. As he arrived home, the sun had set. They put the food on the dining room table, opened a bottle of wine, and gave a beer to Mark, who was not a wine drinker. Special Agent Souza, off duty, also cracked a beer. Neptune sniffed the air, forced his body between the chairs, and found a spot under the table.

Tim took a head count. Three believers and two non-believers. The conversation would have to be generic. "Mark, Mr. Block told me you played football. Where'd you go to school?"

"Michigan."

"Very nice. I'm a Bo Schembechler fan."

"Thanks. Yeah, Coach is a great man. I'll never forget him."

"Did you turn pro?"

"Yeah, the Oilers and the Patriots. I hurt my knee in my second year with the Patriots, though."

"Ah, bummer. Well, at least you landed a job in Hollywood."

"Ha. Sort of." Mark was a man of few words. They opened the first pizza box, and the smell of pepperoni filled the room.

"I think I'm starving," said Holly, happy to talk about anything other than Mildred. The pizza smelled so good that even Andrew, who ordered the salad, grabbed a slice. A minute later, Tim continued the conversation.

"What about you, Agent Souza? It's Lucas, correct? Can we call you by your first name after hours?"

"You can call me by my first name whenever you like."

"Okay, Lucas. Did you play football? You look like you could be a receiver."

"No, I played soccer."

Tim noted that Souza was a man of few words. Even off duty, he acted like an FBI agent. The conversation died as everybody chewed their food. Neptune, meanwhile, began to whine.

"Neptune, stop begging," Tim commanded. "Does he have to go out?"

"No, he just came in before you returned with the pizza," said Holly.

Andrew sniffed the air and turned to the kitchen doorway. Mildred, the dead woman, was there.

"Whoa, something reeks!" said Mark. Neptune continued to whine. "What's up with the dog?" Mark pushed away from the table and caught Tim and Holly's gaze. As he was about to turn, Tim spoke.

"Mark, don't move."

Mark smiled, wondering what Tim was talking about.

Suddenly, the lights went out, and Holly screamed. Souza stood and pulled his pistol but it disappeared from his hands.

"Oh, come on! Turn the damned lights on!" said Mark, who stood to find the wall switch but was sat down by a quick yank on his shoulder, the chair cracking under his weight. "Hey!" Mark turned to see who had him and screamed.

Nobody moved as Mark's life hung in the balance. Mildred tossed Souza's pistol in the kitchen and moved on to Andrew.

A fly landed on Andrew's hand, and he left it there. He held his breath, praying she wouldn't grab him like she grabbed Mark. She was even worse than Thomas described. The flies, the rotten flesh, the smell; Mildred overwhelmed the senses. Souza backed away from the table, looking for something to use as a weapon, but came up empty. Andrew looked at Tim and Holly across the table, reading their faces as they watched the monster pass behind him.

Holly spoke. "Where are the girls, Mildred? Give them back, and we'll leave."

Mildred said nothing but moved on to Souza, who seemed ready to take her on, hand to hand. "Don't come at her, Lucas. Please don't do it. She took your pistol, and she can take your life just as easily."

Souza stepped back.

Mildred rounded the table, saving the best for last. Andrew recalled that Tim and Holly had moved her son's grave, ground his bones to dust, and dumped them in a lake, and it was astounding that Thomas had asked them to do something so dangerous.

Mildred left Holly as is and stopped behind Tim, who couldn't stand the circumstances and spun to face her. Mildred grabbed his throat and pushed him backward over the table. Drinks spilled, and Andrew's salad fell on the floor. Mildred looked up, checking everyone's faces, daring them to interfere. Everyone pleaded for Tim's life except Mark, who hovered near the front door. Jordan Block's movie camera sat in the corner of the room, useless. Tim gasped for breath as the table dug into his back.

Andrew, fearing his mother's reprisal, spoke up. "Let him go!"

Suddenly, Mildred was holding a knife, spinning it like a dagger. Shocked to see the weapon conjured out of thin air, Andrew backpedaled until he hit the wall.

With everyone's attention, Mildred stabbed the blade into the table, stuck her hand in the pocket of her dress, and pulled out Vivian's corn doll. When Tim recognized it, Mildred's face tightened into a grin.

"Where are they?" Tim screamed. Mildred loosened her grip and fled into the living room. Holly held Tim back to ensure he wouldn't follow, then found the wall switch and illuminated all the terrified faces.

"Call Whitlock," said Tim to Souza, who seemed frozen in place. "And what's with Neptune? He didn't do anything!"

"He was scared like the rest of us," said Holly. "She's dead!"

"And you," Tim turned to face Mark. "Mr. Football, where were you? Throw a drink in her face. Hit her with a pizza box! Something!"

Mark Folsom could throw Tim through the wall, yet he said nothing and slipped out into the night, headed for his car.

Holly turned to Tim, mouth agape.

"Where did that knife come from?" asked Andrew.

"She pulls it from thin air," said Holly. "Thomas didn't tell you?"

"No, he didn't. There's no way to defend that," said Andrew.

CHAPTER 206

October 23, 1972

Tim pulled out Jordan Block's business card. "Jordan, it's Tim Russell. Your bodyguard just walked out after seeing our lady face-to-face."

"Slow down. You saw Mildred?"

"Yeah, and Mr. Football took off. He left your camera, too."

"Did he film anything?"

"Not a thing. I don't know what you want to do, but you're down one cameraman, and we're down another set of eyes. You have to tell these guys what they're in for!"

"How am I supposed to tell them?"

"Ask Mark Folsom. Or stop by for dinner sometime. I got a great look at her. She had me by the throat. She snuck in and blew up our dinner table."

There was silence on the other end. "What do you want?"

"Send us another cameraman if you want anything filmed. And tell him the whole story."

Jordan Block hung up the phone. *She had him by the throat. Mark Folsom had seen her and quit on the spot. Did the FBI see her, too?* Things were heating up. It was time to make some phone calls.

Still shaking, Special Agent Souza retrieved his pistol from the kitchen floor and picked up the telephone in Tim's kitchen. "SAC Whitlock, this is Special Agent Souza. We've had an incident. I had eyes on Mildred Wells."

"What about the girls?"

"No girls. She was alone. And ..." Souza stammered.

"And what? Did you get her?"

"She got away." Souza didn't want to tell Whitlock that she'd taken his pistol. "We need—we need—" Souza had trouble requesting more agents. It was like an invitation to death.

"Good Lord, Souza, are you all right?" asked Whitlock.

"No. She's terrible. She's—*not real*. She's *dead*."

Holly wanted to leave, but neither Tim nor Andrew would go with her. Special Agent Souza seemed to be staying, too, but he was in shock. In the end, she felt forced to remain in the house. Being with three men was better than being alone; besides that, Tim was right. If Mildred wanted Holly, she would show up in Laconia.

Andrew wondered if he should leave his bedroom door open. Keeping it open would be more connected to Tim, Holly, and Special Agent Souza, but closing the door would make him feel safer. In the end he closed it, left the shades up, and crawled into bed. He didn't want the night to last longer than it had to.

Tim lay in bed, eyes wide open. Holly was quiet beside him, but he knew she wasn't sleeping. Souza said Whitlock was coming in the morning. Souza was rattled, but at least he didn't run. Tim guessed that they were probably safe for the rest of the night. Mildred had never attacked twice in one day. She probably had to get back to Olivia and Vivian, or at least, that's what he hoped.

CHAPTER 207

October 24, 1972

Thomas Pike woke Andrew up after midnight, whispering in his ear for over an hour. Andrew closed his eyes and Thomas's words became pictures, and Andrew relived the horrible history lesson of the house on Lancaster Hill Road.

Until tonight, Andrew never knew the gory details of little Elmer being drowned in the pond, nor did he know that Mildred spit on Thomas's gravestone after confessing to the murder. The tales continued with David Bonnette sneaking into the house. His death included all the violence the movie camera captured and more.

Andrew sat up, sweating. Thomas was gone, and the house was quiet. Being here was dangerous. Mildred Wells was even meaner than his mother, and Thomas never told him about her knife trick. *I should go.* Andrew packed his things, opened the bedroom door, and peered out. He couldn't let Neptune hear him, or Tim and Holly would wake. Souza was an obstacle, too, but running into Mildred would be even worse. Carefully planting his feet near the wall, Andrew tested each stair before committing.

Six minutes later, Andrew was downstairs on his way to the side door, the furthest exit from the bedrooms. He followed his nose. He'd smell her before anything else. The engine started noisy but calmed to a low idle as he put it in reverse and backed into the corner of the driveway, lights off.

Without stepping on the gas, he let the car coast past the front doors and down the driveway onto Lancaster Hill Road. He tapped the brakes once, but it was smooth sailing after that. One hundred yards later, when the house was lost in the trees, he pulled the lights on, stepped on the accelerator, and breathed a sigh of relief. *Sorry to disappoint you again, Mom, but that one had a knife. If I must be haunted, I'll take you over Mildred Wells.*

Foggy Orchard was an hour's drive. Perhaps he'd find a motel. Maybe the ghosts wouldn't find him, and he would have a solid night's sleep for once. The dashboard lit the car's interior, but the radio was off, so he decided music might lighten the mood. Andrew spun the dial, looking for a radio station halfway listenable—this was, after all, rural New Hampshire after midnight. Soon after, he stumbled upon the song "Thin Line Between Love and Hate" and let it play.

The sweetest woman in the world
Can be the meanest woman in the world
If you make her that way, you keep on hurting her
She keeps being quiet
She might be holding something inside
That really, really hurts you one day

He considered changing the station when the lyrics hit too close to home, but the signal cut out. *Dammit.* Andrew looked down at the dash and saw the radio was off. *Odd.* He reached down and turned the knob again. The dial lit up, but no music played, and in the glow, sitting in the passenger seat, was his mother.

Colleen Vaughn grabbed the steering wheel and yanked it hard. Andrew's car veered on two wheels, off the road and through the brush. Andrew's last moment of consciousness was the split-second realization that he'd misjudged her resolve.

Andrew's car sailed over the gully and smacked into a giant maple. The front end accordioned, and the vehicle was totaled. Andrew had always considered seat belts optional and hit the dashboard hard before continuing through the windshield. His life flashed before his eyes, with added emphasis on his sister's death. Everything on Lancaster Hill Road went dark except for one headlight, which died three hours later.

Holly woke before 6:00 am, needing to pee, a ritual she hated, but at least today, the upstairs was not empty. It was good to have people in almost every bedroom. Neptune was awake but chose to stay with Tim, knowing Holly would be right back. On her way to the bathroom, Holly noticed Andrew's bedroom door open. *Was he downstairs?*

Holly peed and returned to the bedroom. "Andrew is not in his room."

"Is he downstairs?"

"I don't know. I'm not going down alone."

"What about Souza?"

"His door is closed, I don't know."

"Would you be surprised if they both left?" asked Tim.

"Very few things surprise me anymore," said Holly.

Tim dressed and grabbed the shotgun. Their first stop was the front door to let Neptune out, and as the dog did his business, Tim looked down the length of the house, hoping to see Andrew wave from the kitchen with a cup of coffee, but it didn't happen.

When Neptune returned, they approached the kitchen slowly. If a room didn't pass the smell test, they would run. When they got to the kitchen, there was no scent of brewing coffee or Andrew. Tim continued through the breakfast area and looked out the side door into the driveway. Andrew's car was gone, but Souza's was still there.

"Let's hope he went for donuts," said Tim.

"Maybe he couldn't sleep. Last night was stressful, to say the least."

"I think he quit."

Holly shook her head. "I didn't think to check and see if he took his bag." After a quick look, they knew he was gone.

Andrew woke to the red glow of sunlight burning through his eyelids. He hurt all over. Was last night a dream? He couldn't move and didn't dare open his eyes. The wind on his face and his shivering body were sure signs he was not in bed.

His back was stiff and took a moment before it would move, as did his right shoulder. His right arm was over his head and had settled awkwardly on the uneven ground, but it, too, woke with time. Slowly, Andrew rolled, wincing, a dish-sized clump of leaves stuck to the side of his head with clotted blood.

His hand was bloody, too, as was his shirt. Both legs were singing with pain, and his car looked as if it had died trying to climb the tree. Safety glass, plastic, and metal littered the road Blood was everywhere, obviously his. It looked like a truck had hit a deer, and he couldn't remember a thing.

Souza came downstairs just as the coffee finished brewing.

"Hey, Lucas," said Holly. "How are you feeling?"

"I'm fine," said Souza, almost nonchalant.

Tim shook his head in disbelief. "Fine? My God, that was one heck of a night, and you're fine?"

"For the record, I didn't tell Whitlock that she took my gun. I don't think he would believe who we're dealing with yet."

Tim looked at Holly, and both were surprised. "Where have you been for the last year and a half?" said Holly.

"You're going to want to know the whole story now, Lucas. You need to know how to kill her. One of these might be useful." Tim patted the shotgun he had concealed under a dish towel.

"That can't be legal," said Souza.

"No, but it will blow her heart to bits. After we get my daughters back, of course."

"Good to know," said Souza. Just then they heard a knock on the porch door. Neptune barked once. Tim ran to the window. "It's Andrew!"

Holly screamed. Andrew's clothing was soaked with blood, and he wobbled. Just as he was about to fall, Tim propped him up.

"What happened?" said Holly. "Did Mildred do this?"

Andrew tried to speak but couldn't. Holly noticed what looked like a seam running up the side of Andrew's neck. "Andrew, you have stitches! Where were you? Sit down! Sit down!" Holly looked closer. It wasn't just a few stitches—dozens of swollen X's continued up the side of his face.

Andrew ran his hand over the tender puckers. His memory flashed, and he saw his mother in the glow of the dashboard.

"You look like you should go to the hospital, but it looks like you just came from one! What happened?" said Tim.

"My … mother … don't remember much, but she was in my car. Crashed it."

Tim and Holly looked at each other. "Did you go to the hospital? Why are you still covered in blood?"

Andrew rubbed his forehead, as if to revive his memory. "No hospital. She was a doctor. Knows what to do."

"I thought you said your parents ran a funeral home?" asked Tim.

"Before that, she was a doctor."

"Where did you crash?"

Andrew pointed to the road.

"Andrew," asked Tim, "Why did you leave?"

"I tried to quit," Andrew replied.

"I knew it. Andrew, you don't have to stay on our account."

Andrew laughed softly and winced in pain. "I'm not going anywhere. My mom's not going to let me." He lifted his shirt to check the damage from his chuckle and revealed another run of stitches across his abdomen.

Holly gasped. "Andrew, you have to get those looked at! The bruising, the inflammation, there could be an infection!"

"I don't think so."

"You're going! Get in the car, I'll take you."

"Yes, take him. Lucas and I will wait here."

Andrew finally agreed and got into Holly's VW, staining the towel they laid on the seats. A minute down the road, Holly came upon Andrew's wreck, and it was like discovering a corpse. The car was wedged against the tree at a forty-five degree angle, the windshield was blown out, and glass particles sparkled in the daylight in all directions.

A small branch was broken off where the windshield used to be and lay next to the car, covered in blood. Holly pulled over. It looked like a murder scene. Blood was everywhere, especially on the hood, where it ran off in all directions into sticky puddles on the ground below.

"I don't feel good," said Holly. "Andrew, how did you survive this? The blood, your bones?"

"I don't know. All I remember is seeing my mother in the passenger seat, reliving my sister's murder in a dream, and knocking on your front door. I'm in pain, and I think she wants it that way."

CHAPTER 208

October 24, 1972

Holly was nauseous, so Andrew convinced her to return to the house, where he showered and came downstairs looking much better. There was minimal swelling and no sign of infection. The amount of blood on his clothing had exaggerated his condition, but what he suffered was beyond explanation. As he entered the living room, he found Tim on the phone.

"You'd better hurry up with that cameraman, Jordan. It's never a dull moment over here." Tim held the receiver in the air so Andrew and Holly could hear the conversation.

"What do you mean?" said Jordan Block.

"It's a long story, but we have a new visitor. Are you in Wolfeboro right now? I'd love you to meet him." said Tim.

"No, I'm not. Who is it?"

"He claims to have spoken with Thomas Pike, and we believe him. There's more, too, and words won't do it justice. My point is, things are happening, and nothing's getting filmed. I need help finding my daughters and you have a story rotting on the vine. What's the holdup?"

"What did Thomas Pike say?" asked Jordan.

"Hey, Andrew, what's Thomas Pike's plan? I've got Mr. Jordan Block from Hollywood on the phone."

Andrew frowned. Thomas had done a poor job of informing everyone, himself included. Last night's meeting was no direction at all, just a recap of Mildred's sins. Meanwhile, they were all in danger. "We're supposed to keep looking for the girls and await further instruction," said Andrew.

"That's not going to inspire Mr. Block to send more eyeballs, Andrew. You have to *sell it*. Give him a reason to be interested," complained Tim.

Andrew brooded. If Thomas Pike wasn't going to help, then a cameraman or bodyguard might. "I'm as frustrated as you are, Tim. I'm also in pain, and since Thomas isn't helping, I'll share something he didn't want me to mention. Mildred grew up in a cult that used black magick to turn her into a revenant."

Tim almost dropped the phone. "You never told us that."

"Why doesn't he want us to know?" added Holly.

"I don't know, but you told me to *sell it*. I thought maybe we'd get our camera people quicker."

"Did you hear that, Jordan? We need help. Andrew's been here only a few days and he's seen her up close and personal. So has Special Agent Souza. She was raised in a cult! I'm no producer, but hell, I'd watch that movie."

Jordan Block leaned back in his chair, bouncing a pen on his desk. The project had only cost him $150,000 and change so far. He'd get a good chunk of that back when he sold the house. "I'll get you a cameraman. In the meantime, try to film something. Take pictures of the stitches and the truck, too. Mail them to me."

"I can't promise you much in terms of filming, Jordan," said Tim. "We've got our hands full, and I'm not kidding."

Block snapped the pencil in his hand. "Yeah, well, do your best."

"Easier said than done," said Tim before hanging up.

Thomas Pike's absence bothered Andrew. "Tim, we should fortify this place. She walked in here like the door was open."

"Andrew, we can't. Not while she's got the girls."

"Tim, what if she's trying to turn your girls into revenants? She's full of magic tricks, isn't she?"

Tim winced. The thought of his daughters dead or worse was too much.

"This house is a sieve," said Andrew. "She walked up to the dinner table, and not even the dog heard her. Mildred spies on you. She gets in the house. That's why Sheila's dead, and your girls are with her now."

"You're right," said Tim. "I wanted to negotiate, but it never gets that far. Whenever she shows up, we're on our heels. She doesn't want to talk."

"Tim, there's something else Thomas didn't want me to mention."

Holly, recovering on the couch, sat up.

"What's with all the secrets?" said Tim, visibly frustrated. "What did he say?"

"He said he's waiting. It's too early to try and stop Mildred."

"What does that mean?" cried Holly.

"That son of a bitch," said Tim, kicking the telephone across the room. "I thought he wanted us to keep looking?"

"That's what he told me to say. He said it would keep you busy. I'm telling you this because I lost faith in him last night. He's got a plan, but I think your needs come second."

Tim stood and began to pace.

Adrenaline cured Holly's nausea. "Start over, Andrew. What exactly did he tell you?"

"I'm sorry, I was just doing as I was told. I didn't understand what you were dealing with. Thomas told me he wants to get your daughters back, but he wants to wait, and I don't know why. I'm here because I'm supposed to be ready for instructions at a moment's notice. And like I told you, he also mentioned that she was in a cult, and they turned her into a revenant with a magic book."

"Tim, that must be what was in Beverly Farms," said Holly.

"She burned that place down," said Tim. "Let me guess, she stole the magic book, too."

Andrew shrugged his shoulders. "The only time I heard the name Beverly Farms was from the TV show. Thomas didn't tell me that like he didn't tell me about her knife."

"Andrew," said Holly, "If Thomas wants to wait, does that mean he knows where Mildred is?"

"I don't know. I swear," said Andrew.

"Where is this bastard?" screamed Tim, veins bulging in his neck. "I would kill to be able and have some words with him. Do you know?"

Andrew shook his head. "No."

"Coward," said Tim. "He's already dead. What does he care about my girls? Time means nothing to him."

Holly stood and put a hand on Tim's shoulder. "But he wants to wait, so maybe time does matter. Maybe he's waiting for an opportunity. It's too early to count him out. All we can do is be ready."

"But let's stop her from coming and going as she pleases!" said Andrew. "Thomas is not protecting us. Maybe he can't! Let's make her break something to get in. At least we'll hear her coming. Let's nail the unnecessary windows and doors shut for starters."

Special Agent in Charge Whitlock arrived just after 11:00 am with two more FBI agents, and the first thing they did was collar Special Agent Souza and interview him inside the barn.

"All right, cut to the chase, Souza. What's going on?" said Whitlock.

"Sir, we were all having dinner, seated at the table and she appeared out of nowhere. Even the dog didn't hear her. There were five of us. One guy ran out. A big, two hundred and fifty pounder that used to play for the Patriots."

Whitlock looked to the other two agents for opinions. "So you're telling me we're dealing with a ghost."

"She smells bad. Real bad, like a dead animal. Just like a dead animal. Ever smelled one?"

Whitlock paced the floor of the barn. "Dammit, I've smelled dead *people*, Souza."

"That's what she smells like, sir."

"So what did you do when she crashed the dinner party?"

"I pulled my pistol and aimed it at her. Eight feet away. And my gun disappeared, and she had it, like a magic trick. Then she threw it in the kitchen where I couldn't get to it."

"You'd better be joking," said Whitlock. "And what's with that car wreck down the road? Why aren't the police on the scene?"

"Ask Andrew about that, sir. That just happened. We haven't had a chance to call it in."

"I don't know, Souza. I'm having trouble believing all this!" said Whitlock.

"There's a house full of people that saw the whole thing, and the ex-football player that's probably in Los Angeles by now," said Souza. "Bring him in and compare stories. Or stick around; she'll be back. But in the meantime, bring more men. SWAT, maybe. Snipers. People that can hit her in the heart from a hundred yards. You don't want to be near her."

"What is she, a vampire?" Whitlock chuckled, sarcastically.

"No sir, she's a revenant."

CHAPTER 209

October 24, 1972

Special Agent Souza was given the night off and put up in a hotel in Franklin while Whitlock checked his story. Special Agent Harrington took his place in the third bedroom. Andrew prepared for bed, feeling better about the new people on scene and the things they had done to make the house safer. In addition to nailing almost all the windows and doors shut, they moved the dining room table against the porch door so it would make a tremendous noise if pushed.

At least they would know what direction Mildred was coming from. In addition to the fortifications, Andrew moved into the sunny bedroom at the front of the house across from Tim and Holly. The three of them stayed up late, as they seemed to do every night, drinking a little bit and trying to laugh, shortening the time until sunrise. Per usual, the lights went out after midnight.

When Tim heard the noise, he thought it was part of his dream, but he'd been on edge for a year and a half, and his subconscious knew better. *What was that?* He looked over to Holly, who was already awake, proving it wasn't his imagination. Tim looked at the dog. Neptune's ears were perked, and he began to whine.

Tim reached down on the floor and grabbed the shotgun, realizing he might have to use it this time, regardless of the girls. If Mildred were downstairs, he would have to shoot before she could take the gun away.

Tim swung his feet out of bed and stood, listening. He peered out of the bedroom door at the top of the stairs, but still nothing. There was no movement from Andrew's room or Harrington's room down the hall.

Tim crossed the hall, but despite his best efforts, the boards creaked. If Mildred was here, she must have heard him.

Tim peered into Andrew's room and saw him sleeping. For a moment, he considered letting him continue, then thought better. Tim tapped Andrew's foot with the business end of the shotgun, and the young man sat up, startled. Tim held a finger to his mouth.

Andrew put on his shoes and grabbed a baseball bat by the bed. Despite the squeaks and creaks of the floorboards, the four made their way down the hallway. They opened Harrington's door to find him already out of bed. When everyone was ready, they went downstairs. Neptune wondered what everyone was doing up so early.

Tim pointed the shotgun down the length of the house. The kitchen light was on, just as they'd left it. Nothing moved. The entire downstairs checked out, with no sign of a break-in, but still, nobody dared speak. Tim put his finger to his lips again and pointed to the ceiling, reminding everyone that there was one more room to check.

After directing everyone to stand back, Tim opened the door and pointed the shotgun up the stairwell into the turret. A light breeze hit him in the face, and any hope that his mind was playing tricks went up in smoke. He flicked the light switch and the turret lit up. He studied the shadows, and there was movement, but it was only the curtain dancing in the wind.

Tim whispered: "Don't follow me up the stairs. I might have to jump down." Then he motioned with his fingers, 1, 2, 3, and bolted up the stairs. When Tim's eyes were above the floorboards, he swept the room. The turret was empty.

"Nothing?" Andrew asked.

"No, but she was here."

Gooseflesh rose on Holly's skin. Mildred was in the house not ten minutes ago. "She might be watching us, Tim. I don't feel safe down here." Holly and Neptune pushed past Andrew and Agent Harrington and headed up the stairs. Andrew followed and sat on the top step, watching the doorway below.

Holly stared at the open window. *How did she get in?* The four nails Andrew had pounded it closed with were gone, pulled from the wood. She examined the four holes. The wood was undamaged, as if pliers had pulled nails, and the rest of the windows were still nailed shut. On the desk was tonight's horror. Two locks of blond hair bundled in strips of Mildred's dress.

Tim burst into tears. "Do you see this?" He waved the locks at Harrington. "Where is she? Where are my girls? She must be watching! She wants to see me like this." The glare of the light on the windows made the outside invisible, so Tim stuck his head out the window and screamed again. "Where are you?! Where—"

He stopped mid-sentence. Mildred was forty feet away, standing on the crest of the barn, watching everything. Holly struggled to see what Tim was looking at. Andrew cupped his hands against the window as Harrington pulled his pistol. Tim pointed the shotgun and fired both barrels.

The noise was deafening. Holly and Andrew screamed, and Neptune flinched. Harrington tried to open the adjacent window, but it was nailed shut.

"Tim, what are you doing?" Holly shouted.

"Your daughters, man. Don't do it!" said Andrew.

Tim reached into his front pocket and pulled out two more shells. Mildred turned and disappeared down the backside of the barn. With no shot, Tim let his body slump.

"What happened? Is she gone?" asked Holly, shaking.

Tim pulled his head back inside. "She's playing with me. The locks of hair—I lost it."

No one said a word. Holly picked the girls' hair off the floor and placed them on the desk. They spent the next hour checking the house.

Ed Bodwell, vigil leader turned trespasser, heard the shotgun blast from his tent in the grove. The sound of the gun ripped the quiet New Hampshire night in two and sat him upright, wrenching his back. He felt his hip for the clasp on the holster, then slid the gray barrel of his .45 out. He knew he wasn't supposed to have any guns on Tim Russell's property, but he wasn't supposed to be on Tim Russell's property in the first place.

There had been search parties, but he'd dug himself a covered pit that was practically invisible. He did have to watch for dogs, though, so he watched the driveway through binoculars and timed his exits to perfection.

Ed unzipped the tent flap and climbed out, leaving his flashlight off. If Tim and his girlfriend were awake, he didn't want them to see. The grove was, of course, dark, making getting to the meadow tricky. He ran into several branches and stepped on many more, taking one across the face and drawing a bloody scratch.

Just before the tree line, he heard footsteps. Startled, he turned to the direction of the sound. New Hampshire did have black bears, but rarely this far south. Folks up north had to pay special attention to how they disposed of their garbage, but this was seldom the case in Sanborn. It didn't sound like a deer, but he was no expert.

Bodwell took a knee and raised the .45 toward the sound, and the footsteps stopped, which frightened him. *Could it see him?* Worried, he flicked on his flashlight. The row of overgrown spruce lit up loud and bright, shrinking his pupils to pinpoints. Beyond the first row of trees was a shadowy hallway and an even darker second row. Beyond that was blackness.

The flashlight had given away his position, and there were gunshots at the house. There had never been a better excuse to run.

Ed Bodwell stepped into the meadow and looked toward the house in time to see the light in the turret go out. However, the kitchen light was still on, and he could see several adults milling about. Whatever the commotion was, it was over.

Still, Bodwell had nothing better to do and wasn't brave enough to return to his tent. He'd be a sitting duck in that darkness. The footsteps had spooked him, and all he could do was think about that damned TV show. He wished he didn't know Mildred and her son were buried less than a hundred yards from his tent.

Suddenly, the kitchen light went out, leaving the house dark. Then, the living room light went on, and he saw the adults passing through on their way to the staircase. *Whatever it was, is over*, Ed thought. They were going to bed, meaning he should, too. *Dammit.*

Ed hesitated. A mild breeze had picked up, and the noise it made blowing through the trees gave him added pause. He even wondered if he should return to his house, but the thought of it without Alice was unbearable. Until the vigil, he'd been in a deep depression. Without a doubt, they were the worst days of his life.

The drinking he did tonight paled in comparison to the damage he'd done to himself those first lonely months. Retirement, something he had dreamed of as a working man, turned out to be a slow-drip cup of loneliness. At least being on Tim Russell's property was something to do.

When all the lights went out in the house, Ed Bodwell gathered the courage to return to his tent. The first part of the woods was the toughest. Finding the way through the trees without a trail was a recipe for pain. Branches scratched his ear as he ducked through to the grove. When he reached the first row, he clicked on the flashlight and scanned both ends of the corridor.

He did the same for the second row, too, and when he broke through to the third row, he found his tent twenty yards to the south. Climbing in was the equivalent of putting on a blindfold. He heard the night breeze but could not see through the canvas. He couldn't help but listen for footsteps, and the muscles around his ears grew tired of working. Near desperation, Ed took a long, bubbling pull off of the whiskey bottle and waited for the alcohol to heal his worries. Finally, he fell asleep.

CHAPTER 210

October 25, 1972

Holly and Andrew sat bleary-eyed at the counter while Tim fried eggs and Agent Harrington stood watch at the kitchen window sipping coffee. Thankfully, Mildred had not returned, but none of them had slept. Andrew broke the silence.

"I didn't tell you what Thomas showed me the other night, did I?"

"What?" said Holly.

Tim turned, wide-eyed.

"I forgot because of the car crash. It was a history of all the bad things Mildred had done. Like, Elmer's death in the pond, and spitting on Thomas's grave. I saw her kill the cameraman at the top of your stairs, too."

"What did you think?" said Tim.

"I've been thinking a lot about it, actually. Especially since our talk about Thomas wanting to wait."

"*Wait*," said Tim. "Don't remind me. I'm still pissed. Wait for what?"

"That's what I was wondering. What is Thomas waiting for? Well, I think he might have shown me."

Holly put down her coffee. "Aren't you the guy he can talk to? Why didn't he just tell you?"

"Maybe he did, and I missed it. Mildred's little pizza party shook me, and I had nothing but quitting on my mind. Anyway, Thomas showed me all the bad things that Mildred has done, including David Bonnette's murder at the top of the stairs. After Mildred killed him, she sat down on the stairs for like three minutes, and she was thinking with her head down or maybe catching her breath."

"Come show me," said Tim, shutting off the gas. Harrington took his coffee up into the turret for a better view of the property and the three of them went to the spot at the top of the stairs where David Bonnette died. Tim stood in the doorway of one of the back bedrooms and Holly in the other.

"Bonnette was right here in front of the bathroom, and she was over there." Andrew pointed to the balcony and swallowed hard. Playing the part of David Bonnette was more than eerie.

"Bonnette dropped the camera and fell backward. She was on him instantly. Like, snap your fingers, it was over, and then all of a sudden, she pulled that knife and stuck him," Andrew trailed off.

"What happened next?" said Holly, clearly uncomfortable.

"She stepped over his body and sat on the top step. Like this."

"She just sat there?" said Tim.

"I told you. Three minutes at least."

"Give us a real-time reenactment. The entire first minute or so, with body language, the whole thing," said Tim.

Andrew sat like a statue for twenty seconds, then shifted his hands to his face as if exhausted. He remained that way for ten seconds, then removed his hands from his face and placed them on the top step, head down.

"She looks tired," said Holly.

"She didn't feel tired when she pinned me to the dining room table," said Tim.

"I agree with Holly," said Andrew. "I think she's tired, too."

CHAPTER 211

October 25, 1972

Mildred watched as the girls practiced calling acorns. The sixth spell still dulled their senses, and it might be years before she could stop using it. Without it, they asked questions, especially when the smell hit them. *Where are we? Where's Mommy, Daddy, etc.* The facts would have to be discussed at some point, minus the fact that Sheila was murdered, of course.

For now, games were all they had. It was their only distraction as Mildred decided what to do. Caring for the girls took less out of her than the revenge game, but there was no time for what she really needed: extended, healing sleep. It would take stamina to make it as a family now and in the following decades.

The following day, Olivia awoke and roused Vivian. Vivian opened her eyes but was listless as if she might want to sleep more. Olivia attempted to start another game of Pass the Acorn, but Vivian wouldn't have it. Curious, Mildred watched the scene play out.

Olivia set the acorn on Vivian's leg, but Vivian brushed it off onto the ground. Olivia called it to her hand anyway and threw it back, hitting Vivian in the forehead.

"Stop it!" said Vivian, but Olivia repeated the cycle.

"Stop!" repeated Vivian, "Or I'll tell Mom!"

Mildred's ears perked, and she straightened, hoping Vivian might turn to her, but the little girl's eyes remained fixed on her sister.

Olivia threw another acorn. Finally, Vivian turned to Mildred. "Where's Mom? Where's my Mom? When can we go home?"

With a wave of her hand, both girls fell asleep. If Mildred had blood in her veins, it would have boiled. Instead, it felt as if fire coursed through her body. Somewhere beneath the haze of the sixth spell, Vivian had a sense of what was going on. Furious, she left the den. The girls would not be waking anytime soon.

Mildred walked to within a mile of the house and began dropping birds and squirrels in case the dogs returned. Police dogs, specifically, not the handsome Shepherd Holly brought home. Somehow, she felt something for the whiny beast. When they met that first night in the woods, he hadn't shown his teeth, growled, or run. Nor had he done a thing to stop her as she pinned his master to the dining room table. The dog was the first being in over a century to show her an ounce of affection.

On her way back to the coyote den, Mildred killed six more squirrels but picked them up for Vivian to eat. She also raided Tim's overgrown forest garden for whatever nature hadn't killed off. Today had been disappointing, and Mildred needed a lift. When she returned to the coyote den, she built a fire and began cooking.

#Ed Bodwell decided to get to know the surrounding woods better because the nights were getting spookier. If he didn't drink to knock himself out, Ed would spend hours awake listening, and it was all due to fear because he hadn't set up a proper warning system.

Yesterday, he purchased three hundred yards of fishing line and sixteen cat-bells. Today, he marched the grove stringing the line in concentric circles, knee-high around his tent, hanging bells on each length high enough to avoid squirrels and low enough to remain still in a stiff breeze.

He ran out of the fishing line three rows deep, which seemed reasonable enough, but when he was done, he kept walking for lack of anything better to do. Sundown was still more than three hours away, and there was nothing but this walk, dinner, and whiskey between him and bedtime. As he approached the end of the grove, he began to notice dead animals: three squirrels and a crow.

THE LEGEND OF MILDRED WELLS

CHAPTER 212

October 25, 1972

The four adults all went outside with Neptune for his last urination of the day. Each carried a weapon, hoping Mildred had decided to give them the night off.

"Well, what do you think happens tonight?" asked Tim.

Andrew spoke first. "I say Mildred leaves us alone, and Thomas Pike shows up with a golden clue. I'm trying to stay positive."

"I wish I shared that sentiment," said Tim.

Holly's was more severe. "Thomas abandoned us for more than a year. Don't believe for a second you can count on him."

So, what's your prediction?" said Andrew.

"Mildred leaves us alone, and we all get some sleep. I don't want to jinx us. How about you, Agent Harrington? What's your first name, anyway?"

"Kevin."

"Okay, Kevin, this is your second night with us, and you're one-for-one with Mildred sightings. Care to guess?"

"I didn't see her last night, but I'll take your word for it. And as far as that shotgun goes, I never saw it. I'll go with Holly's prediction. No sightings tonight."

"Are you nervous?" said Tim.

"I think *ready* is a better word," said Harrington. "What's your guess, Tim?"

"I'm going to say— Hey! Neptune! No! What are you eating? Holly, shine the light over there. What did he eat?" Tim ran over and tried to open Neptune's jaws, but it was too late. Whatever he found was gone.

"Neptune!" said Holly, frustrated. "Sometimes, he goes for the rabbit turds. Disgusting. Come on, Neptune, pee! I want to go back in."

Holly got her wish, but it only lasted three hours. All four adults fell asleep, catching up on some needed rest. Neptune fell asleep, too, because Mildred's tainted squirrel meat ensured it. Tonight was part two of her fear campaign.

At 3:15 am, Mildred let herself in and listened to the house. Twenty minutes later, she was almost up the stairs. She could hear someone breathing in one of the back bedrooms, so she put her ear to the door and turned the knob.

Mildred crept up on the snoring man and placed the extra pillow over his face. He kicked and struggled but killing him was easy. The horror of discovering his body would be another gift from Mildred to Tim and Holly for dumping Elmer's bones in the lake.

Eight minutes later, Mildred peered in on the frazzled couple. Satisfied they were asleep, she turned for the guest bedroom. By 3:41 am, she was inside Andrew's room and shut the door. Like Harrington, Mildred placed a pillow over Andrew's face and pressed him into the mattress. Four minutes later, Mildred removed the pillow. Andrew's eyes were open, and his face was blue in the moonlight. Soon, but not tonight, it would be Tim and Holly's time, too.

Mildred called the shotgun from Tim's side of the bed, placed it in the hallway, and approached. Tim's eyes opened as the first fly landed on his face, and he screamed. Holly woke immediately and screamed, too.

Holly was so noisy with that mouth of hers; perhaps it was time to prune that branch. She should kill Holly now and leave him with nothing, then hunt him down a year or two later. But something stirred behind her.

"Back off, or I'll blow your heart out of your chest." Andrew was in the doorway. "Take us to his girls, and I won't shoot."

With a wave of her wrist, Mildred took the shotgun from his hands and turned it on him. She could give him both barrels, but this one was strange. He should be dead. *Was he magick, too?*

Holly stopped screaming, and Tim huddled with her on the bed. Mildred backed Andrew into the hallway and using the shotgun like a club, cracked him over the head. After stepping over Neptune, she pulled the security nails from the front door and left.

"Oh my God, Andrew!" Holly rushed to his side. He was already starting to come to. "Can you hear me?"

He blinked. "Yeah, I can hear you. Ow, that hurts." Andrew sat up as the clouds in his head parted. "We were wrong with our predictions. Except Tim because he never made one."

"I made one. I just didn't want to share it," said Tim.

Holly noticed that Neptune wasn't moving. "Neptune! It must be that thing he ate on the lawn!"

"You're right," said Tim. "She left something in the grass. I wonder why she didn't just kill him." Thankfully, the dog was warm and breathing.

"Where's Agent Harrison?" said Holly.

"Oh, no," said Tim and ran to the back bedroom. He felt for a pulse but found nothing. Andrew circled to the opposite side of the bed and attempted the same. "She killed him," said Tim.

"Tim, we have to go," said Holly, standing in the doorway and looking over her shoulder. "You wanted to talk, but she's not listening."

Tim frowned. "Mildred could have killed us too if she wanted. She's saving it for later, making us feel it. I need to call Agent Whitlock. He just lost a man, and he's going to be pissed."

"I can't stay here anymore, Tim. I'm going to my mom's."

Tim hugged Holly tight. "I don't blame you."

"Be near the phone. I'll buy more phones. Put one in every jack." Neptune, as much as it pained her, should stay with Tim. He was, if not a guard dog, an extra chance. There were hugs and tears as Holly packed her things and drove off. Deep down, Holly wondered if being away would solve anything.

CHAPTER 213

October 26, 1972

As soon as Tim called in the death of Special Agent Harrington, a swarm of FBI agents, including Special Agent Souza and Special Agent in Charge Whitlock, took over the property.

"What the hell is going on here, Russell? Step into my office." The two men entered the den behind the living room and closed the door. "You're about to be charged with obstruction of justice, Russell. You haven't been honest with me."

"I'd love to speak freely, Agent Whitlock, but I'll keep it respectful because you hold the power. You've been told what's happening here, and Special Agent Souza will back me up. Let's get him in here."

Whitlock exhaled and looked out the window into the shady backyard. Scare tactics wouldn't work on a man scared of something much worse.

"Besides," said Tim. "You wouldn't have believed me if I told you she was supernatural. Now you're in my shoes and have to explain it to your boss. It's not fun, am I right?"

Whitlock turned and faced Tim. "Are you ready to tell me everything now? I lost an agent last night, and that has never happened. You're right. The higher-ups want answers. The press wants answers, too. I didn't believe Souza or the Bonnette video, but now I have to. Tell me what you think."

In ten seconds, the tension between them evaporated. Tim breathed a sigh of relief, even though their more significant problems were far from over. "She's what is called a revenant, and —"

"Yeah, Souza told me that part. He asked for snipers and people who could hit her in the heart from a distance. She—has a talent for taking people's weapons away."

"I like that plan," said Tim, "but we would never find my girls if you killed her. It's a bitch of a problem, no pun intended."

Whitlock picked up the phone ninety-seven times that day, calling in the best forensic experts, analysts, and support staff to investigate the murder. Sixteen people, six on-property and ten in area hotels, all working to look for Mildred Wells. Whitlock also coordinated with local and state police to ensure that the property on Lancaster Hill Road was tighter than a bull's ass in fly season.

Twenty minutes later, Tim saw Special Agent Souza, who nodded at Tim but said nothing. Tim guessed that Souza had been reprimanded and then reinstated after Special Agent Harrington's death. It was nice to have him back on the property.

Tim and Andrew met in the kitchen. "I feel like this place is still safer than hers," said Tim. "I hated seeing Holly so upset. I hope she comes back."

"You can't blame her," said Andrew. "Mildred comes and goes like she owns the place and Thomas has disappeared. I'm scared for the FBI."

"How do you feel?" said Tim. "You've taken a beating. I'm surprised you can even walk."

Andrew pressed on his stitches. "I think my mother is doing something to keep the swelling down, but this morning, it's all about that shotgun against the head."

Tim's eyes bugged. "Where is the shotgun?"

Andrew returned Tim's stare, dumbfounded. "She hit me with it, and I don't remember. Did she keep it?"

"She must have. How did you end up with it last night?"'

"I found it in the hallway."

Tim stared at Andrew, confused. "Why would she leave it in the open for you?"

Andrew stared at the wall, trying to remember, and when he did, he sat down before he fainted. "I—think she smothered me. She pinned me to the bed, and I couldn't breathe."

Tim poked Andrew's arm. "You aren't a ghost, are you?"

"I wonder. Was I dead? I should be, that's for sure."

"Your mother, again?" said Tim.

Andrew nodded. "Tim, Holly was right to leave. Maybe you should go, too. I'm stuck here. I'll wait for Thomas. There are plenty of FBI agents with me. I can do this."

The two men went quiet, and then Tim spoke again. "Not a chance. Where the hell is Jordan Block's cameraman?"

CHAPTER 214

October 26, 1972

Mildred left the girls asleep as she was in no mood to hear the wrong thing come out of Vivian's mouth again. To settle her anger, she hunted, for they would be hungry when they woke, and while she did, she laid more bait for the dogs even though the police searches had been inconsistent lately. That would change, most likely, after last night.

Mildred brooded over who the young man in the guestroom was. She'd killed him, as she'd killed the other man, and yet he'd popped back up, holding a weapon powerful enough to kill her. Was he here for her? The more she thought about it, the more she suspected Thomas. But weren't he and Elmer gone forever? If they weren't, *Oh, if they weren't.* Well, that would explain everything.

Suddenly, she heard dogs. They *were* back, hunting her, adding to her list of problems. The man that wouldn't die. The girls. Thomas. Dogs. The simple plan would be to kill everyone as soon as possible, but what would she do with the girls? She wanted to turn them into revenants, but that plan had its own challenges.

If she did force the transition, and it didn't go well, she would have to—

Mildred couldn't finish the thought. She never wanted to cross that line again. She felt guilty every time she looked at the pond. But they were chasing her, and she would have to decide soon.

Thomas Pike heard the dogs, too, and saw Mildred's reaction. She'd been on a rampage of late, on the offensive nearly every night, plus the little girls were giving her problems. Her body was weak. Mildred might finally be tired enough. It was time to act.

CHAPTER 215

October 27, 1972

Tim raked a small section of lawn before letting Neptune out and followed him around until he peed. He didn't want any tranquilizing treats waiting ever again. Luckily, Neptune did his business quickly and lay beside the bed. It was hard to feel scared with six agents in and around the property, but Tim knew better than to let his guard down.

At 12:20 am, Andrew woke to Thomas Pike's ghost standing over him. This time, they were going somewhere. Immediately, Andrew's heart began to pound. This was it. Shaking in fear, he dressed, and Thomas led him past Tim's room and down the stairs. After telling the agent at the front door that he was headed outside to smoke, Thomas led him across the property and into the woods.

Occasionally, Thomas stopped and pointed out landmarks, like a stone wall or fallen oak. As Andrew entered the last row of the grove, Thomas pointed into the wild forest beyond and disappeared, leaving Andrew on his own.

Mildred read the book to relax, but it wasn't working. The dilemma of whether or not to make the girls into revenants wouldn't go away. Mildred was tired of flip-flopping. Maybe asking for their forgiveness after the fact would be easier than asking their permission. *Kick the can down the road.* Perhaps it was time to start at the beginning of the Book of Shadows with page one—no more playing with acorns. Start fresh and teach them how to make runes. Maybe together, they could figure out who Andrew was. *Yes*, it was time to begin their education.

But the possibility of Thomas Pike lurking had opened a can of worms, and her anger would not relent. Tired, yet restless, this was madness. Putting the Book down, she stepped into the night to walk it off.

Mildred had already thinned out the wildlife surrounding the den because she didn't want hungry coyotes around the girls while she was away. Now, curiously, came a crunching sound that caught her attention. She stopped and listened. *How many legs?*

Crunch, crunch, crunch, crunch.

Two legs. Mildred called the knife.

Andrew continued through the woods, surprisingly much calmer than when Thomas woke him up. If he turned back, his mother would punish him again. Wherever he was headed would probably hurt, and he could do nothing about it.

Or maybe it wouldn't hurt. Perhaps Thomas only wanted him to remember this walk so he could tell the FBI. Andrew took his hands off his cold ears to part some branches and stepped over a stream. Thomas reappeared at a stone wall and a fallen tree. Finally, Andrew passed through a thick cluster of saplings to find Thomas in a clearing, a finger to his lips, pointing to two spruce trees towering over twin boulders.

Andrew sensed that this was the end of his journey. But where was Mildred? Where were the girls? He hadn't noticed the hidden entrance between the boulders and turned to ask, but Thomas was gone. Andrew was alone, and all sense of well-being vanished. The next move was up to him, and he had no clue what to do. Heart pounding, Andrew approached the two boulders.

CHAPTER 216

October 27, 1972

Tim awoke to Special Agent Souza telling him he had a visitor. He checked his watch: 6:17 am. On his way to the front door, Tim checked on Andrew, who was missing again. *Where the hell is he now?* After stepping over Neptune, Tim peeked outside and saw the silhouette of a gigantic man.

"May I help you?"

The man said nothing but held out a business card. Tim noticed that his hand was twice the size of his. Tim read the card:

Here's your cameraman, Russell. His name is Koji. He's an ex-sumo wrestler from Japan. Sorry, he doesn't speak English, but that might be good if what you say is true. I'll call you when I get a chance. -Jordan

Tim stepped aside and motioned for the giant to come in. "Can I get you any—" Tim suddenly remembered that the man didn't speak English. "Never mind, I forgot you don't—" then caught himself again. *What to do?* Tim brought the man to the kitchen to see if he wanted something. On the way, he wondered if Koji had flown directly from Japan. *Do they drink coffee? Or is it tea? I'll worry about that after we find Andrew. Damn you, Jordan.*

Tim entered the kitchen and saw Whitlock at the counter, using the telephone. Another FBI agent was on the other side of the sliding glass door, watching the side entrance. Koji saw Mark Folsom's movie camera and picked it up, then began to film the house's interior.

Neptune heard people in the kitchen and showed up for breakfast, wagging his tail at the large stranger. Tim pointed to the coffee maker and clicked the machine on. Koji saw what Tim was doing and shook his head once. *Okay, nothing to drink. Now, where the hell is Andrew?*

Just then, Tim heard Holly's car come up the driveway. *Holly!*

Holly was happy to see Tim but didn't look like she'd caught up on any sleep. Her eyes left Tim's and went straight to Koji, who had followed Tim out of the house, still filming.

"Is that Jordan's bodyguard?" she asked.

Tim nodded. "He showed up ten minutes ago. Not a lick of English. I'm not even sure he knows what he's signed up for. He handed me a note from Jordan, who said he'd call when he can."

Holly rolled her eyes. "Great. So, what's he doing? Following you around?"

"Kind of. I was playing charades to find out if he wanted something to drink."

"Yeah, well, we need to do some grocery shopping. Does he like donuts? I brought some." Holly opened the back door and pulled out two boxes and a tray of coffees.

"Where's Andrew?"

"He's gone again! I have no idea!"

"Cut it out." Holly looked Tim in the eyes and knew he wasn't joking. "Is his bag still here?"

"I haven't had the chance to check. Too busy pantomiming."

Holly sighed. "I hate this place."

Suddenly, Koji interrupted, speaking in Japanese. Holly and Tim looked outside. Andrew was stumbling out of the path at the corner of the driveway, assisted by Special Agent Souza. His shirt had a pyramid-shaped triangle of blood that began near his neck and widened until his waist. Twigs and leaves were stuck to the shirt, hair, pants, and hands. Holly gasped.

They rushed outside, all hands attempting to get him in the house without hurting him further. "Tim, he's got fresh stitches across his neck. Some of them are still bleeding," said Holly.

"Okay. Put him down." Tim ran to the house, returned with a glass of water, and put it to Andrew's lips. "Andrew, can you hear me?" Two more agents came outside to help. Whitlock hung up and did the same.

Andrew was unconscious, so Holly took the glass from Tim and began to clean the stitches on his neck. The cold water woke him, and he opened his eyes. "It hurts! It hurts!" Holly put the glass to his lips, but Andrew pushed it aside. "He led me there. He knew I was in danger!"

"Where? To my girls?"

Andrew coughed twice and began to sit up. "Yes. I think I know."

"My God. Agent Stevens, go inside and call an ambulance," said Whitlock.

The crowd on the lawn was growing, and Tim couldn't believe his ears. "What did you say? Do you know where the girls are? Andrew, I know you're hurt, but we have to go. Can you— Do you think you can make it?"

"Tim, look at the blood. They're calling an ambulance!" said Holly.

"I can't, Tim," said Andrew. "Not yet. I saw, I don't know, a cave or something. Get me a piece of paper. I need to write things down. My head."

Holly continued to clean his wounds.

"Do you hear this, Whitlock? Are the girls alive, Andrew?" Tim was manic.

"I didn't see them. I saw two boulders. I was *shown* two boulders. Thomas pointed them out."

"Finally!" Tim paced, frustrated.

CHAPTER 217

October 27, 1972
Three hours earlier

Mildred pulled the long blade from Andrew's chest and watched him slump against the tree, unquestionably dead this time, or at least if he wasn't supernatural. Andrew hadn't heard her coming until the knife crossed his throat. She felt relief, if only temporary. But seeing Andrew this far in the woods was bad news, as were the dogs the previous day. It was time to move, even though hiding places that could keep human children warm in October were hard to find.

Thomas. Tim Russell. Holly Burns. Mildred recited their names to try and rekindle the rage and finish the job. *Nothing's good when you're tired.* Teaching the girls the pages of the Book from the beginning would get the ball rolling, and then she could put them all down for a long nap to heal. They could start fresh in a few years.

Mildred left Andrew's body against the tree. She had a few hours before the sun came up and they came looking for the girls. When dawn came, Mildred remembered that Andrew's body was still outside, which would be the first thing the girls saw. When Mildred climbed out to dispose of him, her head spun. His body was gone, but for how long, she couldn't be sure. He might be bringing the dogs, for all she knew.

There was no doubt that this enigma had been sent to deal with her. Without wasting any more time, she woke the girls and opened the Book.

CHAPTER 218

October 27, 1972

Andrew was taken to the hospital but insisted on being discharged in the afternoon. Colleen Vaughn saw that her son was ready to help Thomas Pike, and the doctors released him, scratching their heads at the miracle they'd just witnessed. Special Agent Whitlock's phone calls and agents on the scene outside Andrew's room expedited the process.

With some assistance from Agent Stevens, Andrew stepped out of the car in front of the porch steps and stood straight. Tim was chomping at the bit and rushed outside to greet him along with Holly and Whitlock.

"How do you feel? Are you ready to show us?"

Holly's eyes searched Andrew's throat, stunned by the number of fresh stitches ear to ear. There were two long scars now, today's and the one from the car crash three days ago, which was mostly healed.

Suddenly, Koji started speaking rapid-fire, "あれは誰？女性。庭にいる女性!"

Tim looked toward the corner of the house. Mildred was there, staring. "Oh, my God, nobody shoot!" Tim motioned to Koji, shaking his head that the woman in the driveway was dangerous. Koji hoisted the camera and began filming.

"I'm in charge, Russell. Agents, be ready, on my command. Don't kill her. Aim for her knees."

Holly ran to Andrew and escorted him inside.

Mildred stood still, taking note of all the weapons pointed at her. Of course, they didn't want to kill her, but that would be their downfall.

"Don't come any closer, Mildred," said Tim.

Suddenly, a gunshot echoed across the meadow. Mildred's shoulder jerked, and she grunted in agony. Koji turned and tackled Tim to the grass.

"Hold your fire! Hold your fire!" screamed Whitlock, yet none of his men had fired a shot. Three more shots rang out as Mildred stumbled.

"Where's Holly?" Tim yelled as he struggled to escape Koji's grasp. He'd heard two bullets hit the house. Tim looked toward the noise beyond the pond and saw a lone rifleman squeeze off another shot. Tim's first thought was Bob Simmons, but Bob Simmons was dead.

Mildred picked herself up and darted into the woods.

"Agent Whitlock, there he is!" Special Agent Souza pointed to the meadow.

"Muller, if he raises his rifle again, take him out," barked Whitlock.

Koji grabbed his camera and took off toward the gunman in bounding strides.

"Dammit, where's he going? Muller, don't hit the big man!"

Koji found a spot halfway to the woods and began filming.

"Is that Ed Bodwell?" said Tim.

"Who is Ed Bodwell?" said Whitlock. Whoever it was continued to stumble over the uneven ground toward the woods, his rifle no longer raised.

"It is Ed Bodwell. Oh my God," said Tim. "I told him no guns!" Tim ran to the driveway, cupped his hands around his mouth, and shouted. "Ed! Stop shooting! You're going to kill one of us!"

Ed Bodwell, still drunk, heard Tim's cries and raised his hand in mock victory. *You're welcome, Russell. I saved your ass, didn't I?* He'd wounded Mildred Wells and sent her running. And who was with him? *Three black sedans. Was that the FBI?* They should thank him for doing their job. Now, it was time to finish her. *Track her, hunt her, and put her down.* He saw the big man had come closer with the movie camera and waved his rifle at it like a war hero.

She entered the woods near the birch, and I was about thirty yards back then, so I should aim for those pines. Eighty percent sure, Ed Bodwell set his sights on a dark patch of pines and stumbled forward, nearly twisting his ankle on the cloddy tufts of meadow. His right hand touched his holster, felt the Colt, and popped the snap. The pistol on Ed's hip could blow Mildred's heart to bits if what they said about her was true, and Ed believed it was.

It appeared that Ed Bodwell was done shooting toward the house. Tim breathed a sigh of relief as he watched the vigil-goer continue toward the woods. Was he going in after her? "Ed! Stay away from the trees!"

Bodwell ignored him.

"Ed, she's dangerous!" *Oh no.* Ed Bodwell was going in for the kill.

As swift as the wind, the figure in the long black dress emerged behind Ed Bodwell, her arm raised high, holding her hatchet.

"Behind you, Ed!" screamed Holly.

Mildred was on Bodwell before he knew she was there. Her hatchet fell, catching him hard in the back of the head, and the old man was dead before he hit the ground.

Koji screamed something in Japanese, but it was too late. Mildred stood over the body, her right shoulder drooping, and looked back at the house.

Mildred disappeared into the woods, but Tim knew that didn't mean they were safe. Backpedaling, He kept her eyes glued to the path at the bend in the driveway. If Mildred were coming, she'd show up there in about fifteen seconds.

"Koji!" called Tim. The big man stopped filming and wasted no time returning to the house.

"Emerson, LeBlanc, and Stevens: go check on the downed shooter. If anything comes out of those woods, shoot," said Whitlock.

"What?" said Tim. "Did you see how fast she is? They'll be sitting ducks."

Special Agent Souza spoke out of turn. "He's right, sir. She'll take their weapons."

Whitlock exhaled, still recovering from what he'd witnessed. "All right, cancel. The perimeter is the driveway. Spread out evenly and maintain visual contact." Whitlock went inside and picked up the telephone. There was a dead or dying man in the field, and they needed more firepower before heading out there.

CHAPTER 219

October 27, 1972

Mildred returned to the coyote den, careful not to leave a trail. Luckily, she didn't bleed because the damage to her shoulder was extensive. Her collarbone was shattered, and while there was no pain, there was little function. She needed rest more than ever, but there was no time. *They will come now.* Using strips of her dress, Mildred stitched up what she could and fashioned a sling to limit the movement of the arm. As she did so, Vivian opened her eyes.

"Mommy, I'm thirsty." Mildred eyed her carefully, trying to determine if the girl was addressing Sheila. With some difficulty, she poured a cup of water and handed it to Vivian, who drank deeply. "Thank you, Mommy. Can I have more?" Mildred perked up. Vivian was clearly awake.

Mildred's lips curled into what once would have passed for a smile. She was tired, yet the affection gave her energy. Mildred hadn't felt love in over a century, nor had she loved back.

"Mommy?"

Mildred let the word linger, enjoying the way it felt. She cleared her throat and managed to answer. "Yes?"

"When can we see Daddy again?"

Mildred's heart sank. *One step forward and two steps back.* There was no time to dwell. They had to move. Mildred attempted to scoop the girls up with her good arm, but it was too much pressure on their tender bodies. Searching the woods for something to drag them on, she came up empty. But Elmer used to own a sled. A big one, too. It took her a moment to remember where it might be.

CHAPTER 220

October 27, 1972

Andrew was starting to look better but still couldn't move well. Holly looked at the fresh stitches on Andrew's abdomen—two clean puncture wounds, freshly dressed *before* he arrived at the hospital. Tim was tense, as he couldn't wait for Andrew to take them to find the girls, yet they couldn't move until more help arrived. Ed Bodwell's body was still in the field.

Everyone watched as the ambulance attendants fetched Ed Bodwell's body from the meadow with the assistance of six well-armed FBI agents. Koji stood guard at the corner of the house, and Holly tied Neptune out next to him for an extra set of senses, but all the dog did was nap under the overcast sky.

Due to a bank robbery in Manchester, it took nearly all day for the SWAT team to arrive. When they did, it was dusk, and the team looked spent, hardly ready for the hike in the woods. Three state police cruisers had arrived with dogs, rounding out the best search party yet.

Still limping, Andrew led the way, wielding a machete. A mile in, he made an announcement. "Uh … I need everyone to shut off their flashlights. Everything looks different with the lights on. It's only for a few minutes."

Whitlock murmured to Tim. "We're chasing a murderer, and he wants us to shut off the lights?" Thankfully, all eight SWAT members had night-vision goggles, but this was the first time they had used them in the field. The New Hampshire SWAT team was only a year old, and today was their first two calls in over four months.

Andrew meandered before returning to retrieve everyone. "I found it. It's this way," he stammered.

"Andrew," Tim whispered.

"What?"

"Are you all right?"

"I'm nervous. I can't see a thing, and with every branch I duck under, I feel like I'm going to take a knife to my liver. Other than that, cool as a cucumber."

Tim thought he saw a bead of sweat on Andrew's brow. Holly squeezed Tim's hand while leading Neptune by his leash. The group was twenty-one, including eight SWAT team members, six FBI agents, and three state troopers. There were also four dogs, including three German Shepherds and Neptune.

An hour later, Andrew made everyone turn their flashlights off again. Nerves were tense as 9:00 pm came and went. Andrew held his finger to his lips. Finally, he gave the signal to turn the flashlights back on, and it wasn't another two hundred yards before their beams shined on the two boulders beneath the spruces.

The SWAT commander understood that they had arrived at ground zero and began giving nonverbal commands, but Andrew waved them off, pointing to himself. Dumbfounded, the commander set his men up to train their guns between the two boulders. Tim and Holly watched in horror.

Andrew crouched down, staring into a small dark hole, machete raised. After two minutes of listening for noises, he pressed the button on his flashlight. The hole was tunnel-like, with a bend to the left. The light shone on the far wall. Andrew tossed a rock but heard no reaction. Finally, he crawled in, craning his neck to see around the bend. Some animal skins were piled in the corner, but nothing else.

Andrew stood tall between the two boulders, holding two blankets sewn from squirrel pelts. "This is all I found. No one's there, but the den is big enough to hold three people."

CHAPTER 221

October 27, 1972

Mildred pulled the sleeping girls behind her, dropping every living animal from the trees. She made several misdirections along the way, knowing there would be dogs and they would follow her scent. For this reason, she was sure to pick up sticks and rocks and touch them to the open wound on her shoulder, then discard them. At least the scent of the girls would not be on the ground.

The old drunk with the rifle was unexpected, a margin of error Mildred never considered. She'd gotten careless, thinking she was invincible, the same thing that had killed every other revenant. Her anger had gotten the best of her, and she had attracted too much attention.

After six miles of misdirections and double-backs, Mildred headed for her next home base. She'd found a farm with a crumbling barn no longer in use. She would tuck the girls where they would be safe as she settled the details.

Two FBI agents were on the front lawn when Mildred arrived at the house, so she watched from a distance. Where were Tim and Holly? Were they out searching for her? The driveway was jammed with official vehicles, so she had to imagine so. Did they think the bullet killed her? That they could track her blood like a deer? Even if Andrew had recovered, he didn't know she had moved the girls.

It was midnight before the mob of humans and dogs emerged empty-handed from the woods. Not only had she doubled back countless times, but she'd lived in this forest since returning from Beverly Farms. Her scent was a part of this forest.

Half the search party left in their vehicles, and the rest went inside.

Minutes later, the turret light came on, and Mildred saw Tim's head appear, turn around, and head back down the stairs. *Looking for me*, she thought. When the light went off, she moved. It took no time to cross the roof, pull the nails from the window, and let herself in. Now, she would listen to their frustrations one last time.

Their murmuring came from the living room, but the giant man and the six government agents could be anywhere. Quiet as a cat, she descended.

Tim, Holly, Andrew, Koji, Whitlock, and Souza went to the living room, where Holly clicked on the lamp. Agents Stevens and Emerson remained in the kitchen and LeBlanc and Muller went upstairs, having pulled second watch. Everyone was exhausted, including Koji, who plopped into the chair by the fireplace.

Tim sat on the couch against the windows, looking as terrible as he felt. Holly sat beside him with Neptune at her feet. Always nervous, Andrew stood by the bookshelf in the back of the room. Whitlock and Souza sat on the couch against the wall.

"Andrew, what you did was so brave. Thank you, thank—" Tim broke into tears. Holly hugged him and stroked his hair.

"Don't mention it," said Andrew. "At least we know where the girls were. Sunlight will make things a lot easier."

Tim nodded as he wiped his eyes. "She has to be close. It can't be easy taking two young girls through the woods. And she's wounded!"

Andrew shrugged his shoulders. There were so many things they didn't know.

"Tim, the search party returns in seven hours. We should try to rest." Holly couldn't believe she was sleeping in the house again, but tomorrow was already here. The girls were close. Despite their disappointing day, hope was alive.

Tim was quiet, lost in thought. Suddenly, his face hardened. "Andrew, what happened to Thomas Pike?"

"What do you mean?"

"Where was he today?"

Andrew paused. "I haven't seen him since yesterday. Once a flake, always a flake."

"Maybe he doesn't want Mildred to see him," added Holly.

"There are two little girls' lives in the balance, not to mention all of us and Ed Bodwell. Thomas Pike doesn't deserve the burial we gave him."

"Maybe he's not done?" Holly wanted Tim to calm down.

"A passive Mildred and Elmer running around was heaven compared to this."

"Wait a second. Mildred turned your kitchen into a bloodbath. Don't forget that," said Holly.

"That's because Thomas Pike let her down, too. That was a bad day, but she didn't want to kill us back then. Thomas Pike got in our heads and made us dream things we didn't want to dream. All he did was pass his problems on to us."

Andrew shook his head. "So, Thomas tricked you and took off?'

"Yes. Thomas tricked us into stealing Elmer from Mildred. He stabbed her in the back and did the same to us. I'd be pissed too."

Holly was about to remind Tim that Mildred had drowned Thomas' son in the pond when Mildred stepped into the room.

Koji, whose eyelids had grown heavy, woke immediately and attempted to stand, but as soon as he rocked his weight forward, Mildred flashed her knife. Koji froze in a half-standing, half-sitting position, then fell back, testing his nose for blood. Everyone drew a breath.

Mildred waited, daring, pointing the knife to be sure he'd quit, and looked around the room. Neptune began to wag his tail. It almost seemed like he was smiling. Mildred stepped over him and stood between Andrew and Koji by the doorway to the den. Neither Whitlock nor Souza moved.

Andrew shivered, wondering what he was supposed to do. Mildred's odor brought back memories of the knifing in the forest and the smothering in the bedroom. He recalled the flash of the blade and her iron grip. He wanted no part of her, yet his machete was by his feet.

Agents Stevens and Emerson heard the commotion from the kitchen and appeared in the doorway.

"Turn around, boys," said Whitlock. "Go back to the kitchen and call for backup."

Before either man could move, Mildred took their pistols and put them in the tattered pocket of her dress. The two men disappeared into the darkness of the dining room.

Tim watched how easily his nemesis had taken command of the room. *So fast, so quiet.* They never stood a chance against her, wounded or not. There would be no reunion with the girls. From its conception, the house project was a pipe dream, a fool's errand that cost him everything. Others lost, too. Sheila, Holly, Andrew, Koji: Olivia and Vivian, most of all. Tim stared into Mildred's cloudy eyes. "Make it quick, Mildred."

Andrew fidgeted, wishing he had a shot of bourbon or a hit of something more potent. Mildred was to his left, facing Tim. Whatever she was here for, she was about to do it. Fearing his mother's reprisal, Andrew counted to three, picked up the machete, and lunged.

The blade arced as Mildred caught Andrew in her peripheral vision. Wounded or not, she was a monster, and he was only human. A bullet wound was an inconvenience, not a death sentence. With the grace of a fencer, she sidestepped and plunged her knife into his ribs.

Andrew fell, and Mildred hovered, hoping she had bought enough time to finish things properly.

"Stop!" Tim stood, ready to beg.

Mildred turned to him as Andrew's blood found her foot, and some of her buzzing entourage found something fresher. Mildred pumped her arm once, and Tim's missing shotgun appeared. Everyone gasped.

Mildred raised the weapon, and when Tim didn't reach for it, she returned her knife to Beverly Farms and wagged the gun again, repeating her offer. Tim Russell might deserve one chance.

She's toying with me, thought Tim.

Mildred held the shotgun at arm's length, butt end first. The trigger was close enough to touch, but it couldn't be this easy. *She's mocking me. She'll flip it at the last second and blow me to bits in front of Holly.*

She waved the gun at him, daring him to take it. Tim reached slowly, grasped the handle, and wrapped his finger around the trigger. For a moment, they held the shotgun together, eye to eye. Then, as if he were dreaming, Mildred released her grip.

Mildred, now weaponless, turned and walked through the dining room. Seeing her in the darkness was still a nightmare, and the agents in the kitchen backed into the breakfast area when they saw her coming. It took all of Tim's willpower not to raise his weapon. Mildred turned to make sure he followed and reached for the doorknob.

"Looks like I'm going somewhere," said Tim. "Stay here. I have to go."

"Not a chance. I'm going," said Holly. It was barely a whisper. Andrew's body lay a foot away, his blood filling the cracks of the floorboards. Holly bent down and checked his pulse. *Nothing.*

"Holly," Tim protested, "I'm going to bet he'll be okay."

Holly picked up the machete. "I'm ready," she whispered. Koji stood behind her, shaken but also ready. Whitlock and Souza pulled their pistols but pointed them at the floor. Mildred stared at Holly's machete. "It's coming with me, Mildred. Take it if you want, but that's the only way I'm letting it go."

Mildred opened the front door and waited by the path to the grove to be sure they were following. Tim hung back fifteen feet, sweat soaking his shirt. Suddenly, Neptune bounded out the door and joined the group. Mildred turned for the woods as if she had been waiting for the dog.

They passed through the trees and up the dark path. The ten of them weaved their way through forest, thickets, and over marshland, toward a place only Mildred knew. She never looked back or gave Tim a reason to raise the shotgun. Holly followed, gripping the machete, waiting for Mildred to end her charade and kill them all, but it never came. Koji followed, bound by honor and duty, even though he knew he couldn't help if the chips were down. Neptune brought up the rear with a dead squirrel hanging from his mouth.

Nearing dawn, they saw an artificial light coming through the trees. The forest was ending, and civilization appeared as a sleepy farm with a streetlamp illuminating the barnyard. The house was dark, and the rooster had yet to crow. Tim saw a street sign: *Varney Road*. They were nearly in Belmont.

Mildred led them toward the abandoned barn, ducked through a collapsed doorway, and pointed to a rotting mound of hay. Tim regarded Mildred, realizing his daughters were close, and ran to the pile. Tim put the shotgun down and parted the straw. There, for the first time in over a month, was Vivian's face. He began to cry. She was warm and breathing. Clearing the hay off Olivia, the little girl's eyes opened for the briefest of moments. "Daddy …"

"Oh, my girls! Are you okay?" Both girls stirred but wouldn't wake. "Oh my God, you're alive!" Tim caressed Olivia's face, noticed the blankets from his bedroom, and realized Mildred had cared for them. Knowing Mildred's history with Elmer, Tim's heart went out to her, and he turned to thank her, but she was gone.

"Tim!" said Holly.

"What is it?"

"She's leaving."

Tim grabbed the shotgun and stepped outside just in time to see Mildred's black dress merge with the dark forest. He hugged Holly and began to cry again. "She wrapped them in blankets," he said.

"She what?"

"They're warm and healthy. I thought they'd be—worse."

As soon as Tim finished the words, the shotgun disappeared.

CHAPTER 222

October 28, 1972

Andrew dreamed he was lying in a rain puddle. His mother looked down on him and said four words: *She's gone. Go home.*

Suddenly, Andrew felt a shock rip through his chest and fade through his extremities. His body rocked, and his back arched, then went still. He opened his eyes, alone. The light was still on in the living room, and everyone was gone. Mildred was gone, too, thank God, and then he remembered how it had all gone down. He felt a searing pain beneath his rib cage. It took him several minutes to stand, and when he did, he felt light-headed.

She's gone. Go home.

Andrew tried to make the words stop, but Mother wanted otherwise. After clearing his mind, he picked up the phone and called George. Home, finally, but what would that be like? He'd helped Tim, but he didn't save the day. There was no way she was satisfied.

George told him he would arrive in an hour and a half. In the meantime, Andrew limped his way upstairs and stripped. Showering was slow and took nearly an hour. George pulled into the driveway just after he'd dressed.

Andrew decided he would leave now and call Tim and Holly later. The funeral home was shorthanded, and there was work to be done. George saw him limping and scrambled out of the car to help.

"Are you all right? I heard about your car."

"I'll tell you on the road. We have to go."

She's gone. Go home.

As soon as they left the driveway, the chatter stopped.

CHAPTER 223

October 28, 1972

With the house empty, Thomas set to work. It was time to extend the olive branch. Mildred was worn and tired. Many things had caused her anger. Some were his fault, but many happened before they met. He would probably never know everything that happened in Beverly Farms, but that didn't matter anymore.

Blood was everywhere. The authorities would impede, hopefully not more than a day or two. Tim, Holly, and the girls might return too, probably just long enough to pack their things and leave. It wasn't even Tim's house anymore. *Why would they want to stay?* Hopefully, his message on the bookshelf would find its audience.

The shelf was still stocked with Annette Smith's books. Tim wasn't much of a reader, not that he had the time even if he wanted to. Thomas thought for a moment about Annette Smith, the brave woman who stayed even after her husband Henry was slain in the grove. If it weren't for her, nothing would have been resolved. Mildred might still be chasing Elmer's ghost and reliving her tortured anniversaries.

Thomas studied the top shelf and found the brown book with a leather-bound cover. The only words on the jacket read *Inspirational Quotes*, and one had to look inside for more information. It was a simple book, each page adorned with a famous quote and the person who said it. Thomas had read the book countless times, waiting decades for the right people to arrive.

Thomas pulled the book from its spot, leaving a noticeable gap, and opened to the page that fit the bill. Then he set the book down and weighed the pages open with the object he'd brought up from the cellar.

CHAPTER 224

October 28, 1972

The girls were out of her life, and Mildred didn't know how to feel. Her walk had become a stumble, but she didn't bother to dig a hole. Why wake up alone again in twenty, thirty, fifty years with nobody to share it with?

It was time to end it, but it would not be suicide this time because it was not fair to call it that. Suicide was for living people who'd lost hope. She'd tried at age thirty and, in retrospect, should have explored other avenues. Mildred was in limbo. She'd been brought back unfairly, unnaturally, *undead*.

Today was not about quitting. On the contrary, Mildred had hope. All she wanted now was one last tour of the property to remember the good years and go out on a high note. Maybe somewhere along the tour, she would decide where and how, but it would have to come naturally.

Mary began in the grove, passing through the rows, realizing it would be the last time she ever walked it. Her old name had popped into her head along the way. *Mary.* She'd buried it for a while when it was too painful to hear, but no more. Her mother Alice had given her that name. Why should she let Gideon Walker steal such a wonderful memory?

As the final row passed, she said goodbye, looking through the wild forest to the meadow ahead. It was overcast, but that didn't matter. Mary's strides lengthened as she passed through the trees and into the field. She bowed her head as she approached the pond, reflecting on her greatest mistake. Mary ascended the front steps, opened the door closest to the road, and looked up. Blood splattered every step. It was not someplace she wanted to go, so she turned to the living room.

Blood was here, too. Andrew must have gone upstairs for something. It was no surprise that Andrew had survived, but she didn't care. Hopefully, he wouldn't surprise her. She still had the shotgun and the knife to ensure her final moments were peaceful. Mary's eyes swept the room, one more glance at the heart of the house before she went to the turret.

But something on the bookshelf caught her eye, an object from long ago, a distant memory, deliberately placed. It wasn't there eighteen hours ago. It was Elmer's toy drum. Mary hadn't seen the drum in over a century but remembered it well. She remembered taking it away from him as a little boy because he beat it until she couldn't take it anymore. One night, after he went to bed, she hid it in the cellar and lied the next day when asked.

Mary whirled. Was someone watching? Finding no one, she turned back to face the bookshelf. The drum sat on a book; a page had been ripped out and left on top.

Anger is an acid that can do more harm to the vessel in which it is stored than to anything on which it is poured. -Mark Twain

Mary dropped the book. *It's him.* He was speaking to her. *Still here, Thomas?* She turned, slower this time, and looked out the front windows. *Where?* she wondered. Mary left the house and limped down the lawn, searching the field and trees for any sign of the sender. She reached the pond and paused, offering plenty of time for someone to show themselves. A minute passed, and nothing but the willows moved.

Mary looked at the pond's surface and saw her reflection. No wonder Elmer had run from her all those years. Mary dropped her eyes, dead tired. It was time to move on before her mind began to eat at her. She stepped into the pond, felt the silt squish between her toes, and waded past the cat-o-nine tails until she was chest-deep.

Sensing it was time, she called the shotgun and placed the two barrels over her heart. She watched for a moment as the barrels bounced to her heartbeat. When she was sure she had everything lined up, she tilted her head back and pulled the trigger.

The buckshot left the barrel and tore through Mary's chest. She felt no pain as her heart disintegrated, and her double life of nearly one hundred and fifty years came to an end. With no revenant heart, the magick died. When her head went under, the flesh dissolved from her bones, the bits and pieces sank, and her body disappeared. Mary ceased to exist, and her flies were left to find new filth.

Mary woke as if from a long sleep, her head foggy at first and then clearing. She was sitting in her favorite spot, the turret, with no recollection of how she'd gotten there, but something was missing. She exhaled, savoring the comfort, and stared into the meadow she used to haunt so pathetically.

For the first time in forever, the meadow was there to enjoy. Even the pond deserved a glance. Death was no longer the end. Death was an anxious transition, and she'd never have to suffer it again.

Mary noticed that her dress was clean. Her hands were pale on the arm of the chair, no longer weathered, worn by time, or by digging. Suddenly, it struck her, the thing that was missing. There was no buzzing. The flies were gone. At last, she could think.

CHAPTER 225

October 28, 1972

Tim hung up the hospital phone. Andrew had found him somehow and called to say he was back home in Sugar Hill.

"Guess who that was?"

"Andrew," replied Holly. It wasn't hard to guess. Neither she nor Tim were stunned when Agent Whitlock told them he wasn't there when the FBI returned to the house. Andrew's mother wouldn't let him die. Theirs was, without a doubt, the most dysfunctional mother-son relationship she had ever known. Well, *top two*.

"Correct," said Tim, shaking his head. "I told him I would tell Whitlock where he was, but he's probably all set."

Holly nodded. "How'd he get to Sugar Hill?"

"Somebody picked him up. I was just wondering if we would ever see him again."

Holly looked at Tim as if trying to imagine a time when they would even want to get together. *Would it be a celebration or remind us of darker times?* "Let's wait and see," she replied.

Olivia and Vivian were checking out of the hospital. Both girls were in surprisingly good condition. Mildred had taken good care of them despite terrorizing everyone else. Olivia was getting dressed in brand-new street clothes and exited the bathroom. Vivian, who put on her clothes much slower, remained inside.

"Close the door, Olivia!" Vivian snapped.

"I am!" replied Olivia in a huff.

As soon as the door was shut, Olivia faced her father. "Daddy, can we go home now?"

"Well, we're going to Holly's house."

"Yay! How come? Did you paint your house again, and it stinks in there? What about Mom's house? Can we go there? I miss Mommy."

"No, honey. I sold my house!" Tim avoided the *Sheila* question for now. He would want to tell both girls in a more appropriate setting. Olivia looked disappointed.

"Aw. I liked your house. It was so much fun! Especially the grove. We had a lot of fun playing with Mildred." Olivia paused as if she'd said too much.

Tim glared at her, but decided to forego any follow-up questions. It was over, and he didn't want to know.

"It was okay, Dad, she was nice. She showed us how to make corn dolls."

"You can't talk to strangers, okay? Not unless I meet them first."

Olivia nodded as Vivian emerged from the bathroom. "Dad sold his house, and we're not going back. We're going to Holly's house."

"What about the things we left? My sneakers? What about your tables and chairs, Daddy?" asked Vivian.

"I'll get you some new sneakers. The man who bought the house bought the whole house and everything inside." Tim looked at Holly as he finished his sentence. Holly nodded, relieved.

"Can we just get my sneakers, though? They're my favorite ones …"

"I'm sorry, honey, but we can't."

"Can I call Mommy?"

"Let's get to Holly's house first, sweetie."

CHAPTER 226

October 28, 1972

Sitting in the turret, Mary couldn't remember what happened to the Book of Shadows. It was in the coyote den, and she'd taken it with her when she moved the girls, but where? *Was it in that old barn? Somewhere in the house?*

She'd read from it intensely in the final days, looking for strength to see things through. She'd read it aloud and to herself, backward and forward, reciting to the girls, keeping them sedated, letting the words soak in.

Suddenly, she noticed a red kite soaring over the meadow. *Elmer?* Mary stood for a better view, feeling lighter than usual. Two figures, a man and a boy, emerged from the woods—a father helping his son. Thomas and Elmer. Thomas looked to the turret, smiling. He was waiting, after all. *The patience on this one,* she thought.

Thomas tapped Elmer on the shoulder and pointed. Elmer followed his father's finger, recognized the figure in the turret, and handed him the spool. After what appeared to be a brief conversation with a moment of hesitation, the boy began to walk toward the house.

EPILOGUE

George turned down the long driveway to Foggy Orchard, and Andrew, asleep in the passenger seat, stirred. He'd slept the whole way home, but that was to be expected. Andrew had showered, but a red stain seeped through his shirt.

"Where are we?" asked Andrew, "Oh, home. You can drop me off over there." Andrew was still groggy, attempting to play host. He had no idea how settled George was or the plans that had been made.

"Andrew, I'm coming with you. You're injured. You have blood on your shirt."

Andrew looked down, then raised his hand to press the stain. He winced. "You don't have to. I'll be fine, and you have a long drive back to Hull. But you can stay overnight if you li …"

"Andrew, I'm staying. I told you I'm your new full-time employee."

Andrew stared at him, then opened the passenger-side door and got out. The two men shuffled to the house, Andrew holding his ribs.

"I remember now. My mother invited you?"

"That's right."

"Why? I mean, why make my life easier? An experienced funeral home director like you is a godsend for me."

George glanced sideways at Andrew. "Maybe she wants to free you up for other things."

Andrew stopped at the front door. "What does that mean? I died three times in Sanborn. I took a knife through the ribs. I've got stitches all over my body. What else does she want?"

"You'll have to ask her."

ACKNOWLEDGEMENTS

Writing a book is a solitary endeavor—until it is not. Ultimately, a writer needs help and attention. Many people have helped or listened along the way, and I appreciate you all.

First, I'd like to thank my editor, MJ Pankey. Your keen eye for detail, insightful suggestions, and constructive criticism are like having a silent partner, and I thank you for keeping this yarn with one foot planted in reality.

To Heather and Steve at Brigids Gate Press, thank you for believing in this project and for publishing me not once but twice. It is always a pleasure working with you.

I'd also like to thank Kendall Reviews for one of my first-ever Twitter reactions. Your support came at the right time. Keep doing what you're doing.

A special thank you goes out to Well Read Beard, Mother Horror, George Ranson, Ross Jeffery, Erica Metcalf, and Tom Rimer for additional support, attention, and enthusiasm.

Thanks to Scott Reid for helping me get my first cover made. To my wife, Josi (my early Mildred cover model), thank you for putting on that farm dress. A huge shoutout to James at GoOnWrite.com for making those pictures of Josi into something that belongs on the top shelf. Your eye is amazing.

And to Francois Vaillancourt, thank you for your latest masterpiece. Your artistry adds an extra layer of magic to this book, and I am thrilled to have worked with you.

I want to extend my appreciation to all the past and present podcasters, BookTubers, and Bookstagrammers who have graciously allowed me time on their shows. Your platforms have provided me with invaluable opportunities to share my work and connect with readers.

Last but certainly not least, to everyone who has ever read one of my books or taken the time to leave a review, thank you from the bottom of my heart. Your engagement and feedback are what keep me going.

Until the next book!

- Mike

ABOUT THE AUTHOR

Michael Clark was raised in New Hampshire and lived in the house where this book takes place. The bats really circled inside the barn, and there was a grove hidden by the forest. He even snuck onto the property forty years later and was mildly disappointed that it wasn't exactly as he remembered. Such is life.

He now lives very happily with his wife, Josi, and his dog, Bubba, and they walk in the woods every single day.

MORE FROM BRIGIDS GATE PRESS

Prepare for adventure as Juliana, a nineteen-year-old Brazilian, finds herself forced to run from an occult overlord, leaving her sister in peril. Temporarily safe, Juliana works to save money for Vilma's rescue—and along the way, meets Patrick, a rich-boy mountain climber with friends in high places.

Angus Addison wants to see his corporate flag on the summit of Mount Everest—carried there by the first woman in history—but the Himalayas are no joke. Failure could cost both sisters their lives.

Juliana weighs the risks and rewards—for even if she raises the cash, she still must figure a way to free Vilma from the same man she ran from—a man known to his disciples as *The Farmer.*

It's Seb's last day working in Turkey, but his friend Oz has been cursed. Superstition turns to terror as the effects of the ancient malediction spill over and the lives of Oz and his family hang in the balance. Can Seb find the answers to remove the hex before it's too late?

From Kev Harrison, author of *The Balance* and *Below*, journey with Seb, Oz and Deniz across ancient North African cities as they seek to banish the *Shadow of the Hidden*.

A family's relocation looked like a chance to relax and regroup—but as they settle into their new home, teenage Kimmie Barnes' special senses make her the target of something primordial, evil, and utterly malign.

Darkness...

Golden Oaks, California is a sleepy town on the shores of Oro Lake, and the residents have no idea what horrors lurk below the glittering waters.

Beneath the waves...

One by one, as people begin to disappear, the once quiet town is soon in the grips of a waking nightmare. An unimaginable horror consuming everything before it.

Hungry...

All while echoes of an ancient evil spread out like malignant spider webs, like dead hands reaching, grasping...

SEETHING...

During the Spring Solstice, four people enter the caves underneath London.

Garth: a shy young man, who seeks to save the girl of his dreams.

Cassie: a beautiful young woman, who seeks to use the dark magic of the caves for her own purposes.

Bill: an older man with a terrible secret, who seeks to find Garth and Cassie before it's too late.

Sienna: a con artist with a dark past, who seeks to escape her fate as a chosen sacrifice.

Four people enter. Each of them must battle their personal demons before facing the White Lady, who rises each year during the Spring Solstice with a hunger for human flesh.

Only one of them will survive.

Visit our website at: www.brigidsgatepress.com

Printed in the USA
CPSIA information can be obtained
at www.ICGtesting.com
JSHW080229030824
67318JS00001B/1

9 781963 355109